PRAISE FOR STINA LINDENBLATT

Decidedly Off Limits

"...I was captivated by the shenanigans of this duo. Not to mention laughing out loud and blushing. Boy do these two turn up the heat."—The Subclub Books

"A feel good, sensual, intoxicating and sexy love story; if you love contemporary romance you do not want to miss Decidedly Off Limits."—Slick, Guilty Pleasures

"Sweet, sexy and invigorating, Decidedly off Limits is a friends to lovers story that is truly a breath of fresh air!"—Read & Share Book Reviews

Other Books By Stina Lindenblatt

"So many laugh out loud moments that you do not want to be reading it in public or be ready for some weird looks. I speak from experience here."—The Subclub Books (*Decidedly with Baby*)

"Oh my goodness this book was so much fun!!!"—For the Love of Books (*Decidedly with Baby*)

"...a truly unique and utterly swoon-worthy romance." —Mary Dubé at Frolic/USA Today's HEA (*Decidedly by Chance*)

"Decidedly By Chance is a well written emotional story that

will tug on your heart strings."—MI Bookshelf (*Decidedly by Chance*)

"Stina Lindenblatt writes an emotional, heartfelt story about single parenthood, friendship, and love. Add to that great chemistry and tons of feels and this is a great book for anyone who enjoys this trope."—Ari at Red Hatter Book Blog (*Decidedly by Chance*)

"...it's an opposites-attract romance that will evoke all the feels."
—Mary at USA Today HEA/Frolic (*Fix Me Up, Cowboy*)

"I just love this book!...add in some tense situations and five (YES FIVE!) hot, sexy, alpha, ex-navy SEALS and you got me!"
—A Book Lover's Emporium Book Blog (*While You Were Spying*)

"While You Were Spying is a heart pumping sexy read! You've got action, intrigue and suspense and then on the other hand you have sexual tension, swoony romance, and sassy banter."—Julia Red Hatter Book Blog (*While You Were Spying*)

"It's light, it's fun, great characters and a little dash of conflict for spice."—Red Hot Blue Reads (*Fix Me Up, Cowboy*)

"Everything – the plot, the characters and the dialogue – made this story captivating."—Harlequin Junkie (5 star Top Pick review for *My Song For You*)

"A well-written story that kept me entertained from start to finish."—Harlequin Junkie (4.5 star Recommends review for *This One Moment*)

"I love that Stina Lindenblatt was able to layer this book with so much depth, mystery, hurt, friendship, and of course love."—Four Chicks Flipping Pages (*This One Moment*)

ALSO BY STINA LINDENBLATT

Contemporary Romances

Carson Brothers Series

One More Chance

One More Secret

One More Betrayal

Pushing Limits Series

This One Moment

My Song For You

I Need You Tonight

Spicy Romantic Comedy Novels

By The Bay Series

Decidedly Off Limits

Decidedly with Baby

Decidedly with Love

Decidedly with Mistletoe

Decidedly by Chance

Decidedly with Luck

Decidedly with Wishes

Visit stinalindenblattauthor.com for more books

DECIDEDLY OFF LIMITS

A SPECIAL EDITION BOXSET

STINA LINDENBLATT

Decidedly Off Limits and *Decidedly with You* are works of fiction. Names, characters, places, and incidents are products of the author's imagination or are used fictitiously. Any resemblance to actual events, locales, or persons, living or dead, is entirely coincidental.

Decidedly Off Limits Copyright © 2016 by Stina Lindenblatt

Decidedly with You Copyright © 2023 by Stina Lindenblatt

Excerpt from *Decidedly With Baby* by Stina Lindenblatt copyright © 2017 by Stina Lindenblatt

ALL RIGHTS RESERVED

No part of this book may be reproduced, scanned, or distributed in any form without written permission from the author except in the case of brief quotations for the purpose of articles or reviews.

ISBN 978-1-990177-40-8

ISBN 978-0-9958139-0-8 (ebook for *Decidedly Off Limits* only)

Cover design: Stina Lindenblatt

Editing: Bev Rosenbaum and Flat Earth Editing

*To the readers who fall passionately in love
with their favorite book boyfriends.*

DECIDEDLY OFF LIMITS

DECIDEDLY WITH YOU

Decidedly Off Limits bonus prequel.

The short story was originally part of the *Chasing Holiday Tails* charity anthology in 2023. The heroine in "Decidedly with You" is the younger sister of the hero in *Decidedly Off Limits*. She is also the heroine's best friend.

Proposing to his girlfriend on New Year's Eve was supposed to be magical. Too bad the universe has other plans.

1

ERIN

What was the best way to spend New Year's Eve? Or rather, early afternoon on New Year's Eve, at the community center's indoor basketball court.

That's right—face painting at the Cause for the Paws Festival with your best friend.

"There you go," I told the cute four-year-old girl sitting in front of me. I picked up the hand mirror and showed her the flower designs on her cheeks.

She inspected them like an art connoisseur examining a fine painting. A bright smile curved across her face. "Pretty!"

I helped her down, and she skipped to where her family was waiting.

Kelsey's phone pinged next to her paints. She checked the screen, tucking her blond shoulder-length hair behind her ear. "Jasmine confirmed she and her husband will be able to come to the party." They must have finally found a babysitter.

"I can't wait," I said, waving for the next kid in line to take the newly vacated seat. "It's going to be so much fun."

Kelsey released a soft sigh but still managed a smile for the five-year-old boy sitting in front of her. "It will be fun." The disappointment in her voice hit me in the chest like a wobbly Frisbee.

"What's wrong?" I asked.

"Owen had to cancel." Owen being her fiancé.

"Let me guess. He has to work." I stopped myself from rolling my eyes—just—but Kelsey no doubt heard the equivalent of it sneak into my tone.

She shrugged as she finished the paw print on the boy's face. "He's busy trying to make partner."

"And once he's made partner, what then? Face it, Kels, he'll still be too busy to spend time with you. You deserve better than that." Owen hadn't always been that way. In college, he'd been a great boyfriend, sweet and funny and always there for Kelsey.

She high-fived the boy and helped him down from the chair. "There's nothing I can do about it. He's my fiancé."

"He might be your fiancé, but you aren't married yet." The way Owen was going with picking a wedding date, Kelsey and I would be old women rocking away on the porch, before she got to walk down the aisle with him.

"Would you like flowers and paw prints on your cheeks?" I asked the little girl now seated in front of me.

She replied with a rapid bobbing of her head.

"Not all of us have found such a devoted love of their life like you have." Kelsey flashed me a smile that said I was the luckiest woman alive.

Now it was my turn to release the slow leak of a sigh. A sigh that hopefully no one else heard.

"What's wrong?" she asked, echoing my earlier question.

I dabbed my brush in the purple paint and began creating petals on the girl's cheek. The girl's mother was chatting with two other women. All were oblivious to Kelsey's and my conversation. "I think Darren's having second thoughts about me."

"What do you mean?"

"I think he might be trying to find a way to end things with me."

Kelsey's shocked-eyed expression almost had me doubled over in laughter...if my heart wasn't stumbling over what I suspected.

"Why would you even think that? The man is absolutely in love with you. I wish Owen looked at me like Darren looks at you."

"How does he look at me?"

Kelsey's expression turned dreamy. "Like you're his world, sun, and universe wrapped up with a shiny gold bow."

I'd always thought that was how he looked at me. But lately?

"He's been acting weird," I explained. "And secretive."

"In what way?" She handed the mirror to the boy so he could check out the paw prints on his face.

"It's hard to explain. It's just...well..." I glanced at the line of kids waiting their turn. Now wasn't the time to go into why my gut was telling me something was wrong.

The same gut reaction I ignored when my last boyfriend started acting strange. What happened? Turned out he'd been offered a job in Tampa. Not exactly San Francisco's next-door neighbor.

Oh, and he didn't tell me the news right away.

Nope. He hadn't been ready to give up sex with me quite yet, so he'd kept that info to himself.

I found out about it two days before he moved away.

Nice, huh?

What if Darren was getting ready to dump me because he'd been offered a job across the country? He was a brilliant electrical engineer with a graduate degree in robotics. Who wouldn't want him?

Asha, a tall curvy woman with magenta protective braids knotted on top of her head, approached our table. The coordinator for the animal rescue shelter wore skinny black jeans, a bright green tunic, and a worried frown.

"Kelsey. Erin. You haven't seen Mashed Potato, have you?" Her faded Jamaican accent lifted her vowels.

"Mashed Potato?" I asked. "Like the food?"

"No—as in one of the dogs up for adoption." Asha held up a piece of paper with the picture of a small dog. His hair was a mix of cream-and-golden fluffy curls. "He was accidentally let out of his enclosure, and we don't know where he went."

My heart squeezed at his cuteness. "Oh, he's adorable."

"He is. And very curious. His curiosity has a habit of getting him into trouble."

He sounded like Darren.

According to Darren's mom, her son's curious nature had landed him in all kinds of trouble growing up. He was always figuring out how things worked, taking them apart, and putting them back together again. For the most part.

As a kid, he hadn't been into sports. Books—especially science books—had been his passion.

Yep, Darren and Mashed Potato had something in common.

Well, not so much the reading part. Or putting things back together.

"We'll keep an eye open for him," I tell Asha.

"That would be great. Thank you." She hurried off to the next table.

"Speaking of Darren." Kelsey nodded toward the entrance of the indoor basketball court.

My boyfriend—hot as always in jeans and a dark green Henley—was walking our way. His wavy hair looked as if he'd recently ran his fingers through the light-brown strands. My heart and horny bits let out a lust-felt sigh.

Four and a half days. That's how long it was since I'd last seen him. He'd been in North Carolina for work.

I finished painting the pink flower on the girl's cheek while my heart pounded happily in my chest. Much like it had when I'd first met Darren.

How did we meet?

Kelsey and I were sitting on the ground at the park, eating lunch and watching a group of guys playing Frisbee. Okay, I was ogling them. Kelsey had been texting Owen. She said something to me—I don't remember what—and I turned to look at her.

Something smacked me on my forehead, and a Frisbee landed on my lap.

A shadow fell over me as I picked up the Frisbee. I glanced up, and a pair of friendly blue eyes met mine. The man's hair glowed in the sunlight, and for a heartbeat I thought perhaps he was an angel.

He kneeled in front of me, shirtless, his skin pale like he'd spent a fair amount of time indoors. He said something to me, but I missed what that was. I was too busy appreciating the view. The guy obviously worked out, his muscles long and lean.

"Are you okay?" he repeated. I assumed that was what he'd said the first time.

"I'm fine thanks." I smiled, even though I was still a little dazed from the Frisbee collision.

His mouth curved into a grin, and I had an impossible time tearing my gaze from his lips. I was vaguely aware of Kelsey coughing back a giggle.

"I'm glad you're all right." He picked up the Frisbee and jogged back to the men. They went back to playing the game, but he kept coming over to make sure I was okay. That I didn't have a concussion.

It was the third time he came to check on me that he'd asked my name.

The fourth time, he told me his name.

And the fifth time?

The fifth time he came over to our blanket, he'd knelt in front of me...and asked me out on a date.

"Hey," Darren said, bringing me back to the present. He gifted me with the goofy grin that usually turned my stomach fluttery. This time was no exception.

I rocked onto my toes so I could reach his mouth. His spicy scent that was all Darren draped around me like a cozy blanket on a cold rainy day.

His phone rang in his pocket. He put his finger up for me to hold my thought and answered the phone. I dropped back onto my heels.

Without saying a word to me, he turned and walked away.

Hot disappointment oozed through me. I flashed Kelsey a *see-what-I-mean?* look.

She rolled her eyes, the meaning behind the action directed at me. She probably had a point. Answering the phone wasn't weird behavior.

But that didn't stop the nagging feeling things were about to change between Darren and me.

Something bad. Something that would rock my world...and not in a good way.

2

DARREN

What was it with bosses and their bad timing?

I'd driven straight to the community center from the airport just to see my girl and kiss her. Well, straight here after a quick stop at my apartment to shower and grab the ring.

That's right. *The* ring.

The two-carat diamond engagement ring. I'd planned to propose to Erin as we counted down the new year.

New year. New chapter of our life.

"Are you planning to keep me in suspense?" Jamieson, my boss, asked. "Did Craigson agree to the changes?"

You would think the two men could've hammered this out on Zoom. But nope. Jamieson had felt it would be better if I flew to Charlotte and talk to Craigson in person.

"He did. He was impressed with the suggestions and wants to go ahead with them." It had been my idea to make the changes to the surgical robot arm.

"Glad to hear that."

Various booths had been set up throughout the gym. Booths with games and other activities to entertain the kids.

Booths selling foods and crafts. My friend, Conner, was headed my way from one of the tables as I ended the call. His volunteer shift at the festival finished a few minutes ago, which meant Erin would also be finishing her shift soon.

"So? You're still planning to propose tonight?" He jerked his head to where Erin was painting a pink flower on a redheaded girl's cheek.

"Yup. During the fireworks." Erin happened to be a big fan of romantic gestures. I was notoriously known for being a romantic doofus.

But not this time.

This time, I would prove to her and everyone else that I could be romantic.

"Isn't that kinda cliché?" Conner's mouth twisted into an annoying smirk.

"Ha! What do you know? I bet McKenna"—his girlfriend— "would love it."

He lifted a yeah-I-don't-think-so eyebrow.

"Proposing during the fireworks is a great romantic gesture. Women lap that stuff up." Besides, even if it were cliché, it wasn't like Erin would say no. We'd already talked about marriage and about having kids. It was something we both wanted. But since we hadn't discussed it in a while, she wouldn't see my proposal coming.

Conner's phone pinged, and he checked the screen. "Speaking of McKenna, she's ready for me to pick her up from work. I won't be long." He smacked me on the arm, his way of saying *later*, and walked toward the exit.

And I headed to the face painting table.

"If you had a pet unicorn," Erin said to the four-year old girl in front of her. "What would you name it?"

The girl seemed to ponder the question, her lips twisted to the side, her expression thoughtful. "Bubble Gum," she replied with a big grin.

"That's a great name."

Erin continued painting the pink flower on the girl's cheek, and the image of her one day doing the same to our kids popped into my head. Without a doubt, she'd be an amazing mother.

My chest grew warm thinking about it.

The girl scooted off the chair, the flower completed, and ran over to a woman waiting to the side. Erin pushed to her feet and turned to face me. My favorite smile spread across her face, and my heart stammered like it always did when she aimed the smile my way. "I've officially finished my volunteer shift."

I pulled her into my arms, her light floral scent reminding me I was home. Her arms and sweet body were home. My lips met hers in a kiss that wasn't the hungry, soul-satisfying kind I'd been craving for the past four days. It was a quick, family-festival-friendly kiss that left me unsatisfied.

"A dog has gone AWOL," she said, her eyes wide with an emotion that made me think of hope. "I thought we could help search for the poor thing. He's waiting to find his forever home, and I'd hate for him to miss out on that."

The one thing I'd learned when it came to those beautiful green eyes of hers?

I could never say no to them...or her.

"Of course. Whatever you want."

She smiled, and there went my heart stumbling again.

"I'll go tell Kelsey." Erin walked over to her best friend, spoke briefly with her, and returned to where I was standing. "She'll join us once her replacement shows up."

"Any idea what the dog looks like?" I asked.

Erin showed me a picture on her phone of what looked like a photo printed on paper. "His name is Mashed Potato."

I chuckled. "He looks more like a twice-baked potato minus the skin."

"I think he's adorable." She smiled lovingly at the phone. The little dude had clearly won her heart.

We set off on our mission.

Erin threaded her fingers with mine and led me to the tables several yards away. Pamphlets had been spread across the tablecloth. In the background, a recent Taylor Swift hit played through the gym speakers. The music wasn't loud to drown out conversation—just loud enough to be noticed. A group of little girls were jumping around to the song. "How was your trip?"

"It was good." It would have been better if she'd been with me. "Glad to be home though."

"How about we play a game?"

Okay, not what I was expecting. "What kind of game?"

"Word association. I'll start." She crouched in front of a table, picked up the edge of the tablecloth, and peered underneath. "Missing."

"Dog."

Erin looked up at me, her mouth curled adorably to one side. "I hope not all your answers have to do with Mashed Potato."

I returned her smirk. "Guess that depends on the word. My turn. Table."

"Chair." She pushed to her feet. "Job."

"Income. Kisses."

We walk toward the next table.

"You." She lifted the edge of the tablecloth and checked under the table. "City." She shook her head, letting me know the dog wasn't there.

"San Francisco. You know, there are more fun games to play," I said, pulling her to her feet. "Like strip poker." I shot her a teasing glance. She laughed.

We continued searching for Mashed Potato. We were on the other side of the gym, with no clue to where the little dude could have gone, when Erin's brother, Trent, and Kelsey approached us from opposite directions. Kelsey wore jeans and a lightweight sweater. Trent had on a business suit and had obviously come here straight from work.

Kelsey stopped walking and her eyes went wide. She stared at Trent as if he was the last person she'd expected to see, which made sense. Erin's brother was a notorious workaholic.

A blush reddened Kelsey's cheeks. *Interesting.*

Erin searched for Mashed Potato behind a pile of shipping boxes. Without saying a word to Trent, Kelsey rushed over to join her.

A friendly grin curved across Trent's face. "Hey, Darren. How are things going?"

"Good. You?"

"Can't complain. I'm looking forward to tonight's party." He glanced at Erin and Kelsey, except I got the impression he was staring at Kelsey...or more specifically, her ass. His best friend's sister's ass. The best friend who was a Navy SEAL.

But even if he was interested in Kelsey and her brother didn't care if they hooked up, Erin would never go for it. Trent wasn't allowed to date any of her friends. That was her number one rule when it came to her brother. He'd been involved with one of her friends in college. From what I'd gathered, things had not gone well. Something about his ex-girlfriend going psycho on Erin after Trent ended things.

"Can I ask you a question?" I said, distracting him from watching Kelsey.

"Sure. What's up?"

"I'm planning to propose to your sister during the fireworks. Do you think that sounds corny?"

He pressed his lips together as if trying not to burst out laughing. "You really want to marry her? Your funeral." He wasn't saying it to be malicious. He loved Erin. Both her brothers loved her. Luckily, he and I had always gotten on well.

Amusement crinkled the corners of his eyes. "In truth, it's not Erin you have to worry about impressing. It's me. And Curtis. As a retired SEAL, he's not easy to impress." Trent crossed his arms, flashing me a devious glance. "How are you planning to impress us, lover boy?"

I rolled my eyes. Trent was not the one I had to impress.

Not by a long shot.

That honor went to the woman I was in love with.

The woman on the floor, looking under another tablecloth.

3

ERIN

I checked behind the cardboard boxes. Still no sign of the missing fluffball. "I'm not getting anywhere when it comes to pumping info out of Darren," I told Kelsey. "I still have no idea why he's acting so weird."

But what did I expect? The word association game? Not exactly high on the list of the CIA's most used interrogation techniques. Had I really expected him to spill everything when I said *job*?

Apparently.

Kelsey didn't respond. She seemed to be staring at my brother, Trent, but that couldn't be what held her interest. She'd known him since we were little kids.

I shrugged off the feeling I was missing something. She probably wasn't even looking at him. "Kels?"

She gave her head a small shake, as if waking from a trance. "Huh? Sorry. What did you say?"

"Where were you?"

She looked down at her feet and then up at me. "Right here."

"That's not what I meant." And she knew it. The twitching

of her mouth gave that away. "You were a million miles from here. Were you thinking about Owen?" And how her dumbass fiancé wouldn't be bothering to show up for our New Year's Eve party this evening.

"Yes...that's...that's it. What were you asking me while I was daydreaming about my wonderfully sweet fiancé?" A cheery smile brightened her face.

"I tried to find out why Darren's acting weird, but I struck out."

"What did he say?"

"I didn't ask him. I played a word association game with him to try to figure it out."

"A word association game?" Kelsey sounded out each word as if attempting to make sense of them, but the corners of her mouth were twitching again. "And how did that work for you?"

I lifted my shoulders in a half-hearted shrug. "Not very well. It's hard to know what words to use if you don't know what's going on in the first place."

Kelsey and I continued searching for Mashed Potato, checking under the tablecloths and behind boxes. Trent and Darren were talking. Trent looked amused. I couldn't see Darren's face.

Kelsey got down on her stomach and peered under the stage, where a group of actors were performing a skit for the kids. "Why don't you just ask him why he's acting strange?"

I groaned—the sound drowned out by the kids' laughter. "I can't do that."

"Why not?" She pushed to her feet and we turned around.

"Because no one likes being told they're acting..." My sentence came to an abrupt standstill, and I stared at the man approaching us. Kingston Bourne. Yes, *that* Kingston Bourne. "Oh."

He was the boyfriend who'd crushed my heart when he moved away because of a job opportunity. He hadn't changed much in the past three years, other than his golden hair was a little longer around his ears, enhancing his rugged good looks.

He still smelled the same. His sandalwood scent used to make my body go tingly.

And now?

Not even a teensy tiny tingle.

"Erin?" He looked at me as if I were an illusion. "You look as beautiful as always. Are you also here to adopt a pet?"

Mashed Potato's image flashed in my head, and my heart melted. "No. I was volunteering as one of the face painters. Kelsey and I were."

He smiled at her. "Good to see you again, Kelsey."

"You too, Kingston." Her voice sounded slightly off-kilter, as if she was being diplomatic to him while at the same time giving me a mental big hug.

Something moved in my periphery, and I glanced down. The missing dog was sitting by my feet, looking up at me expectantly. He cocked his head to the side.

"Mashed Potato!" I crouched and stroked him. "Where've you been all this time?"

He barked and scrambled to his feet, his tail wagging.

I scooped him up. He licked my face. His tongue tickled, and I giggled.

"I'm going to check out the kitties' room," Kelsey told me. "Will you be okay?"

I knew what she meant. She was asking if I was okay with her leaving me alone with my ex.

"Yes. I'll be there in a few minutes, after I give Mashed Potato to Asha."

She nodded and hurried off.

"Yours?" Kingston scratched Mashed Potato behind the ears.

"No, he's one of the dogs up for adoption." I turned Mashed

Potato so I could see his face. "Aren't you? And some amazing person is going to be your human parent."

He licked my face again.

"He seems to like you." A smile curved across Kingston's face.

"Are you here to adopt a pet?" Yes, I might have been a little curious at what he was doing here.

"That's right. I moved back to San Francisco before Christmas. Figured I could use a companion. So here I am." He spread his arms wide, indicating to the festival.

"I thought you had a great job in Florida." The way he'd talked it up before dumping me, it had been his dream job.

"I did. But my girlfriend and I went separate ways at the beginning of the year. Tampa wasn't the same for me after that."

Wow. I hadn't even known he had a girlfriend. It wasn't like I'd kept up-to-date with his life on social media.

Truth?

I'd unfollowed him right after he told me he was moving to Tampa. "So you moved back to San Francisco?"

"Yep. A job opening recently came up for here. I've always liked the city"—his gaze flicked briefly to my lips—"so coming here was a no-brainer."

"You found Mashed Potato?" Darren's deep voice had me turning my head. The voice that always sent my heart executing somersaults that would've impressed even Simone Biles.

"He found *me*," I explained. "I was just about to return him to the dog adoption room."

Kingston scratched Mashed Potato behind the ear again, his fingers accidentally brushing mine. "I'll come with you. I was headed that way to check out the dogs. We can catch up on the way."

Darren glanced between Kingston and me. The small frown

that popped up whenever he was puzzled about something—the frown I thought was adorable—appeared on his brow. "I take it you two know each other?"

"Kingston, this is Darren." I nodded at the man I was in love with. "Darren's my boyfriend." Despite him acting weird lately, my insides turned gooey at the boyfriend reference.

"Erin used to be my girlfriend," Kingston said with a grin, as if he was proud of the fact.

"Before he moved to Florida," I pointed out. I could tell the second Darren pieced things together. He knew about the past relationship that had left my heart broken until he came along.

Not wanting to skip farther down memory lane, I left the gym, Mashed Potato in my arms. Darren and Kingston flanked me. By the time we entered the dog adoption room, Kingston and I had only skimmed the surface on how our families were doing.

"Good luck with finding your forever home," I whispered to Mashed Potato and kissed the top of his head. Smiling at him, I handed the sweet dog to Asha.

She grinned at him. "You really are a little rascal." Her gaze flicked up to mine. "Thanks, Erin, for locating him."

"You're welcome." I skipped over how he found me... because that would have sounded like I was adopting him when I wasn't.

Darren's phone rang, and he answered it. From what I could tell, the call had something to do with work.

"I'm going to find Kelsey and Trent," I mouthed to him, figuring the call might take a few minutes. They usually did when they were about his job—especially when his team was approaching a project deadline. He nodded.

Kingston was talking to Asha when I slipped out of the room.

"Darren has accepted the position in Charlotte," a familiar woman's voice said.

I glanced at where it came from, and my heart walked into a brick wall. Katarina Dewitt. One of Darren's supervisors. She was talking on the phone but didn't seem to have noticed me. "That's right. He'll be a tremendous addition to their team."

She walked off, preventing me from hearing the rest of her conversation, and climbed the staircase to the main level of the community center.

Damn. Darren hadn't mentioned the position or that he'd accepted a job offer. Guess that explained why he'd been acting weird.

The air in my lungs whooshed out on a hard breath. I felt like a partially inflated lawn Santa left up after Christmas, my legs weak and wobbly.

By some small miracle, I got my feet moving and entered the cat adoption room.

Kelsey was over by the cages. Trent was on his phone, standing near the wall on the opposite side of the room. Work, no doubt. Trent took being workaholic to a new level. Even more so than Darren did.

At least Trent and Darren were here. At least they'd be coming to the New Year's Eve party—unlike Kelsey's fiancé.

Darren came into the room and joined me. He leaned down, his warm breath brushing my ear. His smell—a mix of his spicy cologne and him—sent my body into tingling overdrive. And for a heartbeat I forgot all about the phone call I'd overheard.

But reality rudely intruded on the moment, and I opened my mouth to ask him about the new job.

My airway tightened, preventing the words from coming out.

"Christ, Erin, I'll go crazy if I don't get to kiss you soon." The husky need in his voice was all it took for my thoughts to splutter to a standstill.

"I want to kiss you too," I told him. And not the G-rated kisses from earlier.

If I were smart, I would break up with him now since he was moving away soon. But, as the devil on my shoulder so keenly pointed out, I might as well make the most of Darren's and my remaining time together.

I'd worry about my broken heart later.

Darren threaded his fingers with mine and led me out of the room. Doors lined either side of the hallway. He opened them one by one, but none of the rooms were empty. All were being used for the festival.

He opened the last door and peered inside. "In here."

"The janitor's closet?" It wasn't even that big. There was only enough room for two people to stand in each other's space and grab supplies from the metal shelves.

Or to kiss.

I stepped inside, tugging Darren in with me, and clicked on the single light bulb.

He closed the door behind him, and his lips crashed into mine.

My mouth welcomed him in, my tongue playing the gracious host. Stroking. Tasting. Teasing. My arms hooked behind his neck, and I stretched up on my toes.

He grabbed the backs of my thighs and hoisted me up. My legs wrapped around his hips.

He turned in the cramped space and pushed my back against the door. The soft thud was the only noise that permeated the air beyond our panted breaths and equally soft moans.

"God, I've missed you," I murmured, our lips barely parting.

I pressed my aching core against his hardening length. Hunger burned in my veins, pulsated between my legs. I shifted, my body accidentally rubbing along his hardness. The resulting ache, desperate with longing, sent a thrill through me.

"I want you so badly," I whispered.

"I want you too." His thick, gravelly voice sent another wave of need spiraling through me.

I traced my fingers down his torso to between my thighs and brushed his cock. "We can't be long," I reminded him. "Trent and Kelsey will wonder where we vanished to."

"So a quickie?"

"God, yes," I moaned, every inch of my body on board with the plan.

"You'll have to be quiet." He grinned, and the devilish quirk of his mouth came close to incinerating my panties. "Do you think you can do that?"

No. "Absolutely." I flashed him an innocent smile. I wasn't known for being quiet during sex. That wasn't my fault. No one knew how to give me orgasms the way he did.

Darren lowered me to the ground. I kicked off my boots and shimmied out of my jeans and panties. His gaze traveled over me, his light-blue eyes dark, ravenous, but he didn't appear to be in a rush to do anything, other than to stare at me. A deluge of heat coursed to between my legs, turning me wet.

"Hi," I whispered. "Staring at me like that doesn't make this a quickie."

"Right." He tore his gaze from me and lowered his jeans and black boxer briefs to his ankles.

He hoisted me up again. My legs encircled his hips, and I hooked my ankles against his taut ass.

His fingers slipped between us and teased my clit. A soft moan fluttered from between my lips.

"You're gonna have to be quieter than that." His chuckle brushed my ear.

"Okay." My reply came out more like a squeak than a whisper.

"You're already soaking for me." His words poured out on a rumbling groan, which I swear made me wetter. He lowered his forehead to mine. "I need to be inside you, Erin. Now."

I nodded, incapable of doing much else, teetering on the edge of an orgasm.

He pressed the thick head of his cock against my opening and eased his way in.

Oooooooh, God. He'd only been gone four days, yet my body was acting like I hadn't had sex in four years. My body hugged him, loved him, worshipped him while I silently pleaded for him not to move to North Carolina.

I dropped my head back on the door. Darren thrust inside me. The door banged against the jamb.

"Oops," I giggle-whispered and double-checked the tiny space. But nothing had changed in the last few minutes. The only spot without shelves was the door and the gap near us where a mop leaned against the wall.

"Are you sure you want to do this?" he asked once more. I nodded, the movement eager. I wasn't going to last much longer. Stopping wasn't an option.

He thrust again. *Bang. Bang.*

Five more thrusts, then my world imploded, the fireworks lighting up the sky. The New Year's Eve ones? A pale kissing cousin.

My soft heat squeezed tight around Darren's cock, unwilling to surrender it. And I watched his face as his own orgasm powered through him. He looked so beautiful, so breathtaking, so free.

I blinked away the tears that misted my vision.

I'd never loved a man like I loved Darren, and I would soon be losing him.

A goodbye fuck...that's what this was. Or should be. But I couldn't...not yet. I needed to make love to him one more time before I ended things with him. Because that was what I needed to do once the new year began. End things between us. To make leaving easier for Darren.

But even if it made things easier for him, when it came to me, there would be nothing easy about what I had to do.

My heart would shatter. Shatter into a million unfixable pieces.

Darren kissed me one last time, stealing my breath and my wit, and lowered me to my feet.

I bent to retrieve my clothes. Something glinted on the floor, Darren's jeans partially covering whatever it was. I nudged the denim aside, revealing a ring.

A gorgeous diamond ring. *Wow.*

I hadn't noticed it when we came into the closet, but I hadn't exactly been looking at the floor.

I picked up the ring, the silver warm against my fingertips. "Wonder who this belongs to."

4

———

DARREN

The engagement ring between Erin's fingers gleamed in the light from the single bulb. Her eyes were wide with emotions I wasn't sure how to label. Shock? Curiosity?

Fuckity damn.

I'd wanted the proposal to be magical. Romantic. Something Erin would never forget.

True, being proposed to in the janitor's closet—next to a dirty mop, no less—might be something Erin would have a hard time forgetting. But that wasn't the story I'd envisioned one day telling our children.

So I did the only thing I could. "It's Conner's."

Erin blinked, her jaw practically hitting the floor. "Conner is proposing to McKenna?" Her surprised expression quickly morphed into confusion, crinkles creasing her forehead. "If he's proposing to her, how did the ring end up in here?"

Good question.

"Because..." My voice lilted up at the end in almost a question but not quite. "He gave it to me. For safekeeping. He was worried about losing it before he could ask her. And...and he

25

gave it to me when he got here." I rubbed the nape of my neck, hoping Erin would buy the lame explanation. "It must have fallen out of my pocket."

She chuckled, handing the ring to me. "You're not doing a good job so far keeping it safe."

"You're probably right about that."

"But the orgasm was definitely worth it." She flashed me a grin. "It's a gorgeous ring. I'm sure McKenna will love it." There was something slightly off about Erin's voice at the last part, but I couldn't place what it was. "Haven't they only been together two months?" She started to put on her clothes. "I didn't realize they were that serious."

I pulled my underwear and jeans up my legs. "I know. I was surprised too." I zipped up my jeans.

"So when's he planning to ask her?"

"During the fireworks." I stuffed the ring in my pocket.

"Oh, that's so romantic."

Ha! I was right. I knew Erin would love that. "We should probably get out of here before someone wonders what we're doing." Especially if anyone heard the closet door banging. Repeatedly.

"Good plan. I'm going to see how Kelsey's doing with the cats."

"Okay, I'll catch up with you there. There's something I need to do first." Like warn Conner that Erin thought he was proposing to his girlfriend tonight.

I walked with Erin to the cat room, and then returned to the room with the dogs for adoption.

Mashed Potato was sitting next to a Black woman with magenta braids tied in a knot on top of her head. She was talking to another couple.

The couple thanked her and walked away.

I strode over to her, dodging past a young child patting a

medium-sized dog on the head. Several dogs in the far corner of the room let out a series of small barks.

I wasn't the only person heading toward the woman, but Erin's idiot ex beat me there.

"I'd like to adopt Mashed Potato," he told her.

Oh. Shit.

Mashed Potato looked up at his name and barked.

"Really?" The word shot from me, a sarcastic tone singeing the edges. Erin's ex turned, his eyebrow raised. "You don't seem like the small-dog type," I got out by way of an explanation. Except, hell if I knew what type of dog lover he was.

"Well, you know what they say about not judging a book by its cover." He turned to the woman from the animal shelter. "The woman I care about has fallen in love with this dog. And he's won my heart over too."

"My girlfriend has also fallen in love with Mashed Potato," I explained to her. "Maybe we should see who *he* would prefer to live with." That would make the most sense.

"I'm pretty sure Mashed Potato has made it clear he likes her."

Something about the way he said that set off sirens in my head.

"You aren't talking about Erin, my girlfriend, are you?" I asked, hoping I was wrong. If he adopted Mashed Potato because of her, it meant he wanted to be in her life again. And what man adopted a dog so a woman could friend zone him?

"Doesn't matter who the woman is," he replied. "The main thing is finding Mashed Potato a loving family to go home with."

"I couldn't agree with you more." The woman from the shelter smiled at Erin's ex, as if he'd had offered her the contents of Fort Knox.

I'm planning to one day have a family with the woman in question,

I wanted to throw in his face. But I had already let Trent and Conner in on my plans of proposing to Erin. Did I want these two strangers hearing the news before I could ask Erin to marry me?

Hell no.

"Here you are," Erin said from behind me. I turned to find her and Kelsey approaching us. Kelsey had a box in her arms. A box that let out a plaintiff meow.

"Don't worry, Mr. Kitty Whiskers," Kelsey said. "We're going home very soon."

"You adopted a cat?" I asked, not all that surprised. Kelsey loved cats.

"It was love at first sight. Plus, I've been planning to get one for a while."

A short laugh powered from Erin. "She's had the supplies for several months now."

Erin's ex leaned in and said something in her ear that I couldn't hear. She giggled. Actually freaking giggled. Like she'd used to do when we first met and she flirted with me. Her cheeks pinked, and she ducked her head.

What the hell?

I was about to step in on their private moment when I spotted Conner coming into the room with McKenna in tow. Erin also noticed them, and she flashed Conner a grin that hinted she knew his big secret. *Oh. Shit.*

"I'll be right back," I told the two women, crossing my fingers that Erin's ex didn't adopt Mashed Potato while I was gone.

I didn't slow my pace when I reached Conner. I kept going, grabbing his arm and pulling him along. "I need to talk to you. Now."

He must have sensed my urgency. He didn't protest or pull his arm away. McKenna continued over to Erin and Kelsey. At least Erin wouldn't blurt the engagement news to her.

We stepped outside the room, and Conner leaned against

the wall, amusement tilting one side of his mouth. "So, what's up?"

"Erin found the engagement ring." I patted the pocket where I kept it. "And now she thinks you're proposing to McKenna tonight."

His amused expression didn't budge. "Why does she think that?"

"I panicked and told her it was your ring."

Conner groaned. "You're an idiot. You realize that, right?"

"It was that or propose to her in the janitor's closet," I grumbled.

His face was free of emotion for a fraction of a second, then he burst out laughing. "Christ, you were busy while I was gone. I'd better give McKenna the heads-up or else she's gonna wonder why your girlfriend's acting weird around her."

"Good idea."

"Just so you know," I said with a grin. "Erin thought your fictitious plan to propose to McKenna during tonight's fireworks was romantic."

He snorted a laugh. "That's only because she believed it was me proposing to McKenna." He smacked me on the chest and went back inside the room.

Maybe he was right about the proposal. Which meant I needed to come up with a new Plan A—especially since I'd already told Erin about Conner's fictitious plan to propose during the fireworks.

What I needed was to do something unexpected.

And that was where Mashed Potato came in.

But first I needed to convince the shelter to let me adopt him instead of them giving him to Erin's ex.

5

___

ERIN

"Are you still interested in adopting Mashed Potato?" Asha asked Kingston.

"You're adopting him?" I failed at keeping the high-pitched surprise out of my voice.

"That was the plan...but your boyfriend also wants to adopt him."

"He does?"

Darren and I had talked a few times about getting a dog, but that had been more like a hypothetical. We didn't even live together. I was living with Kelsey while she waited for Owen to pick a wedding date.

Kingston nodded. "Got the impression he wants to adopt him for you."

"Really?" Any warmth inside me was snuffed out like a flame in a storm.

Was Mashed Potato a consolation prize because Darren was moving to North Carolina? *Thanks for being a great girlfriend. Enjoy your new companion.*

"You sound surprised." Kingston crossed his arms, looking a tiny bit smug. "You don't want a dog?"

"No, I would love to have one."

"So, about Mashed Potato?" Asha asked as Darren and Conner joined us. "Are either of you still interested in adopting him?"

"I am." Darren glared at Kingston as if to dare him to argue otherwise.

Kingston lifted his chin. "Me too."

Asha glanced between the two men, her eyes wide, seemingly at a loss at what to do.

"Maybe they could arm wrestle to see who gets to adopt him," Conner suggested with a chuckle.

"That's. Um." Asha cleared her throat. "That's highly unusual."

"It's not a bad idea." Kingston leveled a testosterone-loaded gaze at Darren. "Unless you're afraid you'll lose."

Darren pierced him with the unwavering glare. "Bring it on."

A laugh erupted from Conner. "Unusual or not, looks like the competition is on. Gentlemen." He pointed to an empty table in the corner of the room.

Darren and Kingston didn't wait for Asha to voice her concern. They walked over to the table, both looking prepared to go to battle. Determination smoldered in Darren's expression.

They took a moment to warm up, jogging on the spot and stretching their arms and shoulders.

"Are they planning to win at arm wrestling or enter an Olympic event?" McKenna asked, laughter cozying up in her tone.

"Men!" I muttered. McKenna and Kelsey snickered.

Darren and Kingston sat in the chairs opposite to each other and put their elbows on the table.

Conner placed his hands flat on the table between the two men. "Is it the best of one or three?"

Darren and Kingston eyed each other up, possibly to calculate the odds of winning on the first go. Their builds were similar, so it could go either way. "One," they said simultaneously.

"Okay. Get into position, and I'll count you down."

They did as instructed.

"On the one," Conner told them. "Three. Two. One."

The muscles in Darren's and Kingston's upper body tensed as they fought for dominance. Their faces turned red from the strain, but their arms remained in an upright position, barely swaying a fraction of an inch in either direction.

My heart beat rapidly as if I was the one arm wrestling. I pressed my teeth into my bottom lip, the anticipation too much.

"You can do it, Darren!" I cheered, louder than I probably should have, given we weren't the only people in the room.

Kingston's arm moved two inches, gaining an advantage over Darren. My stomach dropped to the tile floor.

I gasped. I might have whispered, "No!" I wasn't positive.

And then it was Darren who, in a sudden burst of energy or by some divine intervention, was pushing Kingston's hand toward the table. The back of his hand touched the surface.

Darren's stunned expression wasn't that of a man who had won due to a burst of energy or divine intervention or anything like that. Kingston shrugged, but I recognized the look on his face. He'd let Darren win—and Darren knew it.

"He's all yours." Kingston looked between Darren and me, as if asking which of us would be Mashed Potato's owner. As if he also knew Darren would soon be breaking my heart and moving away.

He doesn't know. Only I know the truth. Tears clouded my vision. *Happy thoughts. Don't let them see you cry.*

Not that it mattered. Everyone would assume these were tears of joy because Darren had won Mashed Potato.

"Perfect," Asha said. "Do you want to start the paperwork now?"

"Yes," Darren told her as Mr. Kitty Whiskers let out another plaintive meow.

"I should get him home," Kelsey said. "And finish setting up for the party."

"I'll walk you out." I needed to tell Kelsey, before my world fell apart, about the phone call I overheard. I tugged a smile onto my lips, straining to keep it from falling flat on its face, and directed the smile at Darren. "I won't be long."

Kelsey and I headed for the exit. "I can't believe you guys are getting a dog," she said, her voice all breathy. "That's a huge step in a relationship."

"It's Darren's way of breaking up with me."

She adjusted the box in her arms. "He's not breaking up with you. The man loves you. He's adopting Mashed Potato because you love the dog."

I shook my head. "I overheard his supervisor earlier talking on the phone. Darren accepted a job in Charlotte."

The last time I'd seen Kelsey this surprised....well, I'd have to get back to you on that. But I could guarantee it had been a very long time. "Are you sure? Did you talk to him about it?"

"Not yet. I guess he's waiting till tomorrow to tell me. He didn't want to ruin my New Year's Eve." My heart stumbled and tripped and my chest just thinking about it.

I pulled open the door, and we stepped into the hallway. A few people walked past us, heading toward the indoor basketball courts at the other end.

"That does sound like something he'd do," she said. "I'm so sorry, Erin. And as soon as I put this box in my car, I'll give you a big hug."

"Thanks. I definitely need a hug." More than Kelsey could've possibly realized.

6

DARREN

As I filled in Mashed Potato's adoption paperwork, I was hit with a new-and-improved idea for proposing to Erin.

"Can I buy the ribbon in your hair?" I asked the white college-aged volunteer who'd handed me the papers. "I want to tie a surprise to Mashed Potato's harness for my girlfriend." His big floppy ears would hide the ring.

"If you promise to give him a good home," she said, untying the blue ribbon from her ponytail. "I'll throw in the ribbon for free."

"I promise."

She gave it to me, and I handed her the completed paperwork. She checked it over. "Congratulations! You're now his lucky owner."

I'd be even luckier if Erin said yes when I propose to her at midnight.

I kneeled next to Mashed Potato and secured the ring to his harness.

All right, maybe that wasn't a great idea. I still had to pick up supplies for him on the way home.

I took hold of the end of his leash, and we headed out of the room.

A white cat darted out of nowhere, bolted past us in the hallway, and barreled up the steps to the main floor of the community center.

Mashed Potato barked and lurched forward, straining on his leash.

And a second later, the leash went lax in my hand with Mashed Potato bounding up the stairs, leaving his end of the leash on the floor in front of me.

I snatched it up and went after them, taking two steps at a time. Luckily, the door to the main entrance was shut so they couldn't escape the building that way.

The cat hightailed it around a corner. Mashed Potato followed in pursuit, seeming to have the time of his life.

Erin entered through the glass double doors in time to witness the butt end of her dog disappear around the same corner.

"Mashed Potato's leash came unhooked," I said in a rush and sprinted after the two animals with Erin right behind me.

He vanished into a room farther down the hallway. I chased after him.

The large room had clearly been set up for a New Year's Eve party. Long tables lined the periphery of it, their black tablecloths decorated with glittery gold runners. Pearlized helium balloons in black and silver and gold crowded the ceiling, their ribbons dangling in the air.

Afternoon sunlight shone through the picturesque windows along the outside wall, giving the room a warm, magical glow.

"Wow, this place looks incredible," Erin said behind me, her voice an awed whisper.

"Guess we should get those two out of here before they cause trouble." I assumed the cat was also in here.

"They couldn't have gotten out of this room. They must be under the tables. Mashed Potato?" Erin called out.

A loud hiss came from under a table opposite us. Followed by a bark.

A blur of white shot out from under a table, then Mashed Potato poked his head out from under the tablecloth. He scampered out the rest of the way, his small body dragging the cloth with him.

I darted to the table in time to prevent a decoration tragedy, but I wasn't fast enough to catch Mashed Potato. He went chasing after the cat again, but this time at a more leisurely pace.

"Mashed Potato!" Erin beckoned. He turned and bounded over to her, his tail wagging, the cat quickly forgotten.

Erin crouched and scratched behind his ear. A small divot formed between her eyes, and she lifted up one of Mashed Potato's floppy ears. The ear over where I'd attached the diamond ring.

This was it. Forget fireworks and proposing in front of our friends. This...the room, the private moment between us, Mashed Potato as our witness—it all felt more right than anything I could have planned.

I walked over to Erin, kneeled in front of her, and untied the ring.

Outside the window, the clouds separated, casting a bright ray of light on us like a spotlight. "Erin Taylor Salway. I love you with all my heart. I love waking up next to you in the morning, and I love falling asleep with you in my arms at night. I miss you when you're not by my side, and I count down the seconds until you're with me again. I want to spend the rest of my life with you. Will you marry me?" The words came out easily, without a hint of hesitation.

Did Erin look happy? Overjoyed? Not exactly. More like taken aback. Confused.

Definitely not the reaction I was expecting.

"Um, wow," she said, stumbling over her words. "Why are you proposing with Conner's ring?"

"It's not Conner's ring. He's not proposing to McKenna. I am."

Erin's eyebrows shot up, wrinkling her brow. "You're proposing to McKenna?"

Damn. "No, I meant I'm the one doing the proposing. To you." Which I had just done. Did she miss that part?

Erin stared at me.

Shit. Did I get that all wrong? I'd thought she wanted to one day get married and have a family. Maybe she did. Just not with me.

My heart dropped, taking my stomach with it.

"B-but you're moving to North Carolina," she said, her voice so soft, I barely heard her. "You didn't even ask me if I wanted to go with you. You just accepted the job."

Now it was my turn to be confused. I shook my head. "I'm not moving anywhere. I'm staying in San Francisco. What job are you talking about?"

"I don't know. I overheard Katarina Dewitt on the phone. She was telling the other person you had accepted the position in Charlotte and you'll make a great addition to the team."

"I'm not going anywhere. I promise. Darren Carmichael was offered a job there. Not me."

"Carmichael?" Erin dropped her head in her hands. "God, I heard her say Darren and assumed she meant you. I thought you were going to break up with me and move there."

I pulled Erin's hands away from her face. "Hey, if I was offered a job, I would talk to you about it first. It would be both of our decisions. I love you, Erin. I have no intention of going anywhere without you."

"You don't?" Her eyes shone in the sunlight streaming through the windows.

I caressed her cheekbone. "Never. The only place I want to be is with you."

She released a featherlight breath from between her parted lips. "Okay, ask me again. Ask me if I'll marry you." Hope filled her eyes, her voice, the lines of her body.

"Erin Taylor Salway. Would you do me the honor of being my wife?" My voice caught on the last part, the emotion of the moment catching up with me. A moment that couldn't have been more perfect.

"Yes. I'll marry you, Darren." She laughed, her eyes glistening, but fortunately for a different reason this time. "I want to be with you. Forever. With you and your dog."

"*Our* dog." I looked down at the fluffball and up at the balloons covering the ceiling. My gaze snagged on the clock on the wall. The hands were seconds away from 2 p.m. our time.

Seconds away from Athens welcoming in the new year.

I slipped the ring on her finger, the diamond glinting in the sunlight, and my heart inflated like the helium balloons.

I cupped Erin's face with both hands and kissed her. The tender brushing of lips set off fireworks inside me that none other could compare to—not even the ones ringing in the new year.

"I love you." I deepened the kiss, my tongue worshipping the woman who had my heart and body and soul.

And who would always have them—now and forever more.

DECIDEDLY OFF LIMITS

1

———

KELSEY

Quick, name the top ten sounds you never want to hear while in your car—especially when said noise happens on the way to your best friend's parents' anniversary party.

Willing my car to cling to life for a few more feet, I pulled over to the curb. Cars, trucks, and SUVs rushed past, racing to get home for the weekend. The moment I made it to the side of the road, my car abandoned its will to live. The once purring engine took its final purr—well, more like a groan—then I was met with a deafening silence.

"*Fuck.*" Because, really, is there a better word?

I think not.

The car stuck behind me honked. My poor baby didn't care if Impatient Guy had somewhere more important to go. She wasn't going anywhere. I might not have known anything about cars, but even I could tell that much.

I checked over my shoulder at the busy lane next to me. I could have escaped via the driver's side—if I didn't mind risking my life and becoming roadkill.

Since neither was currently on my daily to-do list, I went

with Plan B. I flipped on the hazard lights, stretched my leg over the gearshift, and tried to climb onto the passenger seat. Tall Victorian houses stood sandwiched together along the street. If they were human, they would have been snickering at me.

The hem of my short dress scooted up my thighs, and that sadly neglected part between my legs accidentally brushed against the gearshift. Naturally, it wasn't too thrilled that this was the only action it would see. Which was a helluva lot more than it had seen for the past 460 days.

But who was counting?

Still awkwardly straddling the gearshift and doing my best not to dry-hump it, I performed a graceful face-plant onto the passenger side. My knee landed on the seat; my face almost smashed into the window. On the bright side the sidewalk was empty of pedestrians. No one had witnessed my moment of humiliation.

I shifted my body and opened the door. With my skirt still hiked up my thighs, I performed a complex move of climbing out while shimmying the hem back into place. The Russian judge would have given me a 2.5, mostly due to lack of technical skills...and well, grace. But at least this time I didn't land on my face.

Why I climbed out of my car was anyone's guess. To scowl at it, maybe. That was about the extent of my mechanical skills.

Since Erin—my best friend—and her husband were already at the party, I called AAA and pleaded for them to send someone. Preferably now.

Apparently, 5:00 p.m. on a Friday afternoon was NOT a good time to need AAA. The soonest they could send someone was in four hours.

The sun peeked from behind a cloud, reminding me there was indeed always a bright side. The party wasn't far from here, and AAA would phone me when the cavalry was on the way.

Now, I just needed to get to the party.

In romance novels, this was the moment when the hero pulled over and offered to help the heroine. In thrillers, this was the moment when the serial killer pulled over and added another notch in his...well, whatever serial killers added a notch to.

A familiar black BMW pulled in front of my car and option B would have been favorable at this point. I inwardly groaned as Trent Salway exited his vehicle.

"Hey Kels, you need help?" Six-foot-plus of dark-haired male hotness in a black business suit walked up to me, and the ache between my legs let out a dreamy sigh. Clearly it hadn't forgotten how I had been crushing on my best friend's big brother for as long as I could remember—only for him to see me as nothing more than a little sister. More specifically, his best friend's little sister.

Trent's gaze dropped to my lips and the ache between my legs drifted into its own fantasy land. *It's not what you think*, my brain pointed out, always the party pooper. *Your lip gloss is probably smeared.*

Unconsciously, I ran the tip of my tongue along my lower lip. Trent's sexy green eyes darkened, and his Adam's apple shot up then slid back down.

His passenger door opened, yanking me out of my lust-filled moment, and a pair of never-ending legs, with shiny red stilettos attached, stepped out. Then in slow motion—or at least it seemed that way in my head—the rest of the body appeared from the car. At the sight of her, my heart clambered out of my chest and crash-landed on the asphalt with a big *splat*.

Whoever this woman was, she was the opposite of me. Her black dress clung to her slim body and her auburn hair was swept up in an elegant bun. Her makeup was smoky and made her look like a Hollywood starlet. My ex-fiancé used to call me kitten sexy—a nice way of saying I was cute—but I was nothing compared to this woman.

I had to admit, though, as my heart climbed back into my chest, she was perfect for Trent. She was sophistication on a stick.

Sophistication-on-a-stick smiled her perfect red lips at me. "Hi."

I wished I could say her voice was like claws being dragged down a chalkboard. I wished I could say she didn't have an Australian accent that would cause every guy within a ten-mile radius to blow his load at the sound of it.

"Kels, this is Holly," Trent said. "Holly, this is my sister's best friend, Kelsey."

Holly offered her manicured hand and I shook it. "It's nice to meet you." The voice was so sincere and friendly, it was hard not to instantly like her, even if she was dating the man whose lips I craved.

"It's nice to meet you, too." Was I supposed to say that Trent had told me so much about her? And maybe he would have if I hadn't spent the last ten years avoiding him. Which, I should point out, wasn't easy when his family was pretty much the only family I had left, other than my older brother Liam.

"So what's the deal with your car?" Trent asked.

I shrugged. "No idea. She started making funny noises and died."

"What kind of funny noises?" Holly said.

I described them as best as I could, not that it mattered if I was correct or not. It wasn't as if she could tell me what was wrong with the car.

"Sounds like a broken fan belt."

I stared at her. "How do you know that?"

She laughed like a hyena in heat and I mentally did a happy dance. At least there was one not-so-perfect aspect about her.

"When you have two brothers who are obsessed with cars, you learn a thing or two."

If Holly's interesting laugh bothered Trent, he didn't show it. He was too busy nodding at what she had said, even though he wouldn't know what it meant any more than I did. Cars had never been his passion. Not like with some guys. I suspected he only had a BMW because of the status associated with owning one. Which was kind of funny. The Trent I remembered couldn't have cared less about status.

"Have you called for help yet?" he asked.

"Yep. They should be here in about four hours." I glanced down the street, as if that would magically speed up the tow truck's arrival.

"In that case, you can come with us. I'll drive you back before they get here." Without waiting for a response, he headed for his car. That was Trent for you. Once he made up his mind, end of discussion.

Holly flashed me another friendly smile, then followed him.

I looked back and forth between the two cars. I didn't like the idea of abandoning my poor baby—but I didn't have much choice.

"C'mon, Kels," Trent said, his smooth, deep voice causing the ache between my legs to let out another dreamy sigh. "Erin will skin me alive and feed my carcass to a pack of wild dogs if we're late."

Even though my fate wouldn't be quite as dramatic, I grabbed my purse from my car, locked the doors, and joined Trent and his...girlfriend? Erin hadn't mentioned that he had a girlfriend, or maybe she didn't know about her yet. Or she didn't think I'd care either way, since I wasn't supposed to be lusting after her brother.

As we drove toward Trent's old home, Holly twisted around

in her seat to talk to me. "How long have you two known each other?"

"Since we were kids," I said. "Our families used to live near each other. I spent as much time at his house as he did at mine."

"Kelsey's brother, Liam, has been my best friend since fifth grade," Trent explained. "You'll meet him at the party."

"Will your parents be there too?" she asked me.

The car accident that stole my parents from me and tore my life apart happened when I was eighteen, but even though I had long since moved on, a flash of pain in my heart stirred at her question. "No. They're dead."

Her face twisted into the pitying look I was more than familiar with. I missed it as much as I missed writing exams. "Oh, I'm sorry to hear that."

"It's okay. They died ten years ago."

"What does your brother do?"

"He's a Navy SEAL."

Deep furrows formed across Holly's forehead. She understood what most women chose to ignore when they fantasized about the heroes in romance novels—that my brother's career was damn dangerous.

"He's a hero," Trent added and a small smile graced my lips at that truth. "He once saved my brother's life when they were on a mission together."

Holly's gaze shot to Trent. "Your brother's a SEAL, too?"

"Not anymore. He was injured and honorably discharged from the military. Now he works in Silicon Valley."

"Will I get to meet him today?"

Trent shook his head and parallel parked on the street near his parents' home, a two-story, light-blue Victorian house with white trim. "No, his wife's pregnant and due any day now. They couldn't get away because of that."

Even though I already knew this, disappointment rolled

through me. Unlike with Trent, I had never crushed on Curtis. His claim to fame was that he could make me laugh. Usually during dinner.

Usually to his mom's chagrin.

As Holly and Trent walked toward the front door, I slowed down for a minute, working hard to get air into my lungs.

And it had nothing to do with them being together.

Okay, it might've had a smidgen to do with that.

Trent was introducing Holly to his parents when I stepped into the house. The place hadn't changed much over the years, with its nautical-themed decorations and antiques. As always, his father's arm was around his mother's waist. I almost sighed out loud at seeing them this way. There was never any doubt how much he worshiped his wife—and vice versa. My parents had been the same way.

"Mom, Dad," Trent said, "This is Holly Whittaker. She's an investment analyst at my firm."

So not only was she gorgeous, she was smart. And let's not forget super nice. Darn it. Why couldn't she have at least been bitchy? Then it would've been easier to hate her.

"It's nice to meet you," Joanne said, smiling at Holly.

Trent's father shook Holly's hand as my best friend walked into the foyer, hand resting on her protruding stomach. Whereas I was tall, Erin was short, which made her look more pregnant than her current four months.

She grinned when she saw me and hugged me. "You're late."

"Sorry. My car broke down on the way."

"And if I hadn't done my civic duty and rescued her, she'd still be stranded." The corner of Trent's mouth jerked into a one-sided grin, his usual look when he was teasing me.

"Holly," Joanne said, "have you met Trent's sister yet?"

Holly shook her head while Erin eyed the woman like she was a curious science experiment that could go wrong at any second. She quickly glanced at me and I shrugged. Not that she knew how I felt about her brother. As much as she loved him, she had never considered him good boyfriend material—as his track record with girls clearly illustrated.

And there was also that incident back in college, when She-Who-Shall-Not-Be-Named (AKA Michaela, Erin's former classmate and close friend) dated him. Let's just say it didn't end well for all parties concerned. After that, Erin made it clear that none of her friends were allowed to date Trent. *Ever*.

After the introductions were over, Erin grabbed my hand. "C'mon," she said, and dragged me into the living room where my brother would be waiting.

As soon as I spotted him near the couch, talking to Erin's husband, my body put the brakes on and refused to keep moving.

2

TRENT

K elsey stood frozen in the doorway—and shit, all those feelings I had for her from high school slammed into me, hard. Those feelings that had temporarily done a number on me when I first saw her stranded on the road. Those feelings that Liam, her brother, would've pounded on me for if he knew about them.

Best Friend Rule #1: never fuck the guy's sister.

Best Friend Rule #2: never think of fucking the guy's sister.

Best Friend Rule #3: never think about her naked while *not* thinking about fucking her.

My dick twitched, reminding me why these were all great rules for self-preservation. Especially when your best friend was a Navy SEAL trained to fight and win. Those assholes he was sent to take down during a mission? They would have it fucking easy compared to what he would do to me.

And then once Liam was done, my sister would finish me off. Together, those two would make a killer team.

Kelsey continued standing in the doorway. I longed to rip the elastic from her ponytail and knot my fingers in her soft

49

blond strands. Maybe tug on them and see how she responded as I kissed her long and deep.

Holly placed her hand on my arm, snapping me from my fantasy, the fantasy I often thought about while jerking myself off in the shower. *Sorry to disappoint, Mom. Holly's only a friend.* She and I had an agreement for events such as this.

And no, I hadn't fucked her yet. Wasn't planning to either. She was my colleague, for Christ's sake. A brilliant one at that. And I'd already witnessed the carnage left after the last office romance exploded.

It wasn't pretty.

They both got fired. That wouldn't happen to Holly and me. We were too good at our jobs. The firm needed us. But it still didn't mean I wanted to get involved in something messy like that.

Besides, I preferred keeping things casual with the women I dated. Want a commitment? Then you were chasing the wrong guy.

Want a great fuck? Then I was your man.

Another reason why I was all wrong for Kelsey.

Kelsey finally moved into the living room and I saw what made her freeze up. Liam was standing there with my brother-in-law, Darren, talking and laughing. While they seemed to be having a good time, the heavy feeling that always sat in the air just before Liam left on a mission was denser than the San Francisco fog. My heart pinched, understanding what Kelsey was going through, having lived through it myself numerous times with Liam and my brother. It was the feeling you had, no matter how positive you tried to be, that he might not return home in one piece...or might return home a different man.

Kelsey hugged her brother, and for a moment I was positive she would never let him go. Liam held her equally tight. It wasn't because he feared he would never return. Their parents died while he was away on a mission. Kelsey had also been in the car and had come close to dying too.

His biggest fear wasn't the assholes he was sent to fight. He was afraid of something bad happening to his sister and not being here for her.

I approached them as Kelsey pulled back, her eyes shiny. She blinked away her tears, and the sun returned to her face. "Just remember to kick some major ass, all right?"

Liam laughed. "I'll be sure to do that." Then he spotted me and the familiar smirk appeared on his face.

I gave him a one-armed hug. "Hey, you made it."

"Of course I made it. I wouldn't miss this party for anything." He glanced in Holly's direction. "How come you never mentioned your gorgeous girlfriend?" He draped his arm around her shoulders. "Forget Trent. He's just a boring portfolio manager who spends his day making nice with numbers." Liam pounded his fist against his chest a few times, King Kong style. "I'm a man of adventure who likes long walks on moonlit beaches."

A laugh burst free from my lungs. "You need to work on your cheesy pick-up lines, bro. Then you'd have a better chance of getting laid." I could guarantee Liam wasn't the moonlit-beach-walking type.

"Hello? I'm standing right here," Kelsey piped in. "I don't need to hear about my brother's sex life. Just like you don't need to hear about what brand of tampon I use." She laughed, and the tension I'd felt from my best friend putting his life at risk again eased off at the sweet sound. I hadn't realized just how much I'd missed it until now.

"Point taken," Liam said.

"Holly and I work together," I explained, voice low. "She's only here to keep Mom from asking about my dating life. So please don't make a bigger deal of this than it really is."

Kelsey looked slightly taken aback by that. Holly's smile

wavered for a second, then returned full force. It was the smile she always had whenever the stock market was having a bad day and I went shopping for discounts. She knew days like that gave me a hard-on.

Metaphorically speaking.

Or not.

"So, do you have a boyfriend?" Holly asked Kelsey. She glanced around the room, as if expecting some guy to magically appear. Most of the men here were my father's age and no way would Kelsey go there.

Kelsey shifted on her feet, looking ready to run. I fought back the urge to pull her into my arms and stroke her soft skin, to comfort her.

"I was engaged but I ended it a few months ago," she explained.

Holly's eyes went wide. "Why? What happened?" She then blushed. "I'm sorry, that was rude. It's none of my business."

That might've been true, but I was curious too. Neither Erin nor Liam had told me what happened.

"No, it's okay. Owen wants to become partner in his law firm. That means putting in never-ending hours. He rarely had time for me, and I got tired of feeling like I was no longer worth the effort, and of him constantly canceling on me because of his job." Kelsey held her chin high, proud of her strength to walk away from a guy she loved but who was too much of a douchebag to appreciate what was in front of him.

"I understood why he had to do it, why the long hours," she added. "He had worked hard to get this far. I was proud of him. I really was. But he just didn't seem interested in finding a way to make room in his life for both his job and me." She jerked her shoulders in a what-can-you-do shrug.

Holly chuckled. "That sounds a lot like Trent. I swear he spends more time at the office than he does at home." Said the woman who spent almost an equal amount of time at the office as me. Maybe even more so lately.

But I at least had a reason. Several, actually. First came Angela.

She'd faked a pregnancy just to become the first Mrs. Trent Salway.

Then came Roselyn.

And Carrie.

Carrie's claim to fame was cheating on me—with an eighty-year-old man. I provided the cock; he provided the lifestyle she craved.

I'd long since realized I wasn't meant for love. Love meant trust, and I didn't have a good track record with that. Work was the one thing that wouldn't let me down at the end of the day.

Erin approached our small group. "Kelsey, can you help me for a minute?"

"Sure."

They walked away as Darren asked Holly a question about her job. While they were busy talking, Liam pulled me away to a quiet corner.

"I don't know how long my mission will be this time," he said, tone sullen, like he was going to a funeral, possibly his own. He glanced toward his sister, who was now organizing the food on the dinner table, and let out a slow breath. "Can you keep an eye out for Kelsey? Make sure she's okay while I'm gone."

I started. He'd never asked this of me before, even after the accident that claimed his parents' life. But I knew that he worried about her every time he left on a mission. More so than he worried about his own safety.

Normally a "hell yes" response would be appropriate to a question like this.

Remember Best Friend Rules #1-3?

I did. I also remembered how Kelsey had done everything

in her power to avoid me after I came home from college one summer. It was the summer I'd hooked up with one of my sister's classmates, who I swear had been Velcro in a former life. "I can try. But it's not like I see her much."

"I know." He let out another slow breath. "But she seems restless lately. I'd just feel better if someone makes sure she at least isn't dating assholes. The last thing she needs is to fall for some guy like you, you know, only interested in a good time. Not interested in anything beyond that. She deserves better than that."

Good thing I wasn't drinking at that particular moment. I would've spewed my beer all over Mom's prized tropical plant if I had been. Did he seriously expect me to vet Kelsey's future boyfriends? I doubted she would've let her father do that if he were alive—and I doubted she would've let Liam have any say in it if he was still living in San Francisco.

And yes, his assessment of me stung a little, even if it was true.

But since I hadn't heard anything about Kelsey even being remotely interested in dating just yet, I said, as we returned to where Holly and Darren were standing, "Okay. I can do that if you want."

I mean, how hard would it be?

"I swear, you'll like this guy," Erin said as she and Kelsey approached. "He's super sexy and eager to go out with you."

My sister jerked her eyebrows in a comical dance—and Liam gave me a meaningful glance, reminding me of my promise.

Shit.

3

———

KELSEY

I n everyone's life there is that one person who thinks she's an expert in all matters of the heart. You know the one. Sometimes she knows what she's talking about...most times she doesn't. Her "knowledge" is based on her many failed relationships.

Her goal? To stick her nose into your love life, whether you want her to or not.

"When was the last time you kissed a man?" Chloe asked. Her long, curly red hair was pulled back in two loose pigtails, and she watched me with her large brown eyes.

That's right. My love expert came in the form of a six-year-old patient.

"I can't remember." I'd long since learned that trying to change the topic didn't work with Chloe. You just had to go with the flow and hope for the best.

"You *have* kissed before, right?" She tossed the beanbag at me while attempting to balance on the wobble board. She swayed, her arms flailing madly about as she tried to regain her balance. "Kissing is important for a strong relationship." Her foot touched the ground and she grunted her annoyance.

"Where did you hear that?" I asked, because there was no way a six-year-old would know that. Most believed kissing was gross.

"Ewww. Kissing is gross," Lindsay said. See what I mean? Whereas Chloe was the love expert, Lindsay thought boys were dumb.

"Grandma," Chloe said, ignoring Lindsay. "She also said that boys won't buy the cow if you give away the milk for free. I don't have a cow to sell, but I did try to give my chocolate milk to Joey. He didn't want it. He's lactose intolerant."

A laugh burst free, and I had to cover my mouth with my hand to keep from cracking up. "I can see how that would be a problem."

"I love chocolate milk," Lindsay helpfully pointed out while wobbling on her balance board. "I wouldn't give it to a dumb boy."

I bit my lip to keep from laughing again. "Good for you, Lindsay."

Chloe tossed another beanbag at me. "Do you loooove anyone?" she asked me.

"I love my friends, my brother, and my cat."

She fisted her hands on her hips and flashed me an exasperated look. "No, do you loooove a man and want to marry him?"

Trent's face immediately popped into my head as I was about to tell her "no." I must have made some kind of lovesick face because Chloe sing-songed, "Ooooh, first comes love, then comes marriage, then comes Kelsey with a baby carriage."

Given that I couldn't see Trent ever settling down, let alone with me, I attempted to shove his image from my head. It didn't budge.

"Does he like bugs?" Chloe loved bugs.

"There is no guy."

Hence why Erin was trying her darnedest to rectify that. Her mission? To help me find Mr. Right.

Naturally Trent wasn't at the top of the list.

Or on the bottom.

Or anywhere in between.

"Did you want one?" Chloe asked.

Was I tired of being alone? Yes.

Did I want to waste time dating guys who didn't set my body on fire with just once glance? Not really. But I wasn't about to admit that to Chloe.

"You don't need to be in love with a man to be happy," I said.

Chloe didn't look too convinced. Lindsay nodded her approval.

I indicated for the two girls to sit on the oversized balls. They bounced on them, working their core strength, while I retrieved the beanbags scattered across the floor.

"You could find a boyfriend like my Grandma did," Chloe said. Lindsay just bounced higher.

"How did she do that?" I asked.

"She joined a lawn-bowling club."

And there you had it. Chloe and Erin were never allowed to meet. Ever.

"But remember," she added, her tone serious, "you're not supposed to give him your chocolate milk if you want to sell him your cow."

I pressed my lips together, fighting back the forming grin. "I'll keep it in mind."

While the girls worked through the rest of the session, I did my best not to think about the metaphoric chocolate milk. Just like I had tried not to think about it for the past 463 days.

The only reason I was even contemplating letting Erin set me up was because I was hoping for one night of meaningless sex.

One night to end the record-shattering draught.
One night to distract me from my fantasies of Trent. Naked.
Under me.
Over me.
Inside me.
God, I was a lost cause.

NEXT TO ME ON HER COUCH, ERIN FLIPPED THE MAGAZINE PAGE and checked out the quiz: *Are You Confident Enough To Make Guys Come At The Sight Of You?*

Okay, maybe that wasn't the exact title, but you got the general gist. I had already read *48 Moves To Drive Your Man Crazy In Bed*. Want to learn how to make a man truly happy? Read erotic romance. Nothing was more educational than that.

"Why are you reading that?" I glanced at the clock to see how much time was left before *Outlander* started. Jamie Fraser in a kilt was usually enough to distract Erin from my love life. Call me paranoid, but I had an uneasy feeling she was reading the article for my benefit, not hers.

"It's not for me," she said, not even looking up. "I'm checking it out for you."

See what I mean? "Me? I don't need that."

"Tell me, what is *your* purpose in life?" She pointed at the title on the cover, for an article about creating a fulfilling life before entering a relationship, and waited expectantly for me to answer.

"You seriously want me to answer that?" I shoved a handful of popcorn in my mouth, buying time in case she really did expect me to tell her. Hell if I knew what it was.

"I wouldn't have asked if I didn't want to know."

"Well...I guess it's to help kids with their physical rehabil-itation."

"And?"

"And what?"

"That's your job description, but it can't be your only purpose in life. There's more to you than just helping kids, right?"

"Er..." I drew a blank. Even my cat could have done better.

"What about your hobbies? I play the piano and create jewelry. What about you?"

"Let's see. I took violin lessons when I was ten." Which she knew about. Like she knew about my other non-hobbies. "I sucked at it and gave it up. I'm not athletically inclined." Far from it. "I can make a decent fire. Does that count?"

Erin snorted. "Not really. So what do you do when you're not working?"

I shrugged, too embarrassed to admit that I spent my evenings reading romance novels, hanging out with my cat, and watching TV. But I didn't need to tell her. That was why she'd been trying to set me up on a date. "I go to the gym after work." It must count for something.

"Okay, so your purpose in life is to be in shape." At first I thought she was serious, but then she smirked.

"Hey, being in shape is a good thing. It means I'm healthy and will have a long life." A long unfulfilling life, apparently.

Erin closed the magazine and placed it on the coffee table. A breeze from the nearby window ruffled the cover, causing it to either wave at me or mock me. It could have gone either way.

"Let's look at this another way," she said. "If you're gonna be dating, you need to have common interests with the guy."

"Who says I'm gonna be dating? Maybe I like being single. Single is good." Now if only my voice sounded like I was fully on board. "It beats being in a relationship and still being alone." Something I was an expert on.

"True. But you'd feel differently if you dated the right man.

Owen wasn't the right man." A fact Erin had harped on when I first started dating him in college.

At the time, both Owen and I had been busy with classes and didn't have much time for anything else. Back then it had been fine, but I had foolishly thought that once we were out and working we would've had more time for each other.

Silly me.

"You're right," I said. "He wasn't the right man for me. But I haven't exactly met the right man. All the good ones are already taken."

"And that's why I've made it my personal mission to help you find the perfect guy. I love you, Kels, and I just want you to be happy like I am with Darren. Are you sure there's no one you're interested in?"

I wavered for a moment, lips parted. Trent's name sat on the tip of my tongue, waiting for me to say it.

I bit back the words. "Nope, no one."

"Don't worry," Erin said, "I'm positive you'll love Stephen. He's really excited to meet you."

Inwardly I cringed. I didn't need to go on the date to know it would be an epic failure. Since when did blind dates ever work out?

Never. That's when.

Ugh.

4

TRENT

Sweating from my workout, my T-shirt sticking to my skin, I strode through my apartment, taking in the expensive decorations and furniture that didn't feel like me. I had hired someone to decorate the place at the recommendation of my boss. Something about the condo reminded me of how far I'd come, and how hard I'd worked my ass off to get to this point—the point of being one of the youngest and hottest portfolio managers around.

By hottest, I meant I knew my shit when it came to the stock market and it showed. My mutual funds had outperformed everyone else's in the company for the past two years. I'd been quoted a number of times in the financial sections of respected newspapers—which I could guarantee the girls I'd slept with over the years had never heard of or read.

But I did refuse an interview last year with *Forbes Magazine* because they wanted to talk about my success. I didn't want to risk a money-hungry bitch painting a big fat target on my chest, and scheming to be the first Mrs. Trent Salway.

I'd already traveled down that path.

A path filled with thorns and poison ivy.

I quickly showered and grabbed an equally quick dinner. Now, I wasn't ashamed to admit it...but my cooking skills were greatly absent. But hey, it wasn't like they had cooking classes at Columbia. Or at least if they did, they hadn't existed in my program while I was there.

Which was why Mom had given me leftovers from the party.

Yep, I was her favorite child.

I chuckled, knowing Mom loved us all equally. We'd never given her a reason not to. Well, most of the time we hadn't given her a reason.

I loaded the dishwasher and headed back to the office. If I had a T-shirt that said, "Workaholics Need Only Apply" I would wear it with pride.

By the time I arrived, the place was empty except for Holly (of course) and one other guy who was packing up for the day.

You know how every company has that one asshole who is a step away from being slapped with a sexual harassment complaint? A jerk-off who thinks all women were hired for his own personal pleasure?

Meet Dick Head. Or as Human Resources knew him, Brent Dickinson.

He jerked his chin toward Holly, who was standing at her desk, papers in hand, then winked at me. His face wore a leer I would've liked to wipe off with my fist. It wasn't like that with Holly, and I didn't want him believing that it was. I didn't want him fueling the office grapevine with his blatant lie. While it wouldn't have hurt my reputation, it would've destroyed Holly's. She worked too hard to prove herself in a testosterone-dominated world to deserve that.

Before I could say anything to him or push him against the wall and tell him where he could take his douchebag attitude, he walked past me and left through the main door to the elevators.

At the sound of the door clicking shut behind him, Holly looked up and smiled. "Hey. Did Dickinson finally leave?" She visibly shuddered, leaving me to wonder what he'd said to her.

"You mean old Dick Head?"

Holly laughed and I did my best not to cringe. How could someone so beautiful create such a hideous sound? I swear there were male cats who wanted to hump her whenever she laughed.

And of course thinking about her laugh made me think of another laugh. One that I used to live for. There were days when it became my personal mission to make Kelsey laugh, just so I could hear the sweet sound. The downside was my cock always got excited when I heard it. It was both sexy and sweet, even back when she had been only sixteen—back when she'd been too young for me to consider dating (if you ignored the part about Liam being her brother and my best friend). Back when I had believed love was possible for me.

"He's not sexually harassing you, is he?" I asked Holly.

She shook her head. "No, he's just being a jerk. He's pissed that Ted Callahan is impressed with my work and hasn't given him the time of day."

"He should be impressed."

"Ted mentioned that he had recommended my name for Richard's job, but that's just between you and me, okay? I know there'll be a lot of other qualified candidates, but it's nice to be recognized." She smiled at me, but not with the typical I'm-proud-of-what-I've-accomplished-so-far smile that I would've expected from her. This one was shy, not at all what I would've anticipated from someone so smart and market savvy.

"Either way, congratulations!" I said. "We should go out and celebrate."

"I haven't got the job yet."

"Doesn't matter. The fact that Ted is recommending you for the position is reason enough to celebrate. He's not easy to impress, not like that." I thought for a moment about Kelsey's social calendar for the next few days, which Liam had told me about when he reminded me of the promise I'd made him about his sister's dating life. "What are you doing Friday night?"

"Nothing." Holly picked up the file she had just put down.

"Good. I'll pick you up at six thirty."

Holly grinned, her teeth white and perfect. Unlike Kelsey. Kelsey had a slight gap between her two front teeth, which looked damn sexy and adorable on her. Not all girls could pull it off, but she did.

"Okay," Holly said. "You've got yourself a date."

"Sounds good." I returned to my office and called Antonio's —Kelsey's favorite restaurant.

5
____

KELSEY

Studying my reflection in the bathroom mirror, I let out a long breath. Mr. Kitty Whiskers jumped on the counter and meowed at me.

"What do you think?" I asked him.

He meowed again. I wasn't sure if that was a good thing or not. The shell-pink cotton fabric of my favorite sundress skimmed my body and made my legs look longer than normal. The downside was that it didn't exactly scream, "Hey, I want to get laid tonight."

I brushed my hair. The light blond hinted at my Scandinavian roots, as did my light-blue eyes. Didn't guys think Scandinavian women were hot? Although that might've had more to do with their accents than their hair and eye color.

"Does this say that I want to get lucky tonight?" I asked Mr. Kitty Whiskers in my best fake Swedish accent.

My phone pinged from my clutch bag and I checked to see who had texted me.

Liam: Hey, Sis, how's it going?

Relief rushed through me, like it always did whenever Liam contacted me while he was away on a mission.

> Me: Great. Have a date soon. How about you?

> Liam: You're still going out on that blind date?

> Me: Yes.

I figured if it sucked, then Erin would think twice before setting me up again.

> Liam: What do you know about him? Maybe you should cancel. He could be a serial killer.

> Me: Right. Because Erin knows so many serial killers.

> Liam: There's always a first for everything…

I rolled my eyes.

> Me: I'll be fine.

> Liam: Couldn't you make it a double date? Maybe go out with Erin and Darren.

> Me: Well, considering my date is due here any moment, I'm going to say that's a no. :)

> Liam: I'd feel better if you went on a double date with Erin and Darren.

> Me: And I'd feel better if you weren't with the SEALs, but we don't always get what we want.

No matter how much we might've wished for it.

We texted back and forth a few more times before signing

off. Liam had to get back to duty...and I had a date to get ready for.

I retrieved my clutch from the bed and walked downstairs. I slipped on my sandals, and once again wished I could wear stilettos like Holly. The sandals had a heel, but nothing that made me look sophisticated or sexy.

But maybe looking sexy had nothing to do with the type of shoe you wore. Maybe it was all about your attitude.

I puffed my chest out. I was confident. And there was nothing sexier than confidence.

Or so I'd once read in a romance novel.

As I was thinking sexy thoughts, the doorbell rang. *I'm a sexy Norse goddess. I can make guys come at the mere sight of me.* I giggled at the last one and opened the door.

And then my mouth flopped open. The guy in front of me could've been a Viking, if we still lived in that era. His straight blond hair brushed against his unshaven jaw. Height and build? Definitely that of a Viking.

The only difference between Stephen and a real Viking was that his hair was combed and he wore black dress pants and a white dress shirt.

"Hi, Kelsey?"

I nodded, my ability to speak temporarily on hiatus.

"Are we still on for tonight?"

Again, I nodded.

The Viking, I mean Stephen, chuckled. "Erin never mentioned that you couldn't speak." His warm laugh caused an equally warm reaction to hum through my lower body.

My lips finally decided to cooperate and a smile broke out on my face. "That's because I can. You...you weren't what I was expecting."

He leaned his hand high against the doorframe. "And what *were* you expecting?"

Not a hot Viking, that was for sure. "Well, considering this was a blind date..." I let the rest of my sentence hang, figuring he knew exactly what I meant.

He chuckled again, and my girlie parts grew even more excited. "I'll admit, I wasn't sure what to expect either. But Erin insisted you were gorgeous and I would thank her profusely for setting us up. She even told me where she was registered for her baby-shower gifts."

I grinned until my cheeks hurt, in a good way. "That sounds like Erin."

"So, are we still on for dinner?"

"Definitely."

No, Stephen hadn't arrived at my house on a horse or dragon. He'd pulled up in something much better. I didn't know much about cars, but I knew guys had wet dreams over the sleek black sports car in front of me.

"Nice car," I said, because it was true and because I could tell the car was his baby. Judging from the way it gleamed, he obviously worshiped it.

That annoying, know-it-all voice in the back of my head whispered, *But would he worship you as much as he worships his car...or is there only room for one girl in his life?*

I gave the voice the cold shoulder. This was just a date. We weren't getting engaged.

He opened the passenger door for me. I sat on the seat and sank into the soft black leather. Wow. The seat was comfier than my couch.

"How do you know Erin?" I asked as we drove to the restaurant.

"Through the ad agency she works for. My company is a client of hers."

"Oh, aren't there rules against best friends of ad agency employees dating the employees of their clients?" I joked.

Stephen laughed. "Erin said you were gorgeous. She never mentioned you were funny too."

"That's me. A two-for-one special."

He flashed me a quick grin. "Erin told me you're a physical therapist at the children's hospital. That must be a tough job."

"It is, but it's worth it."

"How so?"

"Well…" I thought about the teen I'd been working with for the past few weeks after she had been involved in a motorcycle accident. Her boyfriend had been driving. He died and she ended up with brain damage. "When you know you've made a difference in the patient's life. When they take their first step after a serious accident that left them unable to talk, walk, or do the smallest of tasks. When they smile for the first time after taking that step." I blinked back the tears at the memory of the girl's half smile from accomplishing something the rest of us took for granted.

"Erin's right. You are an amazing woman. And I can see why you like your job."

"All right, so you know what I do. What about you?" Unless he had a trust fund to pay for his expensive car, he must have a job that paid a lot more than mine.

Not that it made a difference to me. If anything, it was a strike against him. As I'd already learned the hard way, a high paying job came with equally high costs—and I didn't want to go there again.

"I'm the owner and CEO of a small software company."

A growing sense of déjà-vu planted itself in my throat, and refused to budge when I swallowed. "I guess it keeps you pretty busy, huh?"

He nodded. "It does, but I still find time to have fun." He flashed me another smile, which drew up short of reassuring.

At Antonio's, he opened the passenger door and helped me out. I gazed at his lips. They were nice lips, but they weren't Trent's lips. Trent's lips were fuller and screamed, "Kiss me. Now."

Stephen leaned in and my lips parted slightly. But just as I thought he was going to kiss me, he backed away. "Ready to go in?" he asked.

"Yes, sure." *Congratulations, Kelsey.* And that was what I got for thinking about kissing Trent when I was on a date with another man. Maybe Stephen had sensed that, which was why he changed his mind about the kiss.

We entered the restaurant. As usual the place was busy. If Stephen hadn't made a reservation already, we would've been waiting for at least an hour.

"Have you eaten here before?" I asked.

"Never, but Erin told me it's your favorite restaurant."

The hostess showed us to our seats, a quiet table for four in the corner. I glanced around. There were a number of cozy tables for two, all occupied. Maybe when he booked the reservation, those tables had already been booked for the night.

Stephen frowned at the table, pulled back the seat next to the wall for me to sit in, then sat in the chair opposite mine.

The hostess handed us the menus and told us the specials. After we'd studied the menus for a few moments, Stephen asked me, "What do you recommend?"

I opened my mouth to list a few of my favorites, but didn't get that far.

"Hey, Kels."

I looked up and blinked, the air in my lungs catching at the sight of Trent. And that's what I got for thinking about him in the parking lot. I'd somehow summoned him—along with Holly. Cue the *Twilight Zone* theme music.

He was even hotter than the other night. And once again, I noticed how perfectly matched he and Holly were. She wore a short black dress that was both sexy and elegant. It made what I had on look like a little girl's dress. Although in her case, she looked better suited for a five-star restaurant than for here.

Trent had been here before. That was why he wasn't over-dressed for the place, unlike Holly. Like Stephen, he wore black slacks, but instead of a dress shirt, a thin, dark-green sweater hugged his body just right. It let anyone checking him out see that he was in great shape, but without being overly tight.

"Hey, what are you guys doing here?" I asked, even though it was obvious why they were at the restaurant. Of all the places in San Francisco that Trent could've taken Holly for a date, he had to go pick the one Stephen had chosen for *our* date. Go figure!

Please don't sit near us, I silently pleaded.

"We came here to eat, but there was a mix up with our reservation. And now there's a two-hour wait. You don't mind if we join you, do you?" Trent turned to Stephen and held out his hand. "Hi, I'm the best friend of Kelsey's brother. You know, the brother who serves with the Navy SEALs."

Shoot me now. Why the hell did he have to bring that up? From the quirk of Stephen's eyebrow, it was clear this was the first he'd heard about Liam's career. Erin wouldn't have told him. No point scaring him off prematurely.

Oh. God. Did Liam put Trent up to this? That would explain why my brother had been so interested in my dating life. It was like that time when I was sixteen and Liam had a "talk" with my date while I was getting ready. There wasn't a second date after that. It wasn't until a few months later that I found out my brother had threatened to break both of the guy's legs if he hurt me.

Some things never changed.

Before Stephen could object to them joining us, Trent sat next to me. His leg accidentally brushed against mine and it was like a jolt of electricity had hit the spot. A happy buzz hummed through my body.

Whoa, definitely not a good thing.

I jerked my leg away from his—and instantly missed his touch.

Holly looked between the two guys, shrugged, and sat on the chair next to Stephen. At least Stephen was a gentleman and had pulled the chair out for me. Trent's mom would have berated her son for such poor manners. She had taught him better than that.

"Stephen, this is Trent and Holly. They work together." And were no doubt here to discuss work, both being the workaholics that they were.

Except that Holly was dressed as if it were a date.

"Nice to meet you," Stephen said, more to Holly than to Trent.

A few tables over, a waitress carrying two slices of cake, one with a lit sparkler in it, approached an elderly couple. The man, who must've been in his eighties, stood and grinned at the woman. He picked up his wine glass and tapped it with a spoon. The deep, crisp sound broke through the noise from the nearby tables.

"I'd like to make an announcement." His voice was strong and proud and held several dozen photo albums worth of nostalgia. "Sixty years ago today, the most beautiful woman in the world became my wife." He lifted his glass to her, and every woman in the restaurant melted into sticky goo at his sweet words and the way he worshiped her.

I sighed in that way you do when you watch a sappy love story and wish it were yours.

"So how do you know Kelsey?" Trent asked Stephen, breaking my attention from the happy couple. Something felt off with the question and the way he'd said it. He wasn't asking out of interest. It was more like an interrogation. God, this didn't sound like Trent. It sounded more like my brother.

"Erin introduced us," I said. Technically she hadn't but close enough. "You remember Erin, right? Your sister?"

Trent ignored my dig, his attention focused solely on my date. "How do you know my sister?"

"My company is a client of her ad agency."

Trent hummed, his gaze penetrating Stephen's. I squirmed in my seat. Stephen held his own.

"Isn't dating a friend of someone who works for the company considered a conflict of interest?" Unlike when I had joked about it, Trent was dead serious. What was his freaking problem?

"I don't think there's a law against it, if that's what you're asking," Stephen smoothly replied.

"Holly," I said, grasping for anything to end Trent's interrogation. "I love your dress. You look great." I turned to Trent. "Doesn't she look great?"

He glanced at her for a brief moment, long enough to smile at her and agree that she looked great, before returning his attention to Stephen. "And what exactly do you do for the company?"

Stephen didn't have a chance to answer. The waitress arrived to take our drink orders. I ordered a glass of my favorite Chardonnay. Holly did the same. The guys both ordered beer.

"Kelsey," Holly said before Trent could grill Stephen further. "How's your car doing?"

"Great, thanks. Turns out you were right about the fan belt." And then I had an idea. A way to get back at Trent for being such an ass on *my* date. "Your brothers would *love* Stephen's car. It's gorgeous and hot."

"What is it?" she asked him.

"A 2015 Ferrari 458 Spider."

I had no idea what that meant, but apparently Holly did.

Her mouth dropped open in awe. She wasn't the only one. Trent gawked at Stephen and was temporarily rendered speechless. *Finally.*

Sitting back in my seat, I waited to see who'd recover first. I figured from the way Trent had responded to the news about my date's car, it meant Stephen had passed whatever test Trent had thrown at him, courtesy of my brother.

And now that Trent was appeased, this date could go on as planned—other than the part where it had become a double date.

"Statistics show," Trent said, "that owners of sport cars tend to be reckless."

Oh, God, someone find me a brick wall to bang my head against.

6

TRENT

I knew I was being an asshole to Kelsey's date. I couldn't help it. Just look at him. It couldn't have been more obvious from the way he was scoping her that he had only one thing in mind—and it wasn't to discuss the latest in physical therapy news.

It was official: I was going to kill my sister.

And it had nothing to do with my promise to Liam. Kelsey deserved more than this jerk-off. He was only interested in fucking her. He didn't care about the amazing woman in front of him.

I shifted in my seat, letting my leg brush against hers again. The jolt that I had experienced the first time, when I'd sat down, hummed up my thigh and through my body.

Kelsey inhaled a sharp breath, too soft to be heard by anyone but me. For a second I let myself believe that my touch affected her the same way her touch affected me. For a second I let myself believe that Liam and Erin wouldn't have an issue with me being with Kelsey. For a second I let myself believe that I was the right man for her.

But then the logical voice in my head reminded me that I

was a workaholic who didn't do commitments—for good reason.

Kelsey did commitments.

I moved my leg away from hers, doing my best to ignore the loss of contact between us.

"Does that mean you aren't a careful driver?" she said to me, a smirk in her tone. "You have a sports car."

You heard the *ding-ding-ding*, right? That was Kelsey scoring a point.

"That doesn't count," I said.

"Why doesn't it count?" The smirk was still there.

"Because I happen to like my life, and I'm not going to risk it by driving like an idiot."

"I feel the same way," the jerk told me. Then to Kelsey he said, "There are other ways, more fun ways, to get an adrenaline rush." Though from the way he was looking at her, it was clear what he meant.

I clenched my hands under the table to keep from introducing them to his face. There might've also been the need to keep them off Kelsey, since I itched to place my hand on her thigh and soak in her warmth, to re-experience the jolt. A few other ideas as to what I wanted to do, involving my fingers and the heat between her legs, also came to mind.

My cock hardened in agreement, hoping to get a piece of that action. It took everything inside me not to groan out loud. *Focus.*

"You still haven't mentioned what you do for a living," I said, my tone five steps from being cordial. This resulted in a sharp kick to my lower leg. *Ouch!*

Both women gaped at me like I was crazy, so I had no idea who was responsible for the bruise now forming on my leg. Although based on Kelsey's expression, I wouldn't have been surprised if she tried to lure me down a dark alley and murder me.

Holly widened her eyes at me, her message clear: *Why are you trying to sabotage your friend's date?* But it wasn't as if I could tell her—although I was sure her brothers would understand why I was doing this on Liam's behalf. The last person I would admit my feelings to when it came to Kelsey was another woman. While Holly wasn't the type to date much, she was still a woman. She would tell me to get my head out of my ass and ask Kelsey out instead of being an asshole.

Right. She wouldn't have put it quite as crassly, but the sentiment was the same. And if Kelsey was anyone but my best friend's sister, I would've done just that. It didn't bother me that she was *my sister's* best friend. Much.

Erin was a different situation. She would've crushed my balls with a baseball bat if she even suspected I got hard over her best friend. She'd worry about what would happen if things between Kelsey and me didn't work out.

And she had a good point. History was a bitch.

So that brought me back to my original dilemma: Kelsey's douchebag date.

"I'm the owner and CEO of Dinemar," he said. "My company creates software for various companies, including hospitals and medical offices."

A twinge of admiration settled on my shoulders. The company wasn't part of my mutual fund portfolio, but I'd heard one of the other guys in the office talk about it. The company was doing great things for his portfolio.

But hell if I'd admit that to this loser.

The elderly couple celebrating their anniversary stood up to leave. My heart warmed at the love they shared. Just like it was with my parents. You'd have to be a moron not to see how important the woman was to her husband. But I doubted she was anything like Angela. I doubted she would have pretended to be pregnant to trap herself a husband with a great future earning potential.

"That's nice," I said to Kelsey's date, whose name I could no longer remember. "And what about your free time? What do you enjoy doing?" This would be the deal breaker for Kelsey. Being owner and CEO of a large successful company meant he wouldn't have free time for Kelsey. Which meant he would be no better than her ex-fiancé.

"I enjoy all kinds of activities. I'm a firm believer that it's important to have a life outside the office, or else the stress of the job can kill you. That's what happened to one of my uncles. He was so obsessed about his job, he forgot to live his life, to enjoy himself, and the stress became too much. He died of a heart attack. He was only thirty-nine when it happened." He listed the hobbies and activities that he enjoyed, and shit, the list was long.

Way to go, shithead. Make me feel like a slacker.

Kelsey's eyes were wide and she seemed a little paler than before. She probably figured that with all his activities and hobbies, he wouldn't have time for her if they dated—and she was probably right.

As I mentally patted myself on the back for saving Kelsey from making another mistake she would regret, Holly said, "I used to practice tae kwon do in college, but haven't done it in years." She smiled at the loser.

Somehow I managed not to laugh. Holly wasn't the kind of woman to steal someone else's date, or at least I never believed her to be that kind of woman. But here she was flirting with the jerk. Interesting.

I leaned back in my chair, waiting to see what he would do. Maybe I could give him Holly's phone number so they could hook up. That would save Kelsey the grief of being with someone again who didn't have time to appreciate her.

"Kelsey, you should give it a try," Holly said. "I used to love it. It's a lot of fun."

What the hell?

"That's a great idea," the douchebag piped in. "You can come to the studio where I go. It's a mixed group, so it doesn't matter if you've never done it before. We have new members join us all the time."

That wasn't a great idea. It was a terrible idea.

"I might do that," Kelsey said. "Thanks."

Holly and the jerk-off started discussing the things they enjoyed doing. Kelsey listened with rapt interest, every so often asking questions.

"And what do you enjoy doing in *your* spare time?" the jerk asked, turning the question back on me.

Holly laughed and the table next to us looked to see what had caused the weird sound. "Trent is a workaholic. If he hadn't brought me here tonight, he would still be at the office, crunching numbers." She flashed me a teasing smile. What could I say? She was right.

"I'm not that bad. Besides, I love my job." It made me feel alive.

Or at least it used to. The thrill I used to feel had faded a bit over the past year and I couldn't figure out why. So I pushed myself harder, spent more hours at the office, looking for the exhilaration I used to experience every time I showed up for my job.

The jerk didn't say anything. He didn't have to. His expression said it all: *Well, it's your funeral.* Literally.

For the rest of the meal I remained somewhat quiet, pretending to listen to what everyone had to say, but at the same time I couldn't get out of here soon enough. So far I'd failed in screwing up this date between Kelsey and the guy. I still wasn't convinced he was good enough for her, and Liam would want a full report.

And more importantly, I wanted to ensure their date didn't end with him going home with her. The thought of him fucking her was enough to drive me crazy.

I was so focused on trying *not* to imagine them having sex together, I almost missed the sound of a cell phone interrupting their conversation.

The jerk answered it. The only thing I could tell was that the call was urgent and had to do with his company.

"All right, I'll be there as soon as I can." He hung up. "I'm sorry," he said to Kelsey. "I need to leave, but I'll drive you home first." He indicated for the waitress to fetch the bill.

"I can do that," I quickly said before Kelsey could respond. "We haven't had dessert yet." I nodded at the next table over where the waitress was serving Kelsey's favorite. The girl loved her chocolate cake, and no one's chocolate cake outdid the one they made here.

She glanced over at the table and I could tell she was thinking the same. I wouldn't have been surprised if she'd been fantasizing about it while eating dinner.

The jerk-off must have sensed it too. "All right then." His thumb skimmed the back of her hand and he smiled. "I'll call you."

Did you spot it? The dejection in her eyes? I didn't think he'd seen it because she was great at hiding what she was thinking—but it didn't escape my notice.

He paid for their meal and left. I winced at the anger now flashing in her eyes that was directed at me, and waited for her to unleash the temper I had experienced more than once from her while growing up.

I would definitely be dropping Kelsey off first.

But instead of unleashing her temper, she smiled at Holly. "Okay, I'm ready for chocolate cake. And lots of it." She mumbled the last part, along with what sounded suspiciously like, "Since I'm not getting laid tonight."

That smile on my face? That was me inwardly high-fiving myself.

7
———

KELSEY

Late Monday morning, I sat outside in the hospital courtyard, enjoying a quick break before my next patient. The sun was warm on my face, the breeze a slight kiss.

Pathetic as it was, this was the most action in the kissing department I'd seen in a while. Lucky me.

"Is someone sitting here?"

I glanced up from my E-reader. Next to one of the white plastic chairs at the table, holding two cups of coffee, stood a tall, good-looking man in a suit.

"No, you can have it," I said, figuring he needed it for the next table over, where a family now sat.

"Thanks." He put the coffees on the table, one in front of me. "I bought you this. Linda said it's your favorite. Hope that's okay?" Linda was a barista in the hospital cafe. Her four-year-old daughter had been a patient of mine for a short time last year, and Linda and I were on friendly terms because of it.

Which meant she didn't think he was a serial killer if she'd told him what I liked to drink.

I inhaled the subtle sweet scent wafting from my skinny

81

vanilla dolce latte. *Mmm.* "Thanks, but really, you didn't need to do that."

"Sure I did." He pulled back an empty chair, scraping the plastic against the cobblestones, and sat down. "I figured we could count this as our first date." The smile on his face was that of a man confident in who he was, and confident no woman would ever reject him.

Pretty much like Trent.

"And let me guess," I said, "you're expecting a kiss at the end of this so-called date?"

He laughed, but it wasn't the same sexy laugh that came from Trent so easily. The same sexy laugh that always turned my panties damp.

It was more like a giggle.

Oh, boy. Strike one.

"I certainly wouldn't protest," he said, "but I can wait for our second date if you'd prefer."

I tilted my head slightly to the side, in potential flirt mode.

Not that I was skilled at flirting.

"And you're expecting a second date?"

"More like hoping for one."

A quick glance at his ring finger told me he wasn't married. He didn't have a wedding ring on, nor was there a tan line. "Are you visiting a patient?"

"No. I work here, in finance."

Ah, so the guy responsible for my paycheck.

I slipped my E-reader into my purse on the chair next to me and sipped my drink. "How come I haven't seen you before?"

"I only started a few weeks ago, and every time I saw you, you were busy reading. So this time I came bearing a gift."

I laughed and lifted my cup. "Ahh, a bribe so I'll talk to you?"

He giggled again. "Pretty much. So what were you reading?"

Heat rushed to my face at what I had been reading. Or more specifically, the scene I'd been reading.

There might have been dirty talk involved.

And possibly a silk tie.

Don't think about Trent and his long strong fingers strapping you to the bed with his ties.

This fantasy had already visited me more times than I cared to share. The fantasy where Trent ripped open my blouse, too impatient to waste time unbuttoning it.

He spread his warm hands across my breasts, partially hidden by my black lacy bra, and squeezed them. I whimpered with need and my nipples ached for his hot breath, ached for his tongue.

He unhooked my bra and let it drop to the floor, then pressed me against the door. His talented tongue lashed against a needy nipple. Heat surged between my legs. "Oh, God," I moaned.

With a sexy smirk that made my panties wetter, Trent pulled away and started to undo his tie.

"Are you still with me?" A male voice jerked me back to reality.

A reality that didn't involve Trent and me, naked.

My girlie parts all groaned in unison, aroused, achy, and cussing like a horny sailor. *Sorry, girls.*

"Sorry," I told the man. "I was just thinking about something I have to do after my break. What did you say?"

"What were you reading?" He jerked his chin toward my purse.

"Trust me, nothing that would interest you."

He smiled. It was a nice smile as smiles went, but my panties stayed dry. "I'm Craig, by the way. And you're Kelsey, right?"

"That's right."

"And what kind of food do you like?"

Odd question—unless you were getting ready to ask the person out on a date. "All kinds. I'm an equal opportunity eater...minus weird stuff, like bugs." I made a face and he giggled. God, what was it with that giggle? "I love chocolate, but what woman doesn't? But I'm not a fan of chocolate ice cream." Although I could be persuaded if the flavor was to-die-for.

"I don't like ice cream."

My eyes widened. "How can you not like ice cream?"

He shrugged. "I just don't."

Strike two.

Seriously, who didn't like ice cream?

I mean, unless you were lactose intolerant.

"So what do you do in finance?" Not exactly a flirting-type question, but him not liking ice cream had me momentarily stumped.

Six minutes later, after he droned on and on and on about his job, I couldn't get away fast enough. I checked the time on my cell phone and scrambled out of my chair, even though I still had a few minutes before I needed to leave. "Sorry, I have to get back to work."

Craig unfolded himself from his seat with the same confident smile he had worn earlier. "So where would you like to go for our second date?"

Anywhere you won't be.

This was never my favorite part—not that I had a lot of experience turning guys down.

Maybe there was a *Dummies* book on the topic I could quickly Google.

"I'm sorry. But...but you're not my type. I'm a lesbian," I blurted. Something told me that excuse would *not* be in the *Dummies* book.

His confident smile transformed into a confused frown. Confused why his gaydar had malfunctioned, no doubt.

"Well, I'll see you around." Grinning on the inside, I picked up what was left of my coffee and high-tailed it out of there.

8

———

KELSEY

I watched Chloe attempt to balance on the wobble board while doing my best not to check my cell phone for the tenth time in an hour.

And no, I wasn't waiting for the Viking to call me.

Not really.

Okay, maybe I was just a little.

I was also waiting for Erin to return my call. I needed to go out and have some fun...and more importantly, forget about my failure of a date.

The one with the Viking. Not the pseudo date with Craig, the ice-cream-hating guy from this morning.

Yes, I was still annoyed at how the evening with Stephen had ended. Not that I had been too thrilled with the rest of it either once Trent had shown up. What the hell had my brother said to him prior to shipping off? It had to be because of my brother, otherwise why else would Trent have shown up at the same restaurant out of the blue?

And when would Liam finally realize I was an adult who was capable of taking care of herself? I didn't need him sending the interrogation squad while he was away. Heck, I didn't need him interrogating my dates in person, either.

I fiddled with the owl necklace he'd given me for my twenty-fourth birthday, as if by touching it I could tell if he was still okay. He had given me his special code word last night, warning me that he would be away on a secret mission for who knew how long—which meant no calls from his beyond-irritated sister, demanding that he get Trent to back off.

My phone played Erin's pre-programmed tune. "Hello," I said, answering.

"As if you even have to ask," Erin replied in response to my earlier text, asking if she wanted to go shopping. "When do you want to meet me there?"

"Say, in about thirty minutes? I'm almost finished here." I tossed the beanbag at Chloe and gave her a thumbs up when she caught it.

"Good. I'm starving and have a major craving for french fries. I'll meet you in the food court. And be prepared to give me details about your date."

I inwardly groaned, suspecting she would grill me on how it went. But maybe then I wouldn't have to kill her brother.

She'd do it for me.

"Oooh. Is that your boyfriend?" Chloe asked after I ended the call, and made kissy noises.

"Didn't I tell you that I don't have one?"

"And that's why you need my help."

I could feel my eyebrows jump up my forehead. "Your help?"

"Yes, my help. You're pretty and you need a boyfriend."

I choked back a laugh. It was like talking to a six-year-old version of Erin, but with curly red hair instead of it being straight and brown. "And how exactly are you gonna help me?" I tossed another beanbag at her. She caught it. Just.

"I was watching the Disney Princess movies, and now I'm a pro when it comes to getting a boyfriend."

"Oh, you are, are you?"

She responded with an I-mean-business nod and threw the beanbag back at me. "It's simple. You just have to kiss your true love."

Immediately my thoughts went to Trent.

Nothing will ever happen between you and him, I reminded myself. Maybe in another universe it might've worked out between us, but too many elements were working against us in this one.

As I walked to my car after finishing work for the day, my phone pinged.

Are you still mad at me?

I didn't recognize the number.

Me: Who is this?

Trent. Why, are you mad at other people too?

Yeah, my brother.

Me: Maybe.

Trent: Maybe your date from Friday?

Before I could respond, he sent another text.

Trent: Have you heard from him yet?

Me: It's only been 3 days.

Trent: What, is he scaling Everest?

Based on what Stephen had talked about on Friday, I wouldn't be surprised if he *was* scaling Mount Everest.

Me: Ha ha! What about the 3 day rule?

Trent: What 3 day rule?

Me: The rule where you don't phone the girl for 3 days so not to come off as desperate.

I followed the text with another one.

Me: Aren't you supposed to be working, Mr. Workaholic?

Trent: Yes, but I wanted to see how you're doing.

That was the same Trent I'd known for as long as I could remember. He used to come to my house all the time to hang out with Liam. Sometimes he'd get there before my brother showed up. Instead of going home and waiting for Liam, he'd ask me about my day, give advice to whatever problem I was dealing with at the time (which in retrospect wasn't always the greatest advice), and I'd listen to him talk about his day. Even before I started crushing on Trent, I'd sometimes (often) willed my brother to come home late, just so I could get in more alone time with him.

Me: I'm fine, but do me a favor.

Trent: What?

> Me: Next time I'm on a date, please DO NOT crash it.

He didn't answer immediately, so I figured that was the end of the discussion and he'd gone back to work. A few minutes later I received another text from him.

> Trent: So you want a second date with him?

> Me: I didn't say that.

> Trent: So you don't want to go out with him again?

I sighed.

> Me: Yeah, that's exactly what I'm saying.

Except I was only now realizing that.

My car sat at the far end of the staff parking lot. I'd just opened the door when Trent sent me another text.

> Trent: How come you don't want to go out with him?

Wow, what was with all the questions about my date? Oh, yeah. My brother.

I wouldn't be surprised if Trent was writing a report on this for Liam, like I was a company he analyzed for his job.

> Me: I don't know. I just didn't see it going far.

Other than some fun under the sheets for one night.

Which I never got to experience in the end.

Trent never responded to the text, not that there was anything to say. I had made his job that much easier. His report for my brother? Completed in triplicate. The Viking had been my only prospect for a relationship, unless I wanted to go out with someone who didn't like ice cream.

And that was never going to happen.

I drove to the mall and met Erin at the food court. She had already bought a large order of fries and was sitting at a table, eating them.

"I swear I'm going to give birth to a giant french fry." She stuffed another one in her mouth. "I didn't even like fries until I got pregnant."

I giggled. "And you probably won't be able to stand the sight of them by the time you give birth."

She huffed. "I hope you're right. God, at this rate I'll be incredibly fat by the time the baby comes."

I reached into the bag and helped myself to a fry. "No, you won't," I said, pointing it at her. "You'll look just as adorable and as hot as you did before." I stuffed the fry in my mouth.

After she'd finished her snack, we wandered through the mall, stopping at whatever store caught our interest. We weren't looking for anything specific. I just wasn't ready to go back to my lonely house.

We entered Victoria's Secret and checked out their thongs. I held up a light pink satin one. "Um, this looks comfy."

The corner of Erin's mouth quirked up. "Yeah, if you like dental floss stuck between your butt cheeks."

"And yet guys get hard-ons just thinking about women wearing these."

"That's because they don't have to wear them. They might feel differently if they were the ones with the fabric stuck up their asses. Could you imagine them stuffing their junk in this?"

Ugh. I'd prefer not to, thank you very much.

I put the pink thong down and picked up a purple one.

"You must have another hot date with that guy Trent and I

saw you with Friday night," a familiar Australian accent said behind me.

I whipped around, thong dangling from my finger. Holly was smiling, shopping bags in hand. "Actually I don't," I said. "We were just checking them out." I had already told Erin how my date with Stephen had gone, both as to why he hadn't been right for me and how her brother had sabotaged the date.

Holly scanned the colorful pile and picked up a forest green pair. "I love thongs. I don't know what it is about them, but they make me feel sexy."

I barely held back a snort. She was the epitome of sexy. She didn't need thongs for that.

"Really?" Erin said, eyeing the pile. She grabbed a black and red pair, then looked at me. "Hey, I can use all the help I can get." She scanned the pile again and pulled out the pink pair I'd been examining. "Here, you can use all the help you can get, too."

I blinked. What the heck?

"You've always been confident, Kelsey," she went on to explain. "But when it comes to projecting a level of sexiness that drives guys wild, it wouldn't hurt you to dial it up a few notches."

She selected another thong, black this time, shoved it at me, and grabbed my wrist. "C'mon, Holly and I are gonna find you some equally sexy bras to go with those." She dragged me to the racks of bras and searched through them. For some reason I didn't protest. Maybe because I knew there was no point trying. "You're a thirty-eight C, right?" she asked.

Holly looked me over. "That sounds about right." Apparently she had another skill I didn't know about. Was there anything this woman couldn't do? Other than laugh without making people cringe.

Twenty minutes later, we walked out of the store, with me now well stocked when it came to sexy lingerie. According to them, this was part of the makeover to create a new sexually confident me.

"You're not expecting me to wear these to work, right?" I asked.

"Is there a chance you could meet someone worth dating there?" Holly responded.

"Not really. And maybe I'm not ready to date after all. I only just broke up with Owen."

Erin looped her arm with mine as the three of us headed to the restaurant for dinner. Darren was away for a conference, so she didn't have to go home right away. And I was positive Mr. Kitty Whiskers was napping, not pining for my return any time soon.

"You dumped him six months ago, and you weren't in love with him," she pointed out. "So don't even try to tell me you're still dealing with a broken heart."

I grunted. "I was in love with him."

"No, you weren't. You were in love with the idea of having someone there for you, but he wasn't there for you. And he hadn't been there for you for over two years."

No, I didn't sound pathetic and needy at all. But she was right. Until she said it, I had ignored the truth all that time.

"Do you think if I'd been sexy, things would've been different?" This wasn't the first time I'd felt that way. If I had worn sexy underwear and been sexually confident, would he have spent more time with me than at the office?

"Owen is a self-absorbed ass. So no, sexy clothing wouldn't have made a difference to him. He only cares about his career."

So all I needed was to find a guy who was neither a self-absorbed ass, nor a workaholic.

"Well, since the perfect candidate for the position hasn't applied yet," I reminded her. "I think we can agree that my dating life is non-existent...and that won't improve anytime soon."

We entered the restaurant. Several people were waiting just inside the door to be seated.

"At least you've got Darren," I said to Erin, then looked at Holly. "And aren't you dating Trent? You guys don't know how lucky you both are."

Holly opened her mouth to speak at the same time the hostess asked how many people were in our party.

"Three," I replied. She checked her seating chart, grabbed three menus, and told us to follow her.

It wasn't until we were seated at the table by the window and the hostess had left that Holly said, "I'm not dating Trent."

"You're not?" I said, slightly stunned. After Friday night, I'd been certain there was maybe something going on between them...and they hadn't been at the restaurant to discuss work after all. That Trent had changed his mind about not dating her. No one dressed like Holly had been that night just to hang out with their co-worker.

She shook her head. "Don't get me wrong. I would love to be his girlfriend. But so far he sees me as nothing more than his friend and colleague." She perused the menu. "That doesn't mean I've given up on him, though. I just need to be patient and hopefully he'll eventually see me as something more."

I wasn't sure which was worse: Holly being his girlfriend or hoping to be his girlfriend. At least if she was already dating him, that meant he was taken and I had no chance with him— not that I had a chance with him either way. Now that it looked like she could become Erin's and my friend, it meant we were supposed to help her land the guy of her dreams. Wasn't that what friends did? Wasn't that why Erin was so determined to help me find Mr. Right?

Swallowing back my feelings for Trent, I smiled at Holly. "I'm sure he eventually will." Each word felt like barbed wire clawing its way up my throat.

But why wouldn't he eventually come to his senses—or at

least open his eyes to the possibility of him and Holly becoming romantically involved? They both worked in the same office and were both workaholics. The only reason Holly had been at the mall was because she needed to buy a birthday present for her mom. Otherwise she would've been at work with Trent. And while his workaholic status would've been an issue if he and I were involved, it wouldn't be for them. At least whenever they needed a quick breather, they could have hot office sex long after their colleagues had gone home for the day.

My heart pinched painfully at the picture I painted in my head of their hot office sex. You know the kind, where the man shoves everything off the desk and takes the woman right there.

The kind of sex every woman fantasizes about...even if she refuses to admit it to herself.

"Can I get you ladies a drink?" a sinfully deep male voice asked, thankfully breaking into my I-freaking-need-to-have-sex-soon thoughts.

Too bad the sinfully deep voice didn't help my dilemma.

I looked up from my menu. "I'll have a strawberry margarita." I needed something to numb the image of Holly and Trent now taking residence in my head. And of course, Holly's new thongs played a starring role.

Erin and Holly ordered the same—Erin's being a virgin. We also ordered our food, not that I cared about food at this point. I just needed the drink. And if I hadn't driven to the mall and I didn't have to work tomorrow, I would've skipped the food and just ordered drinks.

The waiter left to fetch our margaritas.

"He's hot," Erin said, nodding over my shoulder. I turned to see if she was talking about the waiter or if she had seen someone else.

Yep, it was still the waiter.

"Hey, the last I heard, you're married," I said, dryly.

"One, I'm married not dead. Two, I'm a hormonal mess and incredibly horny all the time. So even though I won't act on it, I will notice hot guys. And three, I was thinking about him for you."

She winked—and I knew right then I was in trouble.

Again.

TRENT

Well-known fact #1: men hate admitting to themselves when they're wrong. Just ask any female. We would rather have our eyeballs gouged from our head and fed to a great white shark than admit the truth to ourselves.

But shit happens—and it doesn't matter who's wrong and who isn't, it comes down to doing what's right.

And messing up Kelsey's love life was the right thing to do. She deserved better than the asshat from Friday, a fact her brother would've agreed with.

Pushing aside thoughts of whom she could possibly deserve, I returned my attention to the presentation I was preparing for tomorrow's meeting. But as much as I tried to focus on the numbers, thoughts of Kelsey popped into my head. Like the way she looked in her dress on Friday, with her deep cleavage that I wanted to explore with my tongue.

Yeah, I know—the irony wasn't lost on me at how I'd been pissed at the jerk-off for having the same thoughts I currently entertained. The difference between us was that I wouldn't follow through with my lust-filled thoughts. I wouldn't hurt Kelsey. Could he claim the same?

Yep, I didn't think so either.

I spent the next hour analyzing numbers. One of the best things about working long after everyone else had left for the day was that no one was around to interrupt me. No one was phoning or emailing me, demanding my instant attention. Normally Holly would've been here, but she'd left hours ago to shop for her mom's birthday present.

I was finishing the final points to the presentation when a knock on my open office door startled me.

"Hey, how's it going?" Holly entered, a Victoria's Secret bag dangling from her hand.

"You got your mom sexy lingerie?" Christ, I couldn't imagine doing that for my mom. That was wrong on so many levels.

Holly shook her head and removed two satin thongs—one dark green, the other black—from the bag. "I got these for me. What do you think?" She held up the black one with both hands.

"Nice," I said, squirming slightly. We were friends, but unless the guy was gay, this wasn't the type of conversation you had with your male friends—except if you were hoping to get laid.

"I bumped into your sister and Kelsey there. They got some too."

I immediately blocked out the part about Erin. TMI. Instead, visions of Kelsey in nothing more than a black thong danced in my head.

And my cock instantly responded. I discreetly adjusted myself, unseen by Holly thanks to the desk. No point in her guessing where my lust-filled thoughts were when it came to my best friend's sister.

"I really like Erin and Kelsey," she said. "They're nice."

"Erin can be a bit of a pain in the ass at times, but other than that, you're right. They are...nice." If only my thoughts about Kelsey were on the nice side too. But with memories of the black thong flashing in my head, they leaned more toward naughty than nice.

"We had dinner together, which is why I'm so late getting back to the office." She grinned. "Did you miss me?"

"Of course. Did you have fun?" *Did Kelsey mention me?*

Holly nodded. "We even managed to get Kelsey another date." She dangled the thong in the air again. "I think I'll go slip this on." She said something else, but I was too busy seeing stars to hear what it was.

"Okay," I mumbled, biting back the urge to call my sister and ream her out. What the hell was she thinking after the last disaster of a date?

I was so busy fuming on the inside about the date, I hadn't noticed Holly leave my office until I looked up and discovered she was gone. I grabbed my cell phone and dialed Erin's number.

Before she had a chance to say anything, I blurted, "What's this about you getting Kelsey another date?" I cringed as soon as the words were out. The last thing I needed was for Erin to know how I felt about her best friend.

As it was, it had taken her a long time to forgive me for what happened with her crazy classmate back in college.

A mistake I still regretted to this day.

A mistake I had made after returning home for the summer, ready to make a move on Kelsey now that we were older and the age difference didn't seem so great...only to find out she had a boyfriend.

You guessed it. Her now ex-fiancé.

What about Liam, you ask? This was back before I realized

making a move on my best friend's sister wasn't okay. Blame it on my horny hormones, if you must.

"And hello to you too," Erin said.

"Sorry," I mumbled.

She chuckled. "I'm sure you are. Anyway, what's wrong with me finding Kelsey another date? Her last one was a flop, but it doesn't mean the poor girl has to remain single for the rest of her life."

If I couldn't be with Kelsey in the way that I wanted, then yeah, I thought her remaining single was a great option. "So who is this guy?"

"We met him today at the restaurant where we ate dinner. He's a waiter there."

I felt my eyebrows pinch together. "She's going out with a waiter?"

"He's not just a waiter. He's also a fitness model."

I sighed. Of course he was. "So when's this date gonna happen?"

My sister snorted a laugh. "I heard what happened when you crashed Kelsey's date with Stephen. Don't even think for a second that you're gonna get any info out of me on this one. Kelsey deserves to be happy, and you wrecking another of her dates isn't going to make her happy."

I gritted my teeth. I wouldn't have been surprised if she'd heard it on her end. "Do you honestly believe that going out with a waiter will make her happy?"

"I'm not suggesting she marries him, but she can at least have some fun." The humor in Erin's voice had vanished, to be replaced with a tinge of irritation. Nothing I hadn't dealt with before. "Why are you so concerned about her dating life anyway?"

Fact #1 about women: never tell them the truth when your family jewels are at stake.

Yes, Erin was hoping for more nieces and nephews one day,

but she had long since written me off as being the provider of them.

Which meant the family jewels were very much at risk.

"Because…Liam wanted me to keep an eye on her while he's away." That was both the partial truth and the safe answer.

"And did he ask you to crash her dates? Oh, who am I kidding? Of course he did." She grunted. "You do realize it's up to Kelsey who she goes out with, right? It has nothing to do with you or her brother."

Said the woman who kept setting Kelsey up on dates.

"She might get hurt."

Erin sighed. "You and Liam always were overly protective of us. But guess what? We're big girls now and know how to take care of ourselves."

I scowled at the phone—not that my sister could see me. "What do you know about this waiter?"

She didn't answer and I knew I'd gotten to her. "This guy could…could…" I didn't want to even think of what this potentially deranged man could do to Kelsey.

"Yes, this guy could end up being into Fifty-Shades-of-Grey type sex, and not only will Kelsey have fun, she'll be a lucky girl."

I hadn't read the book, nor had I seen the movie, but I'd heard enough from the women (and some of the guys) in the office to know what kind of sex Erin was referring to. The image in my head of Kelsey in a black thong switched to her wearing leather and satin and handcuffed to my bed—and my cock strained against my zipper.

And now thanks to the thoughts parading through my head, my goal of quickly finishing my presentation was met by some tough competition, and it didn't look good for the presentation.

"Tell you what," I said. "When Liam returns home, you can

tell him why you were so eager to get his sister laid. I can guarantee he won't be impressed."

She snorted. "It's not like Liam's gonna do anything to me."

She had a good point.

It was my ass that would be whipped.

And not in the Fifty-Shades-of-Grey sense.

10

KELSEY

My doorbell rang, signaling the commencement of Operation Let's Make Kelsey More Sexually Confident. It had been Holly's idea when we were at the restaurant. At the time it had sounded like a great idea.

Now? I wasn't so sure.

She and Erin walked into the small foyer, their hands filled with supplies. After the restaurant, they had dragged me to the makeup counter at Macy's and then to a shoe store. There, they had convinced me to buy stilettos even though I couldn't walk in them.

They placed everything onto the kitchen table. Holly then stood there taking in the house. I'd bought it a few years ago, after I'd finished studying to be a physical therapist, and furnished it Scandinavian style. A nod to my Swedish heritage. The only items that weren't a nod to my heritage were the cute and colorful owl pictures, pillows, and ornaments scattered throughout.

"Nice place," she said, smile genuine as always.

Erin placed a pile of women's magazines on the table. "This is your homework assignment."

"Homework?" I squeaked. "You never said anything about homework."

"These magazines have great articles on sexual confidence and ways to please a man. And this..." She removed a book from the bottom of the pile.

"You got me *The Joy of Sex*?"

"No, I'm loaning it to you. I'm gonna want it back."

Somehow I managed not to groan. This sure as heck wasn't what I had signed up for. I thought they would apply some makeup on me and call it a day. "You're not quizzing me on any of this, are you?"

"No, unlike our high-school teachers, I trust you'll study the info."

"Remember, it's not just about pleasing the guy," Holly said. "It's about knowing what *you* enjoy. If you know what makes you feel good, you'll feel more confident. And if a guy does ask you what you like, you'll be able to tell him. Trust me, guys eat that up. It's like a major turn on."

"And don't be afraid to ask him what he likes," Erin piped in. "Guys love that too."

I nodded, mentally taking notes, wondering what I'd gotten myself in to. Wondering what Trent enjoyed when it came to sex.

Ugh! I couldn't go there. Holly liked Trent. Holly was amazing and sweet and intelligent. She was perfect for him. He just needed to open his eyes and see what was in front of him.

Even if it did break my heart.

"Okay, first things first." Holly grabbed the bag with the new makeup. "Your makeup is perfect for the daytime, but for a date, it needs to smolder. I'm going to teach you how to do that."

"Then come these." Erin held up the stilettos.

"What do you mean?" I asked.

"You're going to practice walking in them."

"Can't wait," I muttered under my breath. "Jeff is just taking me to a movie. I won't have to wear them for that, right?"

"Wrong," Holly replied, spreading out her supplies on the table. She gestured for me to take a seat. "Erin and I came up with the perfect movie outfit—including the shoes."

"And what exactly is this perfect outfit?" Visions of micro minis and low-cut tops danced in my head, mocking me. It was one thing to stand around in a super-short skirt. It was another to sit in a movie theater and have the world get a sneak peek at your underwear.

Or thong—they had already insisted that I would be wearing one for the date.

"You'll see once we're finished," Erin said before disappearing from the kitchen.

The next twenty minutes involved Holly making up one side of my face, then getting me to replicate the results. Her goal wasn't to make me look like someone on the cover of Vogue, with more makeup than I wear in a week. But the end result was two steps above my usual level of sexiness—which was pretty much non-existent.

"If you were wearing an evening gown and attending a gala event, you would want to wear even more makeup than this," she explained. "But glamorous sexiness isn't the right look for you. You should play up the innocent sexy-kitten vibe you pull off so well."

"But remember, you don't want to come off as easy," Erin said, jumping into the next part of my lesson on sexual confidence. My head was spinning from all the information they were throwing at me. "You want to be friendly, approachable, and non-intimidating, but never easy."

"That's right. The goal is for him not to wham-bam-thank-you-ma'am you and you never see him again. You want him unable to stop thinking about you after the date."

I nodded as I tried to absorb everything they'd been telling me for the past hour.

Wow, being sexy was a lot of work.

But they did have a point. While I was dating Owen, did he ever think about me when he was supposed to focus on his classes, focus on his internship, focus on his cases? I doubted it.

He'd never texted me just to let me know that he was thinking about me.

Nor had he ever left Post-It notes around the house like Darren did for Erin.

No, when it came down to it, there had been only one person who had done all of that during the six years we dated.

Me.

Holly took a sip of her frozen strawberry daiquiri. "What's the best sex you've ever had?"

Now here's the thing. Say you've only eaten burgers from a fast food chain. They aren't bad, but they're all the same. There's no variation. None stand out from all the other ones you've eaten there.

Welcome to my former sex life with Owen.

That wasn't to say it was bad—but there hadn't been anything earth shattering about it either. There was no one time that stood out in my mind, because like with the fast food chain, each sexual act was exactly the same as the ones before it...and the ones that followed.

Plus, sex with Owen had been vanilla—nothing like the sex in the erotic romances I'd been known to read.

So there lay my dilemma. What was I supposed to do? Be a guy and exaggerate the truth? Because from the looks on Erin's and Holly's faces, they were expecting something worthy of a romance novel.

I let out a long how-do-I-answer-this sigh.

"Ohmigod," Erin said in a rush. "Please tell me you at least had orgasms with Owen."

"Sure I did." Most of the time.

Okay, truthfully?

Fifty percent of the time.

Except near the end of our relationship. Drop the five from that number and you had how many orgasms I'd experienced in the final three months. And by three months, I meant the three months we were still having sex, which, by then, had fizzled to once or twice a week—if even that.

While I sipped on my frozen strawberry daiquiri, giving myself a happy buzz, Erin and Holly shared about the best sex of their lives.

And color me jealous. I wanted *their* sex lives.

Because it wasn't just one story each.

There had to be a least ten altogether. And that was just for starters.

"All right then, what's the worst sex you've ever had?" Holly asked, and they automatically turned to me, suspecting I had a lot of stories to share, no doubt.

"I guess it had to be when Owen and I first started having sex," I said, feeling a little guilty at what I was going to tell them. But not too guilty, given I didn't have any "great sex moments" to share with them. "I was living in the dorm and he was still living with his parents. So we had to have sex in his car. And...um...he came but didn't realize I hadn't, and that was the end of that."

Erin's eyes went wide, like the end of a stick of dynamite, fuse lit. "This was just the one time, right? Please tell me sex wasn't always like that for you."

"No, it got better." Once he finally got his own apartment.

Holly raised her daiquiri glass. "We need to make a toast." She indicated for Erin and I to pick up our drinks. "To Kelsey finding someone who rocks her world when it comes to sex, so that next time we don't have to feel so sorry for her."

I laughed and raised my glass. "Here, here."

11

—————

KELSEY

S tanding in the steamy bathroom, wearing only a towel, I held up the black thong. Holly had told me to wear it tonight for the date, and maybe she was right.

Yeah, yeah. I remembered the part about not being "easy" in that long list of advice Holly and Erin had given me. And yes, the "old-fashioned" way was to go out with the guy a few times and then have sex. But had the creator of that dumb rule ever tried to survive for over a year sex-free?

No, I didn't think so either.

And it wasn't like I was going to *be* easy. I was going to be everything they'd said. But if he asked...well, then I was prepared to have some fun. Wasn't that what being sexually confident was all about?

I slipped on the thong and matching black satin bra, then repeated several times to my reflection, "I've got it going on! No man can resist me."

It didn't matter how many times I said it and it didn't matter if I was wearing sexy underwear, the words didn't sink in. It didn't help that Owen had never treated me like I was sexy. And it also didn't help that his interest in doing the deed had gone south for the winter (and never returned) during the last nine months of our relationship. Maybe that had been partly my fault. If I'd been more confident like the magazines suggested, I would have found out what excited him and our sex life would've been better, richer.

Existent.

I quickly finished getting ready for the date, slipping on my skinny low-rise jeans and the sexy sleeveless top Erin and Holly had insisted I buy when we were shopping. I left the top buttons undone so my cleavage showed. The white fabric clung to my body, and revealed a thin strip of skin between the hem of my top and the waistband of my jeans. My black bra was visible through the fabric, but they had insisted that only made me look sexier.

I headed downstairs. As I reached the bottom step, my cell phone pinged. Thinking it was Jeff telling me he would be late —or worse yet, canceling—I checked the message.

It wasn't from Jeff. It was from Trent.

Trent: What are you up to?

Me: Going out

Trent: With Erin?

Me: No, I have a date

Trent: Anyone I know?

Me: Doubt it.

And even if he did know the guy, I wouldn't tell him. Not after what happened during my date with the Viking.

Trent: So where are you going?

> Me: Out

Trent: Out where?

> Me: Out out.

Yeah, I was being a bitch. Could you blame me?

Trent: Be careful, okay?

I knew he was only saying that because of Liam and Erin, but a warmth flickered inside me at his concern.

> Me: Thanks. I will.

The doorbell rang, ending any further conversation.

At the sight of Jeff wearing black jeans, a black leather jacket, and a black T-shirt, my jaw dropped open, killing the sexy look I should've been aiming for—unless my goal was to go for the let-me-give-you-a-blow-job-now look.

I snapped my mouth shut.

"Hey, Kelsey." His gaze skimmed down my body. His lips curved up and his handsome face became breathtaking. "You look great."

I smiled, and every sexually confident cell in my body high-fived. "You look great too."

"You ready?"

Slipping on my stilettos, I nodded, then stepped out of the house and locked the door behind me.

I followed him, my heels clicking against the stone path.

And then I froze.

Do you see it? Yes, that's it. The motorcycle sitting on my driveway.

Crap.

My heart jumped into my throat, ready to make a great escape. I'd never been on a motorcycle before. It hadn't even been on my bucket list.

Jeff didn't notice that I had stopped. He grabbed the two helmets sitting on the bike. I took a deep breath, let it out slowly, and joined him. He handed me a helmet and climbed onto his bike.

Where's your sense of adventure, Kels?

Thank God Trent didn't know about this. The same for my brother. Both would've had a fit if they knew I was about to climb onto the bike with a near stranger. A friend of theirs in high school had been killed while riding a cycle. After that, my parents had made me promise never to ride one.

But my parents were gone and Trent and Liam weren't here. Praying that I wasn't about to make a mistake of epic proportions, I climbed on behind Jeff. He started his engine.

And we were off.

Racing down the street.

With me trying not to scream.

I clung on tightly, my arms around his waist. Unfortunately, his jacket prevented me from feeling the amazing abs I knew he was sporting.

How did I know? Erin might have possibly looked him up on the social media sites. And I might have accidentally on purpose looked over her shoulder while she was oohing and aahing over his abs.

At the movie theater, Jeff bought the tickets while I purchased the drinks. Neither of us was interested in popcorn.

And it didn't take long to figure out why Jeff didn't want any popcorn. Does the word octopus mean anything to you? The movie had barely begun when his hands were all over me. They started off innocently at first. The subtle glide of his finger against the back of my hand. That progressed to hand holding, which rapidly progressed to his hand on my upper inner thigh.

He shifted his hand and placed pressure on my clit through my jeans, which responded with a chorus of "Ohhh yes!"

Remember, you don't want to come off as easy. You want to be friendly, approachable, and non-intimidating, but never easy, Erin's voice echoed in my head.

But was this really me being easy? He was only touching me. We hadn't ripped off any clothing, yet. And I wasn't going to let that happen in the middle of the movie theater. That wouldn't be about being sexually confident. That would be crazy.

He continued touching me, the pressure through my jeans inching me closer to coming. This had to stop before I started moaning. Sure, the movie was loud, especially with the car-chase scene currently going on, but I was positive the people in front of us would hear me moan regardless of the movie's volume.

I interlaced my fingers with his and shifted his hand to my knee. Undeterred, he moved our hands to his crotch and placed mine over his hard length. Pride rushed through me that I had that effect on him.

I smiled and leaned in. "Not now. Not here."

He let go of my hand. Disappointment stomped through me like a stubborn child. Even though I wasn't comfortable taking things further in the theater, that didn't mean I wanted him to stop holding my hand. To give me a sign that this wasn't all about the sex for him.

I exhaled a long breath. Why did dating have to be so hard?

I sat through the rest of the movie, only half watching it while silently debating whether I should call Trent to pick me up and forget this night ever happened.

The devil on my shoulder voiced her opinion loud and clear. Yes, Jeff was only interested in one thing, but at least it would be fun—and I could finally end this super-long dry spell.

The angel on the opposite shoulder leafed through a beauty magazine, stopping only long enough to say that the devil made a very good point.

The movie ended and we walked outside to the local pizza place for dinner. At least Jeff didn't expect us to go straight home to have sex. We would have a chance to get to know each other first.

As expected, the restaurant was busy, but the hostess seated us after a few minutes. We ordered a Mediterranean pizza and beer from the waitress who was eyeing him up. As far as she was concerned, I wasn't here.

While he was preoccupied with her flirting with him, I subtly turned on my phone and discovered Trent had texted.

Trent: How's the movie?

I smirked, knowing what he was really asking, and returned my phone to my purse. "So beyond modeling, waitering, and working out, what else do you do?" I asked Jeff.

"I love gaming with my friends."

"That's great." I waited for more, but there was either nothing more to him or he wasn't going to tell me.

The conversation kind of stalled after that. I asked him questions about his gaming, even though I couldn't have cared less about the answers. Unfortunately, once I began asking questions, he couldn't stop talking about it. He failed to notice what was no doubt my glazed-over expression.

After dinner, we returned to my house. I handed Jeff back his helmet and he walked me to the front door. As soon as we were inside and the door shut behind him, he pushed me against the wall and kissed me hard.

I pretended the kiss was all kinds of hot. I also pretended that I didn't wish it was Trent kissing me instead of Jeff.

Jeff pulled away long enough to kick off his shoes and ask

me where my bedroom was. After returning my stilettos to the hall closet, I led him upstairs and had barely stepped into my room before he was all over me again.

He walked me backwards to the bed, until my calf brushed up against it. And before I knew it, my jeans and thong had been practically torn from my body to join his jeans and underwear on the floor.

Jeff rolled on the condom that he kept in his wallet. Before I could ask him what he liked, he was on the bed, leaning over me...then he was in me. I grunted more from surprise than discomfort. When it came to size, the god of penises hadn't been his friend—not even close. Good news for me, I guess, given how long it had been since I'd last had sex and given that foreplay was not in his vocabulary.

He pumped inside me a few times and groaned his release.

He then pulled out of me, tossed the condom in my trash, and was dressed before I could even blink.

"That was great," he said, zipping up his jeans without sparing me a second glance. "We'll have to do it again sometime." And then he left me on the bed, naked, exposed, empty.

A minute later, the revving of a motorcycle engine cut through the night. As stupid tears filled my vision, I pulled my blanket around me, shielding me from the world.

Shielding me from more rejection.

Shielding me from more crappy sex.

KELSEY

Needing to get started on my fabulous pity party for one, I snatched my underwear from the floor and slipped on my fuzzy white bathrobe. Downstairs, I grabbed an open bottle of Riesling from the fridge, a wine glass, and a bowl of strawberry ice cream.

Then my consolation food and I watched a romantic comedy. I know, weird choice given the situation, right? You'd think I'd prefer a horror movie in which the guys never made it out alive. But no, witnessing two people fall in love despite all odds gave me a smidgen of hope.

Yes, I chose to ignore the part about how this was fiction. Of course the heroine would live happily ever after. It wouldn't be a romance if there was no happily ever after.

At least that was my opinion when I started the movie. By the third glass of wine, my opinion had completely twisted around. The only man I truly loved was the one I couldn't have.

The one man no other man would ever measure up to.

That's right—love sucked.

My cell phone pinged from my purse on the floor. I ignored it and reluctantly peeled my eyes open. They felt like the moisture had been sucked out and they hurt—but not as much as my head.

Daylight streamed through the bedroom window, torturing me with its cheerfulness. Easy for it to be so happy, its life didn't suck.

Barely resisting the urge to stick my tongue out at the sunlight, I pulled the covers over my head and let myself drift back to sleep. It wasn't like I needed to get out of bed anytime soon. I could stay here the entire weekend for all I cared.

My head wholeheartedly agreed.

I don't know how long I'd slept when I stirred awake again, to the covers being slowly pulled away from my head.

"Hey, Kels." Trent's deep voice, which was soothing enough to calm even the crankiest of toddlers, eased my aching head slightly. "Are you okay?"

I peered up at him, grunted, then ripped the bedding from his hand and yanked it back over my head. "I'm not here," I grumbled. "And how did you get in?" I could've sworn I locked the door last night.

"Liam gave me his key for emergencies. Are you sick?"

I pushed the cover away from my face. "Define sick."

"I've been texting and calling you all morning to see how the date went."

Not exactly what I would define as an emergency. But if I were Erin, he would've done the same.

I pushed myself up to sit. The bedding pooled around my waist, revealing my robe, which had come untied while I'd slept. The front gaped open, exposing my black bra and thong.

Trent's eyes widened for a brief moment before he looked away. Redness crept up his neck. He had seen tons of women in various stages of undress, so seeing me this way shouldn't have embarrassed him—unless he saw me as nothing more than a little sister.

He reached out, as if to close my robe, but his long strong fingers accidentally brushed against the top of my breast. Flames flared where he had touched, licking me with their dizzying heat.

God, I wanted him so badly.

"Sorry," he said, dropping his hand. His voice was deep and rough, the kind of voice that would've had even nuns renouncing their religion.

"It's okay." My voice was equally rough and I coughed to clear my throat.

I pulled my robe together and shifted my legs over the side of the bed. He sat on the edge of it, and I subtly breathed in his warm spicy scent and the scent that was all man—all Trent.

Now, if only someone could figure out how to capture it in a bottle, I'd be all over it.

"So how was the date?" he asked.

"It was awesome. Can't wait for another one."

His eyebrow quirked up. A very admirable talent, I might add. I couldn't do it. "Really? Better than the last guy you went out with?"

"Well, considering my last date had a freaking chaperone who kept me from getting laid..." I leveled my gaze at Trent.

Trent's hands shot up in surrender. "Hey, I had nothing to do with that. He left, in case you're forgetting. And it's not like I drove him away with a pitchfork."

"You might as well have."

Trent grunted. God, why did his grunts have to be so goddam sexy?

"So let me get this straight, you were actually hoping to fuck that Stephen guy?"

I shrugged. "Kinda."

"Even if he wasn't looking for repeat business?" If you were to pile up all the apples in the grocery store, you would've had a lot less than the disbelief in Trent's tone.

To him, I was sweet, innocent Kelsey.

All right. Maybe I was innocent, given I could count on two fingers the number of guys I'd had sex with. And neither would have given the heroes in erotic romances a run for their money when it came to performance techniques.

"Do you know the last time I fucked a guy?" I asked.

He-Who-Got-Sex-Whenever-He-Wanted shook his head.

"Let's just say it's been a long time. A very long time."

"How long are we talking about here?"

"Well, given that Owen lost interest in me months before I broke off our engagement, I'd say my body doesn't remember what an orgasm feels like." My lips jerked up into a smirk. "And after what happened last night, it still doesn't remember."

Trent chuckled, looking almost relieved. "So no sex last night either, huh?"

"Oh, no, there was sex involved. Well, I think you could classify it as sex." I shrugged once more. Great—even my shoulders were getting in more action than my girlie parts had received last night.

"What do you mean?"

"If the Olympics had an event called sprint fucking, my date would've won the gold medal. He didn't even stick around to make sure I came. He was out the door before I was even close to singing Hallelujah."

Trent cringed. "I'm sorry, Kelsey. The guy was an asshole." Then he tilted his head to the side, like a curious puppy, amusement creasing the outer corners of his eyes. "But let's go back to the part where you don't remember what an orgasm feels like. Haven't you at least gotten yourself off?"

I fiddled with the edge of my robe. "It's not something I've ever done."

"Really?"

"Yes, really." Yeah, it might have been my hangover talking. Sure Trent and I used to talk about things when we were younger, Trent in his wise, "older brother" way. He had always been great to go to when I needed advice but didn't necessarily want to ask Liam.

But never in a million and one years would I have talked to him about sex. That would've been embarrassing...especially once my body started craving him.

However, that didn't stop the next words from leaping out of my mouth. "So you're saying you've never treated a date the same way?"

"Never. When I'm with a woman, I always make sure she has a good time. I never leave her sexually frustrated." He kissed my temple, surprising me, and a tingling warmth spread through my body at his touch.

Or maybe that was because of what he had said.

If I had sex with him, I would never be left wanting.

I would only be left wanting him more.

He pulled away, his breath slightly ragged like mine. "Why don't you shower and come downstairs. I'll make you something to eat." He unfolded himself from my bed and left the room.

It took me a few minutes to collect myself after his tender kiss. Once I had, I stood in the shower, the hot spray raining over my body. I finally turned off the water when the temperature started to cool.

A few minutes later I was dressed in yoga pants, an oversized sweatshirt, and no makeup. My hair was sloppily pulled back in a ponytail. I was the poster girl of someone who didn't currently give a damn about her looks—and it felt good.

As I walked downstairs, the smell of cooked eggs greeted me. Trent cooked me breakfast? Oddly enough, my stomach didn't protest at the thought of food. If anything, it rubbed its hands in glee, waiting for the slight queasiness still plaguing it to ease.

Trent was dumping a pile of some sort of brown mess onto a plate as I entered the kitchen. "I made you some scrambled eggs."

I took the plate from him. "They look…" I thumbed through the Rolodex in my head for an appropriate adjective—preferably one that spared his feelings.

"Overcooked," he filled in. He rubbed the back of his neck. "Sorry 'bout that. I'm not a very good cook."

Something we had in common. "Me neither." Although I didn't remember my scrambled eggs ever being this brown. But it was the thought that counted, right?

My stomach wasn't so sure about that, but it let me eat the eggs without putting up a fight. "Thanks," I said, finishing off the last bite. Then I gulped down the orange juice he'd placed in front of me, washing away the not-so-great texture of the eggs.

"You're welcome." He eyed my body, and his gaze slightly glazed over. He blinked, grabbed my glass, and returned to the fridge. "Is that my old sweatshirt?"

Was it? Now that I thought about it, I did remember him lending it to me when we were in college. I had gone to Erin's apartment but had gotten caught in a downpour. Because I hadn't paid attention to the weather forecast, I wasn't dressed for it. My body-hugging T-shirt had been drenched and I was shivering. Trent gave me his sweatshirt, and I'd forgotten to give it back…and then it just became a permanent addition to my wardrobe.

I started to remove it.

"Don't worry about it. It looks better on you anyway."

I let the soft, faded-red fabric drop back into place.

The stack of fashion magazines on the table mocked me. I grabbed the top issue and spotted an article I hadn't paid attention to before: *Be Your Own Woman*. I read it, and something inside me shifted. Angels sang in gleeful chorus as beams of sunlight streamed into the kitchen.

Remember that article Erin had shown me about creating a fulfilling life before entering a relationship? Yes, that's the one. I didn't need to be told more than twice to realize I'd been going about this all wrong. As much as Holly and Erin would disagree, I was still a mess after my breakup with Owen.

"I'm done with men," I declared, forgetting that Trent was in the room.

"You mean you're gonna bat for the other team?" He didn't laugh. Instead, his voice sounded...off.

"Nope. I definitely prefer penises over...um, pussy." My face heated up and I looked away before Trent noticed. Definitely the hangover talking. But it also felt oddly natural to talk to him this way. "I mean, I'm tired of dating guys who don't care about me, who are only interested in me the wrong way." I guess I was kind of guilty of that too. Hadn't I wanted to have sex with the Viking and the waiter? Which just proved my decision was the right one.

Even if the ache between my legs wasn't on board with the program.

"There isn't much to my life right now. I work all day and come home to hang out with Mr. Kitty Whiskers and read a novel. I don't have any interests. I'm boring."

Trent leaned back against the counter. "You're not boring."

"Thanks, but you're wrong. Other than my job, I have nothing I'm passionate about. I have nothing that defines me. How can I expect a guy to appreciate me when there isn't much to appreciate?" I nodded, convinced I was doing the right thing. Until I sorted out who I was, there was no point being in a relationship. "I need a hobby. Something to get excited about."

Trent didn't look entirely convinced, but at least with my new goal in life, I was making things easier for him. He wouldn't have to play the role of concerned brother while Liam was away. "What kind of hobby?"

Good question. "I have no idea. Maybe if I sign up for a bunch of different classes, I might find something that excites me." I thought about it for a moment, then dug through the recycling bin.

After a few minutes of searching, I found what I was looking for and held the flyer up for him to see.

He frowned. "Cooking lessons?"

"Yes, it'll be perfect. I'm not a very good cook, so this would be a great start." I searched for the website on my smartphone. "Here's one. French bistro. It's three hours of hands-on lessons that will teach me how to make a three-course meal. Then I could host a dinner party."

Trent removed the phone from my hand, studied the screen for a moment, then handed it back to me. "That doesn't sound like a bad idea."

"It's the perfect idea."

The know-it-all voice in the back of my head grumbled that maybe I should start with something simpler.

I ignored it.

13

TRENT

There comes a time in a man's life when he realizes the old adage is true: If you can't beat them, join them.

I walked into the classroom to the rich scent of French cuisine, and spotted Kelsey sitting at a table near the front, reading a piece of paper. The seat next to hers was vacant.

I hadn't planned to sign up for the class when she first showed it to me, but then I realized she had the right idea about taking it. My scrambled eggs proved I needed help.

There was also the issue where I couldn't keep away from her. She was like a drug. Only a lot healthier.

I pulled out the seat next to hers and accidentally (not) bumped her arm with my hip. Like a junkie craving his next fix, I couldn't get enough of her soft body and just wanted to touch her.

Her head turned to me, then her eyes went wide and her jaw dropped open. For a heartbeat it looked like she had stopped breathing.

"Hey, is this seat taken?" I asked.

"What...what are you doing here?"

Assuming that was a "no" to my question, I sat. "Same as you. I figured a cooking class might do me some good."

She nodded, no doubt remembering my disastrous eggs.

"And I thought we could wow our friends and my sister by hosting a dinner party together," I added. It was just an excuse to spend more time with her, but I would take whatever sweet, Kelsey-scented scraps that were scattered my way.

"That might not be a bad idea. We could invite Holly."

I could only imagine what Holly would say if she knew I was here...once she stopped laughing. "I'm sure my friend Josh would also be interested."

"Josh?"

"You probably know him better as Joshua Hoffer from the San Francisco Rock." The city's NHL hockey team.

If I thought she had been surprised when I showed up unannounced in class, that was nothing compared to now. She stared at me as if I had just announced I was running for the Presidential office. In my underwear. "You...you know Joshua Hoffer?"

"Erin never mentioned it, huh?"

She shook her head slowly. "No, somehow she forgot to mention that."

I wasn't too surprised. Erin had pointed out several times that she thought he was an ass after meeting him one time with me at a charity event. I guess she did have a point there. He could be one when it suited him, which was more often than not.

Which meant I didn't have to worry about her asking me to set Josh up with Kelsey. An eternal blizzard would hit hell before that ever happened.

We didn't get to talk beyond that. Chef André started the class. After explaining how the class would be conducted, he motioned for us to join him up front for the first demonstration.

"We'll begin with French onion soup," he announced. "Because it takes forty-five minutes to an hour to caramelize the onions, I will only demonstrate how to make it. The recipe is included in the package I've given you."

He showed us how to cut the onions and how to cook them. Then he set the saucepan aside and removed another one from the stove, with onions that had been cooking for an hour.

"The next step is to deglaze the pot with the sherry." He poured the alcohol in and scraped the onions sticking to the bottom with a wooden spatula. "Next comes the beef consommé..." Which he also poured into the saucepan. A delicious, rich aroma filled the classroom. "And then the vegetable stock, apple cider, thyme sprigs, parsley, and bay leaf." He dumped in each ingredient as he listed it. "I will now allow it to simmer for fifteen to twenty minutes. And while it's cooking, I'll prepare the topping."

He demonstrated how to cut the bread so that it fit the tops of the soup crocks, then ladled the soup into the bowls and covered them with the bread. "And for the finishing touch, we add grated Gruyère and broil for a minute or two, until the cheese is bubbly and brown." He put the cookie sheet with the four crocks in the oven, and removed it a minute later.

And my taste buds pleaded to sample some.

"That wasn't too bad," Kelsey murmured.

"I think we can manage that," I said, even if I had tortured a couple of innocent eggs in an attempt to make breakfast for her.

Next came mushroom ravioli.

"To make the ravioli, I recommend a pasta maker, but you can also just roll out the dough," André explained. "For this class, we will be using pasta makers." He finely chopped a shallot.

Kelsey leaned closer to me. "How does he do that without slicing off the end of his finger?"

"Good question." The man looked like a martial arts expert with his knife-wielding skills. Mugging assholes, beware!

"Next are the mushrooms. You can use any type you like. I prefer a mix of portobello, oyster, and shiitake." Like with the shallots, he finely chopped them. Then he sautéed the mixture, along with garlic and other seasonings, and demonstrated how to make the ravioli. It was hard to focus on what he said when the only thing my stomach was interested in was eating. The woody yet robust aroma of the mixture tormented me, and I tried not to look like an idiot by sniffing the air too much. But it wasn't just the food I could smell. Kelsey's scent was damn good too.

Once the demonstration was over, we were sent back to our workstations so we could make the ravioli ourselves. Kelsey picked up the knife and studied it for a moment. The way she was eyeing it, you'd have thought she expected it to come alive and attack her.

"Do you want me to do the chopping?" I asked.

"Sure." She handed me the knife and watched me chop the shallots then the mushrooms. "Have you done this before?"

"Nope."

"Really?"

I shrugged. "It's not that hard. You try."

She took the knife from me and began chopping the shallot. Unlike Chef André's and mine, her attempt yielded pieces that were far from finely chopped.

The corner of my mouth jerked up to one side. "I'm sure you have other talents." Then I winced at how that sounded.

To my surprise, she grinned. "You better believe it, chopper boy. Just watch me nail the pasta."

Naturally my brain and everything south of the equator perked at the thought of getting to "nail" Kelsey. It took everything I had to redirect my attention back to the ravioli.

Now, there's something you should know about making

pasta from scratch…it's nothing like opening a package of dried pasta and dumping it into boiling water. The mixing of the flour with the egg was a breeze. Kelsey rolled the dough out into a rectangle, but when I tried to thread it through the pasta maker, it was too wide. It took her several attempts to get it narrow enough to slip in.

But then I forgot to flour the counter during the last assault with the rolling pin. When I went to peel the dough off the granite surface, it held on tight.

"Nooo," Kelsey said in a goofy, squeaky voice as I tried to convince the dough it was better off surrendering to its fate. "Don't make me go in there." She giggled.

After some careful peeling and a few patch-up jobs, we finally managed to thread the dough into the pasta maker. She cranked the handle while I lowered the dough in.

"Aaaaaahhhh," she said in the same funny voice as before.

"You definitely work with kids."

She laughed. "That obvious, huh?"

I grinned at her. Not because of her goofy voice and not because of her laugh. Her cheek had flour smeared on it.

Unable to help myself, I stepped closer and brushed my thumb against it. Her skin was as soft and as enticing as I imagined it would be. Her lips parted, an invitation for me to kiss her, and her beautiful blue eyes drank me in. If I didn't know better, I could've sworn she wanted me the same way I wanted her.

The crash of a pot lid against the floor snapped us out of our daze. I dropped my hand from her cheek.

"You had some flour there." I swallowed hard, pushing my lust back down, and returned to what we'd been doing before, a new tension now peering over our shoulders.

We continued working the dough with the machine until it was thin enough, then made the little ravioli pillows stuffed with the mushroom mixture.

"Wow, that wasn't so bad," Kelsey said. "You think our friends will be impressed?"

"Surprised might be a better word. We're not exactly world renowned for our cooking skills."

One corner of her mouth twitched up. "Good point."

"So is now a good time to ask why you spent the past few years avoiding me?" I casually asked as we prepared the creamy mushroom sauce while the ravioli was cooking. We'd been fairly close as kids. But ever since that incident with my sister's crazy friend, she'd seemed to go out of her way to avoid me. Whenever we had shown up at the same family events, Kelsey had kept her distance, then came up with a lame excuse so she could leave early.

"I don't know what you're talking about. I never tried to avoid you." She kept her attention fixed on the sauce I was stirring on the stove. Not once did she look up at me.

"Really? So all that time you said maybe twenty words to me, that was you at your yappiest?"

She shrugged, her face growing flush. "Maybe I didn't have anything interesting to say."

Did you buy that? I sure as hell didn't. She'd never had issues talking to me before, even about the most mindless topics, but I also knew I wouldn't get anywhere with her when it came to finding out the truth. Fort Knox could learn a thing or two from her when it came to keeping secrets locked away.

"Mmmm. That smells so good," Kelsey said, eyes closed. I had to agree with her there.

I poured the creamy mushroom sauce over the cooked ravioli, grabbed a fork from the counter, and pressed it into a square, cutting it in half. Then I speared a piece with the fork and offered it to Kelsey.

She opened her sexy lips to welcome it in—and for a second, I forgot it was the food and not my tongue that she wanted in her mouth. I caught myself before I had a chance to lean in and suck her lower lip into *my* mouth.

She closed her mouth around the morsel and moaned a sound that made my cock take notice—craving for her luscious lips to wrap around it. "Oh, God," she said with another moan. *You're not helping me here, Kels.* "That's amazing."

I ate the other half. Christ, she was right. The ravioli was amazing.

The final demonstration was for a French apple tart. Like with the soup, there wasn't enough time for us to make it in class. Chef André showed us how to create the pastry, then removed a previously made one from the fridge. He rolled it out, prepared the dessert, and popped it into the oven, then removed one he'd been baking while we were working on our ravioli. The sweet aroma of baked apples wafted through the room.

"The final step is the glaze," he said. "Take a cup of apricot jam and heat it so that it melts into a liquid." He demonstrated how to do this and brushed the liquid onto the baked apples. He then cut the tart into pieces and passed them around the group. Like everything else today, it tasted heavenly.

I must admit that when I first registered for the class, I had only done so to keep an eye on Kelsey. I hadn't expected it to be fun, especially with Kelsey by my side.

I also hadn't expected to be so turned on by it. Although that might've had to do with the new fantasy parading in my head—one involving Kelsey in her thong and black lacy bra.

And possibly a kitchen counter.

14

KELSEY

Remember when you were a kid and Santa didn't bring you the one gift you had really hoped for? The one gift that would change your life (or so your seven-year-old mind would've had you believe)?

That was how I currently felt.

I'd enjoyed learning to make the dishes, and I looked forward to cooking them again with Trent for our friends. But as I took the last bite of the dessert, I realized the spark I'd hoped for still wasn't there. I wanted to find something I was passionate about—and cooking fancy dishes wasn't it.

So now what? There had to be something beyond Trent that got my blood pumping.

I squirmed at the effect he still had on me, evident by my reaction when he'd brushed the flour off my cheek. At least that was better than the panic attack when he'd asked me why I had ignored him for all those years.

I would've rather had my head waxed than have *that* conversation.

For one, it meant telling him about the feelings that I'd had for him back then and still had. Guys who put their career first and avoided having girlfriends weren't interested in hearing things like that.

Only women like Holly could handle him being a workaholic, especially since she wasn't much better. But what about the commitment part? Was she okay with being only a short-term girlfriend? Or maybe once they got together, Trent would realize she was the right woman for him and would be eager to settle down.

Pain worse than having an elephant step on your foot taunted me at the thought. I quickly reminded myself it shouldn't matter that I was falling for him all over again. Trent's happiness? That was the trump card when it came to my heart.

Besides, I wasn't interested in dating until I had my life figured out.

But Trent isn't just anyone.

I ignored my heart's lovesick mutterings.

We cleaned our workstation, the odd tension that had sprung up between us when he'd brushed the flour off my cheek still lingering in the air.

"So?" Trent asked as we exited the room.

I waited for him to elaborate.

"What did you think of the class?"

"It was fun, but I don't think cooking really does anything for me."

"Any other ideas then?" He pulled the main door open for me. I stepped out into the cool evening air.

"I've always wanted to surf, but my balance isn't great." Not to mention it was spring and I was more of a hot-tub-temperature-type person. The cold ocean at this time of year didn't appeal to me. "And let's not forget the sharks," I added. "Knowing my luck, a great white would decide I'd make a tasty lunch."

"You know, the odds of being attacked are pretty much zero."

"And you know this for sure?" At his quick shrug, I said, "Yeah, I thought not. Maybe I could do something craft related."

"Good idea. I'm sure your brother would get behind it more than you surfing in shark-infested waters." He chuckled and I punched him in the arm.

"Ha! Very funny."

As I drove home, the idea of learning a new craft started to appeal to me more. By the time I pulled into my driveway, I couldn't wait to see what I could find. I went online and studied the arts and recreation catalog for the local community college. Erin had gushed last year about the jewelry-making class she had taken there.

Belly dancing. Hmmm I wasn't too sure about that. It might be fun as a class, but I couldn't see myself doing it as a long-term hobby.

Drama. My 2.5 in high-school drama said that was a no.

Bookbinding. People did that for a hobby?

Drawing for Beginners. That might be fun. I had always wanted to learn to draw.

The next session started in a few days and the class wasn't full yet. I registered for it and studied the list of supplies I needed to pick up before the first class.

My cell phone pinged.

Trent: Have you considered bull riding as a hobby?

Me: Haha! I'd fall on my butt before the bull even left the chute.

And knowing my luck, some hot cowboy would witness my disgrace and tell all his hot cowboy friends about it.

I texted back.

> Me: I just registered for a drawing class.

> Trent: Can you draw?

> Me: No, but I'm hoping I'll be able to by the time I'm finished.

We texted back and forth a few more times, organizing the upcoming dinner for our friends.

Holly phoned me the next evening. "Trent told me you guys are having a dinner party. Is there anything I can bring?"

"No, just you. I thought..." My throat squeezed tight, like a Shrinky Dink picture shrinking in the oven. Holly and I had become friends, and I wanted to help her win her man—even if the man was the same one I was falling for. "I thought I could help you with Trent."

Maybe then I could finally move past my feelings for him.

Or not.

"What do you mean?" she asked.

"Well, he's asking his friend to join us and Erin's bringing her husband. It will almost be like couples night." Only I wasn't planning to hook up with his friend.

I told Holly to do whatever she could Saturday night to steer the conversation away from work. And I would do what I could to create a romantic atmosphere—for Holly and Trent's sake.

The annoying voice at the back of my head pouted and acted like a petulant four-year-old over my plan.

I mentally locked it away in one of my colorful little owl boxes and threw away the key.

15

———

TRENT

Normally I was a confident man. I had to be for my job. And when it came to women, I had long since learned from the time I turned sixteen that it didn't take much for them to be interested in me. A smile here. A compliment there. A brief touch.

But as I waited for Kelsey to answer the door, my confidence took a hike. Why was it that the one woman who wasn't interested in me was the only woman I wanted?

On the positive side, thanks to Liam, I got to spend more time with Kelsey now than I had since returning from New York City. Maybe I could send him a card. Would porn be too much, to thank him for making it easier for me to hang out with his little sister while fantasizing about her?

Yeah, I thought so.

Kelsey's front door opened. "Do you have everything?" she asked, then bit her lip.

Did she look adorable? Damn right she did—and I wasn't talking about how whenever she did that my cock tightened. No, it was the rest of the package that did it for me too. She was wearing black yoga pants and a tank top that showed off her sexy curves. Her hair was pulled back in a high ponytail. She looked ready to attend a yoga class instead of cooking a three-course meal for our friends.

She looked perfect—other than her eyes, which were red and watery. Panic plowed through me, almost knocking me onto my ass. "What's wrong? Is it Liam?"

"Nothing's wrong."

"Then why are you crying?"

"I started chopping the onions before you got here."

I stepped into the house, carrying grocery bags filled with what Kelsey didn't already have. I'd gone into the office this morning and bought the fresh mushrooms for the ravioli on my way here.

She closed the door behind me and I followed her into the kitchen. "Did you cut them face down on the cutting board? Like Chef André told us to do?" I asked.

She scrunched up her nose. "No, I forgot that part. God, I must look a mess." She wiped her fingers under her eyes, which probably wasn't such a bright idea given she might've had onion juice on them.

"No, you look good." *As always*. I placed the bags on the counter.

She went back to chopping the onions while I unpacked the groceries. This time she made sure to chop them like we'd been taught to do.

I dumped what she had cut into the large saucepan and retrieved my own knife from a bag. Impressive, huh? I thought so. I'd bought it when I picked up the food. Because I hadn't bothered to do much cooking before, my knife supply had been woefully lacking.

Not anymore.

Now that I'd had a taste of how much fun cooking could actually be, I'd already watched a few shows on the Food Network and was eager to try out the recipes.

Of course, I didn't plan to tell Josh this. Otherwise he'd accuse me of trading in my nuts for a pair of ovaries.

"Nice knife." Kelsey looked at the pitiful thing she was using and then back at mine. "It's so big."

"Well, you know what they say about the size of a man's knife," I said, unable to resist.

Her blush? Totally made the comment worth it.

A comfortable silence blanketed us as we focused on slicing the vegetables and not our fingers. But despite that, the air sizzled with the same energy that had crept up between us during the class. And it was taking every inch of inner strength not to lift her up onto the counter and show her how I felt about her.

To taste her skin.

To explore her.

While the caramelized onions and the rest of the ingredients simmered, Kelsey and I got to work on the ravioli. Neither of us owned a pasta maker, so we had to roll the dough out the hard way.

Using the rolling pin, Kelsey flattened the dough while I prepared the filling. When she tried to remove it from the counter, part of the dough stuck to it and ripped in half. "That's not good. It was a lot easier with the pasta maker."

Had to agree with her there.

I mixed the chopped shallots and mushrooms and added the cream. Kelsey continued working on the dough. The finished product wasn't quite like the one from class—the dough nowhere near as thin—but I didn't think our friends would complain. Hey, as long as it tasted good, that was all that mattered.

And, Christ, I hoped it tasted good, or else I'd never hear the end of it from Josh.

Next was the dessert.

"You wanna make the dough?" she asked, reading the recipe.

"Sure, unless you want me to slice up the apples." I was fine doing either one.

"No, I can do them." She grinned that smile that always made my heart trip over itself. "Can I borrow your knife? Mine's too wimpy."

"You think you can handle it?" *Good going, dumbass.* There was no missing the innuendo in my voice.

Kelsey's blush from earlier was nothing compared to now. "I'm sure I can handle your knife just fine," she replied. But in contrast to her blush, her tone held a your-place-or-mine breathlessness—and my cock got excited.

Before I could stop myself, "I'd be all for that" slipped out.

She bit her lip, her gaze raising to *my* lips. But just as I was contemplating tossing my best-friend rules out the window, she flinched. "Ouch!"

Blood dripped from a cut on her finger. I grabbed a paper towel from the roll perched on the table. "I don't think you were supposed to cut off your finger."

"Oops! I must have misread the instructions." Despite the stinging pain she was no doubt experiencing, her tone was like a helium-filled birthday balloon floating free in the sky.

Fighting back the urge to kiss her silly, I rinsed the wound and wrapped her finger with the paper towel. "Where's your first aid kit?"

"Downstairs bathroom. Top drawer."

I returned a few minutes later, removed the paper towel from her cut, and replace it with a bandage. "It's not too bad. You'll survive."

The corner of her mouth quirked up. "I guess chopping isn't one of my hidden talents."

"What can I say? You just weren't ready for such a large knife."

Kelsey sighed. It wasn't a frustrated sigh. It was the kind of sigh a girl does when she's thinking about a certain part of the male anatomy, and how it would feel inside of her. Only, it wasn't my anatomy she was thinking about. That much I knew.

Or maybe I was wrong.

Maybe I hadn't imagined her reaction just before she cut herself.

Don't go there! I warned myself yet again.

Once the dessert was assembled, Kelsey placed it into the oven. "I'm going to have a shower now. Can you keep an eye on the apple tart?"

I'd rather keep an eye on her...in the shower. "Yeah, okay."

She returned forty minutes later, and I barely kept my mouth from flopping open at the sight of her.

Holy fuck.

Remember the pink dress she wore the night I crashed her date? The one she'd looked sexy in? That dress was nothing compared to the one she now had on. This sleeveless dress made the other one look like it belonged on a little girl. Black lace covered the nude fabric, and the floor-length dress skimmed Kelsey's curves in a way that had my cock ready to stand at attention.

I recited the equation for determining the return on equity in my head five times—fast.

My cock's response wasn't anything new when it came to Kelsey lately, but it was a little unnerving just how often it was happening.

Inwardly I cringed at what Liam would say if he knew how my body reacted when it came to his sister. Hell, forget what he would say. It was what his SEAL training would mean to me that I was worried about—or more specifically, what it would mean to my cock.

"You look good," I said, suddenly feeling underdressed in jeans and a dress shirt.

"I know it's a little too much. But since I've sworn off dating for a while, I knew this would be my only chance in who-knows-how-long to dress up."

She said something else, but visions of Kelsey in her black thong under the dress surfed around in my head, and I missed what she had said.

I might have also been busy visualizing removing said thong and exploring her hot, wet pussy with my tongue.

Whatever she had said couldn't have been important. She didn't look like she was waiting for me to respond...which was just as well since it was a well-known fact that men couldn't multitask. Responding to whatever she had said while I was thinking about her pussy was asking too much.

Add to that the image of Liam kicking my ass to the next state, and I was just too occupied to understand what Kelsey was up to.

But once imaginary Liam had kicked my ass as far as Colorado, I realized she was setting the kitchen table. In the center, two candlesticks sat on either side of a short vase crammed full with red and white roses. If I didn't know better, I'd say she had planned a romantic dinner—for six.

The doorbell rang and she smiled. "Showtime." She rushed out of the kitchen and answered the door. I followed her like the good host that I was.

Erin stepped into the house, hugged Kelsey like they hadn't seen each other for several weeks, and handed her a bottle of white wine. "Wow, what have you guys been cooking? It smells amazing."

She gave me a funny look, but I had no idea what it meant—which was nothing new when it came to my sister. I might have lived with her for most of our lives, but that didn't mean I always knew what she was thinking.

Kelsey led Erin and Darren into the kitchen as the doorbell rang again. I opened the door and let Josh in. Unlike Erin and

Kelsey, both dressed for a night on the town, Josh was also wearing jeans and a dress shirt.

He sniffed the air. "Hey, that actually smells good. Were you shitting me when you said you were actually going to cook dinner, or did your friend do the cooking and you're taking credit for it?"

I laughed. "Since when did I take credit for something I didn't do?"

"True."

We entered the kitchen. Erin and Darren were standing by the island with Kelsey, holding the drinks she had already served them. Milk for my sister and beer for my brother-in-law.

"Josh, you've met Erin and Darren, and this is Kelsey." I gestured at her.

Kelsey stared at Josh as if she couldn't believe he was in her kitchen. I hadn't realized she was a hockey fan.

Or maybe she wasn't.

It wasn't as if she could've missed seeing his picture. His good looks made him popular with the local media, even if he wasn't one of the team's star players.

The doorbell rang again and since Kelsey was pre-occupied with Josh (translation: she was still gaping at him), I answered it and let Holly in.

She was also dressed up and looked ready to hit a gala, if the long, floor-skimming dress was any indication. Her forest-green gown hugged her body. The front formed a deep triangle that traveled past her breasts, and flashed more of her skin than I'd ever seen on her before. The side slit in the skirt continued to mid-thigh, making her legs look never ending. Her auburn hair cascaded down her back in smooth waves.

Smiling, she handed me her jacket. "Thanks for inviting me. I can't wait to see what you made for dinner. It smells delicious."

"Thanks," I said, hanging her coat in the hallway closet. "You...you look great." Like she always did.

I followed her into the kitchen where everyone was still hanging out. Kelsey took a step back, and Josh placed his hand on her lower back.

And I saw red.

Fucking fiery-pits-of-hell red.

16

KELSEY

Holly stepped into the kitchen with Trent right behind her. Regular Holly was sexy and gorgeous. This version put that one to shame.

I'm not sure why I took an uncertain step back at the sight of her, but I did...and because I still wasn't used to stilettos, I wobbled and almost lost my balance.

Josh placed his hand on my lower back to steady me.

The smile I gave him was more on the grateful side than the Ohmigod-Joshua-Hoffer-is-touching-me side of things. He was good-looking, but he didn't have the same effect on me that Trent did.

Would I have almost sliced my finger off in Josh's presence? I doubted it.

My smile widened. "I bet you're used to women falling over you all the time."

"Sure, but usually they're drunk when it happens. You'd be the first sober woman to do that." He winked, and my face heated.

Note to self: practice walking in reverse while in stilettos.

I turned to Trent and Holly, and waited for Trent to introduce her to his friend. Instead, Trent watched Josh, a scowl on his face. Weird.

But then everything lately when it came to Trent had been weird. Off-kilter.

Or possibly just my imagination.

My wishful, lust-filled imagination.

"Holly," I said, "have you met Josh?"

She shook her head, but it was clear that she also wasn't lusting over him. A wave of disappointment surged through me. If she had been, I could have switched to hooking her up with Josh instead of with Trent.

Josh did the standard nod guys did to acknowledge someone without having to say actual words, and rubbed his thumb against my back as I asked her what she would like to drink.

I expected Trent to pour Holly a glass of wine, but he just glared at Josh's arm. God, hopefully he wasn't planning to be an ass tonight on my brother's behalf, especially since Josh and I weren't on a date.

Shaking my head to myself, I removed the bottle of Chardonnay from the fridge and poured Holly a glass. "I love your dress," I told her. "Don't you love her dress, Trent?"

Was that a little obvious?

"Yes, it's very nice," Trent responded halfheartedly, and it took everything inside of me not to roll my eyes.

"Your dress looks great," Josh said to Holly. Then to me, he said, "I love your dress. It's sexy." Enough seduction oozed from his words to fill a giant birdbath.

Trent continued scowling at him.

Having no idea what Trent's problem was, I smiled at Josh. "Thanks."

While Holly asked Josh about the current hockey season, I finished making the French onion soup. She then said something to Trent and leaned into him. My heart slumped against my ribs with an echoing thud, knowing that by the end of the night he would finally find out how she felt about him.

The fear that had plagued me while I was engaged to Owen re-ignited. Even engaged, I'd been alone. Sadly, from the looks of things, nothing was going to change.

I would always be alone.

Cue the violin music.

More than anything, I wanted what Erin had. She was loved, admired, appreciated. Not once did Darren ever make her feel like she was a forgotten toy, temporarily played with only when the child remembered she existed.

"I'm currently taking a drawing class," I said as I slid the cooking sheet with the soup bowls into the oven. I glanced at Josh to see his reaction and got the confirmation I was expecting. Guys didn't find that sexy or exciting. "...but I don't think it's the right hobby for me. I was thinking that maybe I could find a class on how to...to rebuild classic cars."

Okay, that was kind of random.

Both Josh and Trent looked at me as if I'd announced I was joining Cirque du Soleil. Although in Josh's case, he looked more turned on than surprised.

"Since when were you interested in doing that?" Trent asked.

I shrugged. "I love classic cars and I thought it might be fun." Or not.

"That would be cool," Josh said. "The closest I've come to rebuilding a classic car are the model cars I build in my free time."

Oh sure. Even Josh had a life outside of his career.

Trent gave me a funny look but didn't say anything else. Instead, he checked on the soup. The cheese was bubbling and had turned light brown. Perfect.

"God," Erin moaned. "That smells so good."

I directed everyone to the table, where I had set up place

cards, purposefully making sure Trent and Holly sat together. By default, that meant I was sandwiched between Trent and Josh.

I filled a saucepan with water and placed it on medium heat for the ravioli.

"I thought you weren't interested in dating anyone for now," Trent said, his voice low so no one else could overhear him. His body pressed lightly against my back—his clean scent a warm caress—and I sucked in a soft breath.

If this had been Josh, I would've said he was coming on to me.

But it wasn't Josh—it was Trent.

"And that's still true," I told him, unconsciously leaning back against him.

Oops. My bad.

Kinda.

But it wasn't like you could blame me. You'd have to be made of stone not to react the same way.

"Then why were you flirting with Josh?"

I blinked, trying to figure out why Trent would believe that. I came up blank.

I turned around to face him. "I wasn't flirting with him. I was being friendly. Big difference. Besides, what's the big deal if I flirt with him?"

Rubbing the back of his neck, Trent glanced at the saucepan. "Josh is a player and I don't want to see you get hurt."

"I'm a big girl, Trent. I know how to take care of myself." Most of the time.

He opened his mouth to say more. I didn't give him a chance. I joined our friends at the table. He sat next to me a moment later, and the unspoken tension between us incessantly poked me in the shoulder, like an annoying mosquito.

If I could have, I would have removed my stiletto and splatted it.

Or maybe I could hit Trent instead.

The way he was acting, he deserved it.

Holly took a sip of her soup. "Mmm. This is one of the best French onion soups I've ever tasted." The others agreed with her, which was the first time anyone had complimented me on my cooking. Unfortunately, because cooking still wasn't my thing, it would probably never happen again.

"Do you know Cavalia?" I asked everyone as we began eating the second course—the ravioli—to another round of "Wow, this tastes great," and "I didn't know you could cook."

"Don't they do acrobatics on horseback?" Holly picked up her wine. "Like Cirque du Soleil but with horses?"

"That's the one. They're in town next week. I've heard they're really good."

"I would love to see it," she said, eyes glowing with excitement. "I used to ride horses as a girl. I even did a bit of show jumping."

Wow, what couldn't she do? The closest I'd ever come to riding horses was the carousel ride at Disneyland when I was a kid.

"If you want to go," Trent said, "I could probably score us tickets."

Thinking he meant Holly, I didn't respond and did my best to ignore the disappointment that had come back for an encore. *He's a workaholic and my brother's best friend*, I reminded myself. *He's perfect for Holly.*

And Erin didn't seem to mind that Holly was interested in Trent that way. Apparently she was exempt from the friends-aren't-allowed-to-date-my-brother rule.

Trent said something else but I was too busy staring at my ravioli to catch what he'd said. It probably had to do with the date he and Holly were going on. Together.

Possibly even him confessing his undying love to her, right here at the table.

"Kelsey?"

I jerked my head up. "Huh? Sorry, what did you say?"

"Do you want to come too?"

"That sounds like a great idea." Josh's hand rested on my lower back, startling me. I jerked slightly, but not enough for him to notice. "Can you make that four tickets?" he asked.

With his gaze on Josh, a brief look of annoyance crossed Trent's face, but it disappeared as quickly as it had come. Trent then glanced at me, the annoyance shifting to hope.

I nodded and finished my wine. Without asking if I wanted more, Josh re-filled the glass and unleashed his brilliant smile. It was the same smile that no doubt left women panty-less at the mere sight of it. But when my parents had me immunized against the usual childhood illnesses, it had worked better than expected.

My panties stayed firmly in place.

Holly leaned in and whispered in Trent's ear, then ran her finger along his arm. He chuckled at whatever she'd said and my heart squeezed hard. I sucked down some wine, hoping it would help loosen the tightening in my chest.

It didn't.

"So how come Trent hasn't introduced me to you sooner?" Josh's warm breath brushed against my cheek.

"Maybe he was worried you would steal me away from him." The corner of my mouth curled up to one side to let him know that I was kidding. "And just so you know, I'm not looking for a relationship right now."

He moved his hand to my upper thigh, hidden under the table. And because that wasn't enough, he started caressing my leg. "That's good. 'Cause I'm not looking for one either."

It's not Trent's hand. It's not Trent's hand. It's not...

In my head, it was totally Trent's hand on my thigh.

"How come?" I might have squeaked that as the hand moved higher.

I subtly shifted my leg away from him, removing his hand from my thigh.

"I don't have time for one. My career comes first." Something in Josh's tone warned me there was more to the story, but it also warned me not to go there. "What about you? Why aren't you looking for a relationship?"

"Same thing. My career comes first." Close enough. He didn't need to know the real reason.

"And what is your career?"

I was suddenly aware of everyone's gaze on us, watching us expectantly. And that's when I realized just how cozy the two of us must've looked, with our "private" conversation.

"I'm a physical therapist at the children's hospital," I said, loud enough for everyone to hear.

"So you like kids?"

"Not only does she like kids," Erin chimed in, "she's amazing with them. She'll be a great mother one day." She rubbed her pregnant belly. "What about you, Holly? Do you want kids?"

"Not really," Holly said. "My parents were career-oriented and never had time for me and my brothers. I refuse to make the same mistake."

Erin stared at Holly as though the woman had sprouted another head. "You seriously don't want any children? None at all?"

"I've worked hard to get where I am. I don't want to give that up, but I refuse to be the selfish mother who puts her career before her kids. And, well, I just don't see myself as good mother material."

Disappointment traipsed across Erin's face and I knew exactly what she was thinking. If Holly and Trent ended up together, there went her chance to be an aunt. Or rather, there went her chance to be an aunt to a niece or nephew who lived in the same city as her.

"What about you, Josh?" Trent asked. "You hoping one day to have kids?"

"Can't say it's a top priority of mine. But then neither is settling down," Josh answered, appearing as confused as I felt at Trent's question. It didn't seem like the kind of topic a guy would ask another guy at a dinner party.

Unless he was trying to warn me away from his friend—because he thought I was now dreaming about a white-picket-fence future...with Josh.

Trent's gaze flicked to me. I shrugged and began collecting the dishes. Trent pushed his chair away from the table to join me. Holly offered to help, but I waved her off. The conversation continued with the discussion of kids, with one side of the table being pro-kids and the other side pro-career.

"Nice going," I hissed quietly to Trent as we set the dishes in the sink.

"No problem," he said. "I aim to please." He winked, which was like lighting the end of a stick of dynamite—and the sudden ache between my legs was the explosive.

"What was the point of asking Josh if he wants kids? And don't tell me you were curious." Not that I really cared, but Trent's closeness was starting to unnerve me and the words just tumbled out.

"Why wouldn't I be curious if my friend plans to be a father one day?"

I didn't have an answer, so I shrugged off the question.

By the time we had served dessert, the topic had switched to the unseasonably warm weather.

"I've been dying to go for a hike," I said. "I just haven't had time yet."

"I'm not much of a hiker," Holly admitted. "I prefer hitting the gym or the tennis courts to keep in shape. Do you play tennis?" she asked me.

I shook my head.

"What are you talking about?" Erin said. "You play."

"I haven't played since high school and I wasn't very good at it." Erin should know. I crashed into her a few times when we had to play partners. I must have hit her harder than I realized and she was suffering from tennis-related amnesia.

"You have to join me," Holly said. "I can hook you up with the tennis pro at my country club. He's really hot. You'll like him. He's an amazing instructor."

"Yeah. Okay." If my lack of conviction was obvious in my tone, Holly ignored it and smiled.

The rest of the evening passed without any other issues—other than Trent becoming progressively grumpier and grumpier. He scowled more than he smiled. We had long since moved to the living room. I was sitting on the couch, with Josh sandwiched between Holly and me, his leg touching mine. Trent had claimed an armchair, while Erin sat on Darren's lap on the other chair.

Needing more wine, I returned to the kitchen and grabbed another bottle from the fridge. I turned around, and walked smack into the familiar-smelling wall of lean muscle.

Trent.

"If I didn't know better," I said, "I'd say you're way past your nap time." He reminded me of an overly tired toddler.

He frowned but didn't step back, our bodies close to touching. "What's that supposed to mean?"

I ran my fingertip along the grooves in his forehead. "This is what I mean. What's going on, Trent? You suffering from withdrawals 'cause you aren't at work like you normally would be at this time?"

"I'm not suffering from withdrawals."

"Then why are you so cranky? Dinner was great. And you've got a beautiful woman dying to spend time with you. What more could you want?"

"What do you mean a beautiful woman is dying to spend

time with me?" The frown faded as he studied my face. His gaze drifted to my lips.

I sucked in a soft breath as I imagined his lips against mine, and I temporarily forgot the beautiful woman in the other room waiting for him.

My lips parted—and as if drawn to him by a magnetic force, I leaned forward slightly. If I took a deep breath, my breasts would've pressed against his chest.

17

TRENT

Remember when you were a kid and saw something you really wanted? Nothing else existed beyond it.

Your parents—the voice of reason that they were—tried to help you see why it wasn't good for you. But that didn't matter. You found a way to sneak it anyway.

Well, adulthood wasn't much different.

Kelsey's lips parted and all I could think about was kissing her and making her mine. Without considering the consequences, I lowered my mouth to hers but didn't wait for an invitation to enter—I just did.

My tongue brushed against hers and I was instantly hit with the need to consume her. I knotted my fingers through her silky hair; the other hand went to her lower back and pressed her against me.

The logical, outspoken voice in my head reminded me this was a mistake. I wasn't what Kelsey needed.

Plus, she wasn't looking for a boyfriend—and I wasn't looking to be a one-night stand with her. I couldn't do that. Once I tasted her, once I felt her heat wrapped around me, I'd never be able to let her go.

"Hey, Kelsey..."

At the sound of Darren's voice, Kelsey and I sprung apart faster than if lightning had hit us. Although from the way my body tingled after that kiss, it wasn't much different than being struck by lightning. My nerves still sparked with an electrical charge.

For a dizzying second we just stared at each other, temporarily forgetting why we had stopped kissing as we fought to regain our breath.

"...do you have any more juice?" Darren asked, breaking the spell. He looked between us. "Am I interrupting?"

From the expression on his face, it was hard to tell if he had witnessed the kiss. If my sister had seen it, I could guarantee she would've said something. Immediately.

"Yes...I mean...um...let me get you more juice." Kelsey took the glass from him, her hand shaking slightly.

She put the bottle of wine she was holding on the counter, filled Erin's glass with apple juice, and handed it back to him. Then she picked up the wine and followed him into the living room. Not once did she look at me or give any indication the kiss meant anything to her.

How could I have been such an idiot to believe otherwise? We were friends, nothing more.

Kelsey knew that.

My brain knew that.

Too bad my body refused to get with the program.

I returned to the living room. Kelsey was sitting next to Josh again. Like back in the kitchen, she did everything to avoid eye contact with me. Disappointment and rejection sat heavy in my chest. Josh leaned toward Kelsey and whispered in her ear. A shy smile curved on her gorgeous face—and jealousy jabbed me in the ribs. Hard.

Erin yawned and leaned her head against Darren's shoulder. He murmured something to her and she nodded. He helped her to her feet. "Looks like it's time to get my sleepy wife to bed."

Other than to say goodbye to them, no one else made a move to leave—including Josh.

"Don't you have an early practice tomorrow?" I asked him, one step away from folding my arms across my chest.

It was official.

I had regressed to the Stone Age.

Me caveman. Me club friend for stealing girl.

"No, it's not until later in the morning." He glanced at Kelsey in a meaningful way—and I did my best to keep from snapping at him. It wasn't his fault I hadn't told him how I felt about her. It wasn't as if he could read my mind.

Kelsey smiled at him, but something was off about it, or maybe that was just wishful thinking.

Kelsey and I walked my sister and Darren to the front door.

"Please make sure you take a cab if you're going to keep drinking, okay?" Erin said to me.

"I can always crash on Kelsey's couch if it comes to that." *That should put a damper on lover boy's plans for the night.*

No sooner had the door closed behind them, Kelsey spun around to face me. "You can't crash on my couch."

"Would you rather I crash on your bed?" I was joking… or not.

She didn't answer right away, her gaze dropping momentarily to my lips. Hope flickered in my gut for a moment. "I meant you shouldn't crash here, period. Doesn't Holly live near you? She can drive you home. Maybe you could even crash at her place."

I stared at Kelsey, unable to believe what she had said. I kissed her in the kitchen not fifteen minutes ago, and now she was ready to send me home with another woman.

For a second, pain flashed in her eyes, or maybe that was my own pain reflecting back at me. I returned to the living room. Josh was explaining the finer points of hockey to Holly. He peered over at Kelsey with a hungry look, hinting loudly that he wanted to taste her in a way I haven't yet—the same way Holly was watching me.

Christ, just how drunk was I? Now I was imagining things when it came to the woman I worked with.

The hockey discussion continued, except every time Holly asked a question, she directed it at me instead of Josh.

Kelsey yawned. Josh glanced at me, the message in his eyes clear: *Time to go home Salway, so I can get a little action here.*

To hell with that.

And no, I wasn't jumping to conclusions. Holly confirmed this a moment later when she said, "C'mon, Trent. They want to be left alone."

Kelsey's eyes widened in panic and she scrambled off the couch. Not noticing this, Josh stood up, wrapped his arms around her, and pulled her against his side.

18

KELSEY

"That's not a good idea," Trent said, pushing himself off the armchair and swaying slightly on his feet. "Kelsey's been drinking."

"She's not drunk." Josh tightened his hold on me.

All I could do was stare at Trent, struggling to figure out why he had kissed me and if he'd meant it. But I was also busy thinking about how Holly liked him too.

You remember how when you were a kid and if someone found something belonging to you, they'd sing-song "Finders keepers, losers weepers" and that was the end of that?

Well, some women might still feel that way, even if her friend liked the same guy. Someone else might say the "rule" didn't count if the woman was a long-time friend. The first woman to stake claim to the guy was the winner.

I'd known Holly for no more than a few weeks, so technically there was no statute of limitations—or whatever you wanted to call it—that prevented me from telling Trent how I felt about him.

But none of that was me.

And besides, I had no idea why Trent had kissed me. He

might not have meant anything by it. It might have been one of those seemed-like-a-good-idea-at-the-time moments.

Maybe he didn't even like the kiss.

Holly looped her arm through Trent's and winked at me.

"I'm fine," I told him as I walked the pair to the front door.

He glanced one more time at Josh, then left with Holly. As the door closed behind them, I struggled not to envision him kissing Holly the same way he'd kissed me.

I struggled not to remember the feel of his lips against mine. And I struggled not to think about what might have happened if Darren hadn't interrupted us.

Oh, and I might have also struggled not to think about Trent lifting me up onto the kitchen counter and taking me there.

The door had barely closed before Josh's lips were suddenly on my neck. His lips that were nothing like Trent's. His hand trailed down my arm. His hand that was nothing like Trent's.

"Jesus, you taste good," he murmured against my skin. "I can't wait to taste your pussy."

In my head, Trent was the one who uttered those words and my girlie parts clenched. I closed my eyes.

Then they snapped open and I jumped away from him like a kangaroo who had landed on a thumbtack.

I faked a yawn, which turned into a real one. "Looks like I'll have to take a rain check." A rain check with an expiry date of last year.

Mr. Kitty Whiskers let out a loud meow, ever ready to be my chaperone. Or maybe Trent had shared a brief word with him, to make sure Josh didn't step out of line.

I wouldn't have put it past him (or my brother) to do just that.

I giggled at the thought of either man having that conversation with my cat, confirming Trent was right. I'd drank too much wine tonight.

Josh skimmed his hand down my hip. "I bet I can wake you up."

I laughed shortly. "I bet you can, too. But Trent's right, I did have a lot of wine tonight." I placed my hand on his arm and ushered him to the front door.

"You want me to leave?" His tone was that of a man who wasn't used to having women turn him down.

The poor baby.

He stepped toward me. It wasn't threatening. More like a kitten getting ready to pounce for the first time.

I easily darted out of the way.

"I thought you were all hot and bothered for me," he complained, just this side of not pouting.

"Me?" I laughed. "It's just you're not my type." That much was true.

He stopped moving, looking momentarily stunned. "You're a lesbian?"

I giggled some more. "Just because a woman isn't interested in you doesn't mean she's a lesbian."

"True." He cocked his head to the side. "So you're really not attracted to me?"

I shook my head. "Sorry. But we can be friends."

He winced, but his eyes held a flash of amusement. "You're friend-zoning me?"

"Apparently."

Now it was his turn to laugh. "I guess friends it is."

No sooner had Josh closed the door behind him, Mr. Kitty Whiskers meowed at it, chin raised. I could almost imagine him saying, "And stay out." He rubbed against my leg then walked into the kitchen.

"So which was it? My brother or Trent who told you to chase away all single men from my house?" I called after him with a chuckle.

I followed him and groaned at the dishes piled in the sink. I didn't want to leave them to dry overnight, so I loaded the dishwasher.

As I was finishing the task, my phone pinged from the counter. Trent had sent me a text.

Trent: Sweet dreams

Me: Sweet dreams to you

And please don't break my heart more than it's already breaking.

19

KELSEY

The next morning, I grabbed the sketchpad and pencils I'd bought for my drawing class. Then I made myself comfy on the couch and worked on my shading assignment...only to be interrupted a few minutes later by Holly's tune on my cell phone. For several seconds, I deliberated if I was better off letting it go to voice mail. She was bound to be calling to share her "great" news about Trent.

Curiosity got the best of me and I answered.

"Good news," she said. "I talked to Caleb. He had a cancellation for tomorrow at five p.m. Are you finished work by then?"

"Cancellation for what?"

"Tennis lessons."

Oh. "I'm not—"

"Before you tell me that you don't think it's a good idea or tell me you're busy when you're not, I promise you won't regret it. He's a great instructor...and he's single."

"But I'm not—"

"I know, you're not looking for a relationship, but you might change your mind once you meet him. I mean, unless something happened between you and Josh last night." The ending

159

came out with a small lilt, a question as to what really happened after she and Trent left.

"Nothing happened. I'm not interested in him that way. What about you?" *Shit, why did I have to ask her that?*

She sighed, the sound of someone who had hoped for a wild night of hot sex...and had to settle for a cold shower. "Nothing to report on my front. Unfortunately. I drove Trent back to his place and he didn't even ask me in. Although judging from his foul mood, it was just as well. I don't think anything would've happened either way."

Being the mature person that I was, I totally didn't do a happy dance on my couch. "Foul mood? What do you mean?"

"He spent most of the trip scowling like a kid who'd had his favorite toy stolen from him."

"Did he say anything?" *Did he mention the kiss?*

"No. He was quiet the entire time. I tried to get him to talk, but after a few minutes I gave up." She sighed again.

I mentally cheered. I had no idea what last night's kiss meant to Trent, but Holly's news gave me a glimmer of hope. As foolish as it was, there was a large part of me that wished the kiss meant as much to Trent as it meant to me.

Shit, what are you thinking? Remember Erin? Your best friend? The one who would disown you if something happened between you and her brother?

Never mind that I was nothing like She-Who-Shall-Not-Be-Named. If things didn't work out between Trent and me, I would never start rumors about Erin, and I wouldn't call her every bad name under the sun (and then some).

We ended the call and I went back to my assignment. Mr. Kitty Whiskers jumped onto the couch and tried to sit on my lap. "Sorry, boy, no lap for you right now. But what do you think?" I pointed at the page and was rewarded with a meow.

Or it might have been a critique of my abilities. In which case I don't think he was too impressed.

The doorbell interrupted any further comment he may have had. I put my "artwork" aside and answered the door.

And my breath almost stole away at the sight of Trent in the doorway. He was wearing khaki shorts, sneakers, and a light grey T-shirt that practically molded to his body. His black hair was messy and only served to make him look even sexier than normal—if that was at all possible.

"Love the outfit," he said, his gaze taking in the view. It swept up my cute-cartoon-owl pajama bottoms and landed on my white tank top. His eyes darkened and for a moment I couldn't figure out why—and then the reason hit me. The fabric of my bra was thin and did little to hide my nipples, especially when teamed with my tank top.

I crossed my arms over my breasts.

His gaze continued to my messy ponytail. I hadn't even bothered with my makeup yet, other than a layer of lip gloss. His gaze locked on my mouth and the tip of his tongue traveled along his lower lip. The sexy lip that Holly wanted to kiss. The sexy lip that I *had* kissed.

The thought of Holly broke the spell and I blinked. Trent shook his head, as if to snap himself out of the same daze. Then he glanced behind me. "Is Josh still here?"

"No, he left last night, shortly after you and Holly."

"He did?"

I nodded. "I'm not interested in him that way."

A small smile appeared on Trent's face, and he leaned his forearm against the doorframe. "I'm glad to hear that. He's my friend, but I'll be the first to tell you that you can do better than him, even if you aren't looking for a relationship right now."

I didn't want to discuss Josh, so I quickly changed the subject. "So what are you up to today?"

"Depends."

"Depends on what?"

"You."

"Me?"

He nodded, my favorite sexy grin on his face. "I thought we could go hiking."

"You, me, and who else?"

"Just you and me."

My brain wanted to calmly discuss the pros and cons of accepting his offer. My body chimed in with its own opinion, which was more along the lines of "hell, yes." My brain reminded my body that after the kiss last night, the last thing my lust-filled body needed was to spend the day with Trent. My body gave my brain the finger, and my heart decided it was best to keep out of the discussion.

"Let me get dressed." I opened the door farther and let him in. Mr. Kitty Whiskers rubbed against Trent's legs and purred. I wasn't sure if that meant he was siding with my body or he was just happy to see Trent.

"I picked up some sandwiches and drinks at the deli before the cab dropped me off here," Trent said, "so we're good to go."

I returned a short time later, showered, dressed in shorts, T-shirt, and my hair in a neater ponytail than before. I grabbed my point-and-shoot camera and stowed it in my small backpack. Trent then drove us through San Francisco, across the Golden Gate Bridge, to a popular wooded area. For the entire drive there, we avoided the topic of the kiss, but that didn't mean the memory of it still didn't taunt me. With the clean, familiar scent that was all Trent sitting next to me, it was hard to ignore how the same scent had been wrapped around me just hours before, when his lips were pressed against mine.

"I tried to get tickets for Cavalia," he said. "Unfortunately they're all sold out. The person I know who might've been able to help me couldn't get any either."

"That's too bad."

"So, how's the drawing class going?"

"We haven't done much yet."

He glanced at me. "Are you enjoying it more than the cooking class?"

I shrugged, unsure how to explain it. "I liked the cooking class, but not enough to get excited about cooking. The art class is interesting so far, but it's just not what I was hoping for."

"What were you hoping for?" He pulled into an empty spot in the parking lot near the trail.

"Something that's more fulfilling. Something I can get lost in and that gets me excited. Something that makes me feel more complete. So far none of that's happening."

"Maybe that's 'cause you just started it." He turned off the engine.

"True."

I gathered my backpack by my feet and climbed out of the vehicle. Trent was removing his backpack from the trunk by the time I walked over to him.

Tearing my gaze from him before my heart could let out a dreamy sigh, I studied the light-blue sky and the few puffy clouds drifting by. Including one that reminded me of a penis.

Oh, God. Even out here I had sex on the brain. "I bet the stars look amazing from here at night."

"I didn't know you're interested in stargazing."

"I wouldn't say I'm interested in studying it, if that's what you're asking. But I've never seen the sky before without the light pollution from the city."

Trent looked up at the sky. "I used to believe that the stars were the people we once loved. When they died, they became a star in the sky."

"I remember that." It was one of the many small pieces of trivia that we used to talk about when we were younger. I smiled at the memory of us lying in the backyard, along with Erin and Liam, discussing the stars and various myths and legends. The guys had quite a vivid imagination. "When did you stop believing?"

"When my aunt died of cancer," he said, still staring at the sky.

I gave his hand a light squeeze, knowing how much she had meant to him and Erin.

We began hiking along the trail between the trees. A few other hikers were out, but other than that the area was fairly quiet. I paused and closed my eyes, enjoying the calming sounds of nature: birds singing in the trees, the occasional rustle of leaves, the gentle gurgle of water rushing over large moss-covered rocks. Now this I could get passionate about.

I opened my eyes and continued to where Trent was waiting for me. A little farther ahead, we stopped at a bridge crossing the wide stream. I removed my camera from my backpack and lifted it to take a photo of the forest. But as I scanned the area for a good picture, I noticed Trent lost in thought, gazing out at the water. Thanks to the trees, the light on his face was just right.

Without him having a clue what I was up to, I snapped a picture of him and checked the result in the LCD screen.

I inhaled a soft breath at the image. I had, mostly by fluke, captured him in a way that I hadn't seen in a while. He looked relaxed, at ease with the surroundings. At peace. He wasn't thinking about the stock market and the companies in his portfolio. He wasn't thinking about his promise to my brother to keep an eye on my dating life—and disrupt it if necessary.

He was just enjoying the moment.

And I could honestly say I'd never seen him look more breathtaking than he did right then. My heart sped up. Not because I was turned on from seeing him this way (which I was). My heart got excited at what I had accomplished. The photo had been a fluke. Now I wanted to learn how to consistently take great photos.

"You're smiling."

I looked up from the screen to find Trent watching me. "I am."

"Want to tell me what you're smiling about?"

My grin widened. "I've figured out what I'm passionate about." I showed him the picture.

He looked at it, then his gaze jumped to mine. "You're passionate about me?" His voice came out I-want-to-do-you-against-this-bridge husky, and for a second I forgot what we were talking about.

Yes! I wanted to say out loud. *You're all I can think about.* Instead I said, "Photography." It came out as a croaked whisper and I cleared my throat to hide what I was really thinking. "My friend taught me a few things in college, and I enjoyed playing around with her camera. I guess I'd forgotten about it." Until now.

My mind started to swirl at what I needed to do. I had to figure out what camera and equipment to buy. And I needed to study books...maybe sign up for a workshop.

I could do this.

"I think you might be onto something." Trent handed the camera back to me. "This is the first time since deciding you need a hobby that you've actually been excited about it. You weren't this excited when you signed up for the cooking class."

He was right. I had looked forward to it but that was about it.

We continued hiking until we stumbled across a fallen tree blocking the path, its trunk too massive to easily step over. Trent climbed up first, his long legs making easy work of it, and jumped down on the other side. I followed, but before I could jump down his hands were on my waist. The warmth from them seeped through my T-shirt and spread through my body, concentrating on the area between my legs.

You could gather all the teenage boys on a football team

together, and they would be less horny than I was from his touch.

I jumped down with Trent's help and our bodies almost collided. Like in the kitchen when we kissed, only a narrow gap existed between us.

Neither of us said anything. My brain was having problems piecing together a logical argument for why I should step away. But judging from the battle of emotions dueling it out in Trent's eyes, I wasn't the only one dealing with this dilemma.

Just as I thought he was going to snap out of it and remember who I was, his head lowered to mine and he kissed me.

The kiss was nothing like last night. It was tentative. Gentle. The brushing of lips. Even though it wasn't the same, I still moaned softly. The heat in my body that had begun as a small flicker morphed into a forest fire, and without realizing what I was doing, I parted my lips and let him in.

My tongue brushed his and my previous moan was answered by his own. Or maybe that was a groan as he realized he was kissing his best friend's sister and his sister's best friend.

He pulled away and rested his forehead against mine. "I'm sorry," he murmured. "I shouldn't have done that."

"Why not?" Shit, what was I doing?

"Your brother wanted me to keep an eye on you and make sure you were okay while he was away. I can guarantee kissing you wasn't what he had in mind."

"You never know. Maybe it was exactly what he had in mind." Hello, brain? What the hell were you doing?

I stepped away. "You're right. We shouldn't have done that. Holly's my friend and..." The words faded away as I realized what I was saying. Oops.

I bit into my lip to keep the rest of the sentence from escaping.

Trent frowned. "What does Holly have to do with us kissing?"

A stream of curses paraded through my head, enough to cause even a sailor to chuckle. I started to turn away, but before I could get anywhere Trent grabbed my shoulders.

"What does Holly have to do with us kissing?" he asked again.

"Um." If I were to rank this on a scale between one to ten when it came to awkwardness, it would definitely be a thousand. "She likes you."

And she was going to kill me. Possibly with her stilettos.

He shrugged, clearly not getting it. "Yeah, we're friends. What does that have to do with anything?"

"No, I don't mean likes you as a friend. She *likes* likes you." Great, now I sounded like we were back in middle school.

"Oh." Rubbing the back of his neck, he started pacing back and forth in front of me. Not quite the reaction I had been expecting.

He suddenly stopped. "You sure about that?"

I nodded. "I was trying to get you guys together last night. I figured you just needed a little nudge in the right direction."

"Then why did you kiss me last night?"

My mouth dropped open. "I'm pretty sure you were the one who kissed me." But now that he knew the truth about Holly's feelings for him, that would be the end of the orgasm-inducing kisses for me.

And knowing this was like giving a chocoholic the best truffles ever created, then never letting her have another one—but leaving them in a glass case for her to see every day.

Trent resumed pacing, forming a new path in the dirt.

"So now that you know the truth about Holly's feelings for you, do you think you could forget you heard it from me?" I flashed what I hoped was the equivalent of puppy-dog eyes.

He nodded but continued forging his new path in the dirt.

If he kept this up, he would've dug a hole to the earth's core by dinner. "Shit, what am I going to do?" he muttered to himself.

"Well, for starters, do you feel the same way about her?"

He kept pacing. "She's a great person and, yes, she's sexy." He paused and looked at me. "But she's not you."

My heart suddenly forgot to how to beat, hoping that he meant what I thought he meant.

But how could he have? Holly was everything I wished to be: sexually confident, well-rounded, and great at sports. She was also one thing that I wasn't, but it just made her that much more perfect for Trent. "She practically lives at the office, like you. You guys are made for each other."

"Why? 'Cause we're both workaholics?"

"Exactly." Holly might be well-rounded, but at the end of the day she was still a workaholic, putting in more hours at the office than the average person.

"Just because we're both workaholics doesn't mean we're perfect for each other." He stepped closer to me. Mere inches separated us. He reached up and caressed my jaw with his thumb. "You're the one I keep thinking about at night, Kels—you naked in my bed. Not Holly."

I swear my heart gave up beating at those magical words. Trent, the guy I'd wanted for all those years, was telling me that he thought about me at night? In his bed? Holy crap.

I needed to sit down.

Maybe breathe into a paper bag.

"You...what?" I gasped. He grabbed my arm like I was going to have a seizure. And maybe I was. "Since when?" I asked.

"Christ, have you taken a look at yourself lately, Kelsey? You're gorgeous and sexy and ever since I saw you on the side of the road, I've wondered why I haven't...fuck, I don't know. But it's complicated. You're my best friend's little sister. Liam would kill me if he knew how I've been thinking about you naked in my bed."

Heat rushed between my legs, ignoring what Trent was saying. He had a point, though. Liam would do exactly that. He was way too overly protective for his own good.

"And after he's finished with me," Trent continued, "my sister would rip me a new one, too."

He had a point there as well.

I stared at the ferns growing near us. "And I can't go through another relationship like I had with Owen."

But I also couldn't imagine surviving another day without Trent touching me like I longed for him to touch me. "And then there's Holly. She's my friend. Even if Liam and Erin were okay with us being together, I refuse to hurt Holly because you and I can't keep our hands off each other." I swallowed, shoving down the words I wanted to say but probably shouldn't. Too bad they were stubborn. "But I..."

"But you what?"

"But I also want to be with you. I want to kiss you. I want to touch you." *I want to make love to you.*

20

TRENT

There was something about standing in the middle of the woods, with the warm breeze cheering you on, to help you forget all your common sense. Throw in a cawing crow and you were set.

"Trust me, Kels, I want that too," I said.

She bit her lip in that adorable way of hers, which made me want to push her against a tree and explore her mouth again, except this time more thoroughly.

"But like I said," she pointed out, "I don't want to have a repeat of what happened with Owen. I'm not ready for another relationship."

Neither was I.

"So what are you suggesting?" I asked. "That we become fuck buddies?"

Remember the first three best-friend rules (never fuck the guy's sister, never think of fucking the guy's sister, and never thinking about her naked while *not* thinking about fucking her)? I was positive there was also a fourth rule: no fuck-buddy arrangements with his sister.

But if this was the extent of my being able to kiss her and

170

explore her in ways I could only have dreamed about until now, then fuck buddies it was. And given neither of us was looking for a relationship right now, it worked for everyone.

Everyone except for Holly.

I'd been so blinded by my lust for Kelsey, I'd failed to notice the shift in Holly's feelings toward me. Now things started to make sense, like her long hours in the office when she didn't need to stay so late. Like why she had shown me the thongs she had bought that one day—only it hadn't ended with the reaction she'd hoped for.

"I was thinking more like friends with benefits." Kelsey shrugged at my what's-the-difference expression. "It sounds less crass than your version."

"Even though it's the same thing?"

She nodded, the grin on her face as bright as the sun overhead. But then it disappeared as quickly as it had come—and I knew why.

"We just have to make sure Holly understands where things stand between her and me," I said.

"We?" Kelsey poked me in the chest. "There's no 'we' here. You want to break her heart, so *you'll* be the one doing it, not me. Anyway, it's not like we can let anyone know about us."

"Why's that?" I asked, even though she was right. She wasn't my girlfriend, which meant that what was going on between us was no one else's business.

"Hello, have you met your reputation? If my brother has you calling interference on my dating life, do you think he's going to be supportive of me messing around with someone who changes women as often as he changes his underwear?"

"Hey, I'm not that bad."

"Yes, you are. And your sister wouldn't be too impressed either. Not after what happened with She-Who-Shall-Not-Be-Named."

"Who?"

"Michaela. Just don't mention her name to Erin." She gave a dramatic shudder.

"Why's that?" I mean, I got that things didn't go down too well after I broke up with her, but I didn't get what this had to do with Kelsey and me.

"You really don't know?"

I shook my head.

"Let's just say Michaela was crazy, and after what happened with her, Erin said she would disown any of her friends if they went out with you."

Oh. I just figured she would kill me. I had no idea she had placed an actual ban on me. Which meant it didn't matter to my sister (and probably Liam) that I hadn't slept with another woman in over two months. Not since Kelsey had stepped back into my life again without trying to avoid me. As far as Erin was concerned, I was the forbidden fruit—so to speak.

"All right. But if we're doing this"—I pointed to Kelsey then to myself—"it has to be exclusive. No tennis pro, no Josh, and no other men."

She laughed, which wasn't the reaction I was expecting. "How much free time do you think I have?"

I shrugged because I really had no idea. The concept of free time was foreign to me.

"The same goes for you," she said. "And we can't do anything until you've squared things with Holly. I know you guys aren't involved, but it doesn't feel right for her to think she has a chance with you when I'm the one sleeping with you." Without waiting for a reply, she turned toward the path and continued walking.

"All right. I'll deal with Holly." I hiked after her. "And just so you know, I haven't been with anyone in a while."

"Really? Well, if it makes you feel any better, I can guarantee your dry spell isn't as long as mine—if we don't count the gold medal winner of sprint fucking."

And I didn't. The guy was a goddamn idiot.

"How long are we talking about?" From what I remembered, she dumped her asshole of a fiancé over six months ago. So yeah, she "won" that competition.

"Well, before him, the last time I had sex was with Owen over fifteen months ago."

I stopped abruptly. *What the fuck?* How the hell did the asswipe manage to be with Kelsey that long without sex? That would mean they were together for the last nine months of their relationship without having sex once during that time? What was he—gay?

If she were mine, I couldn't go three days without tasting her. Anything beyond that and I was positive I'd go insane. And even three days was pushing things.

As it were, if we hadn't been in an area popular with hikers, and if the issue of Holly wasn't hanging over us, I would've taken Kelsey deeper into the woods and ended her fucking hiatus.

"The guy was an idiot," I said. "Glad you dumped him. You definitely deserve more than that tool."

She smiled and kept walking, picking up her pace. "You're right. I do," she called over her shoulder as my phone rang.

I checked who was calling. Dad?

"Hey, what's up?" I asked him.

"You remember how I promised your mother I would renovate the kitchen?"

"Not really," I said, watching Kelsey's fine ass walk away from me. The fine ass that I would be exploring (along with her other body parts) in a few hours.

"Well I did, and now I need your help with it. It'll be like the old days, when you used to help me fix things around the house." Meaning a late night, with beer and pizza afterward.

And hanging out with my father.

Who had just earned the new title of cockblocker.

But cockblocker or not, I couldn't say no to him. Helping him out with the renovations was the least I could do after everything he and Mom had done for me over the years.

Now I just had to hope that once the renovations were finished, nothing else stood in the way of me finally getting to experience Kelsey in the way I'd craved for as long as I could remember.

21

—————

KELSEY

For some people, being a member of an exclusive country club was the ultimate status symbol. It was a goal they strived for, even when they couldn't afford it.

Me? I was the exact opposite. Possessing a country club membership meant nothing to me.

But as I pulled into the club's parking lot, I was once again reminded why I didn't belong here. All the vehicles, other than my poor baby, were high priced, much like Trent's BMW. I didn't belong here. I knew that, my car knew that, but try telling it to Holly.

Holly met me at the front entrance, wearing an adorable white tennis outfit. My outfit wasn't quite so adorable. I wore the black shorts I usually ran in and a white T-shirt with a cute owl on it. Even my sneakers weren't meant for tennis. They were the ones I ran in. Yes, I was better suited for running on a track than chasing a tennis ball around the court.

Again, try telling that to Holly.

Besides, the only place I really wanted to be right now was the camera store. After yesterday's hike, I had checked out a dozen or so photography books from the library. I'd even gone online and registered for a portrait class that was starting in two weeks. Which meant between now and then, I needed to buy a camera and figure it out.

But first up? Surviving the afternoon with Holly's tennis pro.

"I promise you'll love Caleb," she said as I approached. "He's a great instructor plus he's really cute. I mean not as good-looking as Josh." She winked at me.

"You know there's nothing going on between me and Josh, right?"

"Perfect, then you're available for Caleb."

I was about to tell her I wasn't available, but the stubborn words clung to the back of my throat. Besides, "unavailable" meant I was dating someone. And if she was anything like Erin, she would want to know who that someone was.

Do you think Chris Hemsworth was available to be my imaginary boyfriend?

Or maybe Ryan Reynolds?

We entered the pro shop and she introduced me to Caleb. Holly had been right. He was hot—and he had a warm smile that lit up his eyes when she mentioned my name.

"I haven't played tennis since high school," I warned him, "and I wasn't very good at it."

"Not a problem. We'll begin with the basics."

Because I didn't own a racket, Holly loaned me one of hers. That's right. She couldn't have just one racket. She had an army of them.

Good thing we wouldn't be dueling (aka playing tennis) to see who had the right to enjoy mind-numbing sex with Trent. And yes, I had no doubts whatsoever that sex with Trent would rock my world.

Caleb had me warm up and stretch first, then he taught me

the basics of the forehand and backhand. Holly was right. He was an amazing instructor. By the end of the lesson, the ball flew in the generally direction I was aiming for. I mean, I was nothing like him and Holly. Both could hit an ant on the opposite side of the court—intentionally. I was lucky (or rather, the ant was lucky) if I could get the ball within a few feet of it. But that was okay—at least I didn't land on my ass at any point during the lesson.

Once it was over, I expected Caleb to walk off to meet with his next student. He didn't.

"Holly mentioned you're a physical therapist," he said. Holly spotted someone she knew and left us. Alone.

"Yes, I am…at the children's hospital."

"They're looking for a physical therapist here, if you're interested."

Okay, so maybe Holly hadn't been trying to set me up with him after all. "Thanks, but I love my job. And I love working with the kids."

We started walking toward Holly and her friend.

"Would you be interested in going out with me next weekend?" Caleb casually asked.

If it hadn't been for what happened during the hike yesterday, I would have said yes. And maybe I was an idiot for not saying yes, given that what Trent and I were going to do wouldn't amount to anything beyond satisfying sex. "I'm sorry, I'm seeing someone."

"You are? Holly said you're single."

"It just happened. She doesn't even know about it."

"Is it serious?"

I laughed. I couldn't help it. "It's serious enough that we've agreed to be exclusive." Not that it meant much when neither Trent nor I wanted a serious relationship right now.

"If you change your mind," he said. "You know where to find me."

Holly approached and glanced between me and Caleb, the eager expression on her face hard to miss.

"I guess I wasn't fast enough," he said to her. "She's already seeing someone."

Her eyes widened to the size of tennis balls, then narrowed at me. Inwardly I groaned. *Brilliant going, Kels*. I guess I should have thought of that before telling Caleb that I was seeing someone.

He left and I braced myself for what was coming next.

"So do you want to explain why you told him you're seeing someone?" Holly asked and I winced.

I couldn't tell her the truth and I had no intention of lying to her. So I did the next best thing—I changed topic.

"How long have you been playing tennis? I knew you were going to be good, but I never expected you to be that good."

Rule #1 for changing the topic: pick one that focuses on the other person and flatter them to death.

"Nice try, Kelsey, but it's not going to work. Spill it."

So much for rule #1.

"It's really no big deal," I told her. If rule #1 didn't work? Try rule #2.

Too bad I didn't know what that was.

Her face glowed, and it had nothing to do with the sun shining on it. "If you're not dating Josh, then who are you seeing?"

"Um, no one you know." Although for all I knew, she did know Chris Hemsworth. Not that she would guess he was my make-believe boyfriend.

"I would love to meet him. Maybe you and I can double date with him and Trent some time."

That was right—all the gods in the universe had planned to torture me. They couldn't have done a better job than if they had tied me up and made me watch a twenty-four-hour marathon of a lame sitcom, minus the commercial breaks.

I glanced up at the sky and silently cursed them.

My phone played Trent's song. The temptation to ignore it wrapped around me, but Holly knew it was his song and was peering at me expectantly.

"Hey, have you talked to Holly yet?" was the first thing he said after I answered the phone.

Talk to her about what? That he was not available for her to date because he and I were having sex? Yes, that had been on the top of my to-do list for today.

Since Holly couldn't hear his side of the conversation, I told her he said "hi" and almost died at the hopeful expression on her face.

"You're with her now?" genius boy asked.

"Uh huh."

"How about you explain to her why I would make a lousy boyfriend."

Why couldn't he have asked me to do something simpler? Like scaling the Empire State Building. I doubted whatever I told her would make a difference. She already knew about the negatives and she was still willing to give him a chance.

"Nice try. You're a coward. You know that, right?" I said with a laugh.

He chuckled. "Damn right I am. Have you seen her shoes? They're registered lethal weapons."

He did have a point (pun intended).

"And Kels?" His voice was low and I-want-to-do-you-now husky. I practically melted on the spot.

"Yeah?"

"Are we still on for tomorrow night?"

Tomorrow night would be the night he and I finally consummated our friends-with-benefits relationship. And yes, my girlie parts were ready to throw a party in honor of the occasion.

"Absolutely." Because I couldn't say anything else with

Holly standing next to me, I told him I'd talk to him later and ended the call.

"So are you going to tell me anything about the guy you're now seeing?" Holly asked.

Face meet palm.

"Hey, I'm single and have to live vicariously through my non-single friends," she said with the same smirk people who tended to say this usually wore. It was the same smirk that was spiked with jealously, humor, and a healthy dose of longing.

But since she had brought it up. "Holly…" I took a deep breath. Not that it helped. "How would you feel if…if Trent was dating someone else?"

"But he isn't."

"Yes, but what if he was? Would you be okay with it?"

"I'd be disappointed, but I'd get over it. Eventually. But since he isn't seeing anyone, it doesn't matter."

I stared at her for a moment, sending her a mental message that yes he was seeing someone—because that was the only excuse I could come up with to dissuade her from him. I also sent her another mental message so she wouldn't guess it was me.

"Wait, are you telling me that he really has a girlfriend?"

I nodded, hoping this was one of those complex one-plus-one math questions she would never solve: Trent + his mysterious girlfriend = my mysterious boyfriend + me.

"Then who's he dating?" said the woman on a mission.

"I don't know her name." I scanned the area, searching for a shovel to help me dig my grave.

Sorry, Trent. But this is what happens when you send me to break Holly's heart, because you're too much of a chicken to do it yourself.

"I can't wait to meet your boyfriend and his girlfriend," she said without a hint of suspicion.

Brilliant. Now Trent and I just needed a fake boyfriend and

girlfriend to keep Holly—and subsequently Erin—from figuring out the truth.

Something told me this situation wasn't covered in the friends-with-benefits manual.

Oh, joy!

22

KELSEY

"How was your day?" I asked Mr. Kitty Whiskers as I dumped the dry pasta into the boiling water. He rubbed back and forth against my legs, hinting he wanted a kitty treat. "You slept all day? And how was that for you?" I asked.

He answered with a meow.

Satisfied the pasta water wouldn't boil over, I returned to the kitchen table and checked out my new Nikon DSLR camera and the photography book I'd borrowed from the library.

Tap. Tap. Tap.

I startled at the noise from high in the corner of the room, then released a relieved breath. It was nothing more than an overgrown tree branch that kept hitting the wall whenever it was windy. I kept forgetting to call someone to deal with it.

Tap. Tap. Tap.

A flash of lightning temporarily lit up the sky outside the window. The overhead light flickered but stayed on.

My thoughts drifted to Trent and how we would finally get to consummate our friends-with-benefits relationship tomorrow. Something that I would've been more than willing to do yesterday while hiking...if it weren't for the risk of getting caught. And if Trent hadn't needed to help his father.

But since I had already been waiting a long time to end my sex drought, what was one more day? Although, with all the built-up sexual frustration consuming me, starting from when Trent and I first began hanging out together, I might combust before I was able to have sex with him.

The ache between my legs thoroughly agreed.

Maybe a nice long soak in the tub would help to distract me.

Yes, because long hot baths were always a great substitute for sex, said no one ever.

Lightning flashed again, followed a moment later by a loud rumble of thunder.

And my thoughts instantly went back to Trent. And sex. And doing it during a lightning storm.

Another of my sexual fantasies.

I pushed myself off my chair and rifled through the utility drawer for matches. Nothing said romantic evening than a power outage, candles, and being alone.

But at least I had my sexy underwear on. Erin and Holly would be proud. You know, in case a handsome stranger entered the house and wanted to ravish me during the lightning storm.

Enough thinking about sex, I reprimanded myself. *And don't even think about Trent. Naked. Lit up by the lightning outside the window.*

God, I was a lost cause.

While I waited for dinner to finish cooking, I lit the white pillar candle on the coffee table in the living room and flipped through the TV channels. The sky lit up again, only this time instead of the room light flickering, the room and the TV went dark—other than candle on the table. "Great." Now I couldn't watch TV or study.

I guess that left me with nothing to do, other than watching shadows dance on the wall or having a candle lit bath...while not fantasizing about Trent.

Yeah, I didn't think the non-fantasizing part was going to happen either.

What did sexually frustrated guys do when they couldn't have sex?

Oh, that's right, jack off in the shower.

Maybe I could exercise instead. I'd taken a yoga class with Erin a few years ago. Too bad I didn't remember anything, other than the downward facing dog. Which for some reason made me think of sex, doggy style.

Which made me think of Trent.

And...yoga was definitely out.

My cell phone rang from the coffee table. Trent, who was no doubt checking that I was still alive.

"I'm fine," I told him.

"Good to know. I'm home now and just heard that the power is out in your area because of a downed tree. So I figured you might as well come over and spend the night, since you don't know how long your power will be out for. And just so you know...I spent all last night fantasizing about everything I want to do to you, Kels, and I don't think I can survive another night just thinking it." His husky voice left my panties ready to sacrifice themselves to a greater cause.

Hot and dirty and definitely-not-nice thoughts took up residence in my head. How I managed not to moan was anyone's guess.

He did have a point though about the power. The last time the power went out in the area, it had remained off for four hours.

"And Kelsey?" The last part came out all hot and bothered and all male. God, he wasn't playing fair.

"Yes?"

"Don't take too long. I've got a surprise for you." He hung up before I could find out what it was.

23

TRENT

The intercom rang and I let Kelsey into the building. I glanced around the apartment, seeing it the way she would for the first time. Unlike her house, which was homey and reminded me of pictures I'd seen of Scandinavian-style homes, with their clean white interior designs, my apartment screamed professionally decorated bachelor pad. My boss had recommended the designer, and yes, I did end up screwing her. The interior designer, not my boss. My furniture was modern, sophisticated, and nothing like me.

That's not to say I didn't like the place. I did, thanks to the extra-large TV screen that I rarely had time to appreciate. But that was pretty much the high point. Even the artwork on the walls did nothing for me. They looked like something I could have created as a kid, with paint splattered onto a canvas by an artist I'd never heard of.

A few minutes later a knock on the door distracted me from my thoughts. I strode to the door and opened it. Kelsey stood there, a small red pull-along suitcase at her heels.

"Hi," she said. "Sorry it took me so long. Slow-moving traffic because of the rain." She sniffed the air. "Wow, what smells so good?"

"You'll see. It's the surprise I mentioned on the phone." I grabbed Kelsey's suitcase. She followed me into the apartment and into the bedroom.

Her gaze took in the tidy room, with its dark, masculine colors and modern furniture. "Wow, this place is amazing. You decorated it yourself?"

"Ladies and gentlemen, please don't attempt this at home without the help of a professional."

That brought a big smile to her face. "Are you telling me you hired someone?"

"That's exactly what I'm saying."

Most women who might've seen my apartment would instantly wonder about my earning potential—which was why I'd never brought the women I screwed back here. Not so with Kelsey. My income didn't matter to her, which made me appreciate her even more.

"Before I forget to tell you..." she said as I proceeded to show her around the condo, "Holly thinks you're seeing someone."

"She knows about us?"

She made a well-not-exactly face. "I was trying to let her know that you weren't interested in her by letting her down nicely. Soooo, I asked her if she would be okay if you were dating someone. And before that, the tennis pro she had been trying to set me up with asked me out, and I told him I was seeing someone. He mentioned it to Holly..."

"And now she thinks you have a boyfriend and I have a girlfriend."

"Yep, that pretty much sums it up."

Inwardly I groaned. "You know Holly and Erin are going to figure it out, right?"

"Not if we throw them off."

"How do you plan to do that?"

"Introduce them to our fake girlfriend and boyfriend." She shrugged. "It might work."

I wasn't so sure about that, but right now I didn't really want to think about that or how we were going to continue sneaking around. Kelsey in my bed, that was all I cared about for now.

I showed her around the apartment. We made it as far as the living room when Kelsey stopped and grinned at the TV. "You know what they say about the size of a guy's TV?" she said, mischief gleaming in her eyes.

"No, what?"

"They're compensating."

I parked my hands on her shoulders. "No compensating for anything needed here." And then my lips crashed against hers —something I'd wanted to do from the moment she'd stood in my doorway.

I didn't have to coax her to open her mouth. It opened in an instant and I took that as a positive sign. My tongue slipped in, eager to explore. But it didn't want to just explore her mouth. It wanted to explore every inch of her, except I didn't think this was the time to do it. Her ex-fiancé, from the sound of it, hadn't bothered to show her how special she was. And that dickwad she recently had sex with—the one who thought speed fucking was an Olympic event—hadn't been much better.

So my tongue remained on its best behavior and stayed in her mouth, savoring her taste. And it might have also sampled her jaw, the sensitive spot under her ear lobe (which, for the record, resulted in a delectable moan that had my cock hard in record time), and her neck.

That's not to say Kelsey wasn't an active participant in our kiss fest. While her tongue enjoyed what my mouth had to offer, her hands did a little wandering of their own. One explored the terrain of my ass. The other cupped my cheek, then knotted in my hair. And shit, that was freaking hot.

I'm not sure how long we had been kissing when she eventually pulled away, her breath ragged, like she'd just run a marathon.

My breathing wasn't much better.

"So, are you going to show me the rest of the place?" She smiled, the move shy yet teasing.

And instantly I envisioned the next stop on our tour, and what I fantasized doing to her there.

On the countertops.

I slipped her hand into mine and tugged her toward the kitchen.

Most kitchens in apartments aren't much bigger than the bathroom. You can barely fit one person in them, never mind two. And forget about doing any cooking that required space.

Not so with my kitchen.

Kelsey stepped into the room, and her mouth dropped open at the sight of the granite counters, stainless-steel appliances, and the two sinks, one located in the island in the middle of the room. "Wow."

"Impressed?"

"I'd say." Closing her eyes, she sniffed the air. The sweet smell of freshly baked banana bread filled the space. "Are you baking?"

"Yep. And that TV you were appreciating? You should see the Food Network on it."

She opened her eyes and a sweet grin spread on her soft lips. "I can imagine it's impressive. So you're cooking now? One class and you've gotten into cooking?"

"Cooking and baking." And I was getting better at it. My scrambled eggs no longer looked brown and rubbery. They tasted better too.

The Food Network? Best. Fucking. Invention. Ever.

"I've got a special dinner planned," I said.

Her eyebrows went on a field trip north. "You do?"

I nodded. "I didn't just invite you to stay until your power returns."

She laughed, and the sound of it caused my heart to warm. I didn't think I'd ever get enough of that beautiful sound. "And here I thought you wanted me to stay for other reasons." She didn't say it, but I knew exactly what she meant.

And maybe she was right about that too.

"How's the photography going?" I asked, purposefully switching topics.

Her face brightened and the warmth in my heart intensified. "I bought a camera today. The manual's huge," she said, not looking all that impressed. "But once I've figured out how to use the basics, the guy at the store said I'll be set. I also bought a tripod and a lens for close-up photography." The words gushed from her mouth, an unstoppable train heading for the final station of the day. It was easy to see she had finally found something to be excited about. "And I've registered for a class on portrait photography. So I have to do a lot of studying and practicing of the basics before it starts."

The excited look on her face was my undoing. I pulled her back into my arms. She let out a small squeak.

Then I savored the taste of her once more.

And in case you were wondering, there might have also been some exploring of *her* ass this time.

24

———

KELSEY

Nothing was sexier than watching a man cook. The way his muscles flexed and rippled as he chopped the vegetables. I could spend an entire afternoon watching Trent cook and I'd be one very happy woman—one very happy *turned-on* woman.

And this was Trent with a T-shirt on.

Could you imagine if he was shirtless?

Or wearing only a towel wrapped low around his hips, with the delectable low cut V of his abs showing?

I licked my lips at the steamy image now implanted in my head.

Trent said something, snapping me back to my current reality. "Can I help you with anything?" I asked, watching him chop vegetables for a stir fry.

"No, I'm good. You can either stay and watch or go play with your camera." Which I had brought with me just in case.

Hmm. That was a tough one. The idea of both was appealing—but watching Trent was even more so.

"Did you want to watch something on Netflix after dinner?" he asked.

The idea of cuddling with him sounded appealing, although I had no idea if he was the cuddling type. From what Erin had told me, there had been plenty of girls in his life, but I had assumed they were all one-night stands or had been very short-term relationships.

"You know about my dating past and my failed relationship." I grabbed a carrot from the counter and pretended to be fascinated with it. "What about you?"

He was silent for a moment, to the point where I thought he wasn't going to answer. "I dated a girl in college for a while." Freezes in Antarctica were warmer than his tone. "She got pregnant in our senior year and I decided to do the right thing and marry her. Because she wanted to be married well before the baby was born, we had planned to get married in Vegas. Then I found out, by accident I might add, that she had lost the baby and was stringing me along, knowing my upcoming job with an investment bank had the potential of being high paying."

"I'm sorry," I whispered, mentally cursing the bitch for hurting him. "Erin never told me."

"She doesn't know. None of my family does. Call it stupidity on my part, but we were going to get married and then tell our families. I knew my mom wouldn't be thrilled. She wanted a big wedding for all of her kids, but it just didn't feel right and there wasn't enough time...or so I thought. Anyway, it's no big deal." He might have said it, but I could tell it was a bigger deal than he let on. "After I graduated Columbia, I studied for my CFA designation and didn't have time for dating."

"CFA?"

"Chartered Financial Analyst. You have to pass three levels of exams, but the failure rate of each is high and the amount of material to study is extensive. I needed it for what I wanted to do, and couldn't fail even just once. Each exam is offered twice a year, and I didn't want to risk having to wait another six months to retake it."

"So she was your only girlfriend?"

"No, there were two others after that. None of them much better than the first one. That's when I decided being a workaholic was better than wasting time on relationships."

Imagine for a second that you're riding up in an elevator and the cable suddenly snaps. Now you know exactly what my stomach did at his words. Yes, I know, it shouldn't have mattered. We had both agreed we weren't looking for a relationship. But a part of me had secretly hoped for more.

Only now that he had revealed this part about his past... well, the Titanic had a better chance of not sinking than I had of having something more—something wonderful—with Trent. He was incapable of trusting a woman after what his past girlfriends had done to him, and without trust he wouldn't be able to love.

After eating the delicious dinner he'd made, we took our wine to the living room and Trent found a movie we both agreed on. As for the cuddling? Before I had a chance to sit, Trent pulled me down between his legs and wrapped his arms around me. It was nice.

Correction. It was like bathing in a tub of melted chocolate.

Nothing else could compare.

Half way through the movie I became more aware of his warm breath against my neck, his familiar spicy scent, the feel of his strong hands tracing a path up and down my bare arm, the movement a teasing caress.

And for the past few minutes, everything about me had become supercharged, right to my core. I bit my lip to keep from moaning. Owen had never had this effect on me. He was more the lets-get-down-to-business type. Yes, there had been foreplay, but there had never been any seduction involved. Nothing like this.

The moment Trent's tongue found the shell of my ear, my plan to keep from moaning died. At his firm stroke, everything inside me caught fire and I arched against him, pushing my butt against his hard length. Closing my eyes, I moaned. He groaned, playing harmony in our sexual symphony.

Trent's thumb brushed against the side of my breast. I don't care how great a movie is, no one could pay a hundred percent attention to it with Trent doing that to them.

Ignoring what was happening on the screen, I shifted around and straddled Trent's hips. His hands cupped my butt. I gazed at his gorgeous warm green eyes, which sparked with mischief and desire, then leaned down to kiss him.

One thing I can say when it comes to kissing Trent—no other experience equals it.

Scaling Mount Everest. No biggie.

Seeing the Seven Wonders of the World. Who cares?

But Trent's kiss? Absolutely sublime.

My hands traveled down his body, exploring the T-shirt covered surface of his chest. It wasn't enough. I wanted to touch his warm skin, feel it against mine.

Still kissing him, I hooked my fingers under the hem of his T-shirt and slowly pulled it up, my fingertips grazing his smooth skin. I shifted away from him, just far enough to get a glimpse of his taut stomach muscles.

His dark, dilated eyes focused on my lips, then his hands crept under the hem of *my* T-shirt. He flattened his palms against my stomach and curled his fingers around my waist.

His touches...his touches were like heaven—each one a new treat.

With my core rubbing against his hardness, he rocked me against him. A breath rushed from my lungs and I paused in my attempt to strip his clothing off him. We both wanted this. Nothing short of a natural disaster could prevent it.

I pushed away all thoughts of Holly, Erin, and Liam, locking them in a safe place for now. I'd worry about them later.

Instead new terrifying thoughts happily took their place. For starters, so far so good when it came to the kissing. But what about once the clothes were off? Sure I'd been reading erotic romances, but was that enough? Would I be able to please him —or would I be a major disappointment between the sheets?

No, my horny inner voice said, channeling the *Joy of Sex* book Erin had loaned me. *It's like riding a bike. You've got this covered!*

Trent reached behind his head, further exposing his abs (and distracting me from my fears). He grabbed hold of his T-shirt and a second later it was on the floor next to the couch. It had barely touched the ground before my T-shirt snuggled up to it—and a pleased grin curved onto Trent's lips.

With an equally pleased grin on mine, I reached behind me and unfastened my bra. It too joined the growing pile on the floor.

Trent's expression was priceless—and hot—as his gaze took in my breasts. He positioned his hands on either side of them and scraped his thumbs across my nipples, the look of awe still there.

Liquid desire shot through me. I gasped and unconsciously arched my back, pushing my breasts against his warm palms. And before I knew what was happening, one of my nipples was in his hot, wet mouth and he was sucking.

"Oh, God, Trent," I somehow managed to breathe. "We should go into your room."

Trent's mouth left my breast and he pushed himself up to stand, keeping a firm grasp on me. Without thinking about what I was doing, I latched my legs around his waist and he walked us to his bedroom.

Once there, he shut the door behind him and lowered me onto the bed. I sat on the edge with Trent standing in front of me, wearing nothing more than a faded pair of jeans. I'd seen him in his expensive suits and he looked fine, but nothing could compare to this Trent.

This Trent was too breathtaking for words.

I reached out, my gaze locked onto his, and fumbled with the button on his jeans. Somewhere in the back of my mind the one-night stand with the gold medalist in sprint fucking replayed in glorious color.

Trent must have sensed my fear. He kneeled in front of me and took my hands. "We don't have to do this if you don't want to, but I promise I'm nothing like the last guy you were with. I would never treat you like that." He lightly squeezed my hands.

I nodded. "I know." And somehow I did. No matter what happened between us, even if this was just a temporary fling and he would disappear tomorrow, he would never treat me the same way the jerk had.

Trent stood and before I could reach for his jeans again, he leaned forward, placing his hands on either side of me, his dark eyes intense. I laid back on the bed, vertebra by vertebra.

And then Trent was kissing me again.

The kisses weren't filled with hunger and need. They were gentle and filled with a million promises—and they contained one simple question: Do you trust me, Kelsey?

I responded to each kiss, letting him know that I did trust him. I always had and I always would.

The kisses quickly deepened and there was no denying the hunger now consuming us. Trent moved away from my lips and I almost groaned in protest. But then his mouth moved to my jaw and his tongue traced its way to my ear. My groan was quickly forgotten, to be replaced with a moan begging him not to stop.

While his mouth was busy turning me into a heated mess, my hands were back to their original mission of undoing his jeans. This time they weren't shaking and it didn't take much effort to pop the button loose from the hole. With growing confidence, I unzipped his jeans and slipped my hand through the opening.

My fingers brushed the thickness straining against his boxers. Trent sucked in a sharp breath and rested his forehead in the nook of my neck. "Jesus, Kels."

Erin's words of wisdom replayed from my lessons on sexual confidence, although I was pretty sure she hadn't meant for me to practice them on her brother.

Ask him what he wants. Guys like that.

I turned my head and murmured in his ear, "What do you like?"

"You're killing me," he moaned softly. "You know that, right?"

I giggled. "I aim to please." I reached for his jeans again.

Trent stopped my hand. "Not yet." He moved off the bed, then offered me his hand and pulled me to my feet. "Do you trust me?"

"Yes."

He traced his fingers along the top of my jeans and slipped them slightly under the waistband. My heart thump-thump-thumped contentedly, while my clit silently pleaded for his fingers to travel farther south.

He unhooked the button and lowered the zipper. His fingers grasped the waistband and peeled the denim down my legs. Once they were around my ankles, I stepped out of them, leaving me in only my thong.

His heated gaze traveled down my body, making me feel desirable, confident, ready to jump this man in front of me. Except now he was the one who looked momentarily unsure of what to do with himself.

After a few seconds, he recovered his composure and stepped closer. "I definitely approve of the thong." His lips returned to my neck and he gently nipped the skin with his teeth.

Pleasure shot through me, making direct contact with the growing ache between my legs. I might have moaned, groaned, or gasped—or some combination of all three. There might've also been an "Oh, God" thrown in for good luck.

One hand moved to my hip, then dipped between my legs. His fingers cupped me and my clit screamed, "Take me now."

Or maybe that was me.

Trent's mouth returned to mine, and he gently tugged my lower lip between his teeth. His fingers moved to the waistband of my thong, and he peeled the fabric off me in the same way he'd removed my jeans.

"Sit on the edge of the bed," Trent commanded, his voice low yet firm. The wetness between my legs increased at the sound. I wouldn't be surprised if it happened from now on, every time he spoke to me that way.

Like Pavlov's dog.

A conditioned response.

Once I did as he asked, he said, "Spread your legs and let me see your gorgeous pussy."

I swallowed, more turned on than I ever thought would be possible. That guy who I was once engaged to (what was his name?) was anti dirty talk.

I opened my legs wider. A small part of me knew I should feel vulnerable and exposed—but I didn't. With the way Trent was looking at me, my confidence continued to grow.

"Now touch yourself, babe."

Chewing my lip, I considered his request. I'd never touched myself before. Never even thought about doing it—especially not in front of anyone. But the way he said it—demanding yet encouraging—made me want to push aside that innocence and do as he'd asked.

To please him. To please myself.

Without waiting for another word of encouragement, I slipped my fingers between the slick folds and slowly stroked myself, my gaze locked on Trent the entire time. His eyes gleamed dark with approval and awareness. Awareness this had been out of my normal comfort zone—but that I'd been willing to try it. For him. For me. The bulge in his jeans was so pronounced, I wouldn't have been surprised if it ripped through the fabric Hulk style.

Trent let this continue for a minute before squatting between my legs. While I continued to touch myself, inching closer to the edge of euphoria, he planted mind-numbing kisses along my inner thigh. Once he was close to the ache between my legs, he positioned his hand on the one getting intimate with my clit and moved my hand to the bed.

His mouth replaced my fingers, and as good as it had been with them, that was nothing compared to his very skilled tongue.

"Oh, God, Trent. I'm gonna come." I threaded my fingers in his hair with the goal of encouraging him to join me in this moment. "I want you inside me."

He chuckled against my clit. The sensation solidly shoved me closer to the edge. "My, aren't you a little impatient?"

"Please..."

He laughed again. "I think I like this side of you."

"What side?"

"The side that begs me for sex."

I rolled my eyes. "I wasn't begging for sex. I was just begging to feel you inside me."

"Same thing."

"Is not."

Trent's grin grew wicked, but at least he decided to give me what I wanted. He removed his jeans and boxers, grabbed a foil square from the drawer of his night table, ripped it open, and rolled the condom along his thick length. While he was doing this, I scooted onto the bed and laid down. He joined me, his body covering mine, positioned himself, then slowly entered me. I swear he was purposefully tormenting me, keeping me on the edge, making me wait for the moment when I would tumble over.

He paused, letting my body stretch to accommodate his width. And hello, it was quite the width. He put the other two guys I'd been with to shame. True, size wasn't everything, but it sure did help. Don't let anyone tell you otherwise.

"Are you okay?" he asked, the concern in his eyes rivaling that of a chef during a kitchen fire.

I smirked. "I'll be even better once you start moving."

"Demanding aren't you?" The extra order of huskiness in his voice inched me closer to the edge I was toeing again.

"You better believe it."

Trent finally decided he had tormented me enough. He started pumping inside me, taking us both over at the same time. He grunted an animal-like sound that was more on the erotic side of things.

And I cried out in pure ecstasy.

25

KELSEY

You remember the old Viagra commercial? The one where the man danced on his way to work to the song "Good Morning"? Well, that was how I felt this morning. And if I could have gotten away with dancing as I entered my office, I would have done that too.

I hadn't stopped grinning since last night, after my body and mind returned from the stratosphere, where they had visited each time I had sex with Trent.

That's right. We didn't just have sex the one time. The second time occurred after we'd cuddled for a bit in bed.

And then again this morning around four thirty, when Trent woke up incredibly horny—and who was I to say no to him?

Best alarm clock. Ever.

So even though I was tired, it was a happy tired.

I sat on my office chair and powered up my computer.

My cell phone pinged with a text.

Erin: Why didn't you tell me you have a
boyfriend????

I cringed. I'd known it would eventually come out, but I had been so busy since blurting to Caleb that I was seeing someone, I'd kind of forgotten about it.

For the most part.

All right, I had hoped Holly had forgotten and Erin would never find out.

So much for plan A.

I stared at the computer screen, hoping a Plan B would magically materialize. When that failed to happen, I typed:

> Me: We just started dating. Didn't want to jinx anything.

> Erin: When do I get to meet him?

Never, given he didn't exist. ONCE I'M READY TO INTRODUCE YOU TO HIM.

And by then fictitious Chris Hemsworth and I would've broken up.

> Erin: So what unlucky woman is my brother currently "dating"?

> Me: Why would I know? And who told you that he's dating?

> Erin: Holly. She figures you know but you're keeping it a secret.

> Me: Why would she think I'm keeping it a secret?

> Erin: She thinks it might be you.

I groaned. I guess I had been asking too much for Holly not to put one and one together and arrive at the correct answer.

Me: She's crazy. Trent is definitely NOT my
boyfriend.

I peered warily at the ceiling, but since I hadn't technically been lying, lightning didn't strike me.

Erin: That's what I said. You know better than
to date him. Plus it would just be icky if my
best friend dates my brother.

Me: LOL It's not like it would be incest.

God, did she really think that it would be?

Erin: Close enough. Besides what would
happen if you guys broke up? Liam and I
would be caught in the middle. This is why
there's that rule about how best friends should
never date the other one's sibling.

Me: Since when was it a rule?

Erin: Since forever. So do you know who he's
dating?

Oh, God, how did I get myself sucked into this conversation? Right. Because when I attempted to divert Holly from her goal of dating Trent, I'd been forced to lie.

Erin wasn't the only one in the mood to text me.

Trent: Why is Holly looking at me like she's
planning to throw me a surprise birthday
party?

Me to Trent: Remember how I told you that
Holly thinks you have a girlfriend...and I have a
boyfriend?

Trent: Yes.

Me: Well, now Erin knows, but Holly thinks I'm the girlfriend.

Me to Erin: I don't know her name, if that's what you're asking. And no I haven't met her, but I'm sure she's really nice.

I couldn't resist the last part.

Erin: That's too bad.

Me: What's too bad?

Erin: That he's seeing someone. Holly would have been good for him.

Me: So you want Holly to date your brother?

Erin: They're very much alike. If anyone could get him to fall in love and settle down, it would be Holly.

Ouch.

Me: Maybe he'll fall in love with his new girlfriend instead.

I tried to convince myself that him falling in love with Holly (or any other woman) would never happen, especially after what he'd told me last night about his ex-girlfriends. Despite what Erin was hoping for, Trent wasn't looking to settle down. Maybe I could get that reminder tattooed on my arm.

26

TRENT

It's funny how you can stare at a computer screen for five minutes and not really see it. The numbers are there, but are nothing but a blur.

What I did see (not so shockingly) was the image in my head of Kelsey touching herself last night after I'd told her to— and fuck, that had been hotter than all hell.

And because of that—and because of the hot sex we'd experienced twice last night and then again this morning—I was having a shitty time focusing on my work.

I entered the numbers into my calculator, pressed the equal sign, and groaned.

$$696969.69$$

Yes, the financial gods were conspiring against me.

My cell phone pinged and I rushed to check if it was from Kelsey.

But it wasn't from her.

Erin: So is it true?

Me: Is what true?

Erin: That you have a girlfriend?

Good question. I had no idea what to call this thing between Kelsey and me, but since we were keeping it a secret, it didn't matter what we were calling it.

What did matter though was that Holly believed I had one.

Me: Yes.

Erin: Who is she?

Me: You don't know her.

Erin: So when do I get to meet her?

Me: When the time is right. And you constantly bugging me about it won't speed things up.

My phone pinged again. Liam. *Fuck.*

Guilt kicked me in the nuts for thinking that. This was the first time in the past few weeks that my best friend had been able to contact me, and it wasn't as if he knew what was going on between his sister and me.

The tension that had been knotted in my muscles since he'd last contacted me slightly loosened its hold. It would only fully go away once Liam was safely back in the States.

Liam: Still alive. How's my sister?

Me: She's fine and keeping out of trouble.

Unless he considered her screwing his best friend trouble, then she was getting into tons of that.

And while I should've felt guilty, I didn't. But it didn't mean I was ready to send him a text, telling him how I felt about his sister. The guy had contacts back home. Contacts who were equally skilled at killing with the snap of a finger.

I wasn't sure who was scarier. Them or my sister—if she found out the truth.

"Need any help?"

At the sound of Holly's voice, my head jerked up. I hadn't seen much of her this morning—and now she was smiling like she had a secret she was excited about.

"No, I'm fine. What's up?" I returned my phone to the desk.

She stepped into my office and closed the door behind her. "You mean other than it's confirmed, I got the job?" Before I had a chance to congratulate her, she pressed her finger against her lips. "Shhh. You can't say anything until Ted makes the official announcement."

"When will that be?"

"Next week. Right before Richard's retirement party."

"Well, congratulations ahead of time."

"Thanks. I thought maybe you, me, Josh, and Kelsey can go out for drinks tonight to celebrate."

"Sure. Let me check with Josh."

"Sounds great. I'll ask Kelsey." She left my office and I sent Josh a text, asking him if he wanted to join us for drinks. He responded forty minutes later with a "hell yes".

I SQUEEZED MY WAY THROUGH THE SURPRISINGLY CROWDED SPACE and spotted the girls at the bar. Josh wasn't here yet. Kelsey was wearing slim jeans and a thin light pink knit top that hugged her curves. She looked both innocent and hot, and I knew from experience both adjectives fit her well.

As I approached them, a guy a few inches shorter than me,

with way less muscle mass, and who looked vaguely familiar sidled up to them. Unlike most guys, he didn't notice Holly standing there. He just smiled at Kelsey.

The smile on her face was best described as awkward, and I stalked over to them, ready to tell him that she wasn't interested.

"Holly, this is Owen. My ex-fiancé."

His gaze was eating her up, as it slid over her gorgeous face and fuckable body, questioning why he'd let her go to begin with. But it hadn't been his choice to make. She had dumped him.

"I made partner," he said, beaming.

"Congratulations." Kelsey hugged him, then she spotted me and a bright smile slipped onto her face. "And Owen, you remember Trent, right?" We might have met once or twice at an occasional family gathering. But usually Kelsey had come to them alone because the dumbass was busy at work.

He nodded at me and went back to talking to Kelsey as if Holly and I didn't exist. "I'm meeting someone, but maybe we can meet up for coffee soon."

"Sounds good," she said.

As he walked away, Josh made his way over to us. "Who's the jackass?" He jerked his chin in Owen's direction.

"I used to be engaged to him," Kelsey explained.

"Used to? So why was he feeling you up like that?" Josh asked.

"Dude, if you call that feeling her up," I said, chuckling, "then you're more hard up for sex than I realized."

Laughing, Josh slapped me on the back. "Never gonna happen." His gaze jumped to Kelsey. "If you're still in love with that dude, then you should get Trent to make him jealous."

Every guy has that one friend—you know who he is—the one who some days just won't shut the fuck up. Josh was that friend and this was one of those days. Not that I had the right to be pissed at him. He had no idea about my feelings for Kelsey.

"Not necessary," she said without a hint of uncertainty. "What Owen and I had has been over for a long time. I've moved on and so has he."

Relieved to hear that, I rested my hand on Kelsey's lower back. Until now, I hadn't realized just how much I'd missed her.

Holly shot my hand a puzzled look, and I instantly realized my mistake. I casually dropped my hand away from Kelsey, trying not to look obvious about it, trying not to look like I was doing anything wrong.

Shit, this was tough.

Since Kelsey and Holly already had drinks, Josh and I went to the bar to order our beer. After he and I returned, the four of us spent the next hour chatting and sharing amusing anecdotes about our jobs. At one point, while Holly was answering Josh's question about Australia, I asked Kelsey about her day.

"It was good, especially after Liam sent me the text to let me know he's still alive." Her face beamed as she talked. "Oh, I forgot," she added, then pushed her lower lip out slightly in the way she did whenever she was bummed about something. "The power's back on at my place." The storm from the other day had done more damage than originally realized, and Kelsey's house had been without power for two days.

Disappointment punched me in the gut at her news. I pushed it aside and checked to make sure Holly and Josh were still pre-occupied. Then I leaned in and brushed my lips against the shell of Kelsey's ear.

"Stay with me tonight," I whispered, voice two-parts husky and one-part beer.

27

KELSEY

rent brushed his lips against the shell of my ear and my entire body went berserk with need. "Stay with me tonight," he whispered.

At the sound of his I-want-to-have-sex-with-you-now voice, a tropical heat wave—complete with luau, Mai Tais, and leis—rushed to my core.

He wasn't playing fair and he knew it.

"I can't," I said, voice low even though Holly and Josh weren't paying attention to us. "I've got tons to do before my photography class next week."

Trent's mouth transformed into the smile I was more than familiar with. It was the smile that claimed he would have me changing my mind faster than I could say pussy.

That, I didn't doubt.

"Then maybe we should go now so you can get in more studying." He might have said that, but the teasing in his tone confirmed what his smile had said. Along with an underlying, "Good luck with that goal."

Because we had both driven to the bar, I followed him back

to his condo in my car. On the way, my body listed the benefits of having sex with him before I returned home.

And the list was lengthy.

My brain even threw in a few suggestions, trying to be a good sport for once.

True to Trent's word (or smile), the moment we stepped onto the elevator, his fingertips skimmed the back of my neck, sending heated tremors down my spine.

With his free hand, he pulled me against his hard body, letting me feel exactly how much he wanted me.

As if there had been any doubt.

He had already proved it to me several times last night. And because of this, my sexual confidence was at an all-time high.

I was ready...ready to be adventurous and wild in bed—just like the heroines in my favorite romances.

As I leaned in to taste his lips, the elevator door pinged open. And yes, I might have cursed at it in my head a few times.

And then a few more times for good luck.

Trent threaded his fingers with mine and led me to his apartment. The door had barely closed behind us and our shoes kicked off before I was pressed against it. My brain attempted to remind my body that we should leave now, so I could experiment with my camera before bedtime. My body shushed it, saying, "Not now. We're busy."

Taking my reaction as a good sign, Trent walked backwards, his mouth still attached to mine, my arms around his neck.

He bumped into something and stopped moving—and I crashed into him.

I pulled away slightly to see what had happened. He'd misgauged where the door was and had walked into the doorframe.

"Oops." I giggled, removing my hands from around his neck, and stepped past him into the room.

Trent followed and closed the door behind him as I walked to the bed. I stood there, waiting for him to join me. He still had his suit on, along with his I-knew-I-would-win smile.

Touché.

He brushed my hair back, exposing my neck. For a heartbeat his lips explored the skin there, gently caressing it. I dropped my head to the side, purely on instinct, purely because it felt so good. His tongue and then his teeth joined the exploration.

Heat flickered throughout my body, starting from where his mouth was and spreading to my core. Moaning, I leaned back against him and placed my hands on the side of his strong, solid thighs. I slowly traced my fingertips against the soft wool of his black slacks, moving them to gently cup him.

But it wasn't enough.

I wanted to feel more of him—to feel his skin.

Preferably against mine.

His arms wrapped around me. Even his suit jacket felt soft against my skin. I swiveled around and my gaze settled on his full, begging-to-be-kissed lips. For several seconds, neither of us moved, other than the shallow synchronized rising and lowering of our ribs.

I peeled his jacket away from his shoulders, my fingertips skimming the even softer fabric of his white dress shirt. Once the fabric was free of his body, I carefully draped the jacket on the armrest of the black leather armchair.

With trembling fingers, I unbuttoned his shirt. Trent stood still, arms at his sides, allowing me to do whatever I wanted.

Once the final button was released, I took a moment to appreciate the fine sculpturing of his abs. Every ripple and every muscle was perfect—like a sunset at the end of the day, with all its color nuances.

I placed my palms flat against his stomach. I didn't think I would ever get tired of touching him. It was like eating the finest chocolate truffles. One was never enough.

I trailed my fingertips along the smooth hardness of his chest, and slipped my hands under his shirt, nudging the fabric away from his body. I continued sliding it past his shoulders and down his arms, until the shirt was bunched around his wrists.

Trent removed it, practically ripping it off in his haste. He tossed it onto the chair, and the corner of his mouth tugged to one side in my favorite sexy grin.

So not to be outdone by me, he removed my knit top, his fingertips grazing my heated skin. Unlike mine, his fingers didn't tremble. I guess that was the perk of being a player at one point. Sex didn't make him nervous. The only emotion he was experiencing, if his dark-green eyes were any indication, was lust. Pure. Hot. Lust.

Next off were my bra, jeans, and panties. They too joined the happy pile of clothing on the chair. He palmed my full breasts, and his touch alone almost had me coming, almost had me dropping to my knees.

I wrapped my arms around his neck, inadvertently pushing my breasts into his palms. He squeezed them then pinched my nipples. And holy-of-all-things-amazing, I thought I'd just died.

While his thumbs continued teasing my nipples, I unzipped his pants and slipped my hand into the opening. My palm met his cock and the thick length jerked in my hand, accompanied by Trent's moan. And yes, it did make me feel powerful. Just one touch—and he started to unravel.

His mouth was on mine again, proving once more that he was the world's best kisser. Don't believe me? That's okay. I wasn't going to let you test-drive him anyway.

Eager to see all of him, I removed my hand and slid his pants and his boxers down his legs, until he was able kick them aside with one swift movement. His cock jutted out, heavy, strong, proud—the swollen tip glistening with a drop of desire.

A different urge whispered for me to kneel before him. I dropped to my knees and palmed his long, thick length. Even in my fantasies it had been nothing like this.

"Shit, Kelsey. You have no idea what you're doing to me."

I grinned at him. "I think I have a good idea what I'm doing to you....And just so you know, my ex wasn't interested in me going down on him. I'm not sure what I'm doing here."

Trent stared at me, his expression incredulous. "Are you fucking kidding me? All I've dreamt about since last night and this morning is what it would feel like to watch you take me into that sweet mouth of yours. And what it would feel like to have your gorgeous lips moving against my cock."

I swear a whimper tumbled from my mouth at his words. His dirty talk had this amazing ability to leave me all shades of turned on.

Or rather, more turned on than I already had been.

"Well, since you put it that way..." I slipped my lips over the broad head and swirled my tongue against the tip, tasting his male saltiness. I kept my gaze on his face, curious about his reaction.

His hooded eyes locked on my lips. The erotic, intimate moment and the way he looked at me caused wetness to flood between my legs. Never before had sex been this hot—this naughty.

I could seriously become addicted to this.

Correction, sex for the fourth time in twenty-four hours screamed: Hi, my name is Kelsey Quade and I'm addicted to sex. With Trent.

Oh, well. I'd deal with the consequences later. Maybe there was a support group I could join, once whatever this was between us was over.

While I sucked and flicked my tongue against the super-sensitive part below the head, he groaned again, leaving me even more heated than before. Thank you, erotic romances, for teaching me how to please a man in bed. And if Trent wasn't so busy trying not to melt on the spot, I was positive he would've also wanted to convey his thanks.

I gripped the base of his cock and moved my palm up and down his length. He enjoyed this too, apparently. With my free hand, I cupped his balls and lightly squeezed them.

"I'm going to come soon, Kels."

I grinned up at him. "That's generally the point."

My mouth slipped over his swollen tip again. He threaded his fingers in my hair, but instead of pushing my head so that more of his cock was in my mouth, he gently yanked on my hair.

A mix of pleasure and pain shot through my scalp, and I moaned my appreciation.

Just as I thought Trent was going to come in my mouth, he pulled away and tugged me to my feet.

He turned me around so my butt was pressed against his cock. His hand slipped around my hip, down the front of my thigh, then to a spot that made my clit get excited.

His fingers moved easily along my slick folds. "Bend over," he murmured in my ear, his breath heated against my skin, "and put your hands on the bed."

As if I wasn't damp enough, more wetness rushed between my legs, which were quickly resembling cooked spaghetti. At this rate, I wouldn't be able to drive home. I wouldn't even be able to walk to his bedroom door.

I was done for.

I did as I was told, bracing my forearms against his bed. I expected Trent to enter me from behind. He didn't. Instead, two fingers slipped inside me and his thumb rubbed against one *very* happy part of me. If it could've broken into cheer, it would have.

He pumped and swirled his fingers inside me. Just as I was close to coming, thanks to those magical digits, he removed his fingers, slipped on a condom, and entered me.

It didn't take much more on his part (or mine) before we both came, hard, mere moments apart. I almost felt sorry for his neighbors.

Almost.

28

TRENT

"What's the child's name?" the receptionist in the physical therapy clinic at the children's hospital asked me. In the background, a child's giggles broke through the reception room chatter.

The pretty blonde behind the desk was about my age, so I turned on the charm and smiled at her. "I don't exactly have an appointment. I'm a friend of Kelsey Quade's. Is there a chance I can talk to her for a few moments?" I flashed her another smile, the same one that usually got me what I wanted when it came to women.

Except with Erin. She always saw right through it.

The blonde smiled back at me. "She's currently with some patients. What is your name?"

I told her and waited while she called Kelsey.

Once she was finished with the call, ending with an "I'll do that," she hung up the phone. "Go down the hallway." She pointed in the direction I needed to go. "You want room PT4."

I thanked her, and a minute later entered what looked like a small gym, with kid-sized equipment on the floor along the mirrored wall. In the center, Kelsey faced two six-year-old girls, all three standing like flamingos. One girl had curly red hair, the other a dark braid down her back.

Kelsey waved me over. The two girls peered curiously at me in the mirror.

"Chloe and Lindsay, this is my friend Trent," Kelsey said, gesturing to each girl.

Chloe, the redhead, grinned. "Did Kelsey give you her cow or chocolate milk?"

The star of my twenty-four-hours-a-day-seven-days-a-week fantasies blushed in the cutest possible way, and it took me a second to figure out why.

I laughed, which made Kelsey turn redder. "I'm not going to answer on the account it will only get me in trouble."

"You aren't lactose intolerant are you?" Chloe asked. "I tried giving a boy my chocolate milk once, but he wasn't allowed to drink it."

The corners of my mouth twitched as I fought back another laugh. "No, I'm not lactose intolerant."

Her face brightened. "So, you can eat ice cream?"

I nodded. "I happen to love ice cream. What about you?"

"Change legs," Kelsey said, and the three of them switched the leg they were standing on.

"You should do it too," Lindsay said, pointing at me, then wobbled for a second before regaining her balance.

I moved into position, which wasn't easy with dress pants and a shirt on. I still had my tie on, but had loosened it before coming to the clinic. My suit jacket was back in the BMW.

The girls giggled, even though my balance was better than theirs.

"I love chocolate ice cream," Chloe said. "And cookies and cream. And mint chocolate chip." She went on to name at least five other flavors.

"I only like vanilla," Lindsay said, swaying worse on the one leg than she had with the other.

"Do you think Kelsey loves ice cream?" I already knew she did. I even knew her favorite flavor—raspberry cheesecake.

"Of course she does," Chloe said, lowering her foot for a second to keep from wobbling too much. "Everyone loves ice cream."

"Do you think she would like to have some with me after work?"

"Yes!" both girls cried out in chorus.

"So what do you say?" I asked Kelsey. "We can go to The Lickery." It was her favorite ice-cream place in all of San Francisco.

"Sounds good."

Did you notice it? The glimmer of excitement in her eyes?

They say the way to a man's heart is through his stomach.

Well, the way to Kelsey's heart was via her favorite frozen dairy product.

Any man worthy of her would know that.

"We just have a few more exercises to do," Kelsey told the girls. "Should we get Trent to help us?"

There was another chorus of yeses, with Chloe jumping up and down like a rubber ball. Kelsey had me toss a beanbag to Lindsay, who had to catch it while standing on one leg. Kelsey did the same with Chloe.

Once they were finished, Kelsey dismissed them, then told me she had to complete some paperwork first before she could leave, but it would only take a few minutes. While I waited for her in the hospital courtyard, I checked my office emails on my phone.

At the sound of voices entering the sunny space, I looked up from the email I was reading. Kelsey was walking toward me with a man wearing a suit. She pointed at me and he waved over a gorgeous redhead sitting at a nearby table. Unlike Kelsey, who was wearing yoga pants and a white T-shirt with the hospital name on the chest, the redhead was dressed in a sleeveless black jumpsuit that skimmed her toned body.

Kelsey and the man approached me at the same time as the redhead.

"Faith," he said to the woman, "this is Kelsey, the woman I was telling you about. Kelsey, this is my cousin."

His cousin's lips curved into a seductive smile...aimed at Kelsey. Her heated gaze traveled down Kelsey's equally scorching body.

And I swear every hot-blooded male's fantasy was playing out in living color in front of me.

Minus the kissing.

Although from the way Faith was checking out Kelsey, it was clear she would've been in favor of that too.

"Nice to meet you," she said, still smiling.

"You never mentioned if you have a girlfriend," the man said to a stunned Kelsey. "But when I told Faith about you, she begged me to introduce her to you. Hope that's okay."

I choked back a laugh. Faith was definitely barking up the wrong redwood tree. But where the hell did he get the idea Kelsey was gay?

Faith laughed. "I wouldn't say I begged. But I did ask him to introduce us."

"It's nice to meet you too," Kelsey said, finally finding her voice. "But I'm sorry. I'm already in a relationship."

Faith was still smiling, but it had changed from being seductive to holding a hint of understanding. What she understood was lost on me. "I had a feeling you were. You have the glow of someone who's in a relationship and couldn't be happier."

She did?

My head spun around to check out this glow I'd apparently missed. But Kelsey didn't look any different.

She looked great, as always.

But that didn't stop pride from surging through me, because I was responsible for this so-called glow.

"What was that all about?" I asked Kelsey as we watched Faith and the man walk away. Faith was laughing at whatever he had said.

"I met him here a few weeks ago. He wanted to go out with me but I wasn't interested. So I might have told him I was a lesbian."

The blush on her face from earlier returned as I threw my head back, laughing.

Once I was able to control the laughter, I asked, "Why weren't you interested in him?"

"He doesn't like ice cream." She winked at me and strode toward the courtyard door.

At The Lickery, we each ordered a double-scoop ice cream in a waffle cone (raspberry cheesecake for Kelsey, cappuccino for me), and headed to an empty bench by the waterfront. In the distance, Alcatraz sat proudly against the blue sky and choppy water.

"Oh, god, this is soooo good," Kelsey moaned. Her tongue flicked against the ice cream and I also moaned. Except mine had nothing to do with my ice cream. In my head, the same tongue flicked against the head of my cock, licking the pre-cum as if it were her favorite flavor.

And then, because that wasn't torturous enough, I visualized her lips wrapped around it—a replay of last night.

My cock instantly responded, hard, pulsating, hungry to escape the confines of my pants. Hungry to sink into her soft heat or her hot mouth—either was fine with me.

"What's one of your sexual fantasies?" Kelsey asked, and for a second all I could do was stare at her, positive she had only asked me the question in my head.

"What's yours?" I said, doing my best not to sound overly turned on. Which was hard given my current situation.

Her gaze dropped to my pants and she chuckled. "I believe I asked you first."

"Is this like show me yours and I'll show you mine?"

This got a bigger laugh from her. "Exactly that."

"Can't say I have any specific sexual fantasies."

"So you don't have any costume fantasies? Like a school girl or French maid?"

I shook my head. "Women dressed like kids doesn't turn me on. And French maids are cliché. I'm more of a sexy-under-wear-on-the-woman type guy. All right, I've told you mine. Your turn."

A sly smile slipped onto her lips and she murmured in my ear, "Being restrained...with ties." She traced her index finger down my silk tie...and I swallowed hard.

"You never did that with your ex-fiancé?"

Licking her ice cream, she shook her head. "Not Owen's thing. And before you ask...no, I haven't done it with anyone else either. Other than Owen, and of course you, there's only been the speed fucker, and I didn't know him enough to trust him with something like that."

That made sense.

The energizing rush of relief, satisfaction, and exhilaration greeted me, like when I had a great day on the stock market and made a shitload of money for my portfolios. Not only had she been with just two other guys before me...she had shared with me this piece of herself.

Given what I knew about her ex, I had a feeling he didn't know. Only I was privy to her fantasy.

I devoured her with a kiss, momentarily forgetting our ice cream. She tasted of sugar and cream and raspberries and Kelsey.

She tasted of heaven.

"Until now, I hadn't realized just how delicious raspberry

cheesecake ice cream is," I said against her lips. "I think it's become my new favorite."

"If you're not careful, you'll be wearing your new favorite." She pulled back slightly. "Our ice cream is gonna melt."

"That's my new sexual fantasy," I said, voice low, rough, eager. "Licking ice cream off my favorite places. Like here." I slowly traced my finger along her jaw.

"And here." Down her throat.

"Here." Down her sternum.

Her breath stilled in her chest.

"Here." My voice had dropped to a murmur and I stroked my finger across her taut nipple. She inhaled softly.

I lowered my hand to her inner thighs, and traced the seam of her yoga pants to her pussy. "And here." I cupped my hand there and she groaned.

Something cold and wet and sticky dripped onto the hand holding my waffle cone, and the distant giggles of a young child snapped me back to the here and now.

I removed my hand from between Kelsey's legs, and we finished our ice cream in a comfortable silence—as I performed difficult calculations in my head, rectifying the situation in my pants.

Afterward, I drove her back to her car and kissed her goodnight...then headed back to the office to put in several more hours of work.

Only instead of focusing on the report I was supposed to work on, I was lost in the new sexual fantasy playing in my head.

The new sexual fantasy that was nothing like the real deal.

Shit. After Kelsey, everyone else would be nothing more than a pitiful replacement.

29

KELSEY

The last time I had attended class was during the final year of my physical therapy program. Back then the students had known each other because we'd been in the same program for the past three years. It had been four years since I was a new student on her first day of class—but that was a lifetime ago.

Even the cooking and drawing classes hadn't felt like this.

And just like back on my first day of the physical therapy program, excitement mixed with a good case of nerves coursed through my body.

I sat on an empty chair in the classroom and parked my purse and camera bag on the floor. At the front, a woman in her forties was hooking up her laptop to the overhead projector. With her chin-length black hair, dressy black pants, and cream-colored blouse, she looked more ready to model in a fashion shoot than to teach a photography class.

Once she was finished, she glanced around the classroom, mentally counting to see if everyone was here. "Welcome to Portrait Photography. For those of you who don't know me..." She moved her mouse and launched into the slide presenta-

224

tion, giving us a taste of her experience: fashion photography (including Vogue), weddings, and child photography.

At the picture of a shirtless athletic male cradling a naked newborn against his chest, my ovaries sat up and took notice—imagining it was Trent in the photo with our child.

Down, girls!

"Will you be teaching us about nude photography?" a guy in the back asked.

"Yes, but if you're expecting to learn to take the kinds of photos you find in Hustler, you'll be disappointed." She returned to her laptop and an image of a young almost naked couple about to kiss appeared on the screen.

The picture was intimate and hot, and the kind of photo I would love to take...if I could find willing participants.

After class, I signed up for studio time. As I was walking toward my car, I heard my name. I turned to see Luke, a guy I'd talked to during our break, jogging toward me.

"Hey, I noticed we've booked back-to-back time slots for the studio. Would you be interested in modeling for me?" He gave me an uncertain smile. "I feel stupid asking someone if they would be willing to do it since I'm only learning right now. I thought maybe then we could figure it out together."

"That's a good idea. That way hopefully one of us can figure out what we're supposed to do."

We talked about it for a few more minutes. Then after saying goodbye to him, I continued to my car. My cell phone pinged.

Trent: What are you doing right now?

Me: Leaving photography class

Trent: Want to come over?

Me: Come over? Are you home?

Trent: Yes

Me: Let me guess. Booty call?

Trent: Well, technically, that would be a booty text. But no. Want to show you something.

Me: Can you give me a hint?

Trent: No.

Me: A tiny hint?

Trent: Just come over, Kels.

Grinning, I typed:

Me: I'll be there soon.

TRENT LET ME INTO HIS APARTMENT AND THE DELICIOUS SMELL OF baking bread instantly greeted me.

I inhaled deeply. "That smells amazing."

He came up behind me and wrapped his arms around my waist, pulling me against him. "Not as good as you smell," he murmured in my ear, turning me into a puddle on his dark hardwood floor. "I've missed you, Kels."

My head fell back against his shoulder, providing him room to nuzzle my neck. *Welcome to heaven.*

Naturally, my brain decided to go on party-pooper mode, reminding me that the pearly gates to my heaven could slam shut at any time. At some point the friends-with-benefits relationship wouldn't be enough for me, but since that was all Trent wanted it to be...

"I've missed you too," I murmured.

"Enough to spend the weekend with me in Napa Valley?"

Darren and Erin had rented a house and had invited Holly and us to join them.

Trent kissed my neck—the place he knew to kiss me if he wanted to have his way—and my body let out a dreamy sigh. "The house even has a hot tub."

I swiveled to face him and my neck instantly cursed my betrayal. Removing his hot lips from my skin was grounds for punishment.

My neck had a very good point.

"Except how are we going to enjoy it if they think you and I are dating other people?" I asked. "As it is, we'll have to sneak around if we plan to have sex. It's not like we'll be able to do it in our bedrooms." Neither of us were good at being quiet.

Trent thought about this for a moment. "So we bring dates with us."

Huh? "The last I heard, neither of us are actually dating anyone. Are you saying you want to start dating other people now?"

He rested his hands on my hips and pulled me to him. "No. But the only way I'm going to get Holly and Erin off my case is if I introduce them to my fictitious girlfriend. And I suspect it won't be any different for you."

True.

"So you want us to bring actual dates with us?"

He nodded.

"And where exactly will these dates be sleeping?" The house was big, but it didn't have *that* many bedrooms.

"They can sleep in one room together and we sleep in the other one. As long as no one catches the wrong person sneaking into the rooms, we should be fine."

I laughed…uncontrollably. Only a man would come up with such a crazy plan. "So you just expect two strangers to not only be okay with pretending to date us, but be willing to sleep together just so you and I can do exactly that ourselves?"

"Not strangers. We'll find a couple who is already involved."

I giggled some more. That's right everyone. The proof was finally in. Trent's mother must have dropped him on his head when he was a baby.

"You're kidding, right?" I asked.

"No, I'm serious."

"And do you have a couple in mind?" I sure as heck didn't.

"I happen to know the perfect couple. They're both actors, so this will be like an acting gig for them."

"Are you sure this is going to work?" I was all for it if it meant getting to sleep with Trent on the trip. Besides, I could only lie for so long about my fictitious boyfriend before Erin and Holly got suspicious.

Trent's lips returned to my neck. "Positive," he murmured, sending vibrations zinging through me.

"At least while we're there, I can practice taking portraits for my assignments." My mind was half thinking through all the possibilities while my body enjoyed Trent's talented mouth.

Trent pulled away from my neck. "Assignments? You have homework?"

I nodded. "And get this, there's even a lesson on shooting nude and semi-nude photos."

His eyebrows shot up. "You're learning to shoot porn?" I couldn't tell if he was excited or not—but I was leaning more toward the excited.

I laughed at his expression. "Down, boy. Not porn. And I wouldn't be doing straight nudity." I'd be too uncomfortable even though I wouldn't be the one who'd be naked. "We're doing semi-nude shots."

"We? Your whole class will be watching. That's kind of

kinky." The sexy one-sided grin of his that I loved so much was back on his face. He was enjoying this conversation way too much.

"No, it's just gonna be me and a guy from my class. I'm going to take photos of him for my assignment and he's going to take photos of me for his."

A slight frown wrinkled in Trent's forehead. "So this guy gets to see you semi-naked?"

I tilted my head to the side and smirked. "Jealous much?"

"When it comes to other men seeing you naked—"

"Semi-nude," I corrected.

"Okay, when it comes to other men seeing you semi-nude, of course I'm jealous. Only I'm supposed to see you that way. It's in the job description."

I laughed again. "Oh, it is, is it?"

"Yup. Check the fine print."

"Well, technically you've seen more of me than Luke will. I'll be wearing my underwear in the photos."

"Hmm. You do realize your brother's going to kill me, right?"

I snorted. "Why is that?"

"Because, one"—he held up his index finger and started counting all the reasons why my brother would want to kill him, although I could've probably added a few more of my own —"some guy is going to see you in less clothes than your brother would approve of. Two, this guy isn't your boyfriend. And three...if Liam had his way, no man would ever date you or see you naked. End of story."

I reached up and gave him a quick peck on the lips. "Well, it's been nice knowing you."

"At least let me come with you so I can make sure the guy doesn't try anything."

"He's not going to try anything."

"Take it from a member of the penis-carrying club, he's

going to be thinking about it. He's a man. That's what we're programmed to do…"

I could feel the smirk return to my mouth. "Does that mean if you come with me, you'll be thinking of trying something while I'm partly naked?"

"Sweetheart, I'm always thinking of trying something with you, naked or not." He traced the pad of his thumb against my lower lip. Heat flared between my legs. I nipped it gently between my teeth and he released a soft hiss. "You don't even have to be in the same room as me for my thoughts to point in that direction," he said, his voice a low, sexy rumble.

"All right," I managed to say, my mind enjoying its own dirty thoughts. "You can come with me. But just so you know, I'm not Luke's type. You're probably more his type than I am."

"Then I guess it's just as well you're the one posing semi-naked and not me." The lecherous smile on Trent's face was a whole new level of sexy. He threaded his hand with mine. "Come check my bread out."

I barked a laugh. "Is that what you're calling it now?" My free hand brushed against his package, hidden in his faded jeans.

He let go of my hand and wrapped his arms around me, pulling me against his body. I might have melted a bit. "Well, as tempting as it might be…" He pinched my ass and grabbed my hand again.

He led me into the kitchen and removed the tea towel from the cooling rack, revealing four small loaves of bread.

"You made those?" I glanced around, as if searching for the true creator of the loaves. On the far counter sat a large shiny mixer I'd never seen before. My gaze snapped back to him.

Grinning, he nodded. "I found a soup recipe online that sounded good, but it's served in bread bowls. So I've been perfecting my bread-making skills. I was hoping you'd stay for dinner tonight." He brushed his lips against my cheek. "I was hoping you'd stay the night." The low, sexy rumble returned to his voice.

"I think that could be arranged," I breathed. "But only because I want to try your soup." I kissed him, which quickly turned heated—and dinner was temporarily forgotten.

But countertop sex? Definitely not overrated.

30

KELSEY

"R emember," I said as Trent pulled up to Danielle's house, two weeks after our conversation about the semi-nude photography, "you promised you'd be on your best behavior."

His expression transformed into one best described as angelic. "I'm always on my best behavior." Then he winked at me.

I groaned. If we had time, I'd remind him of a few of his transgressions when it came to his behavior, starting with the Viking.

As Trent parked his BMW, I released a nervous breath. I wasn't sure which was worse: modeling first or having an audience of one. Sure, Trent had seen a lot more of me than he would be seeing during the photo shoot, but that was different.

I rubbed my sweaty palms against my thighs. *It's no big deal. You won't be naked. It's no different than when you're wearing a bikini at the beach.*

Except my bikini was boring.

It was nothing like my satin and lace underwear.

Once out of the car, Trent reached for my hand and we

walked down the path alongside Danielle's house. The warmth of his skin against mine eased my nervousness. A little.

I led him to the large wooden building that resembled an oversized shed in the backyard. Danielle's studio. I knocked on the door and entered. Luke, who was fiddling with a studio light, looked toward me and smiled.

"Luke, this is Trent," I told him. "Hope you're okay with him being here."

"Sure, not a problem. We could always use an assistant."

"That's me, always ready to assist." Trent leaned into me and murmured in my ear, "Especially if that means I get to taste you."

Inwardly I moaned while the center of my universe did a happy dance. Just what I needed—for him to get me all hot for him just before we started shooting.

I kissed Trent lightly on his lips.

"Woof!" The loud bark came from the oversized, fluffy white dog sitting in the far corner of the room.

"Bear!" I walked over to him and after letting him sniff my hand, hugged the friendly dog.

He barked again, almost deafening me, and I turned around to see what he was barking at.

"Hey, buddy." Trent took a step closer. Bear jumped to his feet and let out another less-than-friendly bark. "Okay," Trent said, drawing out the word. "How 'bout I just stay over here for now?"

"Sit, Bear," Luke said and the dog did as asked, still eyeing Trent like he was the enemy. "Sorry about that. He's jealous."

"Of what?" Trent asked, his gaze warily on the dog.

"You."

Trent laughed. "Why, 'cause I'm human?"

"No, because you were kissing Kelsey. He can get a little possessive."

Trent muttered something that sounded a lot like "I know

the feeling," but stayed where he was. Probably a smart move. That wasn't to say Bear would live up to his name and try to eat him. More than likely Trent was at greater risk of being knocked over by the massive beast.

"Guess I should get changed now." Blowing Trent a kiss (because Bear was probably less likely to take offense to that), I walked over to the small change room in the corner.

Once inside, I quickly stripped to my white lacy bra and panties, and put on my fluffy white robe. Thanks to Erin and Holly's makeup lessons, I had enough makeup on to give my eyes that smoldering look essential for what Luke and I were after.

I exited the change room, carrying a pair of white stilettos and urging my inner Victoria's Secret model to stand proud. Too bad she'd quit last week, leaving me clueless at what I was doing. My entire modeling background consisted of teenage Erin and me practicing our seductive looks in the mirror... because Erin had insisted that would help us get boyfriends.

In case you were wondering, it didn't.

Bear was still eyeing Trent when I approached the bed. Trent gave me a sly smile, his gaze taking in my short robe, practically peeling it from my body. "I never realized how sexy that is until now," he said, and my body tingled from the way his gaze touched me and at the sound of his husky voice.

Bear gave another bark, not as loud this time. More like a warning for Trent to get his mind out of the gutter. He then lumbered over from his corner and squeezed his massive body between Trent and me, almost knocking us over.

"Christ, it's like having a goddamn chaperone," Trent muttered under his breath.

I chuckled. "Now you know how I felt when you barged in on my date with Stephen."

The sexy smirk that always left my panties damp slid onto

his face. "Yes, but I got the girl in the end. The dog isn't gonna get so lucky."

Bear barked again, as if to say, "That's what you think."

"Bear, corner," Luke said, pointing to where Bear had just come from. The dog lumbered back to his spot and laid down.

I let out a long breath, and with my gaze averted, dropped the robe. I had no idea why I was suddenly feeling self-conscious. It wasn't like Trent hadn't seen me in my underwear before. Hell, it wasn't as if he hadn't seen me naked before.

And Luke?

He was busy sneaking glances at Trent's ass (not that I could blame him), which Trent missed because he was too busy staring at me.

Trent flashed me a grin that suddenly put me at ease. It wasn't filled with dirty thoughts of what he wanted to do to me tonight. It was more like a you-can-do-this type of grin. A grin filled with warmth and honesty.

I got into position, sitting on the edge of the bed with my stilettos on. I shook out my hair, giving it the I've-just-had-an-amazing-fuck look. Luke took several photos while Trent held the reflector in front of me—ever the helpful friends-with-benefits friend that he was.

Bear only barked once while Luke was taking the pictures, and that was because Trent had accidentally taken a step toward me.

"Tilt your head a little more to the left, Kelsey," Luke said from behind the camera. "Now let's see some smolder."

Easier said than done.

And based on the cringe on Luke's face, I didn't come close to nailing the look he had envisioned.

"Pretend you're making love to the camera," he prompted.

Again, easier said than done.

Trent inched closer to the camera, and the sexy expression

on his face had my insides turn into heated goo—like roasted marshmallows.

"That's perfect, Kelsey," Luke gushed.

Bear barked as if to agree.

Once Luke was finished taking photos, we checked them on his laptop—with Bear now snoring loudly in the corner. They weren't bad, but there was nothing special about them. Not like my favorite pictures that I'd seen on social media sites.

Those had an intimate beauty about them.

They didn't look like a department store underwear ad.

I turned to Trent, an idea forming. "Okay, assistant, take it off."

His eyebrow quirked up. "Come again?"

With my best come hither smile, I started unbuttoning his dress shirt. "I need this."

I continued unhooking the buttons through the holes. My fingertips might have accidentally crept under the white cotton fabric and there might have been some caressing of his chest.

Never one to miss a party, my body might have hummed happily at the contact.

I glanced at Bear, who was still snoozing, and gave Trent a quick chaste kiss. If it weren't for Luke and Bear, I'd be doing a lot more to Trent than just giving him sweet kisses.

I slipped the shirt on but didn't bother with the buttons.

Trent's eyes dilated to Christ-you-look-fucking-hot-in-my-clothes black. Something to keep in mind next time I wanted to seduce him. He pulled me against him and growled low and rough against my ear, "I want you wearing that shirt and only that shirt when we get home."

Goosebumps prickled across my skin in anticipation of what was waiting for me once we were through here, which couldn't come fast enough if you asked me.

"Woof!"

Rolling his eyes, Trent took a step back and threw Bear a look. "You're really cramping my style here."

Bear barked what could have loosely been translated as "Sorry. Not."

I positioned my knee nearest the camera onto the bed, the stilettos for now abandoned on the floor.

And then we were shooting.

A knock on the door jerked me from my lavish thoughts of what I wanted to do with my tongue to Trent's half-naked body.

"It's me," a male voice said. "I've come to pick up Bear." Ah, Cam, Luke's boyfriend, who I'd met a few times after class, along with Bear.

At the sound of his other owner, Bear gave another loud bark and the door inched opened. "Can I come in?" Cam asked.

On instinct, I pulled Trent's shirt shut, covering myself. "Yes."

Cam entered the small building and Luke introduced him to Trent.

"C'mon boy," Cam said to Bear, taking the leash from Luke. "Hope you've been good."

Still eyeing Trent like he was the enemy, Bear lumbered over to Cam and waited patiently for his owner to click the leash onto his collar, his tail now wagging.

As Cam walked Bear to the door, Trent called out, "Told you I'd be the one getting the girl in the end."

Bear ignored him, Luke laughed, and Cam just looked confused. Once man and dog were out the door, we got back to the photo shoot.

Afterward, Luke loaded the pictures onto his laptop and showed them to us. The photos turned out exactly how I had envisioned them. A large reason for that was because of Luke. He had a natural talent for getting the best from his models—even me.

He looked up from his laptop, and his gaze jumped between

Trent and me, studying us. "I have another idea, but I need you both to be in the photos this time."

"Why do you need me in them?" Trent asked, his heated gaze still locked on the laptop screen.

"Because I have an idea you might like." He explained how he wanted us to pose. As a couple.

After Luke promised none of the photos would end up online without our written permission, Trent climbed onto the bed and I straddled his hips.

Luke adjusted his camera and the lights, explaining what he was doing for my benefit. Then he began shooting the new round of images. For the most part, Trent and I were to just gaze into each other's eyes and pretend we were getting ready to kiss, our mouths only inches apart.

Now, this doesn't sound too tough, right?

Bet you aren't feeling too sorry for us.

Trent and I had kissed a lot during the past few weeks. True. But staring at someone's mouth for at least five minute when all you wanted to do was kiss him and taste him was sheer torture. I was positive this pose had been listed in the *Guide to Effective Torture Techniques* back during the Spanish Inquisition.

But it wasn't just lust that was boiling inside of me, hot and heavy to get it on with him. There was something about staring into his eyes, into his soul, and realizing that everything had changed. The man you liked as more than just a friend, the man you had craved for who-knows-how-long was the man you were in love with.

Too bad for me it was one-sided.

"Okay," Luke finally said, "I'd like to try something else. Kelsey, take off the shirt and your bra. You'll be in the same pose, but your breasts will be pressed against Trent's chest. Nothing you don't want seen will be visible."

"You didn't tell me there would be added perks to this assistant gig," Trent said, his breath a hot kiss against my ear.

"Do you think you can handle it?" My gaze dropped to his package, hidden in his jeans.

"I was hoping you'd be handling it later." He chuckled.

I turned my head a fraction of an inch. "If you're a good boy," I murmured, "I'll be doing more than just handling it later." I brushed my lips against the shell of his ear.

A muffled curse tumbled from his mouth and I couldn't help but grin.

Before Trent could say anything else, I slipped off the shirt, letting it pool around my hips. I removed my bra and stuffed it under the covers so I could easily retrieve it once we were finished.

I shifted forward, pressing my suddenly achy core against Trent's thickening length and my breasts against his chest. "Okay, we're ready," I told Luke, who had been busying himself with his camera while I was removing my bra.

Luke returned to behind the camera and began shooting again. "Pretend you want to make love to each other," he directed.

Pretend? That was one thing I didn't have to pretend.

I ran my lips along Trent's jaw, relishing the feel of his light stubble against my face.

"Wow, you guys are seriously hot," Luke said, the camera still clicking away. "Good thing Bear is gone or else his fur would be singed."

I pulled back slightly and looked into Trent's eyes. My breath caught at the love reflecting back at me, but unlike the feelings I had for him, his were based on what he was projecting for the camera. He was getting into it, giving Luke what he wanted.

My heart slouched in my chest, knowing I would never get that for real with Trent. But this was what I had signed up for when it came to our friends-with-benefits agreement. I just had to suck it up.

"And we're done," Luke said, fanning himself. "I knew you two would be good together. I just wasn't expecting that much heat."

"You mean it was better than when I was pretending to make love to the camera?" I asked, half joking.

Luke burst out laughing. "Girl, it wasn't the camera you were making love to earlier." His gaze slid monetarily to Trent, then he walked away, allowing me time to slip my bra and the shirt back on.

I gave Trent a quick kiss. "I'm just gonna put my clothes back on. I'll be right back." I started to climb off his lap.

He grabbed my hips and dragged me back. "I have a better idea." His eyes held the familiar heat I'd seen so many times with him lately. "How about Luke leaves and I'll be your model." With the way he was looking at me, it was impossible to say no. "On one condition," he added.

"What's that?"

His fingers slipped under the shirt opening and traced along the edge of my bra. "You don't get changed yet."

"Are you sure about this?"

He nodded.

"All right." I turned to Luke, hoping he wouldn't take offense to me turning down his offer to model for me. "It looks like I won't need your help after all. Trent's volunteered to be my model."

"You sure?" Luke asked.

"Definitely."

He jerked his chin at Trent. "Thanks, man, for the pictures. If you want, I can burn them on a CD for you."

Trent glanced at me, the heated expression still in his eyes. "I'd appreciate that."

Luke packed up his stuff, moving quickly, possibly to bail before things became R-rated between Trent and myself. After starving for the feel of Trent's lips during the photo shoot, I was more than happy to kiss him again, only this time deeply.

Which was exactly what I did once the studio door shut behind Luke.

But as my legs began to melt beneath me, I remembered where we were and why we were here. I reluctantly pulled away.

"We should get started," I murmured, my lips close enough to Trent's that I could feel his warm breath on my mouth.

The corner of his mouth twitched up. "I thought we were getting started."

I lightly punched his arm. "I meant the photos."

"That's too bad. 'Cause I was enjoying the kissing part." He wrapped his arms around me and pulled me close again. "I don't suppose there'll be kissing involved with *your* photos. But real kissing. Not the almost kissing crap that practically killed me."

I gently whacked him on the arm. "Sorry, no kissing in these photos. Not unless you want me to call Luke back. But something tells me he's not your type."

Trent rolled his eyes and gave me one final kiss. Then I pulled away and set up the lighting and props for the photo shoot.

With a level of self-control I didn't know I possessed, I told Trent how to pose without touching him.

That wasn't to say I didn't want to.

There should've been a gold medal for *that* level of restraint.

31

TRENT

If you think Robert De Niro has the easiest fucking job around, then you obviously haven't spent the last two hours of your life preparing to convince your sister that the stranger sitting next to you is your new girlfriend.

And that the woman in the back seat isn't the one you really wanted to make love to.

That's right. Kelsey and I were driving to Napa Valley, where we would be spending the weekend convincing Erin and Holly that the two other people in my BMW were our new significant others.

Yes, maybe it would've been easier to just come clean and risk the wrath of Erin. But the thought of what she would do to my balls for screwing around with her best friend was what held me back.

"Just so we have this straight," Jillian asked from the passenger seat, "what's the policy on PDA?"

I peered in the rear mirror at Matt. Did he look familiar? Hopefully Erin and Holly didn't think so. He had recently been on *Criminal Minds* as some Ted Bundy type. Nice, huh?

"Hand holding and hugging is fine," I said. "No kissing."

242

Did I mention Matt was extremely good-looking?

While I was confident I was the one Kelsey really wanted, the caveman part beat his fists against his chest and grunted, "Mine." Any man who claimed he didn't do that when it came to his woman was lying—or just wasn't that in to her.

We all did it.

End of story.

"Got it," Matt said from the backseat, where he and Kelsey had been working on their "story." Jillian and I had been doing the same. How the hell I would remember all of this was beyond me.

Ask me anything about the companies in my portfolio and I could tell you every last detail. Ask me how Jillian and I first met and I was still a little fuzzy.

Fortunately, Kelsey and Matt had only been on a few "dates" (same with Jillian and me), so we didn't need to know each other all that well.

Just well enough to be spending the weekend in Napa Valley with them.

"You owe us big time for this, Trent," Matt said, laughter in his voice. The guy was enjoying this way too much for his own good.

"Says the guy who had me cover his ass big time in college," I reminded him. Not that he had needed to be reminded of that when I'd asked him if he and Jillian could help us out.

"What happened?" Kelsey asked.

"Genius boy decided in college that it would be a great idea to date the daughter of one of our professors." I pointed to Jillian so Kelsey would know who I was talking about. "Never recommended at the best of times..."

"And especially not recommended when your professor already dislikes you," Matt added.

"My father didn't dislike you," Jillian said, looking back at Matt in the backseat. She laughed at his expression, the expression that said, "Yeah, right he didn't." "Okay, the two of you didn't exactly share the same opinions most of the time…"

"Which wouldn't have been a problem except her father always thought he was right and no one was allowed to think otherwise," Matt said.

"All right, I'll give you that."

"So long story short," I said, "I covered for Matt's ass so many times, just so he could continue sneaking around with Jillian until the semester was over. Which got me into hot water a few times, especially when our professor thought *I* was the one dating his daughter."

"Hey," Matt said, "it all worked out in the end."

"But considering what Trent did for us," Jillian added, "there was no way we could say no when he asked us to help you guys out."

"Does your father know you married Matt?" Kelsey asked.

"Yes. He eventually got over it once he found out we were together, but this was long after Matt had finished with the class. And it didn't exactly happen overnight."

The sun was low in the sky by the time we pulled up to the ivy-covered mini mansion. Because Kelsey had a photography class today, the four of us had left after that. Erin, Darren, and Holly had arrived earlier this afternoon.

"Nice place," Jillian said, her voice filled with awe. Not much different to Kelsey's expression.

"I wouldn't get too attached," Matt said. "Not unless *Criminal Minds* offers me a hundred-thousand-dollars-per-episode contract as an agent for the next five years."

"Given you were killed off during your one shot at the show, point taken." Jillian flashed her husband an adoring smile, then blew him a kiss.

"Showtime." Kelsey nodded toward the house as Erin and Holly walk down the front steps, smiling. "God, I hope this works," she muttered, then opened the car door and slid from the back seat.

She hugged Erin and Holly. Jillian, Matt, and I joined her as Darren stepped out of the house. Kelsey moved closer to Matt and lovingly wrapped her arm around his waist.

Lucky bastard.

"So, here he is. My boyfriend. Matt." Her cheeks reddened and she chewed on her lip. The lip I longed to taste but had to wait a few more hours before I could do just that.

She introduced him to Erin, Holly, and Darren, then I introduced them to my "girlfriend." I could tell from the way Erin looked Jillian over that Jillian had already scored points with my sister. She was wearing a simple sundress and had a low maintenance look about her, much like my sister and Kelsey. Her long blond hair was pulled back in a messy bun. But as pretty as she was, she still wasn't Kelsey.

I wrapped an arm around Jillian, and had a whole new level of respect for Robert De Niro. Shit, why did acting have to be so tough? It took everything in me not to glance at Kelsey and give away how I felt about her.

Once the introductions were finished, we entered the house and Erin showed us around.

"This is Kelsey and Matt's room." Erin opened the door and we followed her inside.

The large picturesque window overlooked the local vineyard and its breathtaking view. The room was designed with a mix of mahogany furniture, latte-colored walls, and floral bedding. A forest-green wingback chair sat near the corner— and thoughts of what Kelsey and I could do in the chair and on the four-poster bed left me all shades of excited.

"Wow," Kelsey said. "This is gorgeous."

"The bathroom's down the hallway." Erin pointed in the direction we had to go to get to it. "Holly's room is across from this one. And Trent and Jillian, you're next door."

I let out a relieved breath that Matt and I didn't have to go too far to get to the rooms we were supposed to be in—and to the women we were supposed to be with.

Jillian and I followed Erin down the hall to what was supposed to be our room. "Darren and I are staying in the room at the end of the hallway." She pointed out the bathroom, which was sandwiched between her room and Holly's. "We have the en-suite. There's also a bathroom with a shower on the main level."

Erin showed us our room, then left us alone so we could unpack before dinner. I stepped onto the balcony, which had the same view as Kelsey's. Unfortunately her room didn't share the same balcony. That would've made things easier when it came to sneaking around.

I checked the hallway to make sure the coast was clear. "Don't go anywhere," I told Jillian before leaving the room.

Matt and Kelsey were chatting when I entered their room, her suitcase open on the bed, filled with her stuff and mine. "She's waiting for you," was all I said. Matt slapped me on the back and left the room, closing the door behind him.

I locked the door and crooked my finger, summoning Kelsey over to me. She was instantly in my arms and my lips didn't waste time. They explored her sweet-smelling neck, her jaw, and finally her mouth. My hand cupped her equally sweet ass and I pressed her against my cock, which had come to life the moment I'd stepped into the room and saw her.

I crouched slightly, running my hands down the backs of her thighs, and lifted her. Her legs went instantly around my hips and she rubbed her seam against my straining length. I groaned against her lips and walked to the bed.

I lowered her onto the mattress. Her sundress had bunched around her hips when I'd picked her up. I left it that way and enjoyed for a second the view of her lacy, light pink underwear. Then I leaned over her and said hotly against her ear, "There's nothing I want more than to eat you, but that's gonna have to wait." I ran my fingers along her seam, applying enough pressure to cause her to arch her back.

She whimpered. I grinned.

"Tell me, Kels, how wet are you?"

"Very wet." Her voice was a breathy whisper. My cock hardened that much more. "Just for you, Trent. Only for you."

I groaned against her jaw. "Christ, you're killing me." I slipped my finger past the elastic and stroked her slick lips. "I want you so fucking bad. I always want you so fucking bad."

"And that's exactly what I want. You fucking me." A campfire could've been started by the amount of heat in her voice.

"Soon. But in the meantime"—I hooked my fingers on the waistband of her panties—"you won't need these for dinner." I slid them down her legs and tossed them somewhere on the floor.

I guided her legs apart. "Let me see my favorite pussy, Kels. I need something to think about during dinner." Screw dinner. I wanted to feast on her now.

And then I wanted to fuck her long and hard.

I admired her slick heat for a moment, then brushed my thumb roughly against her core. She bucked at my touch. "You're so beautiful," I told her, and with a shocking amount of self-restraint, I gently brought her legs back together.

I helped her off the bed and kissed her, white-hot desire burning in my veins. In the back of my head, I was vaguely aware of a soft knock at the door but ignored it. I had everything I needed and wanted right now in my arms. Nothing else was important.

For now, the pain-in-the-ass voice in my head warned. Then it was back to reality once we returned to San Francisco—and my job that always came first.

As if hearing my thoughts, Kelsey pulled away. "Yes?" Her voice was louder than before, but still rough with need.

She indicated for me to duck behind the bed. I would have laughed if the person behind the door wasn't someone who was supposed to remain oblivious to what Kelsey and I were up to.

"It's Jillian," the person on the other side of the door said.

Kelsey let out the breath I hadn't realized she was holding, and unlocked the door. She opened it wide and let Jillian in. Kelsey wasn't the only one who looked like she'd had a very satisfying make-out session.

"We're supposed to head down now," Jillian said.

"Thanks," I told her.

Matt entered the room. "Are you ready for this?"

"I think so," Kelsey said, although she did suddenly look as though she was going to be sick.

"All you have to do is pretend you're with me," Matt coached. "Everything else will be simple. Try to keep the conversation away from us as a couple and it'll be fine. It's just another dinner with friends."

"Don't worry, Kels," I said. "You've got this."

"But how long do we have to do this for?" she asked. "I mean, I get why I can't be honest with my best friend, but how long will I have to pretend Matt's my boyfriend?"

"Until you're able to convince my sister and Holly to quit setting you up." Or until she'd had enough of our relationship and was ready to date other men for real.

My stomach turned to lead at the thought.

"We can stop pretending now if you want and tell Erin the truth," I added. "It's up to you. I'll stick by you whatever you decide."

Kelsey shook her head. "No, we're already here and this is for the best. It will keep our friends off our backs for a while."

As long as we could pull it off.

32

KELSEY

Dinner was great. As was the company. Jillian and Matt did a good job convincing everyone that Trent and I were dating them.

Okay, maybe they did too good of a job.

Did you see the look in Erin's eyes? That's right, the one already envisioning Trent's and my future children.

But it wasn't our combined genetics she had mixed together. It was future Jillian-Trent junior and Kelsey-Matt junior she was seeing. Trent was right. I needed to pull up my big girl panties soon, and stop Erin from setting me up with yet another guy I had no interest in.

There was only one guy I wanted—the one I couldn't have. Not in the way that I wanted him. Trent needed to learn to trust me and trust that I would never hurt him like the women in his past had. He needed to be as committed to me as he was to his job, which had never let him down. And after that, we'd have to convince our siblings that we could make it work.

Except it would've been easier to convince terrorists to sing Karaoke with the world leaders. While wearing women's underwear.

Once dinner was finished, Holly, Jillian, and I helped Erin clean up, then we joined the men outside on the deck. There wasn't a lot of room for all of us. Erin cuddled up next to Darren.

Jillian and I exchanged looks, but it was clear we didn't have a choice. Whether we wanted to or not, unless we wanted to raise suspicions, we had to cozy up to the wrong guy.

Resignedly, I sat next to Matt on the loveseat. He played his role well, other than stiffening slightly when Jillian cuddled up to Trent. If I hadn't been leaning against him, I wouldn't have noticed.

"It's been driving me crazy," Holly said to Matt, "but I'm positive I've seen you before."

Matt chuckled, but something was off about it. A quick peek at Erin's and Holly's expressions told me they hadn't noticed, both watching him intently.

Trent was too far away for me to tell if he was breathing—or if like me, his breath had stalled in his chest while waiting for Holly to piece things together.

"You're probably confusing me for someone else," Matt said. "I get that all the time."

Holly didn't look too convinced.

"I can guarantee with your Australian accent I would remember you," he cleverly pointed out.

"I guess that's true."

Erin was looking at him, her head tilted to the side, as if noticing for the first time that he did looked familiar.

Shit.

I didn't think Erin watched *Criminal Minds*, but there was always a chance she had seen the one episode Matt had been in.

Quick, think!

"So, Holly," I said, blurting the first thing that came to mind.

"Maybe Erin can help you find a great guy since I'm officially off the market for one."

Foot, meet mouth.

Erin's face lit up with a grin. "Hey, that's not a bad idea."

Holly shifted in her seat, as though it were made of burning coal. "Thanks...but, um, I think I'll take a rain check. It's quarter end...and I'll be really busy for a while." Holly changed the topic so fast after that, I was surprised none of us ended up with whiplash.

By ten o'clock, Erin was fighting to stay awake. She leaned her head against Darren's shoulder, and a few minutes later she was asleep.

He scooped up his wife. She didn't even stir. "See y'all tomorrow," he said.

Holly uncurled herself from her seat. "I'm up for the hot tub. Who wants to join me?"

"I will," I said, even though the only place I really wanted to be was in Trent's arms. On the bed...or bent over it. I wasn't fussy.

But...

Hot tub safety 101: friends don't let friends hot tub alone under the influence of Napa Valley wine.

Trent, Matt, and Jillian also said they were in, and we headed upstairs to our rooms. Except Matt's swim trunks were in Jillian's room and Trent's were in mine...where they weren't supposed to be according to Erin's sleeping arrangements. The men had purposefully switched suitcases back in San Francisco, to make things easier for once we got here. Trent's clothes were in my suitcase. Matt's were in Jillian's.

So much for that plan.

Matt stood in the middle of the bedroom and checked his phone. He removed Trent's swim trunks from the suitcase and walked out onto the balcony. Curious what he was up to, I followed him.

Trent was already out on Jillian's balcony, with what I guessed to be Matt's swim trunks.

"How are you planning to get them to him?" I asked Matt.

"Like this…" He placed the trunks on the ground, rolled them into a tight ball, and tucked in the ends.

He stood back up and walked over to Jillian's balcony. "Ready?" he called to Trent, arm cocked back as if he was about to throw a baseball.

At Trent's nod, Matt threw an impressive pass and Trent intercepted it. Trent did the same with the makeshift ball he'd made out of Matt's swim trunks. Matt easily caught it.

Jillian pretended to throw him a kiss. He easily caught that too.

I chuckled. "Wow, you're really good."

He let out an easy laugh. "I was an all-star baseball player in college for a reason."

"Yet, you went into acting instead?"

"Call it a twist of fate….Do you want to get changed first? I can stay out here until you're ready."

By the time we had changed into our swim gear, Holly was waiting for us in the hallway. She was wearing a tiny green bikini, with a matching wraparound tied low on her hips. Like with everything else she wore, she looked amazing.

"Love your bikini, Kelsey," Jillian said, walking toward us in hers—a cute, light pink top with black boy shorts accented with light pink.

Did Trent appreciate it? I had no idea. He was too busy staring at my bikini, with the aqua-blue fabric peeking through the black lace overlay. I'd bought it the other day for this trip—and for Trent's benefit.

He swallowed hard, his gaze still on me. And I wasn't the only one who noticed. A light frown formed between Holly's eyebrows.

She opened her mouth but before she could say anything, Matt's arms were around me and he pulled me in for a kiss.

Just a quick kiss. Nothing to make me weak in the knees.

But as he released me, I caught the end of Trent's reaction... and it wasn't a happy one. He scowled at his friend, even though his friend had just saved our asses.

Fortunately for us it wasn't Holly this time who saw what happened. Unfortunately for Trent, it was Jillian. Her elbow jabbed his stomach. Not enough to cause damage, but enough to remind Trent what was at stake.

"Where's the hot tub?" Jillian said, laughter in her voice, although I had no idea if that was part of the act, or if she had actually enjoyed nailing Trent in the stomach.

"Follow me," Holly said.

Jillian and Matt did exactly that. Trent lightly grabbed my wrist, holding me back. My skin tingled at his touch.

"Screw the hot tub." His breath was hot against my ear and my knees felt a little wobbly from the sensation. "I want to take you back to your room and fuck you."

I pressed my lips against his. "Soon. But it'll look a little strange if my boyfriend and your girlfriend join Holly and we vanish."

"I'm going to have to kill her husband for kissing you," Trent growled but it was missing any real anger.

I laughed. "Her husband saved your ass."

"How so?"

"You were so busy staring at me that you almost gave us away."

At least he had the decency to look sheepish about it.

We quickly joined the others before Holly could realize we had disappeared. Jillian deserved an Academy Award for her role in distracting her.

We climbed into the tub, Jillian and I on either side of

Holly. Except Trent forgot who his girlfriend was supposed to be and sat next to me, leaving Matt to sit next to his wife.

My heart rate picked up at the error, but the loud gurgling of the water kept anyone from hearing the thump, thump, oh fuck, thump. If Holly thought it was a little odd that Trent and Matt were sitting in the wrong spots, she didn't say anything or give any hint of what she was thinking.

Eventually my heart rate eased, helped along by the soothing water.

We spent the next fifteen minutes relaxing in the hot water, not talking a lot at this point. Being in a fake relationship was exhausting, and I'd run out of things to say. Instead, I leaned back and stared at the stars.

"So beautiful," I whispered, more to myself than to anyone else.

Trent's fingers brushed against the back of my hand. Without thinking through the consequences first, I smiled at him.

"I'm tired. I think I'll head to bed," Jillian said, and I could've almost hugged her.

The rest of us agreed and headed back inside.

Jillian and I had our showers first in the two available bathrooms. While I waited for Trent to join me in my room, I blow dried my hair, then climbed into bed, naked.

The door eventually opened...and Matt walked in. I let out a small squeal and yanked the sheet up, covering my breasts.

"Sorry," he mouthed and shut the door. "Holly's door is open, so I had to come in here."

He paced the room for a few minutes, then inched the door open to check if she had shut hers yet. Shaking his head, he closed the door again.

I slumped back against the pillows.

Shit, now what?

33

TRENT

Men are generally an impatient species. From the moment we discover our penises as babies, we favor instant gratification.

Which was why Holly wasn't currently topping my list of favorite people. Her bedroom door was open, meaning I couldn't sneak into Kelsey's room.

And it didn't look like she was in a rush to shut it.

Like she wasn't in a rush to shut it thirty minutes ago.

Matt: What the fuck are we going to do?

Good question.

Me: The balcony?

Matt: Might work.

Jillian and I headed outside, to be met by Matt and Kelsey on the other balcony. Thank god Holly's and Erin's rooms weren't overlooking this side of the mini mansion. It was dark out, but the lights on our balconies were like spotlights, preventing us from sneaking around.

Matt and I inspected the one obstacle separating us from the women we wanted to be with. The balcony railings were possible to climb over, and as long as they were firmly attached to the balconies, it was possible to climb between them.

The good news was we were only on the second floor and the ground beneath us wasn't concrete. The bad news? The rose bush didn't look too comfy if hit wrong.

I tested the railing. "They feel secure." Matt tried his and agreed. "I'm coming over first," I said.

"Are you crazy?" Kelsey called out. "You could get killed."

"I'm not gonna get killed." Holding onto the railing, I managed to climb over without maiming the boys.

"Be careful," Kelsey said, gripping her own balcony railing. If she'd had superhero strength, she would've created a sizeable dent in the black metal.

"That's the general plan."

"It better be...or...or else I'll have to kill you if you die."

I snorted a laugh. "I'll take that into consideration."

Still holding onto the railing, I shifted my body. With one foot perched on the concrete, I stretched my other leg toward Kelsey's balcony. Once my footing was secure there, I reached for the railing, and swung my body over, leaving my balcony behind.

Kelsey grabbed hold of my arm and helped me over the railing. Well, more like she tried to drag me over, fearful that I would otherwise fall to my demise.

Once she had assured herself that I was indeed safe, she flung herself at me.

I wrapped my arms around her and kissed the top of her head. "Looks like you won't have to kill me after all."

"Glad to hear it." Her arms went around my neck and she

kissed me long and hard. I was vaguely aware of Matt making the same journey to the other balcony to be with his wife.

"I want you so badly," Kelsey moaned when we briefly came up for air. Matt and Jillian were no longer on the other balcony, having already retreated into Jillian's bedroom.

My cock strained against the zipper of my jeans, hell-bent on giving my woman what she wanted. We barely made it to the bedroom before Kelsey unzipped my jeans and slipped her hand in, cupping me.

At the sensation of her hand pressing against my throbbing length, I saw stars. Unable to wait another moment, I practically ripped her jeans and T-shirt from her body while she did the same to mine.

I paused once she was standing in nothing but her lacy panties. She smiled, but unlike the shy smiles from when we first hooked up, this one was filled with a confidence that almost had me coming at the sight of her.

Yes, sexual confidence was that hot, that powerful.

I kissed her once more—deep, hungry, demanding—then peeled the lacy fabric down her legs. Once they were tossed aside, I indicated for her to lie on the bed and removed three silk ties from my bag. Kelsey's eyes dilated at the sight of them.

Just as I expected they would.

I climbed onto the bed, straddling her. "Put your hands together above your head."

She did as requested and my lips moved into a devilish smile. I lightly dragged the tip of one tie up her stomach and between her breasts, silently promising her nipples that I'd soon be worshiping them, like I would be the rest of her body.

She gasped softly and my smile widened.

I continued along her arms, then gently bound her wrists together before knotting the ends of the tie to the headboard.

"Do you trust me?" I asked. She nodded without hesitation,

and a warmth stirred in my gut at how easily she had given me her trust when I struggled with that myself.

I took the other tie and covered her eyes with it. Once it was secure, I lightly brushed my lips against hers, silently thanking her for giving me this part of her, for trusting me not to hurt her.

She playfully nipped at my lower lip, and everything south of the equator pulsated with need. But as much as I wanted to sink into her, I wasn't ready to end the game just yet.

I rolled up the third tie and stroked it against Kelsey's cheek. Her beautiful lush lips curved into an equally beautiful smile. "That's so soft," she whispered.

"It is, but not as soft as you." I gave her one more tender kiss, before sliding the tie down to a perfect rose-tinted nipple.

I caressed it with the tie until Kelsey was moaning and writhing on the bed. If anyone was to walk past the room, there'd be no question what she was up to.

Once I'd finished having fun with that nipple, I switched to the other one, and was rewarded with the same moaning and writhing. I didn't think I'd ever get enough of this—knowing what I could do to her, knowing she loved it as much as I did.

"Now open your legs wide so I can see your gorgeous pussy," I murmured against her ear.

She whimpered but did as I requested. Got to love a woman who does what you ask of her with a smile filled with longing and amusement.

With the tie, I stroked around her clit, touching her in the way I knew from experience drove her insane with need.

"Oh, God," she groaned and writhed again, her bound hands pulling at the bed frame.

"Do you want me to keep going?" My voice remained low so no one could overhear me and realize I was in the "wrong" room.

"Yes," she breathed.

I slid my fingers between the lips of her pussy and brought them to my mouth. "Christ, you taste amazing, Kels."

Another whimper. She wouldn't last much longer.

And neither would I.

I lavished her clit with my tongue, pushing her further and further to the edge...until she came hard against my face, in all her fucking glory.

Pride sat up inside me. I had done this to her. I had made her fall apart like this. Yes, I had fucked other women before, but never had it felt like this.

Never had they felt like Kelsey.

Once she returned from whatever stratosphere I'd sent her to, I untied her, removed the blindfold and my boxers, and grabbed a condom from the nightstand.

"I want to feel you without anything between us," she said softly. "I'm on the pill. And I'm clean." The longing in her eyes was accompanied by a question: *What about you?*

The last time a woman had told me she was on the pill... well, you know what happened. And yes, the angel on my shoulder that night had given the devil a helluva hard time. He never lived that one down.

But the idea of entering Kelsey with nothing between us sent more blood to my cock. I needed relief from the building ache and I needed it now.

At my hesitation, she stroked her fingers against my jaw. "I would never do anything to hurt you, Trent. And if you're not ready for that, I understand."

"I want you so bad, Kelsey. More than I've ever wanted anyone before." My voice was rough with emotion and a level of vulnerability I'd never felt before. I peered into the depths of her beautiful blue eyes. Nothing but pure, hot honesty shone back at me.

"I'm clean too," I whispered. I lifted her legs onto my shoulders, and pressed the head of my cock against her hot entrance.

Then I slowly eased my way in, allowing her tight heat to adjust to my width.

It was like coming home after being away for so long.

I WOKE UP THE NEXT MORNING TO FIND THE ROOM AGLOW WITH sunlight and a naked Kelsey snuggled up to me, her back against my chest, my arm around her waist. Her breathing was deep and even, not too surprising after last night—and the three times we'd made love. She had fallen asleep in my arms shortly after the final time.

I gently kissed her shoulder, skin warm, soft, and sweet-smelling.

She stirred, her hot ass brushing against my morning wood, releasing a moan from my lips. "Careful, sweetheart. Unless you're recovered from last night and ready for another round."

She turned around with a grin on her face. "I think I could handle it." Her hand moved under the covers and she stroked my length. Her grin grew—as did my cock.

I crawled over her and my mouth headed south for my morning feast. My tongue lashed against her nipple.

"Oh, Trent," she half moaned, half whispered.

A knock at the door intruded on us and I muttered a curse.

"Kelsey," Holly said. "Can I come in for a second?"

"I'm kind of busy right now," Kelsey began to say but the sound turned into another moan as I continued enjoying my feast.

"It's important."

I reluctantly removed myself from her tit and murmured in Kelsey's ear, "She's not going to leave until she's talked to you."

"But she can't see you," she whispered back, pitch raised in panic.

"She won't. I'll stay under the blanket until she goes."

Maybe have some fun while I was at it. No, not that kind of fun...although it would be amusing. "She'll think I'm Matt and she won't stay long."

Kelsey nodded and I pulled the cover over my head and her naked body.

"Okay, come in," she said, reminding me that I'd forgotten to check that the door was locked last night. I had been too eager to be with her.

The door clicked open and shut.

I reached out in the darkness, found the soft skin on Kelsey's thigh, and traced it with my fingertips.

"What's up?" Kelsey asked. I snickered quietly at her unintentional pun and let my fingers explore farther north...aiming for one of my favorite parts.

"How was your night?" Holly asked.

"Good," Kelsey squeaked as my fingers slipped between her wet folds.

"Sounded like you were having a great time. So did Trent."

Warning bells rang in my head and my fingers froze.

"Oops," Kelsey said, with an awkward giggle. "Sorry Matt and I were a little loud."

"Oh, you two weren't loud at all."

Shit.

"You can come out now, Trent." Holly didn't sound pissed, but the blanket over my head could've been deceiving.

"Trent's not here," Kelsey said, doing a good job sounding confused. Matt and Jillian weren't the only good actors it turned out.

"Ahh, so you're telling me Jillian is one very lucky woman, and was having sex with both Matt *and* Trent last night?"

"Why would you think she was having sex with Matt?"

"Because I saw him leave her room this morning to use the bathroom." The last word had barely left her mouth when the bedding was tugged away from my head, exposing Kelsey's and my lie...as well as a good proportion of my ass.

Groaning, I shifted around so that all my valuables were covered.

Then groaned again at her do-you-really-think-I'm-that-stupid expression, eyebrow raised.

I had an economics degree from Columbia and my professional CFA designation, both of which said I was an intelligent man. Yet at that moment, not one intelligent thought traipsed around in my brain. The best I could come up with was "Hi?"

Holly didn't say anything at first. She just sat on the wingback chair, where I had at one point made Kelsey come last night. But now wasn't a good time to point that out to Holly.

Kelsey and I sat up, her arms crossed in front of her to keep the covers against her breasts.

"So, how long has this been going on between you two?" Holly waved her index finger at us to indicate who she was referring to, as if there was any doubt.

"A couple of weeks," Kelsey said, her voice soft. Soft with the promise of a lifetime of groveling to make up for what we had done. To make up for the betrayal that Holly was no doubt feeling, because we hadn't been honest with her to begin with. "I'm so sorry, Holly, that I didn't tell you sooner. We didn't plan for this to happen...it just did."

"Why didn't you just tell me the truth?"

"Because Erin and my brother can't find out."

Holly looked genuinely surprised. "Why not?"

"Because I'm screwing my best friend's little sister," I reminded her. "Liam would be pissed if he knew the truth."

"And Erin would be devastated if she found out," Kelsey added.

"How come?" Holly asked.

"Well, to start with, the last thing she wants is for me to date

Trent. She loves her brother, but he's not her first choice for me."

"But it's not her choice to make," Holly so wisely pointed out.

"I know, and under different circumstances I would tell her that. But it goes deeper than that. And if she knew I'd been lying to her the whole time, she'd never forgive me."

"So you're going to keep lying to her about this?"

"It's not like this is going to last forever." Kelsey's words were a swift kick to the nuts. She had already written off what we had between us. I was a temporary fling—nothing more.

Ready to stamp "hypocrite" on my forehead? The irony hadn't skipped me. She viewed me as not much different than I had viewed the women I'd been involved with. But the difference was I had done it out of self-preservation.

A voice in my head muttered maybe that was what Kelsey was doing too. She had already gone down the workaholic route with her ex. She had no intention of repeating that mistake.

Wasn't that why we had hooked up to begin with?

"Please don't tell Erin," Kelsey said to Holly. "We don't want to hurt her."

Holly nodded and pushed herself from the chair. "I won't. But I really believe you two owe it to her to be honest with her... as well as with yourselves."

She strode to the door, turning back to us once she got there. "I'll let you get back to what you were doing. But you might want to think about getting up soon. I'm sure the four of you"—she pointed at the wall separating us from Jillian's room —"are hungry after all that sex last night." Laughing, she left the room.

Kelsey's phone beeped from the bedside table. She picked it up while I checked the text from Matt, warning me that Holly had seen him come from Jillian's room.

Sure, *now* I saw it.

"Weird. It's from Luke," Kelsey said. "Our photography instructor needs to talk to us."

"About what?"

"No idea. All he knows is that it's about our assignment and it's important."

For some reason, she seemed more nervous about that than what had just happened with Holly.

After her comment to Holly about what we had between us not lasting forever, I should've gotten up and hit the shower. But knowing that this thing between us had an expiry date—as vague as it was—I decided to make the most of the time we did have together.

I took her phone from her and placed it on the nightstand... then slowly, tenderly made love to her one more time.

34

———

KELSEY

L uke's car was already parked on the street when I arrived at Danielle's house. I pulled up in the space ahead of him and turned off the engine.

My cell phone pinged.

Owen: How about that coffee? Say in two hours? There's something I need to ask you.

Me: What's that?

Owen: I'd rather ask you in person.

Me: Okay.

We finalized the details, then I released a long, slow breath, and walked up the path to the house. There was no reason for me to be nervous about meeting with my photography instructor, yet I was more nervous about that than I was at seeing my ex-fiancé afterward.

I rang the doorbell of the large house and a few seconds later the front door opened.

"Come on in," Danielle said, stepping aside to let me in.

The inside of the house was nothing like I had expected. Her studio was organized and tidy. Her house was chaotic in the way that made you feel at home. It was splashes of different colors, with no particular theme in mind. If an editor for a home-decorating magazine came in, she'd be hard-pressed to identify a particular style Danielle had adhered to. It was as if she couldn't decide which she'd liked best and had adopted them all.

Luke was on the floral couch, reading a piece of paper when I entered the living room. His expression was serious, the complete opposite of Danielle. She was smiling like she'd found buried treasure in her backyard.

He peered up at me, stunned—and I had a feeling it had nothing to do with me showing up.

"Luke was a few minutes early," she explained as she and I sat down, me next to Luke on the couch, Danielle on the armchair opposite us, "so I've already filled him in on what I wanted to discuss with you both. First, I want to tell you how proud I am of the work you've accomplished in the class so far. The work you've presented for your assignments has been breathtaking."

"Thank you," Luke and I said at the same time.

She gathered a small stack of eight-by-ten photos from the coffee table and laid them out, side-by-side in front of Luke and me. The first two were the ones I'd taken of Trent during our semi-nude assignment. In one, he was standing to the side of the window, wearing his jeans and white dress shirt. The shirt was open and untucked, revealing his taut abs. He was smiling in the way that had caused my panties to grow damp when I had taken the photo. Even now, the smile still had the same effect on me.

The other photo showed him without the shirt. The side lighting emphasized each muscle in his arms, chest, and abs.

These photos were two of my favorites that I had taken of him that day.

In the other two photos, I was straddling Trent's hips while he sat on the bed. One was with me wearing his shirt. The other was when I had removed it. Trent and I had both asked Luke for copies of the pictures.

"I showed these photos to an editor friend of mine," Danielle explained. "She's involved in a fundraiser for the restoration of an old historic library. They've chosen to target females twenty-four to fifty years old for the fundraiser, and your photos are perfect for it."

"Perfect for what exactly?" I asked.

"A calendar. They're also hoping to include some of the bachelors in an auction."

I blinked. "You want to auction off guys? To do what?"

"To take the highest bidder on a date. You know, dinner and a show. Anyway, my friend recognized Trent Salway. He's touted as one of San Francisco's hot-up-and-coming-under-thirty bachelors."

"And she wants our pictures for the calendar?" I asked slowly, uncertain if I had heard her correctly.

"She wants two of them, and she's hoping he'll agree to participate in the auction. She's positive with his good looks and reputation of being quite the bachelor, the fundraiser will be a great success."

I glanced at the photos then at Luke, before looking back at Danielle. "But what does this have to do with Luke?"

"They want to include one of his as well as one of yours." Seeing my puzzled frown, she explained. "Females love romance. They love the idea of meeting that perfect guy who knows how to make a woman swoon. And there's definitely swooning going on in this photo."

Had to agree with her there, even if it was me in the picture.

"Luke told me that he never got a model-release form from

the two of you"—she casted him a shame-on-you look—"and we need it before they can proceed. Also, she was wondering if you could bring up the auction with Trent. Or she can do it if you'd prefer."

Several thoughts zinged through my head. "What if he's dating someone? Doesn't that make him ineligible for the auction?"

Or did friends with benefits not count?

"Unless you know something my friend doesn't, he's very much single. And it's for a great cause. The women's group wants to convert the building into a spa for women dealing with cancer."

"But what if he is dating someone?" Luke asked, echoing my earlier question, casting me a sidelong glance. A quiet kind of excitement rolled off him. He wanted this opportunity, but he also knew that Trent and I were involved. For the most part. He didn't know Trent and I were just friends with added perks.

"In that case he wouldn't be eligible to participate," Danielle explained, "which would be a great shame. I can guarantee his participation will help raise the money required to finish the project, and to prevent a valuable landmark from being destroyed." She smiled at me. "And they wouldn't be the only ones to benefit. You would both get full credit on the calendar. That will be a huge advantage if you're planning to do any freelance photography."

"All right, I'll ask him," I said, and Luke released a relieved breath. Given that Trent's aunt had died of cancer, I couldn't see Trent turning down the opportunity to help women going through what she had endured.

And like Danielle had said, Trent was a bachelor. Our relationship didn't change that. I was just the woman he was having sex with—nothing more. Thanks to those bitches of girlfriends past, Trent was unable to trust another woman, and without that trust he'd never be able to love me like I loved him.

We never had a chance for a happily-ever-after. Together.

As I walked from my car to the coffee shop, my cell phone pinged.

> Holly: Have you told Erin yet about you and
> Trent?

No, I mentally texted back. It wasn't like I even knew how to bring it up with Erin. "Hey, I just thought you'd like to know that I'm screwing around with your brother." Or, "Guess who I'm in love with? That's right, your brother Trent." There wasn't an easy way to tell her. Stress when you were pregnant was never a good thing.

I know, that was a coward's excuse—but it worked for me.

I entered the coffee shop and scanned the tables. Owen was already sitting at one by the window, with a cup of coffee waiting for me. He was dressed in a grey suit, looking great as he always did. But those fluttery feelings I got whenever I saw Trent in a suit? Zilch, nada, zip when it came to Owen. And now that I thought about it, they never really had existed.

As I approached, he glanced up from his phone and smiled.

Smiling back, I sat down. "Thanks for the coffee."

"You're welcome. And thanks for meeting up with me. I've missed you, Kelsey."

Okay. Not quite what I was expecting.

"I've missed you too, Owen. You were once one of my best friends."

He nodded. "You were mine too."

They say distance makes the heart grow fonder, but I wasn't sure that was true in our case. The love I had once felt for him had long since faded. I loved him, but it was a different kind of love now.

"So what was it you wanted to ask me?"

He took a sip of his coffee. "The wife of one of the senior partners organized a black-tie charity event. I'm expected to attend and show my support. But I need a date for the event, and I'd rather go with you than have to ask someone else."

I clasped my hand to my chest, and in a faked Southern drawl said, "Oh, Owen, you always did know how to sweep a woman off her feet."

"Always the funny girl," he said dryly.

I giggled. "And that's why you miss me...so when is it?"

"May 3rd."

In two weeks. "All right. I can do that."

He fidgeted with his cup.

Owen never fidgeted with anything.

"There's one other thing. I never told anyone at the firm that we're no longer engaged." He flashed me a sheepish grin.

I blinked. "Come again?"

"They're expecting to see you...as my fiancée."

I blinked again, positive I'd misheard him both times. *Who went around pretending they were still engaged when they weren't?*

"Can't wait to hear this explanation," I said, barely holding back a laugh. With Owen, it was bound to be good.

He was a lawyer after all.

"The day you dumped me, one of the guys who was also trying to make partner announced his wife was leaving him. He was a mess, and I overheard one of the senior partners grumble, 'God forbid the next person who announces he was dumped'..."

"So you decided not to tell them about us," I finished for him, somewhat not surprised.

"I figured there was no point in saying anything. Besides, everyone would eventually come to the conclusion on their own, and by then it wouldn't matter. But..."

"But what?"

"But then one of the wives of the senior partners decided to set the poor sap up on numerous dates. Really bad dates with her friends' scary granddaughters. And let's just say I want to avoid that."

I laughed, knowing how that went.

The corner of his mouth twitched up. "Glad you find that so amusing."

I pressed my lips together, attempting to stop the giggles now plaguing me. "I'm sorry." It probably would've sounded more sincere if I hadn't burst out laughing again.

"She'll be at the event," he said once I was finally able to stop laughing, "and I just want to avoid that insanity while I'm there."

"Which is why you need my help?"

He nodded.

"Sure, why not?" It could be entertaining, especially if I got to meet Erin's alter ego at work. "But you will have to tell them the truth, Owen. I can't keep pretending to be your fiancée."

That was right. I had officially joined the hypocrites' club.

New members always welcome.

"I will," he said. "I promise. After the event."

We talked for a while, catching up on our lives. I told him about my photography and he said he would love to see it sometime. The only things I didn't mention were Trent and the calendar.

"You really have changed, Kelsey."

The corner of my lips quirked up to one side. "Is that a good or bad thing?"

"Definitely a good thing. It's been awhile since I've seen you this excited about anything beyond your job. I need to take a lesson from you sometime."

Since he had to return to his office, we stood up and he hugged me. The gesture felt like thick socks on a cold winter night. Nice, comfortable, but nothing beyond that. It was nothing like hugging someone you loved so much, you could barely breathe. That was more like hot chocolate—with a splash of Bailey's and mounds of whipping cream.

Owen kissed my cheek, nothing more than a friendly peck. I pulled away and turned to leave—and was met by a pair of warm green eyes.

35

TRENT

Kelsey's dickwad ex-fiancé kept talking to her, oblivious that she wasn't listening to him.

He must have said something that grabbed her attention because she looked at him again, smiled, then walked toward me, her smile grander than the one she had just given him.

And something stirred inside me. Not jealousy. Fear.

Fear that I would be the next guy she dumped for being a workaholic. Some women attracted the bad-boy type; she attracted workaholics.

Except that wasn't the life she wanted anymore.

"Hey, what are you doing here?" she asked.

"Getting some coffee and fresh air before returning to the office. What about you?" She was the last person I expected to see here, since the hospital where she worked wasn't nearby.

"Owen wanted to tell me something. But I have something more exciting to tell you," she said as we joined the line for coffee. She removed a business card from her purse and handed it to me. "This woman wants to talk to you about a charity she's involved with. My photography instructor showed her the photos Luke and I took of you, and she wants to use them in a hottest-bachelors-in-San-Francisco type calendar. There's also an auction she would like you to participate in. You know, a chance for you to strut that sexy ass of yours and raise money to help women dealing with cancer." The way she was grinning, you'd think she had just won the lottery. Not the fifty million dollar one, mind you.

My body went cold at her words. I had trusted her when she said no one would see those photos. If they had been leaked, it could have damaged my hard earned reputation in the industry. What the hell was she thinking?

"Thanks, but no thanks. Being sold at an auction isn't my thing. Anyway, I've been thinking," I said, knowing that it was time for me to end what Kelsey and I had before I made another goddamn mistake, like I had with my previous girl-friends. "Things are getting really busy at work now. So I think it's time we end our fuck-buddy arrangement. I don't have time for it anymore." I didn't give her a chance to respond. "This is going to take too long." I gestured to the line in front of us, ignoring the couple who was obviously listening to me. "I need to get back to work." I walked away.

Kelsey didn't come after me. Not that I expected her to. Like her ex, I was picking work over her. Only unlike in her ex's case, I wasn't doing it because I wanted to become partner. Work was my safe place—when it came to my heart.

But instead of going back to work, I drove to my apartment building, doing my best not to think about Kelsey. Doing my best not to think about all the times we'd made love. Doing my best not to think about the fun I'd had with her over the past few months.

The elevator pinged open and I trudged down the hallway to my apartment. Inside, I tossed my keys on the table by the door. And for once the emptiness in my life reached up and slapped me. No one was here to greet me and ask me how my day had been. No one was here for me to wrap my arms around. No one was here for me to throw on the bed and make love to.

My life was empty and meaningless.

Melodramatic thoughts and I headed to my bedroom, where I changed into my workout gear. Josh wasn't here to challenge me, but with the way I was feeling, it didn't really matter. My thoughts would be bringing up the rear, yelling at me to get my ass moving.

And yes, they must have attended SEAL training along with Liam and picked up a thing or two. They rode my ass hard as I ran to the park.

After I finished torturing myself with sprints, I jogged to the outdoor workout center and pushed myself equally hard there. The plan was that by the time I was finished, my body would be so tired I wouldn't have the energy to think about Kelsey.

Now, if only my brain had been in on that plan.

I half-heartedly jogged home, which at this point resembled staggering. After showering, I plunked down on the couch and found the channel I needed—The Food Network. Maybe I could whip up comfort food, like Erin used to do whenever she had boyfriend problems.

Too bad the network hadn't been appraised of my plan ahead of time. Whatever the host was cooking looked good, but I didn't possess any of the ingredients. Same deal with the next episode.

Sighing, I trudged into the kitchen and studied the contents of the fridge. A few minutes later, I had whipped up an omelet, grabbed a fork and a beer (to prevent my man card from being revoked), and returned to the couch in time for the hockey game to begin.

My cell phone rang.

Still watching the TV, I answered it. I didn't even bother to check who was calling.

"Hello, is this Trent Salway?" an unfamiliar woman's voice asked.

"It is."

"Hi, I'm Jodi Mckenzie. Kelsey Quade passed your number on to me. I'm involved in the Albright Heritage Charity event." She went on to explain the charity, what the money would be used for, and about the event. She didn't give me a chance to say anything—and I didn't feel like being an asshole and hanging up on her.

The more she talked, the more I thought about my aunt and how she would have loved to see something like what the charity was organizing. Not the part about auctioning off hot bachelors, although she would have thought that was hilarious. No, she would have loved to see a place where women dealing with cancer could go to be pampered and not feel self-conscious.

"Would you be interested in helping out?" Jodi finally asked.

"Possibly. Can I get back to you about the photos?" It was my body and my choice as to what I did with it, but I needed to ensure Bristol Mathews was okay with it too. Especially since there would be no way to keep what I'd done out of the media... if I said yes.

"Does that mean you'll participate in the auction?"

"That much I can do for sure."

I didn't think it would be an issue.

As long as I wasn't expected to do any sort of erotic dance on stage.

Phone Kelsey and let her know you're participating in the auction.

I ignored the pain-in-the-ass voice in my head, the one that always thought it knew best. It wasn't like Kelsey needed to know. She only needed to know if I decided to participate in the calendar, and Jodi could tell her that.

Call me a coward, but part of my decision not to talk to her had to do with missing her. If I talked to her again, chances were good that I would agree to go back to our fuck-buddy arrangement—and that was only if she would even have me after how I had spoken to her.

Regardless, that arrangement would've just left me screwed.

36

———

KELSEY

Life sucked.

That was my new mantra—ever since Trent walked out of my life, proving once again that I was a failure at love.

Granted it hadn't been true love—not when it had only been one-sided—but the sentiment was the same.

My doorbell rang and I opened the door to let Erin in.

"I still can't believe he convinced you to pretend you two are engaged," she immediately said, without even a "hi." The plus side of Trent's and my breakup was that now I didn't have to tell Erin. She never had to learn the truth—that I had ignored her my-friends-aren't-allowed-to-be-involved-with-my-brother rule.

I sighed and followed her to the kitchen. We'd already gone through this a few times about Owen. But at least she had finally gotten past the part where I was attending the event with him. "I'm helping him because he needed someone to go with tonight and save him from the meddling matchmaker," I reminded her.

Her eyebrows pinched together in a dubious frown. "So

there's no way he'll be able to convince you to give him a second chance?"

"I promise there's nothing he could ever say to convince me to change my mind. And I don't think he would even try. He's long since over me." That was part of the reason our relationship fizzled. I suspected he had been "over me" while we had been engaged, but had been too busy to admit it to himself.

"So you're okay with him pretending you're still engaged?"

"It's not a big deal. He's already promised that he'll tell them the truth."

Erin gestured for me to sit at the kitchen table and began searching through my beauty supplies. "When? Right after you two have your fake wedding? Right after you return from your fake honeymoon? Or when you announce your fake pregnancy?"

I snickered. "He's not expecting me to fake a pregnancy."

"How can you be so sure?"

I shrugged. "Because I trust him."

"Like you trusted him to tell everyone the truth after you called off the engagement?"

Point taken. "He knows this is a one-time thing."

"Well, for his sake I hope you're right. I still don't get why you agreed to be his date to begin with."

Because I thought it would help take my mind off the man I was in love with but couldn't have. "Because he's still my friend. And because I'm the idiot who has a hard time saying no." Or else I wouldn't have let Erin hook me up with the Viking and the speed fucker to begin with.

She laughed and picked up the straightening iron. "So what is this event tonight anyway?"

"He had no idea. All he could tell me was that it's some big black-tie charity event."

Erin made a sound that was somewhere between a huff and

a grunt. "Sure, he finally takes you to a black-tie event when you're no longer actually engaged to him."

She had a point, but I didn't want to go there. I was looking forward to tonight. It was a huge step up from my typical evening entertainment—pining for Trent.

Once my hair was straightened, Erin got to work on my makeup. By the time she was finished, I didn't recognize myself. My blue eyes smoldered, like a model straight out of Vogue, but Erin had kept my lips light with a shell-pink lipstick. A little overdone for my yoga pants and tank top—perfect for my gown.

I scooted upstairs to get dressed.

The floor length, nude-colored dress skimmed my body to a few inches below my hips, then gently flared to the floor. Overtop, black netting let the nude underlay peek through, interrupted only by the large black floral designs. My breasts pushed against the fabric of the low neckline, held up by spaghetti straps. My girls were cleverly hidden or highlighted—depending on your view of things—under the elaborate design of black lace and sequins.

I finished the look off with three simple black bracelets that shimmered in the light. Overall, I was a combination of sexy and glamorous. I just hoped it wasn't too over-the-top for my fake date with Owen.

The bedroom door opened and Erin entered my room—looking like she had just seen Santa in a speedo. In her hand was a five-by-seven piece of thin card.

"You okay?" I asked.

She sunk onto my bed. "When were you going to tell me?"

I shook my head, baffled at what she was talking about. And that's when my gaze dropped to the card in her hand. Only it wasn't a piece of card. It was a photo.

Of me.

And Trent.

In a very intimate position.

Oh crap!

"Where did you get that?" I whispered, even though I knew exactly where she had found it.

The corner of her mouth curled up, not quite a smirk, but definitely headed in that direction. "In the magazine where you left it."

"It's not what you think." Okay, it totally was. "Trent was helping me out with a photography assignment."

She glanced down at the picture. "Riiiight. So who was taking the actual photo?"

The words "The Easter Bunny?" hung heavy in the air.

"Luke. A classmate. He took photos of Trent and me together for our photography assignment. Then he left and I took photos of Trent."

"Really? 'Cause it doesn't look like you were modeling for an assignment."

I snorted a laugh. "So what *does* it look like?"

"It looks like you and my brother posed for boudoir photos, like Darren and I did last year."

I'd seen those photos. She had shown them to me when she had gotten the prints. Until now, I'd forgotten about them. "Why would we be posing for boudoir photos like you guys did? We're not married."

Erin's eyes widened, fear and shock taking up residence there. "You're dating?"

"Definitely not," I said a little too fast.

"Good, because the last thing I need is another incident." "Incident" was Erin's code word for Michaela.

I quickly shook my head, but there must have been something on my face that gave me away, because her mouth dropped open, forming a perfect O. "Shit. It is like *her* all over again."

"It's nothing like Michaela."

There are moments in your life when you wish you could yank back the words you just said. They are the ones spoken in haste...sometimes misinterpreted, other times not.

They're the ones that shift your world on its axis.

And never in a good way.

Did you spot my mistake? I can guarantee Erin did. Her expression said it all—"traitor" taking up the number one position.

"You promised me," she said, her voice a pained whisper, her gaze locked on the photo in her hand. "How long has this been going on between you two?" Her gaze snapped up to me and her eyes narrowed. "And what about Jillian and Matt? Are you and Trent cheating on them behind their backs? Or did this happen before you met them?"

Busted. The word might as well have slapped me in the face. The truth of it hurt just as much.

"There is no Jillian and Matt," I said, my chest feeling like I was caught in a giant bear hug by my great Aunt Wilma, had she still been alive. The kind of hug that slowly squeezed all the air out of your lungs, leaving you unable to do much more than squeak. "Well, that's not entirely true. They exist. But they're married."

I didn't think Erin could have looked more confused than she did at that moment.

"They're both actors," I explained. "Trent knows Matt from college."

"But why? Why did you tell us that you were dating them? And why did you bring them to Napa with you?"

"Because it seemed like a good idea at the time." I sat next to Erin on the bed. "Trent and I weren't officially dating, but we couldn't have you and Holly constantly trying to set me up with other guys. He and I had agreed to be exclusive—"

"Why would you want to be exclusive if you weren't dating? What the hell were you doing?"

I shifted on the bed. When had it become so uncomfortable?

"Oh, God, you were sleeping with my brother?"

I flinched at her hash tone. "It wasn't quite like that, but yeah, I guess so." I swallowed back the Ben-&-Jerry's-sized lump in my throat. The one that had taken up residence since Trent ended things between us—because his job was more important to him than I was.

"Wasn't?" Erin asked. "As in past tense?"

I nodded, unable to look at her, and the tightening in my chest tightened some more.

"Please tell me you didn't fall in love with him." When I didn't reply, she powered on, "This is exactly why I didn't want any of my friends becoming involved with him. He doesn't do love, Kelsey. The only thing he's capable of loving beyond his family is his job."

I nodded again, tears leaking from my eyes. Stupid, traitorous tears. "I know." I wiped them away.

Erin threw her arms around me and hugged me tight. "I'm so sorry. But don't worry. I'm personally going to kill him. And once I'm finished with him, Liam will go Navy SEAL on him for ignoring the best-friend code."

"Best-friend code?"

"Yes, the one that prevents guys from screwing their best friend's little sister." So, pretty much the same one that Erin had for me when it came to screwing her big brother.

"That's not going to happen," I said with a groan.

"How can you be so sure?"

"Because Liam won't find out what happened, because there's nothing to find out. Trent ended things with me."

Time for a change of topic. Thinking about Trent was causing my heart to sing cheesy '80s love songs—especially those by Debbie Gibson (something mom had played a lot of while I was growing up). The last thing I needed was for "Lost in Your Eyes" to play on repeat mode in my head while at the charity event.

I smoothed the front of my dress with my hands. "How do I look?"

Erin wiped her thumb under my eyes, no doubt fixing the makeup I'd just ruined with my tears. "That's better." She smiled, the gesture genuine. "You look amazing."

Then she let out a long slow breath. "So tell me about this." She handed me the photo and I told her everything that had led to the last time I'd seen Trent—the modeling, the photos, the charity event, and the calendar.

Once I was finished, her face brightened. "Can I see the other photos?"

"Are you sure you want to see them?"

"Why wouldn't I? I mean unless Trent's naked? In that case, I'll pass, thanks."

I laughed. "No, he's definitely not naked." I grabbed my laptop from my desk, started it up, and showed her the photos I had taken of Trent.

"Wow, you did this?"

I nodded.

"That's amazing. No wonder they wanted it for the calendar. Women would be willing to drop their panties to see it." She made a face at the thought, given that we were talking about her brother.

I then showed her the another photo that Luke had taken of Trent and me together, my naked breasts pressed against Trent's chest.

Her mouth opened and she gawked at the photo. "Ohmigod, this is seriously *hot*. You guys are seriously hot." She tore her gaze from the laptop and glanced up at me. "And they wanted this for the calendar?"

"Yes."

"And you were okay with that?"

"I wasn't sure at first. But it's not like you can see anything that would cause my grandma to go coffin shopping."

She smirked, but then the one-sided smile faded. "What about your job? What will they say? Or are you hoping they won't see it?"

"They've seen it. I made sure it wouldn't be a problem. I didn't want to risk my job over it."

"Smart move."

"Not that it matters. Trent was against the idea, so no one will see the picture anyway." I shut off the laptop. "So you're okay that I'm in love with your brother?"

Another long exhalation—never a good sign. "To be honest, I don't know. I love you like a sister, Kelsey. I just don't want you getting hurt."

Too late.

Possibly seeing those two words stamped on my face, she hugged me, letting me know it would be all right. At least when it came to her and me. When it came to her and Trent, that was a different topic.

"You don't have to worry about me getting hurt," I said, swallowing back the lie. "Trent doesn't love me, and I never expected him to fall in love with me. I knew better than that. So you can't blame him for what happened. We were very clear at the beginning that there were no strings attached. What we had was just for fun.

"And you don't have to worry about me going all psycho bitch on you," I added. "That's not going to happen. Promise."

She gave me a sad smile. "I know. So when's Prince Charming due to pick you up?"

"Anytime now. I should go downstairs." When Owen didn't forget he had to be somewhere, he was always punctual.

"Okay, I'll be right down. I have to go to the bathroom." She patted her protruding stomach.

Erin joined me downstairs several minutes later, stepping

off the final stair as the doorbell rang. Since she was closer to the front door than I was, she went to open it while I slipped on my stilettos.

"Remember, kids," she said as Owen entered the house, "no coming home late." The corners of her mouth then curled up into a smile. Mischief sparked in her eyes. But whatever it was that she suddenly found amusing was something she didn't care to share with me, and for some reason I was too scared to ask.

"You look great," Owen said, ignoring her and smiling like he had the night we got engaged, "but your outfit's missing something."

I glanced down, trying to figure out what was missing. As far as I could tell, I had everything I needed. I glanced at Erin to see if she knew. She looked as perplexed as I felt.

Owen removed a small box from his pocket and opened it. My engagement ring. I'd recognize it anywhere. It was large and fussy and had never really suited me. "You still have it?"

"I wasn't sure what to do with it," he said, reaching for my left hand.

Before he could touch me, I pulled my hand away and placed it behind my back. "No, first you're going to repeat after me, I, Owen Girard, do solemnly swear..." I nodded for him to repeat it.

He looked at me like I had just inhaled weed...something I might add that I'd never done. Ever.

"I'm not going through with this unless you repeat what I say," I said.

He peered over at Erin, cringed, then repeated my words. I glanced at my best friend but she was smiling innocently.

"...tonight is not a date," I continued, "and Kelsey and I are not really engaged."

He chuckled and repeated the vow.

"I now pronounce you and I not engaged, and that we will

never be married to each other for as long as we shall live." Somehow I managed not to laugh at his amused expression.

The same couldn't be said about Erin. "Maybe I should toss some rice at you two to make it official."

Owen laughed. "Okay, you two have had your fun. Can we go now?"

"All right." I let him slide the ring on my finger.

Erin hugged me. "Have fun tonight." A secretive smile crept on her face as she stepped away, "You look gorgeous."

While Owen drove us to the event, we caught up some more on the past eight months since I'd ended things with him. I did my best not to think about Trent and what he was doing tonight. That wouldn't be fair to Owen.

But tell that to my heart.

37

TRENT

As I turned off the ignition, my cell phone rang. I checked who was calling. It was Erin, not Kelsey. Disappointment clenched my heart in its iron fist.

But what did I expect after how I had reacted the last time I saw Kels? What we'd had between us had been about more than just the sex. We had been friends—and I missed that.

I missed her.

I accepted the call. "What's up?"

"So how's Jillian doing?" she cheerfully asked. Maybe a little too cheerfully.

Was I worried?

A tad bit.

"She's good. Why?"

"I hear she likes threesomes."

I almost dropped my phone at that as I climbed out of my car. But could you blame me? Most men at some point in their lives get turned on at the idea of being in a threesome.

That's just reality.

And no, I've never been in one, in case you were wondering.

288

"Not as far as I know," I replied.

"So you weren't screwing her *and* my best friend while we were in Napa?" There was an edge to her voice that set off alarms in my head. The kind of alarms that blared loudly with bright flashing lights.

She knows.

"How could you hurt my best friend like that? How could you hurt the little sister of *your* best friend?"

"I didn't hurt her." Just the opposite.

It was *my* heart that resembled a basketball that had been driven over by a cement truck. Kelsey's heart was fine.

"Right you didn't. You ripped out her heart and didn't give a damn about it. This is exactly why you should never have gotten involved with her. You don't do commitments, Trent."

"That's not true. I've done commitments. It was the women I've ended up with who turned kicking my heart into an Olympic sport."

Maybe I could introduce them to the gold medalist in speed fucking.

They would make quite the team.

"Why would you think I was the one doing the ripping out of hearts?" I asked. If hope was a food group, there was enough in that simple sentence to feed a hungry family for a week.

A couple walked past me and the woman laughed. Before I could tell Erin she had it all wrong, my sister asked, "Where are you?"

"At The Grand Chelsea hotel. I'm participating in a charity event tonight."

"Charity event? What kind of charity event?" Curiosity dripped off her words more than I would've expected. This wasn't the first charity event I had participated in.

I told Erin about it and she laughed. Not the reaction I was expecting. "Well, have a good time tonight," she said. "And whatever you do, don't screw things up more than you already have. Despite what you might think, and despite what I would like, Kelsey feels the same way about you as I suspect you feel about her."

Before I could ask her what the hell she was talking about, she hung up.

38

KELSEY

Owen and I walked through the plushly-decorated hotel lobby to the ballroom. The large sign, propped on a bronze easel next to the open double doors, left my mouth dropping open in an unattractive way.

THE ALBRIGHT HERITAGE FOUNDATION
CHARITY EVENT AND AUCTION

Holy freaking crap!

I scanned the area. Why? Because Murphy's Law clearly stated: anything that can go wrong for Kelsey will go wrong in triplicate.

Don't believe me? Read the fine print.

Which meant that even though Trent wasn't involved in the calendar and auction, there was nothing stopping him from showing up tonight to lend his monetary support.

And since he wouldn't be part of the calendar and auction, it meant he could bring a date. A drop-dead gorgeous date.

Lucky me.

When I didn't see him, I exhaled a relieved breath and

allowed Owen to guide me to a group of people on the other side of the room, none of whom I recognized.

"The woman in the dark blue dress is the one I was telling you about," he said as we drew closer to them. "She's the one who set the guy up on all those god awful dates."

I hooked my arm through his. "Oh, Pookie, we can't have that." I snickered. God, this was going to be fun. Neither of us did pet names.

"Please tell me you aren't going to call me that in front of everyone."

"But, Pookie, how will we ever convince them that we're madly in love if I don't call you that?"

"You're enjoying this, aren't you?"

"Yep. And that's what you get for not telling everyone the truth."

And the kettle and the pot live happily ever after, as friends.

"What a beautiful gown," the gray-haired woman in the navy dress said as we joined the group. A warm smile spread on her face, making me instantly like her. Her dress was modest and elegant, and the perfect backdrop for the large diamonds that adorned her ears, neck, wrist, and fingers. I swear, the woman was a walking ad for Tiffany's.

"Thank you," I replied, smiling back at her. Contrary to what Owen had told me, she seemed perfectly harmless.

Stepping closer to me, Owen placed his hand to my lower back. "I'd like to introduce you to my fiancée, Kelsey Quade." He gave me those adoring eyes that I hadn't seen in what felt like a hundred years—and my stomach turned into a concrete block.

But not because it was Owen giving me those adoring eyes. It was because they didn't belong to Trent.

Except I *had* seen them before on Trent—when we were posing for the photos.

He was just acting for the camera, I told myself.

That's right, because Trent's a talented model. If the voice in my head could've rolled its eyes, it would have.

One man in the group, who must have been in his sixties, held out his hand for me to shake. Only instead of shaking it, he lifted my hand to his mouth and kissed it.

The woman laughed, the sound rich like butter. "Watch out my dear. My husband might be old, but he's still quite the flirt."

I smiled genuinely at her as her husband released my hand. "Thanks for the warning."

He laughed deeply and wrapped his arm around her waist. They clearly loved each other. Just like it had been for my parents. Just like it still was for Trent and Erin's parents.

"So when's the big day?" she asked.

"We haven't set a date yet," I said at the same time Owen replied, "later this year."

She looked between us, confused at our answers.

"We haven't set a date yet," Owen smoothly said, proving why he was a talented lawyer, "but I was thinking fall is a great time for a wedding due to the beautiful fall colors."

I almost snorted a laugh at that. He must have heard his sister say that when she had been planning her wedding a few years ago.

"Well, you'll have to let us know once you've picked the date," she said. "But don't wait too long. The best locations and services book up well in advance."

We both just nodded, ready to move the topic to an easier one.

Like solving global warming.

A murmur of excited voices near our group captured my attention. I turned to see what had caused it, and was met by the gaze of five college-aged girls, all gorgeous and wearing designer gowns.

A girl in a silver gown, which had been practically painted on, glided in our direction. Her friends followed. "We just want to know if this is you." She held what looked like a calendar with Trent on the cover.

By some large miracle I kept my mouth from flopping open. Oh. Wow. Why didn't I know about this?

She flipped the pages and held the calendar up again for me—and everyone in Owen's group—to see.

"Oh, my," a woman behind me said.

"Oh, my" was right. The girl in the silver dress was holding up a picture of me and Trent, with my naked breasts pressed against his equally naked chest. Despite how we were posed, the woman in the picture was clearly me.

Oh. Fuckity. Shit.

Next to me, Owen stiffened. He'd never even received a heads up about the photo. I hadn't seen the point of telling him, not when I believed no one would see them—and certainly not at the event he had invited me to.

"Am I right?" the girl asked. "Is this you?"

For a second I thought about claiming the woman in the photo was my twin.

That was plausible.

If I had a twin.

But before I could say the words, my body betrayed me and I nodded instead.

"Can you sign it for me?"

"You...you want me to sign it?"

"Well, yes. Trent signed it. All the men in the calendar signed their pictures." She held it out for me and my brain finally got its crap together. I took it from her and flipped through the calendar. It contained the hottest bachelors in the San Francisco area, but only Trent was half naked in his pictures. The other men were fully clothed.

Trent's half-dressed state wasn't the only thing that made his picture unique from the other months in the calendar. His photo was the only one with a woman in it.

The girl handed me a Sharpie, and I signed the picture for her, my face heating at the memory of that day...and at being asked to actually sign the picture. The moment I handed it back to her, four other calendars were shoved under my nose.

"Is he your boyfriend?" one girl asked, but she wasn't looking at Owen. She was referring to Trent.

"Of course not," another girl said, rather sharply. "He wouldn't be in the calendar and auction if he had a girlfriend or wife. That's why he's a *ba-che-lor*."

The first girl rolled her eyes, no doubt used to the other girl's attitude. All were too busy to notice my heart had stopped beating at the news that Trent was part of the auction.

"So how come you're in the picture with him?" The girl in the silver dress sighed, as if wishing herself into the photo instead of me.

And right now, I was wishing the same.

"I was helping out a friend," I simply said. "He needed someone to pose for the picture and...and I did." I didn't dare turn around to confirm what I already suspected: the horrified expressions on everyone's faces, especially Owen's.

"I love the picture," she said, "but I love the one on the front even more." The one in which Trent wore low-rise jeans and the white dress shirt, but the shirt was unbuttoned, revealing his taut abs and pecs. He had a come-fuck-me look on his face that made anyone with ovaries swoon.

I grinned. "Thanks."

The girls looked at me like I was crazy. It took me a second to piece together why. "I'm the photographer," I explained.

The calendar was yanked from the girl's hand. She scowled at the thief. "Hey, that's mine!"

The woman studying the cover held up her hand to silence her. "You're extremely talented, Kelsey. I would love to see your portfolio sometime."

"I've only just started doing this. I don't have much of a portfolio."

She removed a business card from her purse and passed it to me. I read it and almost fainted. Jennifer Ashton, CEO of Ashton Crawford Inc.

"You work for an ad agency?" I knew the name. It was a rival agency to where Erin worked, with an impressive clientele.

"Yes. We're always on the lookout for photographers and good stock photos. I'd love to meet you for lunch sometime to talk more about the opportunities available, if you're interested."

"I'd love that, but I also work full-time as a physical therapist at the children's hospital."

That seemed to impress her as much as my photo. "I'm sure we can figure something out."

I thanked her, but didn't get to say much more. An older woman in a burgundy gown walked over and practically kidnapped her from the group.

"I already know which bachelor I'm bidding on," a dark-haired woman not much older than me said as she walked past with her friend, reminding me there was a lot more to this event than the calendar and dinner.

The bachelor auction was still to come.

Which meant having to watch another woman win a date with Trent. I wouldn't be the one spending time with him, something I painfully missed.

The dark-haired woman and her friend stopped close enough to us that I could still hear them.

"Which one?" her friend asked.

"Trent Salway. And I'm prepared to outbid everyone."

Her friend laughed. "Why am I not surprised?"

"Because you know I always get what I want." A greedy smile spread across the dark-haired woman's face. With her long silky hair, light olive skin, and bright green eyes, she was both breathtaking and exotic. "And I definitely want him." *Permanently* was what her expression implied.

"I don't blame you. I'd bid for him too if I knew I had a chance to win against you."

"Kelsey," Owen said, dragging my attention away from the two women. "Can I talk to you for a moment?"

"Sure."

Owen excused us and we left to find a quiet spot down an empty hallway.

"I guess I've got some explaining to do," I said, no longer holding onto his arm. Now that we were away from everyone, we could temporarily drop the act.

He rubbed the back of his neck. "Wow, now I'm engaged to a porn star." His eyes sparkled with amusement, something I hadn't seen in years.

"Ha, ha! I wouldn't go that far. But I am sorry I didn't warn you ahead of time. I didn't know the picture had made it into the calendar until I saw it back there."

"Hey, don't worry about it. I'm proud of you for what you've accomplished." He pulled me in for a friendly, heartfelt hug. "Granted, I wish it were me in the photo, but that was my fault for not realizing what I had until it was too late. I just hope the next guy in your life realizes that before it's too late for him."

I wished that too.

But wishing was best saved for birthday cakes, water fountains, and shooting stars.

I opened my purse and fished around for a quarter.

"What are you doing?" Owen asked as I pulled one out.

"I'll meet you back in the ballroom," I said, already walking away toward the front entrance—and the water fountain.

39

KELSEY

The majestic fountain sat in the courtyard in front of the hotel. At this time of night it was lit up, the coins in the water glinting like lost treasure. In the center, on top of the massive stone base, stood a statue of a young woman dressed in a bed sheet.

Legend claimed that if you threw two coins into the Trevi Fountain in Rome, you would find romance with a Roman. Three coins ensured marriage to him. But since this was San Francisco and not Rome, and I was in love with Trent (who definitely wasn't Roman), I tossed my single coin in and hoped for the best.

Truthfully I knew nothing would happen—but it was the thought that counted, right?

With a sigh (and a quick check for a random shooting star), I returned to the ballroom.

In time.

To see.

Trent walking onstage.

In a tux.

They say when you're in a life-and-death situation, your life flashes in front you. I couldn't say if that was true since I wasn't dying, but my mind was definitely revisiting my past. Except all of the flashbacks were Trent oriented. The first time he helped me with my math homework, and I thought he was the smartest boy alive. Even smarter than my brother. The first time he helped me with the flat tire on my bike. And the second and third time. The first time he was there for me when I fell off my bike and broke my leg. The first time we went to see a movie together, along with Liam and Erin.

The first time I fell in love with him.

What they fail to mention when it comes to these life-flashing-in-front-of-you situations is that walking during them is never recommended.

Especially when a waiter is standing in your way.

Drinks went flying. Glass shattered. Everyone looked at us.

With heat flooding my face, I bent down to help him. "I'm so sorry."

"Not a problem," he said, picking up the broken glass and placing it on his tray. "And don't worry, I've got this. You should go back to your seat. They're starting the bidding soon."

At this point I would've rather climbed into a hole and hid for the rest of the evening. But since that wasn't an option, I stood up and my gaze automatically went to the stage.

Big mistake.

At the sight of Trent, the heat in my face decided it would be better served rushing to between my legs.

Somewhere in the back of my head a desperate voice urged me to keep walking...to my seat. But I couldn't. Trent was watching me and both my heart and my legs had stopped functioning.

Just when I was beginning to think they'd have to rush in a crash cart to restart it, my heart got over the initial shock of seeing him and performed a happy dance.

My body joined the party. Both ignored the memo that my

brain was attempting to send them—the memo pointing out that I needed to move on, both literally and figuratively.

"Ladies and gentlemen...well, especially the ladies. Are you ready for the auction to begin?" Jodi said into the microphone, and the spell Trent had on me was instantly broken.

As I walked over to where Owen and his colleagues sat, the applause at her announcement was deafening. But no more so than from the table next to us, where the woman who planned to outbid everyone when it came to Trent sat.

I took my seat, relieved no one was paying attention to me anymore.

"Are you okay?" Owen asked. I nodded, unable to pull my gaze away from the stage, where twelve men stood in a line, facing the audience.

Did you see who was third in line? That's right. The Viking. Too bad the woman who was after Trent didn't want to jump his bones instead.

I would've been fully on board with that.

I was vaguely aware of Owen talking to me, but don't quiz me on what he said. All I could do was stare at Trent—and try not to imagine my hungry mouth against his, my naked body against his, my tongue tasting everything he had to offer.

Yes, I was seriously screwed.

But it wasn't like I could bid on him. Even if I hadn't been pretending to be Owen's fiancée, I didn't have enough money in my bank account to outbid Miss Eager-to-Get-into-Trent's-Pants, who was currently drooling on the table in front of her.

Plus, there was the part about how Trent had made it clear that he didn't feel the same way about me as I felt about him.

"Kelsey? Are you okay?" Alice, the grey-haired matchmaker, asked while Jodi talked about the charity and the event, and what the money would be used for.

I nodded slowly, my eyes still on Trent.

I glanced at Miss Eager-to-Get-into-Trent's-Pants, and my

heart squeezed hard. All I could think about was the photo in the calendar of Trent and myself, but instead of it being me, it was her.

She licked her lips, and my heart beat harder and louder and minus the big girl panties.

Jodi finished explaining the rules of the auction, then introduced the first man. January. Eventually she got to Trent. Needing something else to focus on instead of on him, I sipped my white wine.

"Trent Salway is one of the hottest and brightest up-and-coming mutual fund portfolio managers on the west coast. His latest hobby involves cooking up something sweet for that special woman."

And my mind instantly landed in the gutter, remembering a few times we'd had sex in his kitchen.

On the counter.

On the floor.

Against the stainless-steel refrigerator.

Damn traitorous mind.

All the men—except for January—walked off stage. January stepped up to the microphone and described what his date would entail. "We'll go out for dinner and a show at Marrakech Magic Theater."

A collective sigh came from the tables behind me.

The professional auctioneer who had volunteered to help with the event stepped to the podium. "Let's start the bidding at a hundred dollars. Do we have a hundred dollars?" he rapidly fired.

About twenty hands went up.

And so began the auction. By the time it got to November (Trent), the winning bids ranged between three to seven hundred dollars, depending on the man and the prize.

October went for six hundred and eighty dollars. Slightly less than the Viking, but way more than I could afford for a date, especially if the guy turned out to be a self-absorbed bore.

"Next up we have November," Jodi announced. Miss Eager-to-Get-into-Trent's-Pants was practically panting—and I frowned. Something about her made me uneasy.

"Because you know I always get what I want."

Trent walked to the microphone. He was typically a man of confidence, which was why he excelled at his job. He had to be confident with his choices or else he might make foolish errors. But as his gaze settled on me, I realized the usually confident man had uncertainty sitting on his shoulder—and I couldn't figure out why.

"The date will begin with a hike in Muir Woods," he said, gaze still on me.

With a perplexed frown on her face, Jodi glanced down at her notes, then flipped the index card over.

"We'll have a picnic at the spot by the stream where I first realized I was falling in love...with the place." Trent's gaze remained locked on my face. It was the same spot we had stopped for lunch when we had gone hiking together a month ago.

Oh, God, was I reading too much into this...or did he feel the same way about me as I felt about him? Owen said something but I didn't hear him past the pounding in my ears, the blood rushing to my heart.

I must have made a noise because Alice turned to look at me. She then looked at Owen and I could tell the wheels were turning in her head, but in the wrong direction. Oh crap! She had no idea that Owen's and my engagement was fake. To her I was the fiancée who was interested in the wrong man. The man she had posed practically naked with for the calendar. She had no idea about my long history with Trent or how I knew him.

"He's my brother's best friend and the brother of *my* best friend," I told her, as if that explained everything. Trent was describing the next part of the date, which included dinner at my favorite restaurant and stargazing. There might have also been something about going on a sunset cruise.

She nodded and smiled knowingly. "He's very good-looking."

"He is. But he's also an amazing friend and brother. He'll do anything for the people he loves."

Note to self: No more dreamy sighs. Best leave that for the women who are allowed to bid on him.

Even if the date was supposed to be mine.

I knew this from the way Trent looked at me and from the way he had planned the date to play out. The hike, the picnic, my favorite restaurant—they were special to me and only me. On top of that, he remembered what I'd told him about stargazing the day we'd hiked in Muir Woods.

The auctioneer took the microphone from Trent. "Let's start the bidding at—"

"A thousand dollars," Miss Eager yelled out. "I bid a thousand dollars." She gave a smug look, expecting no one to outbid her.

Murmurs from the neighboring tables filled the space, along with groans from the women who had planned to bid. A thousand dollars was already higher than they wanted to go.

"I have a bid of one thousand dollars," the auctioneer said. "Do we have one thousand and ten dollars?"

Silence sat heavy in the room, and I willed someone, anyone, to meet the bid. If there had been enough time to run out and throw all my coins into the fountain, I would have.

"Do we have one thousand and ten dollars?...Going once. Going twice."

Before I realized what I was doing, I raised my hand.

"We have one thousand and ten dollars." He indicated toward our table—and everyone sitting at it looked at me with wide eyes. *Brilliant going, Kels.* How was I going to explain this to them when I was supposed to be engaged to Owen? "Do we have one thousand and twenty dollars?"

Miss Eager's hand shot up. I groaned.

"We have one thousand and twenty dollars. Do we have one thousand and thirty dollars?"

Who needed to eat anyway?

Besides the money was going to a great cause. I raised my hand, and almost fell off my chair at the vicious glare Miss Eager leveled at me.

"We have one thousand and thirty dollars. Do we have one thousand and forty dollars?"

"That man," Alice said to me, her voice easily heard by everyone at our table, "he's in love with you...and you're in love with him, am I right?"

I bit the inside of my mouth, keeping the truth from tumbling out.

Was Trent in love with me?

Everything inside me screamed an emphatic "Yes!"

"We have one thousand and forty dollars," the auctioneer continued, which meant Miss Eager had bid again. "Do we have one thousand and fifty dollars?"

A thousand and thirty dollars had been beyond what I could reasonably manage. The new bid was enough to sink the Titanic—if it hadn't already been sunk.

"Do we have one thousand and fifty dollars?" the auctioneer repeated. "Going once. Going twice."

My heart stopped as I waited for him to yell "gone" and slam the gavel down.

"We have a bid for a thousand and fifty dollars." The auctioneer indicated at our table. Huh?

I peered down at my lap. Yep, my hands were still there.

Everyone at our table was gaping at Owen. I looked at him, confusion no doubt plastered on my face.

He gave a quick shrug of his shoulders. "The money goes to a good cause."

"Wait, did you just bid on him?" I said, loud enough that everyone at the table heard me.

"You love him, don't you?" he asked. Everyone at the table continued watching us, their interest at the new turn of events unmistakable.

"I've loved him since high school, but things were too complicated and I didn't think he felt that way about me. But just so you know, I did love you when we were together. At least I did until we grew apart."

Owen smiled. "I know." To the rest of the table, he said, "Kelsey and I were engaged, but she broke up with me last year when she realized we weren't right for each other. I was too much of an idiot to admit the truth to you, and I didn't want you to think I was unable to adequately perform my job because of the breakup."

No one had a chance to respond to his confession. "Sir," the auctioneer said to Owen, "you do understand that Mr. Salway is straight, right?"

Trent looked ready to scratch his head in bewilderment, knowing that Owen was here with me and that he wasn't gay. I nibbled on my lip to keep from laughing at his reaction.

Owen chuckled. "So am I," he called out. "I guess I got caught up in my friend's excitement. But the bid still stands at one thousand and fifty dollars."

"You don't have to do that," I told him.

"Yes, I do. Besides, you don't want her"—he indicated to Miss Eager with a brief nod—"to end up on a date with him, do you?"

His boss laughed. "I think the poor man onstage feels the same way." Everyone else at the table chuckled in agreement.

"Okay, we have one thousand and fifty dollars," the auctioneer said. "Do we have one thousand and sixty dollars?"

Again, Miss Eager's hand shot up.

"Does someone have a belt we can tie her hands to the chair with, so she'll quit bidding?" Alice joked. Or at least I thought she was joking.

"Do we have one thousand and seventy dollars?"

Trent's gaze remained locked on me, as if to tell me how he felt about me. As if willing me to keep bidding and win the prize—him.

"We have one thousand and seventy dollars."

This time it was Owen's boss who had raised his hand. Everyone at the table discreetly pulled money out of their wallets, ready to chip in if the bidding continued.

"Do we have one thousand and eighty?"

Miss Eager was busy conferring with her friends, but none appeared as willing to help her.

"Do we have one thousand and eighty dollars?" the auctioneer asked. "Going once. Going twice. Gone to the...well, gone to table number twenty. Would someone like to come up and claim the prize?"

Laughter filled the ballroom as Owen nudged me to stand. Somehow I managed to walk, legs shaking from the adrenaline rush. Shaking because everyone was watching me again, only this time no bumping into waiters had been involved. Shaking because soon I'd be in Trent's arms—and I didn't think I could wait another second for it to happen.

Before I got past our table, Alice gently grabbed my hand and smiled deviously. "Make sure you kiss that young man when you go onstage. That should infuse some more excitement into this show." She winked at me.

Without glancing back, I made my way past the tables to the stage, silently thanking the fountain—you know, in case it had something to do with this.

At the bottom of the stairs, I lifted my skirt slightly, so not to risk the hem getting caught on my stilettos. With my legs still shaking, I carefully walked up the steps.

Trent was waiting for me at the top, a huge grin on his face. My heart stumbled over itself at the sight of him.

"Hi," was all I managed to say.

His warm green eyes remained on me and my heart practically leapt out of my chest.

"Christ, you're gorgeous, Kels. I'd forgotten just how beautiful you are."

"So are you...I mean you look great."

Trent stepped closer to me, our bodies almost touching. Nothing else but this moment existed. "I'm pretty sure your brother's going to kill me when he returns home, but I love you, Kelsey." His voice was low. The only person who could hear him was me—just the way it should be. "I love everything about you. Your love for your job and the kids you help. Your love of life. Your love of those funny little owls. Your amazing photographs. Your heart. I love it all.

"I know I'm a workaholic, but I promise that will change. I'm hoping you'll give me a chance to prove to you how important you are to me. To prove to you how you mean everything to me."

"I love you too—"

I didn't get a chance to say anything else. Someone repeatedly tapped their wine glass with a fork. The sound of more and more clinking glasses joined the first one, until the room was filled with the musical symphony.

"I think they want us to kiss," I said.

Trent's grin was back. "We probably shouldn't disappoint them."

He cupped my cheek with his hand, his touch igniting a sweet warmth that spread through my body. Then his lips brushed against mine—and I could barely breathe.

My lips parted and I welcomed him in. Welcomed his minty taste. Welcomed his familiar scent.

Welcomed every part of him into my heart—without any reservations or fear.

The thunderous applause filled the room—along with a few whistles that I suspected came from my table.

"I guess I don't need to introduce you two," Jodi said into the mic.

40

———

TRENT

After we paid the "cashier" for the winning bid, we left backstage to return to the ballroom. Although Kelsey had won, I insisted on paying. It was the least I could do.

Did you recognize the woman who had tried to outbid Kelsey? She was Beatrice Peterson, or Reese, as she preferred to go by.

And trust me when I say I owed Kelsey a lot more than a date to thank her—something I had every intention of doing once we could sneak away from the event.

Unable to wait that long, I glanced around the hallway. A few people were milling around, but they were mostly the staff waiting for the auction to finish so they could start serving the food. I grabbed Kelsey's hand and led her in the opposite direction of the ballroom.

"Don't we have to go the other way?" she asked.

"Not for what I have planned."

"What exactly do you have planned?"

Nothing close to what I wanted to do to her once we were

back at my apartment. Fortunately, I was very well acquainted with the hotel.

On the second floor, I pushed open the door to the women's bathroom. Unless you knew where you were going, you could easily miss it. The room was small and elegant, and had a lock on the door.

Very convenient for moments like this.

As soon as the door was locked, my lips crashed against Kelsey's and I kissed her the way I couldn't onstage. There, it had been about making sure people knew she was mine. Now I wanted to prove it to her.

My tongue flicked against hers and every cell in my body hummed with electricity. It had been a very long two weeks without her.

And in case you were wondering, the dream date I'd described onstage hadn't been the one I'd originally planned. The original date had been a five-star dinner cruise around the bay, but the moment I saw Kelsey—the moment I saw how she was looking at me—I knew I had to take a chance and tell her how I felt...in front of everyone.

I had to tell her that I trusted her with all my heart—something I had thought would never be possible after my past relationships.

What I had really wanted to do was tell her that I loved her, everyone be damned. But I couldn't do that because of the charity, as much as I had wanted to. Luckily for me she figured it out on her own.

"The dream date," she said, "you changed it, didn't you? You changed it at the last minute because of me?"

"How did you know?"

She giggled. "Because, one, you threw Jodi for a loop. And two, everything you said and the places you planned to take the winner...well, it was like you had planned the date for me and only for me."

I ran my lips against Kelsey's soft, sweet-smelling jaw. "I wanted to add one more item, but I didn't think the organizers would be too thrilled with what I have planned. Too scandalous." And the last thing I had wanted was to give Beatrice the idea that sex with her was on the table in the event that she won the bidding.

"I'm going to make love to you," I said, my breath against the shell of Kelsey's ear. "That's how our date will end."

She shuddered in my arms. "I'm not sure I can wait that long," she murmured.

"Hmm you might have a point." I certainly couldn't wait that long before tasting her.

Hell, I couldn't even wait until later tonight to taste her.

My mouth was on hers again, and I slowly backed her up until her calves hit the cushioned stool against the far wall. But before I took things further, I needed to know one thing. "Have you been with anyone else since I last saw you?" Her ex-fiancé came to mind.

She shook her head, but it was the truth in her eyes that told me everything I needed to know. "I'm only here with Owen as a favor. There's nothing between him and me and never will be again."

I brushed my lips against her jaw. "For the record, I haven't been with anyone either." I hadn't even been tempted.

Kelsey was the only woman for me.

I ran my hands down her legs to the hem of her dress. Then I traced my fingertips back up, drawing the fabric with me. My cock perked up, eager to join the party.

Once the skirt was bunched around her hips, I told her to sit on the bench. A sexy, confident smile curved onto her lips and she did as I asked.

"You have my favorite thong on." Hell, any pair of panties she owned were my favorites.

I was an equal opportunity type of guy.

It didn't take long before I had them off her and tossed them aside. "Spread your legs." The words rumbled deep in my chest. For two weeks, I'd dreamed about her pussy.

For two weeks, I'd dreamed about nothing but her.

But I guess that doesn't surprise you by now.

"We should be getting back. Everyone's probably wondering where we've disappeared to." Kelsey might have said those words, but they lacked the conviction I needed to stop. I'd been craving this moment since spotting her in the audience.

The corner of my mouth tilted up to one side. "I'm sure they've assumed we've gone off to get reacquainted." I knelt between her legs and pressed my lips to her inner thighs. They traveled along her sweet skin with light kisses—the appetizer before the main course.

And then I found what I had been starving for during the past two weeks. And just like I remembered, she tasted like liquid gold.

I stroked my tongue against her clit, savoring her like fine wine. Once. Twice. A third time. It didn't take long before she was writhing against my mouth and softly moaning.

My cock tried to break free of the restraints of my zipper, less than thrilled that its turn wouldn't be until much later. I slipped a finger inside her...followed by the second one. She groaned the sound she always made when she was close to coming. Her fingers knotted in my hair.

I tormented her for a few more seconds with my fingers and my tongue, then switched things around. My thumb worshipped her clit and my tongue entered her.

It was more than she could take. Her head fell back against the wall as her muscle clenched around my tongue. She let out a soft erotic moan, doing her best to make sure the people in the ballroom on the floor beneath us didn't hear her. The

Kelsey I knew and loved was usually a lot less restrained when it came to noisy sex.

It took her a few moments to recover, and the sight of her with her orgasm-flushed cheeks and drowsy, satisfied eyes almost did me in. My mouth relished the opportunity for one final taste of *her* mouth before I helped her to her feet.

She reached for her thong but I was quicker. I shoved it in the pocket of my tux. "We should go back now before we're missed." I winked and walked to the door before she had a chance to steal the thong from me. If she really insisted, I'd give it back to her later, but for now it would help me get through the night until I had her in my bed again.

Our salads were waiting for us when we returned to the table. Kelsey introduced me to her ex-fiancé's colleagues and his boss.

"Nice to meet you," I said. And yes, I even meant it when I then told Owen that it was good to see him again. How could I not? If he had appreciated what was in front of him when he'd had the chance, I wouldn't be the one sitting here with Kelsey's thong in my tux pocket.

I'd be the poor sap—instead of December—sitting with Beatrice.

Dinner was enjoyable, with Kelsey sitting next to me and knowing that this time she was mine. I wasn't crashing her date. I wasn't hosting a dinner party for our friends while fantasizing that she was mine. And I wasn't sitting on a bed while someone was taking photos of us, when all I wanted to do was make love to her.

She was mine, through and through—and I would happily spend the rest of my life reminding her of that. I would happily spend the rest of my life ensuring that she never had any doubts about how much she meant to me.

She came first.

Always would.

41

KELSEY

Quick. Name the best place in the world to be on a Sunday morning?

Wrong.

It was definitely in bed while snuggling up to Trent—but you'd have to take my word for it.

It was a week after the auction and the sun was streaming cheerfully through my bedroom window. Trent was catching up on the latest news on his iPhone. I was leafing through a photography magazine, a special edition focused solely on portraits. I had contacted Jennifer Ashton this past week, and we had gone out for lunch yesterday to discuss what she was looking for with the upcoming ad campaign she thought I would be perfect for as the photographer.

To say I was nervous was an understatement...but I was also excited for the chance to prove myself.

Without warning, Trent kissed my temple. I smiled sweetly at him. "What was that for?"

" 'Cause you're too sexy for words." The lopsided grin on his face was enough to turn my panties damp, if I had been wearing any. " 'Cause I love kissing you." His mouth grazed

314

against mine. "And 'cause I love how I can now do that whenever and wherever I want. I love how I no longer have to hide how I feel about you."

This time the kiss wasn't just a soft brush of lips. This time it was possessive, hungry.

Divine.

When he finally pulled back, my breath had long since been stolen away. But that was okay. It wasn't like I needed oxygen anyway. The man I loved was next to me, the man who had already shown me that I was the center of his universe and always would be.

"We're not completely there yet," I said. "Erin might be okay about us"—which only came about after Trent promised he would never do anything to hurt me, and she was welcome to cut off his balls if he did. And I had promised never to be a reincarnate of She-Who-Shall-Not-Be-Named—"but I still have to tell Liam."

You know how you're not supposed to break up with someone via text? Well, it's also not recommended you tell your brother that you're sleeping with his best friend the same way. I mean, sure for Trent's own safety it would probably be better if I told Liam the truth via text. It would be a lot harder to physically hurt his best friend that way, unless he called in favors from his SEAL brothers. Some were reported to be the best snipers around—unfortunately for Trent.

"When are you planning to do that?" he asked.

"As soon as he returns home." And by "home" I meant when he came back to San Francisco to visit us. As it was, I still had no idea when he was returning to the US. I hadn't heard from him in the past twenty-four hours, and before that he'd promised me it wouldn't be much longer.

"He's going to kill me, isn't he?" Trent said, only half joking.

"He'll be fine once he realizes how much I love you." I tossed the photography magazine over the side of the bed and grabbed the back of his neck. I pulled his head closer to mine, and reminded him once again with actions and not just words how much I loved him.

Vaguely, in the back of my head, I heard the bedroom door click open. But kissing Trent and feeling his hardening length against my stomach took precedence over paying attention to the sound.

"What the fuck, Salway?"

At the sound of one very pissed off brother, I squeaked like a mouse who had been caught in the expensive cheese. Trent muttered a curse and jerked back. But to my immediate relief, he didn't move completely away, his naked body shielding mine from my brother. The sheet had pulled away, revealing my breasts, when Trent had moved to kiss me. Despite the tense situation, I imagined Liam was also thankful that Trent's body was shielding mine—the only thing he was thankful for.

Although I was positive he would've been happier if Trent's sexy ass wasn't mooning him.

I yanked the sheet up, covering Trent's assets and myself. "Why didn't you tell me you were coming home?" I asked, my voice little more than a whisper. Under normal circumstances I would've rushed over to hug my brother because he was safe and back in the States. Under normal circumstances I wouldn't have been naked and in bed with his best friend.

Oops.

Instead of answering me, Liam glared at Trent, who had carefully shifted away from me, his back no longer to my brother. Smart move.

"What the fuck, Salway?" Liam repeated. "I asked you to keep an eye on Kelsey. I didn't ask you to fuck her."

I flinched at the anger in his tone. And I was positive the hard-of-hearing eighty-five-year-old woman down the street also flinched at it.

"I wasn't fucking her, as you so crudely put it," Trent said, his voice holding the same sharp edge as Liam's, but with the volume at a more reasonable level.

"That's because I interrupted you before you could. Now get out of my sister's bed." Liam didn't even glance in my direction.

"It's not what you think, Liam…" I hurriedly pointed out, and his gaze finally swung to me.

"Does your best friend know you're sleeping with her brother?" he asked before I could tell him exactly what was going on between Trent and me.

I nodded. "She also knows I'm in love with him," I said in what I hoped was a calming voice.

Shock flashed on Liam's face, quickly replaced by a scowl. He turned that scowl on Trent.

"And I'm in love with your sister," Trent said and gazed down at me, his gorgeous green eyes full of love and warmth. "Have been for a while now."

I smiled at him, my brother momentarily forgotten, and cupped my hand against his cheek, his weekend scruff rough against my fingers. As if pulled together by an unknown force, we started leaning toward each other.

"Why is this the first I'm hearing that?" Liam grumbled.

Trent turned his head to my brother. "Because I didn't know Kelsey felt the same way. Because I knew you would pulverize me for feeling that way." Trent's body shifted, the tension in his muscles still there. "Look, I know you're pissed off and you have every right to be. But can we continue this discussion downstairs, once Kelsey and I are dressed?"

Liam looked like he was about to argue, his mouth open.

"Please, Liam," I said, softly.

What was the best way to approach an angry beast? Correct. Cautiously. Never move too quickly and always speak in a soothing tone.

Hopefully that also worked with an angry Navy SEAL.

"Wait, how did you get in?" I asked. "I thought you gave Trent your key." *Or did I forget to lock the door last night?*

"I did. But I had a duplicate made just in case. I'll wait for you downstairs." The don't-even-think-of-fucking-my-sister-once-I've-left-this-room look he threw Trent said it all. With that, he stalked out, not bothering to shut the door behind him.

Well, that didn't go down the way I had hoped.

"Maybe I should work on the eulogy I want you to read at my funeral on my behalf," Trent said, his warm breath stroking my ear. Even when faced with certain death, he still sounded sexy, he still turned me on.

So I did the only thing I could do—I elbowed him in the gut.

"*Oof!*"

"Sorry," I said. "Didn't mean to do that so hard." Which was the truth at least. "What are we gonna do?"

He chuckled. "Guess it's too late for me to climb out of the window, huh?"

"I wouldn't be surprised if he's waiting under it for you. Maybe we should call Erin," I suggested. "She can try talking some sense into him."

Trent scooted out from under the covers. "Don't worry, Kels, I've got this." Naked, but no longer wielding a full out hard-on, he scanned the floor.

"What are you looking for?"

"My clothes."

"Aren't they on...?" Images of the last time I remembered seeing them flashed in my head to the tune of "You Are Royally Screwed." *Oh, shit.* "If I remember correctly"—and I did—"they're on the living room floor and the stairs." Along with mine.

We had gotten a little turned on last night while watching a movie.

Clothes came off.

By the time we made it to my room, we were completely naked.

"Well, that does it." Trent leaned over the edge of the bed and gently kissed me. "I'm leaving some of my clothes here."

"You might not want to open with that when you talk to Liam." I clambered out of bed.

Trent's eyes darkened at the sight of me naked. Clearly forgetting one overbearingly protective brother downstairs, his cock twitched to life.

And my girlie parts cursed Liam for his bad timing.

I padded over to my drawers and removed my underwear, a pair of black yoga pants, and my favorite cute owl T-shirt, then quickly yanked them on.

I didn't have to go far in search of Trent's clothes. His underwear was half way down the stairs, his jeans on the bottom step. His wallet lay on the floor, his driver's license next to it.

That explained why my brother had burst into my room when he knew I was in bed with a guy. Although Trent's BMW in the driveway would've been his first clue before he even bothered to check who the clothes belonged to. If it had been any other guy, Liam would have left and come back later, or done what he should have done either way—called me first.

I let out a long sigh and returned upstairs with Trent's underwear and jeans. The rest he could retrieve once we came back downstairs.

A few minutes later, an almost-fully-clothed Trent and I entered the living room, holding hands...and came to an abrupt stop.

Liam wasn't alone on the couch. Sitting on the other end was Erin—with Trent's shirt now draped neatly over the armrest.

The first thought that came to mind when I initially saw them? Firing squad, with Trent their primary target.

Letting go of Trent's hand, I walked over to the couch and hugged Erin. "When did you get here?"

She gave me an extra tight squeeze that I wasn't sure how to translate. "A few minutes ago. I figured my dumbass brother was here and I wanted to talk to him."

I stood up and found myself immediately in Trent's arms, my back against his chest. "You could have called," he told her, his tone affectionate, the fingers of one hand lovingly stroking my bare arm.

"And miss seeing how cute you two are together?" She grinned, the action just as affectionate. "I still can't believe I didn't see it sooner. I just don't get why you two waited so long to get together."

I choked back a laugh. I had admitted to her the other day that I had fallen in love with Trent long before we finally got together. Long before Michaela had done her part in screwing everything up.

I settled my gaze on my brother. "I know you don't approve of me dating your best friend, but if there's anyone who knows what an amazing guy he is, it would be you, Liam. And no matter what happens between him and me, that should never change your friendship. I mean, unless he cheats on me and breaks my heart."

"And if he does," Erin said to Liam, "I give you full permission to break both his legs. I'll even pin him down if you want." She winked at her brother.

The corner of Liam's mouth jerked up to the side, and his eyes gleamed at the enticing possibility. "I'll be sure to hold you to that," he said with a laugh.

"Okay, now that that's over"—I stepped away from Trent—"do I get a hug?"

The words were barely out of my mouth before Liam was off the couch and I was in his arms. The tears that normally appeared whenever he returned from a mission finally clouded my vision and rolled down my cheeks. "I've missed you."

He squeezed me hard. I wouldn't have been surprised if he cracked a rib or two. Did I care? Not really. My brother was home, safe and in one piece. I would happily put up with cracked ribs just for that.

As long as it didn't prevent me from having mind-blowing sex with Trent.

Once he had finished hugging me, he and Trent shared a one-armed man hug. And that's when I knew everything was going to be okay between them. They both loved me—and they still loved each other like brothers.

Erin and Liam stayed for a while longer, then we made plans to meet up at Liam's favorite restaurant for dinner—to celebrate the end of his mission. And this time, I wouldn't have to fantasize about Trent while on a date.

Fantasy, meet reality.

I shut the front door after Erin and Liam left, and turned around. Trent had that look on his face I recognized all too well.

I stroked the pad of my thumb against the sexy stubble on his cheek. "Can we go upstairs and finish making love? Please?"

"You don't even have to say please, Kels. I'll do anything you want. You only have to ask."

That made two of us. Because whatever Trent wanted, I would willingly give him. I had already given him my heart— and that was only the beginning.

EPILOGUE
TRENT

Six Months Later

What's the best thing about having a girlfriend? The sex.

Let me rephrase that. What's one of the best parts of being in love?

That's right. The sex.

Somehow, being in love makes sex that much better, that much hotter.

"Oh God, Trent," Kelsey said, bent over the kitchen counter, her slick heat tightening around my cock.

The pure sexiness of her voice and her body's response to me was all I needed. I joined her a heartbeat later in a complete state of bliss.

Best. Thanksgiving. Ever.

Do you think the turkey gave a damn what we were doing? If anything, he was jealous that I got to fuck my gorgeous girlfriend. All he got out of the deal was several hours in a 325-degree oven.

I removed myself from her and we fixed our clothing. Then Kelsey wrapped her arms around my neck and gave me a slow, gratified kiss. "I guess we should get ready before everyone shows up."

And shower sex it was.

By the time we were finished—Kelsey flushed from our heated shower and wearing the same black lace dress she had worn at the auction, me in dress pants and a light-blue shirt—everyone was due to arrive.

While I checked the food, Kelsey began setting the table.

At one point, I glanced over to see how she was doing. "Wow, Thanksgiving exploded and left no survivors."

"Ha! You're just jealous that while you were busy with work, I was hanging out on Pinterest and making this."

I walked over to Kelsey and pulled her against me, a pinecone in her hand.

Lucky pinecone. "You got that right," I said with a smirk. "I'm very jealous...jealous your hands were all over them instead of on me."

She smirked back at me. "And that's what you get for working late last week." She stepped away from me and returned to arranging the contents of the darkly stained, shallow wooden box that took up almost the entire length of the table. Cream-colored candles of various thicknesses were scattered on either side of the small pumpkin pie. Ornamental squashes, pinecones, and cypress made up the rest of the display.

I kissed the end of her nose. "It looks great," I said as the doorbell rang. I threaded my fingers with hers. Tonight was a big deal for us. Not only was it the first Thanksgiving we were hosting together, as a couple, but Liam would be here.

Was he over how his little sister had hooked up with his

best friend? Not exactly...but I hoped by now he realized that what she and I had between us was real. In time, I planned to propose to her, but after her engagement to her ex-fiancé, she wasn't ready for that yet. She needed to make sure I wouldn't grow bored of her—of us.

Like that would ever happen.

I opened the front door to find my sister with my adorable three-month-old niece in her arms, my brother-in-law carrying the empty infant seat, Liam, and a glowing Holly.

Why was she glowing? Holly was six-months pregnant.

Liam isn't the father—in case you were wondering.

Who is? Sorry, that's her story to tell, not mine.

I opened the door wider and let them in.

Kelsey hugged everyone while I hung up their coats, then she took my niece from Erin. Most men would freak out seeing their girlfriend gush over a baby. But not me.

In my mind, it was our baby she was holding, and I grinned at the thought. Kelsey would be an amazing mother one day to our kids. That, I never doubted.

"Hey, sweetheart," I said to Samantha. She smiled at me with her toothless grin.

"It smells great in here," Erin said as we walked into the living room.

Yes, I'd come a long way since my scrambled-egg-burning days. This was my first attempt at cooking a turkey, but thanks to my Food Network addiction, I was confident dinner would taste as it should.

Kelsey handed Samantha back to Erin, and everyone chatted while Kelsey and I fetched the drinks.

Mom and Dad were visiting my older brother, Curtis, and his family for Thanksgiving. They weren't the only ones who couldn't make it. Josh was in Montreal for a hockey game, which had started an hour ago. I'd already turned on the TV so we could watch it for a few minutes before we ate.

I sat in the armchair and pulled Kelsey onto my lap. Liam was too involved in the game to pay attention to us. When he finally did notice his sister was on my lap, he just rolled his eyes and went back to watching the game.

Josh passed the puck to Sean Burrows, who nailed it past the Canadiens' goalie. And so ended the second period—with us cheering and the Rock up two-zero.

Kelsey and I ushered everyone into the kitchen. Because Kelsey's Thanksgiving decorations took up most of the table, dinner was buffet style. While Kelsey and I placed the food and plates on the counter, Liam lit the candles. Then everyone helped themselves, with Darren and Erin taking turns holding their daughter.

Ever since Erin and I had been old enough to talk, each Thanksgiving meal began with us saying what we were thankful for. Some of our answers hadn't been quite what our parents had in mind (like my transformer figures when I was eight), but the tradition had stuck. Even when Kelsey and Liam's family joined us for Thanksgiving, the tradition remained.

So it came as no surprise to anyone (except maybe Holly) when Kelsey said, "I've got lots to be thankful for this year. I'm thankful my brother is home. I'm thankful for all my friends. I'm thankful for my job that I love so much and for the great opportunity I've been given with my photography. But most of all"—she moved her hand from her lap and laced her fingers with mine, then she smiled at me—"I'm thankful that the man who's had my heart for so many years loves me as much as I love him."

The adoring look on her face warmed me all over. I leaned toward her and gave her a sweet kiss. The longing sigh in the background? It came from either Erin or Holly—or both.

We went around the table, each person saying what they were thankful for.

And then it was my turn.

"I'm thankful for the same things as everyone else. My friends. My growing family." I glanced down at my niece, currently in her father's arms, and grinned at her. "My job. The Food Network." Everyone laughed.

I turned to Kelsey and cupped her cheek with my hand. "But most of all, I'm thankful the woman I fell in love with is also my best friend, the woman who I've cared about for as long as I've known her. And I'd be even more thankful if she would agree to live with me."

I know, it wasn't a marriage proposal—hell, it wasn't even a question. But Kelsey and I had already casually brought up the topic of living together a few times, so I knew she wasn't against it.

Other than the cooing and gurgling from my niece, the room was silent—either due to shock or because they were waiting for Kelsey's reply.

Her lush lips parted and my breath stalled in my chest. "Where would we live? Your place or mine?" Her voice was quiet like a gentle breeze.

I stroked my thumb against her soft skin. "Whichever you prefer."

She turned her head and kissed my palm. "Mine."

"So, is that a yes?"

She smiled, the brightness competing with the sun on a hot summer day and winning by a long shot. "That would be a yes."

I leaned toward her, intent on kissing her and sealing the proverbial deal, but never had the chance. Liam cleared his throat.

Uh oh. This couldn't be good.

He picked up his wineglass. "I would like to add one more thing I'm thankful for." He smiled at Kelsey. "I'm thankful my best friend, the guy who I trust with my life, loves my sister. And I'm thankful Kelsey fell in love with him. If there is anyone

I trust with her life, it would be Trent." He raised his glass and saluted us...then he smirked. "Now you can kiss her. But try to keep it G-rated, would you? That is my sister you're kissing after all."

Everyone chuckled.

Then my lips crashed against Kelsey's in a not-so-G-rated kiss.

But I didn't care—because kissing her was another thing I was thankful for.

When it came to Kelsey, I was thankful for...everything.

BONUS EPILOGUE

In terms of time frames, the bonus epilogue takes place after *Decidedly with Baby* (the second book in the By the Bay series).

BONUS EPILOGUE
TRENT

I used to believe the idea of settling down with one woman and having a happily-ever-after was for losers. The kind of losers who were ready to give up their lives and their freedom.

Well, I was happy to report that I was ready to join those merry bands of men.

I patted my suit jacket pocket—the one holding the blue box and the two-carat engagement ring. I would have bought Kelsey a five-carat ring as a warning to other men that she was mine and only mine, but since I trusted her, there was no need to go caveman and mark my territory. Plus, Kelsey had never been into expensive jewelry—so a five-carat ring wouldn't necessarily impress her.

And it wasn't like she needed a pricy ring to prove how much I loved her. The Kelsey I loved and worshiped appreciated the little things rather than oversized gestures.

"Are you ready?" the vision before me asked as she walked down the stairs. Kelsey was wearing a black cocktail dress that dipped in the front, giving me a mouthwatering view of her cleavage. If we had time, I would've feasted on her gorgeous breasts...like I'd done before we had to get ready for the Christmas party at my sister's house.

I wasn't *exactly* planning to propose to her in front of our friends and family. When I proposed to the woman I loved, it would be just Kelsey and me and a billion stars gazing down on us. So why bring the ring to the party? My sister's backyard was the perfect place to propose, thanks to the landscaping that provided privacy and created a romantic backdrop.

So instead of running my tongue along Kelsey's cleavage— which I really wanted to do—I softly kissed her on the lips. "I'm definitely ready."

More than she could possibly imagine.

At Erin and Darren's house, I parked my BMW a little farther down the street from where they lived.

"Have I told you lately how much I love you?" I asked after helping Kelsey from the car. Her blonde hair, glowing in the street light, brushed against the shoulders of her long black coat.

She wrapped her arms around my neck. "Not for two hours." Kelsey leaned in, her mouth closer to my ear, thanks to her stilettos. "Not since right after you were pounding hard into me and causing me to see stars." Her voice held a smile as if she too was reminiscing about that quick-yet-awesome fuck.

"That's nothing compared to what I plan to do tonight."

She ran her tongue along my jaw, and my cock twitched with excitement. *Down boy. No time for that.*

"And what's that?" she asked.

"Make slow, delicious love to you."

I could've sworn she shuddered in my arms.

"How long do we have to stay at the party?" she asked.

I knew she was joking.

Mostly.

Erin was not only my sister, she was Kelsey's best friend. And we both knew my sister would skin us alive and feed us to a pack of rabid wolves if we missed her party.

"As long as you want." But hopefully long enough for me to do what I had already planned...with a little help from Darren, Erin's husband.

Does Erin know about my plan?

Hell no. I love my sister, but her keeping a secret like this? Impossible. She'd be too excited and Kelsey would know something was up.

The party was already going full force when we entered the house. Fighting back a smile, Darren took Kelsey's coat from her.

Loud laughter erupted from the living room. Kelsey spun around, and I had the sudden urge to lick her sexy back.

But there was no time to appreciate the taste, the feel, or the sight of her soft, luscious skin. I quickly removed the ring box from my pocket and slipped it into hers.

As planned, Darren sneaked away to hide the coats in the guest bedroom near the back door.

So far, everything was perfect.

Kelsey and I entered the living room where a grand Christmas tree stood. Samantha, my fourteen-month-old niece, was busy admiring the shiny decorations that had been placed at her level. Like Mr. Kitty Whiskers enjoyed doing with Kelsey's and my tree decorations, Sammy batted at one, a big grin on her face. Possibly sensing us watching her, she turned to us and toddled over. She lifted her arms up to me.

Admit it. My niece is the cutest little girl on the planet. At least for now. Once Kelsey and I start our family, I can guarantee any daughters we have will be even more adorable. How could they not with Kelsey as their mother?

I hoisted Samantha up in my arms. "How's my little angel

doing?" I asked her. She waved at Kelsey. Kelsey waved back. I took it to mean she was doing great.

"Are you ready for Santa to visit?" I asked my niece, who had met him two days earlier when my sister threw a party for her and her toddler friends. Travis Hamilton, a defenseman for the San Francisco Rock, had been Santa.

But I wasn't talking about Travis.

I was referring to the "real" Santa, who was due to travel around the world in two days.

Samantha didn't answer. She was too busy squirming in my arms, her attention back on the shiny decorations on the tree. Oh, hell, who was I kidding? The entire living room looked shiny—like an elf had sneezed glitter everywhere. Erin had always been a fan of sparkly things.

Just ask her husband.

Kelsey and I spent the next thirty minutes socializing with our friends and family. Impatience rolled through me as my thoughts went back to the ring box in Kelsey's coat pocket.

I glanced around the room. Everyone was preoccupied—no one would notice if Kelsey and I sneaked out the back door for a few minutes.

"Why don't we go out to the backyard?" I murmured in her ear. "There's something I want to show you."

Kelsey giggled, thanks to the near empty glass of white wine in her hand. "I'm not sure Erin would appreciate it if we made love in her backyard while she's throwing this party. Or maybe you were thinking more along the lines of a quick blowjob?"

"That's not what I had in mind." A smirk grew on my face. "But now that you mention it..." I left that hanging. Who was I to complain if we had a little fun outside? Except it was a bit chilly for that.

All right—it was more than a bit chilly.

I took her hand and led her to the guest room where Darren had left our coats on the bed. I removed Kelsey's, my hand subtly patting the pocket with the ring box.

It wasn't there.

I did the same with the other one, this time a little less subtly.

The box wasn't there, either.

I looked under the bed.

"What are you doing?" Kelsey asked, sounding like she was one step away from laughing.

"Nothing..." Which was pretty much what I found under the bed.

I pushed myself to my feet and scanned the room—in case the box had fallen on the floor when Darren had entered. The door had been open when we came in, but why would anyone go searching through Kelsey's coat pocket? It wasn't like there had been a neon sign saying, "Two-carat diamond engagement ring in here."

"Are we still going outside?" Kelsey asked.

"Yes—but I just need another moment." To do what exactly, I had no idea.

I don't know why I decided to return to the living room, but as soon as we stepped into the large space, I spotted the little culprit who had managed to remove the box from Kelsey's pocket.

Samantha was sitting on the floor near the tree, examining the blue velvet box in her hand. She shook it; I winced—even though the ring wasn't that easy to break.

As Kelsey and I approached, my sister knelt next to her daughter. "Hey, sweetie. What do you have there?"

Remember how I said my sister loved sparkly things? That also meant she knew exactly what the box signified.

Well, kind of what the box signified. I didn't think she had clued in that it belonged to her brother...who was about to propose to her best friend.

Samantha showed her the box but didn't seem too interested in actually giving it to Erin.

That was when I swooped in for the rescue.

Before Erin could remove the box from her daughter's clutches, I snatched it up. "Hey, magpie. What's this?" I thought it was a very apt name given what she had in her hand.

Now, I just needed to get Kelsey outside so I could propose to her.

No problem.

A big pout formed on Samantha's face and she reached up to me. Translation: *Hi, Uncle Trent. Now give that back or else all hell will break loose.*

Shit.

"You should probably give it back to her," Kelsey said, also recognizing the look.

The expression on Erin's face as she peered at me? It was one I was more than familiar with. She knew I was up to something.

"Sammy, where did you get the box from?" Erin asked.

If Samantha understood the question, she didn't show it. She pushed herself to her feet, her diapered butt sticking up first, then toddled behind me to where I was holding the box in my hands.

She made a noise, demanding I return it to its rightful owner—her.

Before I could respond, the box was yanked from my hand.

Not by Samantha.

By Kelsey.

My hand shot out, ready to snatch it back, but I wasn't fast enough.

Kelsey began opening the box as she showed the contents to Samantha.

I knew the exact moment she saw the ring: she gasped.

Except her gasp was loud enough to gain the attention of everyone near us. They peered on, noticed the ring, and congratulated Kelsey.

"Oh, this isn't mine," she adamantly said, her face adorably flushed. She glanced around the room—possibly searching for the ring's owner.

It was at that moment I realized I didn't care if I proposed to her in private or in front of a million people. I couldn't wait another second to find out if she wanted to spend the rest of her life with me. And with the Christmas tree lights glowing on Kelsey's face, a log burning merrily in the fireplace, and music playing softly in the background...

"That's where you're wrong." I removed the box from her hand and got down on one knee. The room went silent...other than the crackling fire and the Christmas music.

I focused on Kelsey—her eyes full of emotion, full of tears. But she was smiling, so I took that as a positive sign.

"I had planned to do this outside, where it was just you and me, but clearly my niece had other plans. But that's okay—because I want the world to know how much I love you. We've known each other since we were kids. We became friends. And then we became something more. Something wonderful. Something I never want to end. Kelsey Samantha Quade, will you be my wife?"

She nodded, tears running down her cheeks. "I would love to be your wife, Trent."

She didn't give me a chance to slide the ring on her finger or even stand. Before I could blink, Kelsey dropped to her knees, flung her arms around my neck, and kissed me. Passionately. Sweetly.

I was vaguely aware of cheering—including from Samantha. Although in her case, she probably had no idea why everyone was cheering.

I moved back slightly—my lips instantly missing the softness and taste of Kelsey's—and helped her to her feet. Then I removed the ring from the box, slipped it onto her finger, and smiled at my future.

Smiled at my soon-to-be wife.

HOLIDAY SHORT STORY

HOLIDAY SHORT STORY
TRENT

Christmas morning, I walked into the kitchen to find Kelsey busy wrapping a present. An hour ago, we'd been making love in the shower while I marveled over her still flat stomach that held my unborn child.

Can you imagine that?

Me, the guy who had made the list of most eligible bachelors in the San Francisco area—a title that landed me in a charity bachelor auction—was going to be a father?

Five years ago, if someone had told me I would one day marry my best friend's little sister, I would've thought they had gone insane. Never mind the part about having a child with her.

But here I was, soon to be precisely that. A father.

I wrapped my arms around Kelsey from behind. Her blond hair was scooped up in a high ponytail, conveniently providing me access to her neck.

Taking full advantage of her hairstyle, I planted a teasing kiss on her soft skin, her pulse beating fast at my touch.

"Isn't it a little late to be wrapping my presents?" I asked, my lips still against her neck.

We hadn't unwrapped our gifts yet. With the exception of the ones for each other, we were saving the presents until later, when we would be celebrating Christmas at my parents' house, with my family and Kelsey's brother.

Liam had been away for the past few days, helping with a search and rescue mission in the Lake Tahoe area. But then he had gotten stranded there overnight because of a snowstorm.

The last Kelsey had heard, he was back in San Francisco... and had a surprise for her.

He wasn't the only one with a surprise. We hadn't yet announced our news to our friends and family. We were saving that for later today, mostly because there would be no hiding the truth once Kelsey passed on the wine at dinner.

"It's not your present," she said, a smile in her voice. She opened the gold paper with snowflakes on it, revealing a navy T-shirt. She picked it up, allowing the top to unfold itself. Large white letters on the front proclaimed *Uncle-To-Be in Training*. "It's for Liam. It's how I plan to tell him that I'm pregnant."

"I guess that's better than announcing that his best friend knocked up his little sister." Did I believe the T-shirt would soften the blow when it came to that truth?

Not at all.

Kelsey laughed, the sound of it making me quickly forget about our conversation. Instead, it made me want to hoist her over my shoulder and return to the shower, or the bedroom, or heck, even the kitchen counter would do. I was all for an encore of what we'd been doing an hour ago.

"I don't think Liam will see it quite that way," Kelsey said. "You and I are married. And in case you're forgetting, he was your best man. While he might not have been jumping for joy when we first hooked up, he's past it now."

"That doesn't mean he's okay with us having sex."

She laughed again and twisted around in my arms to face

me. "Does that mean you're not okay with your sister having sex with her husband?"

"Erin and Darren don't have sex," I grumbled.

Kelsey grinned. "Oh, they don't, do they? And how do you explain your niece and nephew? You do know how babies are made, right? Or do you and I need to sit down so I can explain to you how we created this one?" She placed her hand on her stomach, and I couldn't help but smile.

"I do know how babies are typically made. And I had a great time putting this one in here." I tenderly ran my thumb just below Kelsey's hand, eliciting a soft gasp from her. "But when it comes to my niece and nephew, they came to be because of the generosity of two storks."

My brother's kids, on the other hand, were created via the conventional method. The fun method.

Kelsey's grin widened. "So that's what you're planning to tell Liam? That a stork will be visiting us in seven months?"

"Don't you think he would prefer it that way?"

Kelsey gave me a quick kiss. "If it helps you sleep better at night, you can tell my brother he doesn't have to worry. You and I have never copulated. His niece or nephew will be arriving via Special Stork Delivery."

That worked for me.

But instead of telling Kelsey that I agreed with her idea 100%, I proceeded to demonstrate how much I loved her.

One hand cradled the back of her head. The other pulled her against me. My mouth found hers, and Liam's gift was quickly forgotten.

Our tongues glided against each other in a slow sensual dance. Nothing else mattered in this moment. Not her brother, my best friend. Not my sister, Kelsey's best friend. Not even my parents, who I knew would be ecstatic at the news.

My body stirred to life—like it did whenever I kissed

Kelsey...or when she was curled up against me on the couch, or when I woke up in the morning with her in my arms.

I bent down slightly, hooking my hands behind her knees, and hoisted her up. Her legs automatically went around my hips.

Still kissing her, I carried her into the living room. We hadn't gotten around to opening the curtains covering the windows that faced the street. No one could see what we were doing. The other curtains were open, but the trees and shrubs in the small backyard gave us the privacy we needed.

The only individual to bear witness to what we were about to do was Kelsey's cat, Mr. Kitty Whiskers.

As if guessing what Kelsey and I were planning to do, he jumped down from the armchair he had been snoozing on, and walked off with what I imaged to be a slight huff.

But not to worry. He would get over it soon enough, once Kelsey gave him his catnip-infused gift.

Then he would be one doped-up kitty.

I sat on the couch, still kissing Kelsey. Her legs released my hips, and she shifted to straddle me, brushing against my hard length.

My cocked silently groaned.

Kelsey giggled.

"That doesn't do much for my ego," I said against her mouth.

"I don't think your ego has anything to worry about. But shouldn't we exchange gifts first?"

I flashed her a smug smile. "Maybe my being buried deep inside you *is* my Christmas present. I seem to remember specifically asking Santa for that this year."

Mischief gleamed in her eyes. "Yes, but weren't you on his naughty list?"

"Absolutely. And if I have my way, I'm about to be even

naughtier. And I plan to corrupt you to be naughty, too." I winked at her.

She laughed and grasped the hem of her lightweight sweater, slowly pulling it up her body and revealing my favorite light-pink lacy bra.

"I must have been better than I realized this year." I chuckled and dragged my thumb lightly across one nipple, visible through the lace. The bud tightened, and everything south of my belt followed suit.

Kelsey didn't answer, her eyes dark with need.

"Or maybe we should exchange gifts now," I said, voice low and husky.

"Now? But I thought you wanted to be buried deep inside me." She trailed her hand down the front of my Henley.

"Nope. I've changed my mind. But if you want to open your gifts while wearing nothing but your jeans and bra, I certainly won't complain."

She wiggled her ass, brushing her denim-covered sex against my hard length. Her mouth curled to one side. "Are you sure you want to wait?"

No. "Yes." The word came out in a lusty groan.

You're not making this easy on me, Kels.

If her expression was anything to go by, she already knew that.

"Will we get to make love after we open our presents?" She rested her hand over my heart. I wouldn't have been surprised if she could feel it thumping fast beneath her palm.

I cupped the back of her head and gently kissed her. "I'm counting on it."

Satisfied with my reply, she shifted off my legs and reached for her sweater. Despite my suggestion about wearing only her jeans and bra, she slipped the top on over her head.

I pushed myself to my feet and led her to the Christmas tree, smiling at how next year there would also be presents for our son or daughter. Like for most kids, Christmas had always been a special time for me when I was young—and I couldn't wait to share it with our child.

Couldn't wait to pretend that Santa had visited during the night.

Couldn't wait to experience the magic of the holiday season through his or her eyes.

Kelsey and I sat on the floor in front of the lit tree. I handed her the shoebox-size gift, wrapped in red and gold paper with a large glittery bow.

Her expression was full of curiosity and awe as she carefully unwrapped the present.

She then removed the lid and peered inside.

Her eyes went wide; her mouth formed a perfect O.

A floppy purple rabbit sat inside the box. Hanging from around its neck was a delicate sliver necklace from Tiffany's, with a simple diamond-and-pink-sapphire-encrusted heart.

"The bunny is for our baby," I explained. "The necklace is for my beautiful wife, who will soon be an amazing mother to our child."

"It's so gorgeous," she whispered, fingering the charm. "I love it. It's perfect. Thank you!"

She was right, it was perfect.

Kelsey wasn't big on flashy jewelry. Her diamond engagement ring had been the exception. But I'd wanted to give her something to signify what she meant to me, to signify the new chapter in our life together.

I also couldn't wait to make love to her while she was wearing the necklace and only the necklace.

I removed the rabbit from the box and unfastened the clasp.

Kelsey turned around, and I slipped the chain around her neck and fastened it. She twisted back to face me, the charm resting just above the V-neckline of her sweater.

She threw her arms around my neck, and with a kiss that

seared me to the soul, she showed her love for me and her gratitude for the present. "Thank you," she murmured once we finally parted, her joy unmistakable.

A sweet warmth rushed to my chest at her reaction, soaring like an eagle in the bright blue sky.

This time, *I* was the one who initiated the kiss.

We then opened the rest of our presents, relishing the quiet moment of just the two of us. In a few hours, we would be dealing with family and all the fun and craziness that came with them—especially once we announced our news.

Sunlight shone through the window, painting the area rug with its warm light.

The perfect place to make love to my wife, since taking time to go upstairs wasn't currently an option.

Kelsey drew herself to her knees and set her hands on either side of my face. Her fingers lightly traced against my jaw.

While her hands explored my face, mine were preoccupied with the strip of skin above the waistband of her jeans. Her breaths became ragged with each passing sweep of my fingertips.

Unable to wait any longer before seeing her naked again, I flicked open the top button of her jeans and slowly dragged the zipper down. My fingers moved lower, brushing against the lace of her panties.

Kelsey drew in a sharp breath.

The next thing I knew, we were on the floor, sunlight bathing our naked bodies. The diamond-and-pink-sapphire necklace gleamed against Kelsey's pale skin.

She looked perfect, like an angel. Her ponytail had been dismantled, and her blond hair created a fan against the light blue rug. Her bra had been discarded only moments ago, and her taut nipples pleaded for my attention.

Which naturally I gave them.

How could I not?

I teased them, worshiped them, showered them with my appreciation. And with each flick of my tongue, each scrapping pass of my teeth against her tight buds, my fingers circled Kelsey's clit, delved inside her, did everything I could to bring her closer to the abyss.

"Oh God, Trent," she said on a moan. "I need you inside me. Now."

With a smug smile, I pressed the tip of my hard length against her entrance and plunged deep inside her.

Taking us to the stars and beyond.

Taking us to the place where only those in love go.

THREE HOURS LATER, I PARKED THE BMW ON THE STREET outside my parents' home. Liam's and my brother-in-law's vehicles were already in the driveway.

"Are you ready to be smothered to death once we tell my parents they're going to be grandparents again?" Same deal with Erin once she learned that she would soon be an aunt.

That's not to say she wasn't already an aunt, thanks to our older brother and his wife.

But this was different. Erin and Kelsey weren't just sister-in-laws, they were best friends.

The twinge of regret on Kelsey's face at my question?

It wasn't because she was pregnant.

It was because her parents were no longer alive. They had missed out on becoming grandparents.

I pulled her into my arms and kissed the top of her head. "I know you miss them. They would've been amazing grandparents. But I know my parents will do everything in their power to make up for your parents' absence." They had all been close friends when we were growing up.

She smiled softly at me. "I know. Even though our kids will only know one set of grandparents, they'll be very much loved."

"And my parents will ensure that our kids know all about your parents. They will be thrilled to share all the humorous stories about the four of them. Plus we'll make certain our kids know just how wonderful your parents were."

The grateful smile on her face? It melted my heart. There wasn't anything I wouldn't do to keep it there.

"So how do you want to do this?" I tilted my head toward my parents' house. "Do you want to tell your brother first?"

She nodded.

"Remember, the stork will be delivering the baby in seven months. I didn't knock you up."

Kelsey laughed, shaking her head as if I was being ridiculous.

We began gathering the gifts from the trunk, piling them in our arms.

"You do realize I can carry more than three small presents?"

"You're pregnant."

"So I've heard, but I can still carry a few more gifts."

I studied the packages in the trunk and selected two small presents for my mother. I placed them on the ones in Kelsey's arms. "Is that better?"

She didn't roll her eyes, but I could tell she wanted to.

"I'll get the rest after we tell Liam our news." I shut the back of the vehicle.

We walked up the path to my parents' house. The faint sound of Christmas music wafted through the closed windows.

I didn't bother ringing the doorbell. I opened the door of my childhood home and stepped inside.

A blur of a small child rushed past, followed by a slightly taller blur.

A third child crashed into my legs. Four-year-old Samantha peered up at me, her eyes wide in shock.

Then a huge grin stole onto her face. "Hi, Uncle Trent and Auntie Kelsey."

Kelsey bent down, giving her niece a big hug. "Did Santa visit you last night?"

Samantha nodded and proceeded to tell us all about the gifts Santa had left her under the tree. Her words came out so fast, don't quiz me on what she said.

"Samantha, are you ready to play Hide and Seek?" A familiar blonde woman, whom I hadn't seen in over ten years, entered the foyer from the living room.

Kelsey stared at Ava, as if seeing a ghost, her mouth open but unable to form words.

Ava smiled shyly at Kelsey, and then at me. "Hi." She turned in the direction she had come from and called out Liam's name. "Your sister and brother-in-law are here."

Liam joined us a moment later, the smile on his face bigger than I'd seen in a while.

And it only grew bigger when his gaze landed on his ex-fiancée.

His gaze turned heated, and a light blush spread across her cheeks.

Liam had never really explained why they didn't end up at the altar. I only knew it had something to do with him being in the military at the time. I also understood that whatever had happened, he wasn't happy about it.

He settled his hand on her lower back, making it clear she wasn't just an acquaintance. "You two remember Ava?" he asked us.

Still looking confused, Kelsey nodded.

"It's nice to see you again." I held out my hand to her.

She shook it with ease, then looked at Kelsey, face hopeful.

Kelsey appeared as though she didn't know if she should hug the person who had once broken her brother's heart or defend his honor.

So, she did the first thing that came to mind. "I'm pregnant, but it's not Trent's baby."

For a second, a horrified expression crossed her face as her words sunk in.

Me? I burst out laughing.

Now it was Liam's and Ava's turn to look confused—although I have no idea if it was because of what Kelsey had said or because I was laughing so hard.

"I figured if you're anything like me," I explained, still laughing, "you lie to yourself about your sister having sex... especially with your best friend. So I told her to tell you that a stork would be delivering the baby. Then you could maintain the delusion about her and I not having sex."

Liam made a pained face every time I mentioned Kelsey and I having sex, confirming my suspicions on that topic. "I'm all for that idea," he said. "Stork delivery it is."

Both Kelsey and Ava cracked up laughing...and just like that the two women hugged and fell into easy conversation.

Needing to go somewhere quiet to catch up on the past two days, the four of us escaped outside and walked to the playground where Liam, Kelsey, and I used to play when we were kids.

Liam and Ava explained what had happened all those years ago that resulted in the end of their engagement. And they filled us in on how Liam had found Ava stranded on the side of the road, thanks to a flat tire during the snowstorm.

By the time we returned to my parents' house, you would've thought the past ten years had never happened—minus the part where I'd fallen madly in love with Liam's sister, and now we were expecting our first child.

The house was oddly silent. The Christmas music was still playing, but it was the only sound present.

We entered the living room, to find six adults watching us expectantly. The kids were playing quietly on the floor.

It was like stepping into a scene from the *Twilight Zone*.

Cue the eerie music.

"Is it true?" Mom's gaze flicked between Kelsey and me, her face glowing. "I'm going to be a grandmother again?"

"It's true," Kelsey replied, her voice choked with unshed tears.

This news resulted in a squeal from both Mom and Erin. They rushed over and hugged her.

Then they hugged me—because I did, after all, contribute to their future grandchild/niece or nephew.

And then they switched back to hugging Kelsey again.

Once the hug-fest came to a close, Erin gestured at Kelsey's necklace. "Did Trent give you that for Christmas? It's gorgeous." She said it loud enough for all the men in the room to hear.

My mother, Ava, and Erin gushed over the heart-shaped charm. The younger girls clambered to see it, excited at how the diamonds and sapphires sparkled.

Naturally, the women's goodhearted jealousy resulted in hardy groans from the men.

Not to mention a few *did-you-really-have-to-upstage-us?* friendly glares directed my way, which only made me chuckle.

I swear it was a good ten minutes before Kelsey was finally in my arms again.

As soon as everyone's attention shifted to the kids and the gifts under the tree, I pulled her aside, giving us a moment alone. "How are you doing?"

She smiled at me. "Perfect. Everything about today is perfect."

She was right about that.

So I kissed her, reminding her how much I loved her and our unborn child.

READ ON FOR AN EXCERPT FROM
DECIDEDLY WITH BABY

EXCERPT FROM DECIDEDLY
WITH BABY

HOLLY

Quick, name the one person you'd rather not talk to on a Friday night...while you're still at the office?

First question—what was I doing at the office on a Friday night? Easy. Where else would you expect a workaholic to be?

Okay, I wasn't planning to spend the entire night here. I did have a life after all.

I also wasn't planning to talk to my mother on the phone while at the office on a Friday night—yet here I was doing exactly that.

"I tried calling your apartment." Her tone for the last word was like battery acid with a dash of honey. My mother didn't do apartments. And definitely not apartments the size of—as she had put it—my parents' swimming pool.

She was exaggerating. *Mostly.*

Did I feel that my apartment was too small? Not at all. What did I need a large apartment for anyway? With two bedrooms, mine had plenty of space for me, especially since I spent more time at work than I did there. Besides, it was a nice apartment located in a Victorian house not far from the bay. I loved it, even if my mother didn't.

I didn't bother to point out she'd been calling my cell phone earlier, but I had let her go to voicemail. I hadn't expected her to then phone my work number, which was why I'd answered it.

Although I had no idea, in retrospect, who else would've called me at 9 p.m. at work on a Friday night, which was Saturday afternoon in Sydney.

"I was just about to leave," I said. "What can I help you with?" Even though she and Dad had a financial planner, it didn't stop her from asking my advice.

Not that she necessarily listened to it, but it was one of the few things we could talk about that didn't leave me feeling as though she was judging me in the worst possible way.

"First," she said, "while it's commendable that your career is important to you, you shouldn't be working at the office so late. Especially not on a Friday night."

Said the woman who spent my childhood doing the same thing. Only difference was, she had three kids and I was completely kid free.

I didn't even have a pet.

"I'm meeting up with friends in a few minutes," I pointed out. *I do have a social life, Mum.* A social life that wasn't all about being seen by the right people in the right places—something Mum had specialized in my entire life.

"Good. The reason I'm calling is to inform you that my mother died." A small amount of emotion snuck into her otherwise cool voice.

"Nanna's dead?" The words barely squeezed past shock and despair. I coughed to clear my throat. "What happened?" She had been fine the last time I talked to her.

"Heart attack. The funeral is on Thursday."

I bit my lip to hold back the building sob. "I'll be there."

"Good." Her voice wavered slightly. "Send me your travel information, and I'll have Simon pick you up at the airport."

I smiled a little at the thought of seeing my thirty-year-old brother. "Okay." I had no idea if she'd heard my reply. She'd ended the call the moment the word had left my mouth.

My gaze fell to the small, framed photo on my desk. The woman crouched on the ground with an adorable baby wallaby cuddling a teddy bear? That was Nanna. She had found him injured and nursed him back to health.

The photo had been taken at Christmas, when she was full of life, her cheeks glowing, her eyes holding the mischievous light that was all Nanna. Both of us were wearing ratty denim shorts and had dirt smudged on our makeup-free faces. Surprised? I know—the complete opposite of how people in San Francisco normally saw me.

I examined my perfectly manicured French tips, then brushed my fingers along the light gray pencil skirt and the cream-colored cashmere cardigan hugging my breasts. Nanna wouldn't have recognized me like this.

In San Francisco, I was more like my mother.

I shuddered at the thought—then turned off the computer, straightened my desk, and switched off the office light. Even workaholic Trent had left several hours ago, something that was new for him ever since he started dating Kelsey. I sent her a text that I was on my way.

The bar they'd picked was the furthest thing from a sports bar they could have found. The upbeat jazz music playing in the background? If I didn't know better, I could've sworn Nanna had requested it especially for me. It was one of her favorites.

I grinned at the memory of her humming it while trying to give Marcus, the baby wallaby, a bath. By the end of it, Nanna and I were soaked—Marcus, not so much.

Kelsey and Trent were deep in conversation when I approached the table. Josh wasn't there yet—and wouldn't be for another few hours—but they already had drinks in front of them, and a strawberry daiquiri was sitting at one of the two empty spots. *Gimme, gimme.*

Kelsey glanced up and grinned. "Hey, you actually made it."

I laughed and the people at the next table visibly cringed. That's right. I won the gene pool jackpot. I had beautiful, long auburn hair that looked like fire when the sunlight hit it just right. My skin was creamy and perfect—other than a splattering of freckles on my nose—and I had a great body (which I did work hard at, so there was that).

What I hadn't been blessed with was a beautiful laugh like Kelsey. When she laughed, angels sang. When *I* laughed, they burrowed their heads in the ground and prayed their agony would end quickly—or at least that the world would end soon.

Oh, well. No one was perfect.

But it was that one imperfect trait that turned guys off. I knew it. They knew it. So all was good.

It didn't cause me to stop laughing, though. Life was too short not to laugh. Nanna had taught me that.

"Of course I made it," I said, taking my seat. "I stayed late at the office to watch some of Josh's game." I took a sip of my drink. "Wow, that's good." *Now let's keep them coming.*

How did I meet Josh? Kelsey and Trent had hosted a dinner party a few months ago and he was invited. The two of us had hung out together as friends since then—as in, seeing-a-movie-together, Josh-helping-me-move-furniture, and I-need-a-woman's-opinion kind of friends. Was it possible to be friends with a guy and sex not be involved? Absolutely. And unlike with some couples who invited their single friends out like a matched pair, neither Kelsey nor Trent entertained expectations that Josh and I would become a couple.

Which was a good thing—because I couldn't see it happening. Even if he was hot and my body got all tingly whenever I saw him. Josh didn't come off as the settling-down type. Not that he needed to settle down when women were more than happy just to have sex with him—no commitment required.

How did I know? I'd seen him being hit on a few times; I swear the guy was a magnet for horny women. Did it ever bother me? Not at all. It was always fun giving him a hard time about it afterward. And yes—he did occasionally leave with a few of them.

Was *I* the settling down type? Well, I wasn't looking to get married and I wasn't looking to start a family. My career? That was my baby.

Maybe this was why Josh and I had become friends over the past few months. We were perfect for each other—strictly as friends.

And hopefully my body would eventually be fully onboard with that.

Kelsey, Trent, and I chatted until Josh eventually showed up, looking like he had just finished playing triple overtime. Not once did I mention Nanna. Not once did I let on that something was wrong. I just happily worshiped my drink.

And once I'd finished worshiping it, I started on round two.

"Enjoy life, Holly," Nanna's laughing voice said in the back of my head. "You need to seize life by the horns and all that clichéd crap, and enjoy it while you can. You don't want to be like your parents—miserable all the time."

I raised my glass as if to say cheers to her.

"Did I miss anything?" Josh asked as he sat in the empty chair next to me—and a happy heat that had nothing to do with the alcohol made a mad dash to my girlie parts.

All right, ten percent had to do with the alcohol. But the rest was unmistakable lust.

Down girls. This was Josh—Trent's friend—we were talking about. We were totally not going there.

Somehow the "down" and "going" part got twisted in my

head, and an image flashed across my mind of him actually going down on me.

And that was like tossing gasoline on a fire. *Kaboom!*

ACKNOWLEDGMENTS

First, I'd like to thank my readers and the bloggers who've supported me over the past few years. My books wouldn't exist if it weren't for you.

This book wouldn't have been possible without the support, encouragement, and knowledge of so many people. There are too many to list them all, but that doesn't mean I don't appreciate everything they do for the romance writing community. First, to my editors, Bev Rosenbaum and Flat Earth Editing (Hope and Jessica). Each challenged me to make the book stronger, better, funnier. But it was Hope and Jessica who helped me polish the book until it sparkled—and so you weren't left wondering why certain pieces of clothing suddenly vanished from the hero or heroine during the sex scenes. Yes, my "They're magical clothing" excuse just didn't cut it.

Decidedly Off Limits also wouldn't have been possible without Christina Lee, Jayden Abello, and Brenda St. John Brown. Each tirelessly read the manuscript during the various drafts and helped me with certain aspects of the story. In addition, Brenda was always ready to chat about promo and marketing with me—which often involved pictures of hot guys. Yes, such a tough job we have!

I also want to thank my Facebook reader group, Stina's Sweethearts. Your enthusiasm every time I post something about my books always makes my day.

And finally, thank you to my family. Ralph, Anton, Stefanie, and Anja. You've put up with so much just so I can make my deadlines. I know it's not always easy. Thank you for your love and support. Thank you for believing in me.

ABOUT THE AUTHOR

Born in Brighton England, Stina Lindenblatt has lived in a number of countries, including England, the U.S., Finland, and Canada. This would explain her mixed up accent. She has a kinesiology degree and a MSc in sports biological sciences.

In addition to writing fiction, she loves photography, and currently lives in Calgary, Canada, with her husband and three kids.

For news about her books and to sign up for her newsletter, check out her website at stinalindenblattauthor.com.

facebook.com/StinaLindenblattAuthor

instagram.com/stinalindenblatt

tiktok.com/@stinalindenblattauthor

bookbub.com/authors/stina-lindenblatt

www.ingramcontent.com/pod-product-compliance
Lightning Source LLC
Chambersburg PA
CBHW011409310726
48972CB00011B/2908